THE
SURRENDERED

CHANG-RAE LEE

Little, Brown

LITTLE, BROWN

First published in Great Britain in 2010 by Little, Brown

First published in the United States in 2010 by Riverhead,
part of the Penguin Group

A CIP catalogue record for this book
is available from the British Library.

ISBN 978-1-4087-0238-3

Printed and bound in Great Britain by
Clays Ltd, St Ives plc

Papers used by Little, Brown are natural, renewable and
recyclable products sourced from well-managed forests and certified
in accordance with the rules of the Forest Stewardship Council.

Mixed Sources
Product group from well-managed
forests and other controlled sources
www.fsc.org Cert no. SGS-COC-004081
© 1996 Forest Stewardship Council

Little, Brown
An imprint of
Little, Brown Book Group
100 Victoria Embankment
London EC4Y 0DY

An Hachette UK Company
www.hachette.co.uk

www.littlebrown.co.uk

for Eunei

THE
SURRENDERED

ONE

Korea, 1950

THE JOURNEY WAS NEARLY OVER.

The night was unusually chilly, the wind sharpened by the speed of the train as it rolled southward through the darkened valley. The cotton blanket June had stolen was large enough to spread as a tarp and at the same time wrap around her younger brother and sister and herself, but it was threadbare and for brief stretches the train would accelerate and the wind would cut right through to them. It had not been a problem the night before but now they were riding on top of the boxcar, as there was no more room within any of them, even as the train was more than a dozen cars long. A massive phalanx of refugees had met the train at the last station, and in the time it took her siblings to relieve themselves by the side of the tracks they had lost their place and had had to climb the rusted ladder between the cars, June running alongside for fifty meters until her brother was high enough on the rungs so she herself could jump up and on.

There was a score or so of people atop every car, groupings of families and neighbors, mostly women and the old and the young, and then a cluster or two like theirs, children traveling by themselves. June was eleven; Hee-Soo and Ji-Young had just turned seven. They were fraternal twins, though looked as much alike as a sister and brother could, only the cut of their hair distinguishing them. June knew they could have waited in the hope of another train with room inside but it hadn't been cold when they stopped just before dusk and she decided they ought to keep moving while they had the chance. To keep moving was always safer than lingering in one place, and there was nothing back at the depot to eat, anyway. There were a few scruffy soldiers drinking and playing cards by the depot shack, though their presence could only mean trouble, even for a girl her age. She was tall besides and she was wary of soldiers and any stray men. They were some two hundred kilometers south of Seoul, past Chongju, and June was now thinking that they would make their way down to Pusan, where her uncle's family lived, though she didn't know whether they were still there, or even alive.

The train sped up on a slight decline and June curled her arm around her siblings, spooning them tightly. They lay as low as they could between the ridges of the steel roof of the boxcar. They were on the front end of the car and as such they were fully buffeted by the rushing wind. They were fortunate to have a blanket; many others on top of the cars did not. It was too early to sleep but it was cold and it was better for the twins not to be active, especially given that the two had shared only a few crackers early in the day. June herself had eaten nothing. They had eaten well the day before, as June had found, below a footbridge, a GI's abandoned pack of canned rations, a small bar of chocolate, and a sleeve of crackers. Her brother and sister were so hungry that they'd bolted down the chocolate first as June was smashing the cans open against a rock. She'd cut her finger and gotten some blood on the food but they ate it without hesitation, two tins of stewed

beef and one of sardines in tomato sauce, afterward each taking a turn
to lick the insides, carefully, with the deftness of cats. She made them
save the crackers. They'd been by themselves on the road since their
mother and older sister were killed two weeks before, at first traveling
with some people from their town but then blending in with the endless stream of other refugees moving southward along the pushed-up
roads and embankments of the river valleys. At another time it might
have been a pretty journey, the hills just turning the colors of pumpkin
and hay and pomegranate and the skies depthless and clear, but now
everywhere one looked most of the trees had been felled for fuel and
there was only a hazy, oppressive brightness refracted from the shorn
hillsides. There were formerly cultivated fields of potatoes and cab-
bages, and then the terraces of rice paddies, but all had been stripped
and then abandoned during these first months of the war. The farmers'
houses, if they hadn't been bombed to rubble, were alternately occu-
pied by both sides in retreat and advance, and then by passing refugees
like themselves. It didn't matter that sometimes the owners were present and still living there.

A few days earlier June and her siblings had stayed a night in a house
no bigger than twenty square meters with nearly thirty others, including the old farmer and his wife, who slept in the corner next to a locked
chest of their things. It was raining heavily that day, and when someone
spotted what looked like a house at the foot of a hill a few people began
to run for it, and then others, and soon enough scores. But it was far
in from the road and the three of them were fast and reached the house
in the first wave. The farmer had attempted to camouflage it with a
makeshift cover of netting and reeds and then appeared out front holding a pitchfork, but he pointed the tines downward when he saw it was
no use. The force of numbers held for even the weak and the ragged.
The crowd pushed in until the small house was full, the others having
to hike back to the road and continue their sodden march.

All the farmer and his wife could do was to make certain that they themselves had a space for the night. They were shrewd to share some of their food in the hope that all of it wouldn't simply be taken. Without any prompting, his wife quickly made a large pot of barley porridge and everyone got a half-cup; the three of them had one tin mug between them and June begged the farmer's wife to fill it to the brim, which she did. They took turns taking swallows while sitting jammed in among the rest of the horde, everyone sitting cross-legged and knee-to-knee. Only the smallest children could curl up or recline. Everyone was soaked from the rain, and the smell of so many wet, long-unwashed bodies in the enclosed space was fierce, the air of the single room quickly stifling and sour with an overwhelming humidity, and soon someone asked June to open the window, which was right above them. After eating, she took out a tortoiseshell comb of her mother's and ran it through her siblings' hair; she had noticed before the rain began in the morning how whitish their heads appeared and so combed through to remove the sheets of clinging lice. She flicked them out the window. It was futile work, of course, for she had no special soap to kill the eggs and they would simply multiply, besides the fact that the other people there were equally infested, but now that her mother and older sister were gone it was she who had to keep the little ones safe, keep them as sound as she could, and so whenever she had a chance June wiped their faces, or rubbed their teeth and gums with mint leaves, fed them whatever she could scrounge or barter for, offering them as much as she could without growing too weak herself.

She was always a responsible, filial daughter and, as she was closest in age to the twins, had looked after them for as long as she could remember. It happened that her older brother and sister were also twins and their family had always seemed to comprise her parents and just three children, instead of five, June ever slightly removed from their naturally unitary play. It was a system of orbit that had seemed unlucky to her at first but in fact suited her burgeoning character, something her gentle, thoughtful father recognized. He was a respected school-teacher in their town, and he often told her that there was great strength in her singularity, that she ought to revel in it, an idea that she would see as bitterly ironic years later, when he was falsely denounced as a Communist in the first disastrous, terrifying days of the war.

She combed her own short hair and saw that hers was rife with lice, too, and her sister Hee-Soo offered to do it for her, and she let her. A few of the men lit cigarettes and others began talking. The conversations centered at the start on the rumored movements of the forces (the Americans were advancing quickly north now, the North Koreans reportedly retreating pell-mell), on which were the best refugee camps, on lost family members, but then soon enough turned to subjects like the rain, the recent trend of weather, if the pears and persimmons would be ready by now (if there was any remaining fruit on the trees, if there were any trees at all), the best remedies for certain body aches, all the blithe, everyday talk that might keep at bay for a moment the staggering reality of the dismantled world outside.

But then a man stood up and began berating everyone for their trivial concerns. He was in his early thirties, which was unusual because any other man his age would have been conscripted instantly into military service. He spoke with emotion and passion, and from his accent and verbiage one could tell he was well educated. Didn't they care that atrocities were occurring daily, in every village and town in the river valley? Didn't they care that they were being committed not just by soldiers from both sides but by their own people? He talked about the rampant lawlessness that had swept the land, the raping and maiming and summary executions. A white-haired man near June sharply replied that his accusations were unfair, for what could powerless people like themselves ever do? It was difficult enough just to get by, to simply survive.

"War brought a tide of blood," the older man went on. "And it has swallowed everyone."

"Yes, it has," the man said. He had turned squarely to address the other man and June saw that one of his eyelids was shut and half sunken in the socket, the other eye wide open but clouded gray and aimed off-kilter.

"But it doesn't mean we should so quickly give up our humanity. That we should be so indifferent. Yesterday on the road there was an old woman lying on her side. I can hardly see but it was obvious that she was suffering greatly. Some of you here must have passed by her, yes?" He seemed to pick out June but she couldn't be sure. She had indeed seen the old woman. She was a wretched sight. She had soiled herself front and back and was wheezing heavily with desperate effort, as if a crab apple were lodged at the back of her mouth. It was difficult to know what was wrong with her but she had a terrible color. There was no family beside her, nor any possessions, or even a bag, only what she was wearing, as if she had been magically dropped there onto the road from some place far away. She was barefoot as well, her soles very pale and soft-looking, as though someone had just pulled off her shoes. Ji-Young was curious and slowed as they approached but they had nothing, nothing at all, to give her, and June had tugged her siblings' hands and they had quickly walked on.

"All the woman asked for when my mother and I stopped was to have a drink. A sip of water. That's all. She knew she was dying, and what a horror it must have been for her, to see that no one would even pause so she could have something so meager. Yet hundreds must have passed, before we came to her."

"We have Mother Mary and Jesus here," someone mumbled from

the other end of the room. There were scattered snorts of laughter. The man crooked his head, his one eye widening, craning about.

"I am talking about decency. About something as basic as that. We could offer her only the smallest comfort. She died shortly thereafter but, my God, she was alone and afraid and in misery. Who in this room would ever wish anyone an end like that?"

"So did you resurrect her?"

More laughter, this time full-throated and resonant. The man was about to respond but he went silent, his mother pulling hard on his arm to make him sit down, which he did. His eye was half closed now and his head and neck slightly shuddered, as though he were having the mildest seizure. The small talk resumed and soon enough it was as if the man had never stood up and said anything. The moment had already passed and disappeared. They were all chronically weary and hungry and whenever off their feet and safely sheltered the time paradoxically seemed to accelerate, the periods of rest never long enough, never satisfying, their bodies ready for complete repose but their thoughts restlessly spinning out memories they did not wish to see. Hee-Soo and Ji-Young lay nested together against her lap, the weight of them almost unbearable on her crossed legs. But the dirt floor was damp and chilly and she was afraid they might get sick, and those sick on the road, she knew, only grew more ill and weak and then often enough fell out of sight. She gently patted them on the back in a slow rhythm, lowing *cha-jahng, cha-jahng,* as her mother would do when they had a nightmare or couldn't sleep. The man and his mother sat leaning back-to-back, like many of the others trying to invite sleep, and June wondered whether he'd been in this condition his whole life or if he'd been blinded more recently, since the start of the war.

The rest of the night passed without incident. Despite the torture of having to sleep sitting up, people were accustomed to it, and it was mostly quiet. There were groans, and the anxious, nonsense mutterings of dreams, and then an outcry that would wake them all for a moment before they returned to their difficult slumbers. The half-blind man in fact cried out in the middle of the night, and for a long while afterward June couldn't sleep, her mind bracing for another shout or cry. It was the racked voice that disturbed her most. Someone's miserable song. Now, after all that had happened, she thought she could suffer seeing most anything, whatever cruelty or disaster, but the notes of a human plaint would make her wish she could exist without a heart.

She sensed movement in the dim predawn light. In the near corner an older middle-aged man was huffing and grimacing; he was one of those who had taunted the blind fellow. Everyone else was still asleep. She had heard his breath filtering fast through his teeth. He looked terribly pained and she was ready for him to wail for help when he closed his eyes and exhaled with a final rasp of his throat. His shoulders sagged. He was surely about to keel over, but instead he pushed aside the coat that covered his lap and a woman's head rose up, her expression wan, completely blank. She was around June's mother's age and still quite pretty, despite the sallow, drawn flesh of her face. Without looking at her, the man gave her a few strips of dried fish and then almost immediately dozed off. The woman slipped the shreds into her shirt and turned away. She absently caressed the sleeping children beside her, two young boys and a girl, and it was as if nothing had occurred until she glanced up and met June's gaze. June tried to look away. The woman stopped patting them, momentarily trapped in her shame, but then her eyes narrowed, hardening their focus, and they seemed to curse June through the darkness, as if to foretell of an ever-nearing future, an imminent fate.

With the new light of the day the others were arising, the room echoing with coughs and moans, and the several infants among them were already fretting, their bellies keen for milk. Hee-Soo and Ji-Young were awake now and they were softly whining, too, as they did every morning when they knew there would be nothing on hand to eat. If she had her own milk (if she even had a woman's breasts) she would have surely tried to feed them, but she shushed them, not for the sake of those still sleeping but to keep their thoughts from dwelling on the hunger. Her mother had kept telling them to think only of what lay over the next hill, in the next valley, the coming turn in the road, and though it never quelled a grain of the ache, her command seemed to quicken their pace ever so slightly, make them cover that much more ground on their southward journey to Pusan. From the beginning of their wartime life, their mother was shepherding them constantly forward, no matter the topography, no matter the weather. It was brutally torrid those first few weeks, the July sky a stifling blanket of haze; then the clouds would rend and the road would become a stalled river of mud. The flies and mosquitoes sang furiously in their ears. They'd trudge ahead anyway with their minds in arrest, in the suspension of any future save the one in which they persisted, kept on. Their movement was more inertia than propulsion. A necessary tendency. And yet one did whatever one could. One morning, when her mother was alive, June saw her mother emerge from the cab of an ROK army truck and then turn and accept several pouches of food from the driver. They were dried red beans. As she walked back, June pretended to be asleep, only rising with her siblings when her mother began to cook the beans. Nobody asked where they had come from. They ate them for breakfast, had bolted them down in fact, June filling her gullet so fast she'd actually choked for a few seconds, her eyes tearing as her mother gently rapped her on the back, saying, "Slow down, dear. There's plenty now."

The old farmer stood up with his wife by his side and said he wished he could offer something for breakfast but there was hardly anything left and so asked if they would kindly move on, now that it wasn't raining. He also said he had heard of a newly opened UN refugee camp some twenty kilometers south. No one much believed him about the camp or his store of food, but he'd surely suffered them and people began to gather their things and leave. While her siblings yawned and rubbed the sleep from their eyes, June brushed the smudges of dirt from their clothes. It was of course futile, as they could never do any wash and their clothing and skin were long infused by the brickish color of the valley soils, but she did so anyway because it was what her mother would do if she were still alive. It was how June formulated every decision. Whether to go on and whether to rest. Where to sleep at night. Whom to approach and whom to flee. But most of all it was how she snuffed her own animal impulses, her desire to keep wholly for herself the meager cache of whatever they were lucky to find. It was how she blunted herself from ever seeing her siblings as burdens, or worse, as though they were killing her, if slowly, two blind leeches attached to her heels and drawing the life out of her. It was how she had not yet allowed herself to harden against them. To hate them. For of course she loved them, and just as her mother would she'd give up all to protect them, but what in fact was left of her to give? She felt hollowed with hunger and weariness, only the fear invigorating her blood. She was beginning to realize, too, that they could not go on in this way for much longer, that something would have to change, and soon. They were carefully listening for frogs and crickets at night, in the hope of catching some to eat. They dug for roots and grubs during the day. They begged and stole whatever they could, but three months of grinding war had left little of value. And she knew she was too young and powerless to keep them sound. She could take care of herself but someone else would have to aid them. Otherwise they would perish, or in a moment of weakness she might let them perish, as she would sometimes imagine, letting go of their hands as they waded across some fast-moving river, the sound of the rushing water only partly masking their cries.

The farmer again asked the others still in the house to leave. But some had not even begun preparing to clear out, either remaining on their haunches or lying on the floor and smoking cigarettes. The farmer began complaining, saying he'd been patient and enough was enough. But he was being ignored, those moving on continuing to do so, the others remaining indolently at rest. The blind man and his mother had tightened their bundle and he hefted it onto his back, tying a canvas strap around his chest to secure it. They were shuffling out ahead of June and she saw that they were among the few who thanked the farmer and his wife as they exited. The wife was kind-eyed and spoke softly, and when they reached her, June took her hand and asked if they could remain with them for a while, if for just a few days, explaining as quickly as she could what had happened to their family, that they were now alone in the world. They'd sleep in the outhouse, if they had to. The farmer overheard her as he was exhorting some of the others to leave and he scolded his wife for even listening.

"The whole country is orphaned!" he said. "Get on, now, children, before the day gets too late. You'll be better off for it."

But instead of leaving, June sat down right in front of him, tugging her siblings to sit beside her. He told them to get up.

"Please, Grandmother, let us stay," June said to his wife, addressing her as if she were of their blood. "Don't make us go."

The farmer said harshly, "Did you not hear me, you insolent children!"

"Please, Grandmother!" she cried, her siblings now chiming in, too.

The farmer became enraged and grabbed her brother roughly by the arm, yanking him up like a doll. Ji-Young shrieked in pain and the farmer's wife asked her husband to stop. But he then grabbed June the same way and tried to pull her up to her feet. She resisted and he clasped her shirt and would have almost pulled it off, had she not leaned in and bitten him hard on his bony, darkly tanned forearm. The farmer shouted an obscenity and flung her wildly behind him, sending her crashing against a neat stack of kindling near the step-down to the tiny kitchen. June lay on the floor, her back and side afire with pain. For a moment all in the house seemed suspended, everyone staring at her, before she realized that it was not her they were looking at; part of the stack had fallen away, exposing the lid of a large earthenware barrel hidden behind the kindling. The farmer's wife immediately knelt and tried to gather the loose branches to place them again before the barrel.

Someone barked, "Hey, old-timer, why didn't you show us that last night?"

"Yeah, let's see what's in the jar."

Indeed, when his wife had prepared the pot of porridge, he'd made a special point of showing the inside of a similar vessel, which was practically empty save a cup for scooping.

"It's none of your business!" the farmer said. "None at all. Look here, I've been patient with all of you! We have nothing to give anymore. Now let us have our home again!"

One of the middle-aged men who'd been smoking now stood before the farmer. His cheeks were rough, his eyes lightless and deeply set. He was a head taller than the farmer and much broader, though still thin like everyone else, and he spoke without any hint of jest in his voice: "Just show us what's inside."

"I won't!" the farmer said.

The man brushed past him. But before he'd taken a second step the farmer pulled a wooden baton from under his shirt and hit him in the back of the head. The man fell straight down, as if dropped from a great height. He landed headfirst, with an ugly, hollow sound. June scooted away as some men attended to him; his face was pinched against the hard floor, dark, thick blood streaming from his nose. The farmer stood dazed as they tried to revive him, but it was no use.

"He's killed him," one of them said.

"With his back turned, no less!"

The farmer was already retreating against the wall when they rushed him. He held back the first man with his baton but the others quickly overwhelmed him, punching and kicking him as he crumpled to the floor. His wife was screaming for them to stop. But they beat him until he was curled up in a ball, covering his head, crying out like a pitiful boy in a schoolyard, his mouth webbed with bloodied strings of spit.

It was then that the house was ransacked. Everyone took part. Even many of those who'd begun hiking back to the main road, including the blind man and his mother, returned to force their way back inside. There was no use in doing anything else. It took perhaps all of a few minutes, for how little of value there was. First the hidden earthenware barrel was dumped, which was only half full of dried corn, then the larder of dry goods, and then the kitchen was stripped of pots and utensils and of anything else someone was willing to carry away. June and her siblings scooped up as much of the corn as they could; Ji-Young even used his mouth, jamming it with kernels when his shallow pockets were filled. (Later on he spit them up into June's hand and she rinsed them in the next stream they crossed.) Somebody broke off the lock on the clothes chest and women were rifling through it, June lucky to grab a blanket that fell between two women as they struggled over a silk blouse. The blanket was of light weight but large, and June knew it would be useful. The rest was just old people's clothes, worn and stained. In the end the house was in shambles, the floor a mess of pottery shards and torn fabric, smashed bits of furniture, every last object picked through and taken apart, and if not stolen, then instantly rendered worthless, and as the three of them left, June ordered her siblings to look away from the farmer's wife, who was still kneeling over her half-conscious husband, her face pure madness, screaming as if she were slowly being murdered.

THE TRAIN SLOWED DOWN and halted completely for a moment, then started again, the change in the rhythm waking Hee-Soo from her dreams. June was listening to her and wondering whether to wake her out of them, as she was growing more and more upset. She was calling their father as if he were inside his study but had somehow gotten locked in and was greatly distressed.

"Please hold on, Father," she was half crying. "Please just a little longer. Mother is still looking for the key."

June wound the blanket tightly around them, retucking the tattered ends beneath their feet. The stars were just appearing, moment by moment gaining in brilliance as the sky darkened. In another time, in another life, she would have thought them pretty, might have stirred her siblings to gaze up at their array, but as it was she could only see them as impossibly distant and perfect. Forever uninterested. After the train lurched forward, Hee-Soo fell quiet, Ji-Young snoring lightly the whole time; he always slept well, despite the circumstances. June hoped she might fall asleep, too, for a few hours at least, so that she'd have some strength the next day. But it was futile. She was thoroughly exhausted and her limbs felt as frail and old to her as that farmer's wife's branch-thin arms; and yet her mind still raced at night like a fueled engine, simply running and running, until it ran so hard and long that it forgot all else but this sole reason for being.

Their father had been the first. The last time she saw him he was bleeding from the nose and mouth, from the eyes, kneeling on the ground with his hands tied behind his back, a South Korean army officer standing jauntily above him, pressing the nose of a pistol to his head. The rest of them, except for her older brother, were in the back of a large transport truck, being driven away with the families of the other men who were being rounded up. They weren't told where they were going. It had all happened instantly, in the course of an afternoon, this a week after the war started; the rapid retreat of the South Korean forces was sweeping through the towns and a general panic abounded, everyone fearing what the Communists might do as the front rolled southward, people frantically loading up whatever they could and filling horse carts, wheelbarrows, cars if they had them. But as it happened the ROK forces wreaked as much misery as the northern soldiers, and perhaps more. That morning June's family was packing when the local police captain and ROK army officer and two armed soldiers appeared in their inner courtyard and ordered that her father go to the station with them. At first he simply nodded, as if the sight of them were nothing unusual. When they grabbed him to take him away he suddenly erupted, demanding to know what they were doing, why they wanted him, but they wouldn't tell him. When he resisted, a soldier rifle-butted him in the face, sending him to the ground. His nose was smashed. Her older brother, Ji-Hoon, who was fourteen, wildly threw himself at the soldier but he was easily thwarted and they toyed with him cruelly before corralling him into the back of a sedan, along with his half-conscious father. June witnessed this from the house, having just gathered the few clothes she would take with her, the rest of the family arrayed below in the small inner courtyard, and when her father was struck it did not seem an actual or even possible happening. It seemed to her that she was shouting and screaming along with her mother and older sister (the younger twins were sobbing), but a week afterward, in a quiet moment of rest on the road, her older sister asked her how she could have been so dispassionate and calm. "What is wrong with you?" she'd said, almost desperately, her tone suggesting that June's non-reaction was more a confirmation of her character than any surprise.

June's father and brother were driven away. The rest of the family was ordered to wait. Two hours later a truck pulled up and they had to climb into the open bed, where another fatherless family was riding. The truck picked up two other families and made its way to the public square of their town. In the square was her father, along with three other men. They were badly beaten up, bleeding and swollen about their faces. June's brother was not among them. The police captain announced that these four men were advance spies for the North, which the men had apparently admitted to under questioning. Neither her father nor the others were allowed to deny the charges. A crowd of townspeople had gathered, including some village officials who stood nervously behind the police captain. Then her father and the others were pushed to their knees. The officer paused for a moment and then waved the driver of their truck to pull away. June never heard any shots. They were driven for an hour or so south of town and then told to get out and join the rest of a throng of refugees marching on the road. Unlike the others, they were carrying hardly more than what they were wearing, though her mother had wound a belt of cash around her waist in the last chaotic moments they were in their house. Her mother asked the driver if he knew where her son had been taken, and the driver told them that a truck full of new conscripts had been sent toward the front line. But his expression was odd and her mother pressed him and he finally said that he'd heard the truck had been ambushed and attacked, and that those not immediately killed had been taken prisoner. For the next weeks her mother asked every person she came across if they had encountered or heard of him, the only word coming from a woman from their town who said she heard rumors of young South Korean men who had been reconscripted by the Communists and taken north.

June still asked after her brother whenever she had the chance, though somehow she was certain that she would never see him again. Either he would be killed in the fighting or they would perish on the road. But even at the farmer's house she spoke his name to those sitting immediately around them, perhaps more for the twins' sake than anything else.

The twins were fast asleep. She was flagging, too, and hungry. Sometimes the pangs overwhelmed her at night, after her siblings were asleep, and only then did she allow herself to softly whimper and cry. By the morning her spirit had hardened again, her mind already scrambling, angling furiously as to how they would eat for the day.

They were constantly famished, the hunger risen in them like well water during the spring rains, accruing to them each day until the feeling, oddly enough, was like an unbearable plenitude, this pressing flood of hollowness that would not recede. In the beginning, in those first days on the march, when they still had some money, they might buy rice and dried cabbage from others, her mother making a simple soup or gruel in a small tin pot a former neighbor had kindly given them. Because they'd had no time to gather what they'd packed they had much less than most of the other refugees. At first they did not dwell on the circumstances, for they were surely only temporary, for everyone was quickly moving southward toward the rumored refugee camps set up well behind the front, where people said there was plenty of food, and tents. Once a column of American trucks had rolled by, the soldiers tossing oranges and candy to them, and they could believe they would be all right. But soon enough, within mere days, there was little anyone could sell them, or, if someone was willing, a cup of rice or some strips of dried squid would be so costly that their money was practically worthless. And so the five of them—her mother and older sister and the twins and herself—took to foraging and scavenging, leaving the road for a part of the day to gather whatever they could in the countryside, greens and roots, wild berries and seeds, and then always checking any abandoned or destroyed American armor or trucks, however dangerous that might be, for whatever had been left behind. The Americans seemed to have unlimited supplies and were generous and profligate with them. Of course everyone else knew the same and so it was pure luck to happen upon a vehicle before it was completely, instantly stripped.

One afternoon the twins made a thrilling find, spotting the tail rotor of a helicopter that had crashed behind a bombed-out farmhouse. It had been there for at least a week, to judge from the remains of the pilots scattered about the wreck, the birds and rodents and feral dogs having worked to leave them almost cleanly skeletal inside the torn uniforms. Broken beer bottles littered the floor of the cockpit. But in a crate behind the seats there was a hold of pristine riches: a half-dozen packets of beef jerky and a can of Spam. As with the tins June found, they couldn't help but eat the canned meat right away; their mother refused it, professing not to like its smell as she cut the pinkish block into four thick slices with the edge of the can, though while she was gorging on the salty, slick meat June saw her mother take a taste of her fingertips, her eyes half shut, losing herself for a moment in another time and place.

The days on the road were like that. You could never anticipate what might happen next, the earth-shattering and the trivial interspersing with the cruelest irony. You could be saved by pure chance, or else ruined. That was the terror of it, what kept June awake at night and stole her breath through the day, though it was the terror that was also forming her into her destined shape, feeding the being of her vigilance until it had grown into the whole of her, pushing out everything else.

It happened soon after the twins found the helicopter. It was a beautiful, shimmering day, the sky majestically tufted with high clouds, the slightest cooling breeze filtering down from the hills. Because of the solid nourishment, they were feeling stronger, more lively, and they were covering good distances, the younger ones having less trouble keeping pace. And their mood was light, as light as could be, given the circumstances. An especially haggard-faced woman traveling in their column had even given Ji-Young a soccer ball, of all things; it had been the prized possession of her son, who'd succumbed to a terrible infection several weeks before. They'd traveled all the way from Pyongyang, most every meter on foot. The woman had two daughters with her and all of them were bearing heavy loads on their backs, and she'd held on to the ball but it was a burden as it was impossible to pack, and she was hoping to give it away to another young boy. It was somewhat deflated but almost new and June's mother at first balked at accepting it, for the very reason of having to carry it, but Ji-Young was jumping up and down and she couldn't bear to refuse him. Soon enough they would stop once or twice a day and they would play in whatever patch of field was around, often other children joining them for a kick or two before their families called them back, June's mother and older sister, Hee-Sung, watching them from the embanked road. Everyone was exhausted and hungry, but it was joyous, for a moment at least, to simply watch the children play. That day they were playing with others when a column of trucks and light armor rolled through. It was the Communists, heading north; it was said the Americans were pushing them back now from the small foothold they'd desperately held around Pusan, and the North Koreans were in full retreat. Several hours later a troop of soldiers followed, numbering only in the dozens, scuttling through them in a labored, steady march. The soldiers' condition was poor, some of them worse off, it seemed, than their own civilian ranks, a good number of them wounded, at least every fourth or fifth man unarmed. Still, they paused there long enough to demand food from the refugees, having everyone open their packs, and Hee-Sung, who was carrying the beef jerky, decided on her own to slip down off the road and join the soccer game, to safeguard the food. The packets of dried meat had been tightly strapped to her chest with a long bolt of muslin (they were careful to keep it hidden, given its great value, taking it out only under cover of night, when they could huddle together and gnaw the delicious strips in secret); June's mother had been binding her chest anyway, for at fourteen Hee-Sung's breasts were already full and womanly. She'd cut Hee-Sung's hair short, too, as well as June's, rubbed their faces with dirt each morning, and dressed them with school caps like boys, for there was always that certain danger. They'd witnessed soldiers from both sides kidnap other women and girls, some of them as young as June; they'd simply grab a girl from the ranks and drive off with her, and if she was lucky they wouldn't kill her afterward, abandoning her someplace not too far away where she could be found or still make her way back.

When one of the soldiers reached June's mother she stood up and immediately gave him a tiny pouch each of barley and rice, saying she had only one other for her entire family. He was a corporal, judging from the bars on his uniform, and he shouted for the other one and she gave it to him, whimpering. But June knew she'd just hidden much more than that in a sock of pantyhose beneath her feet and in the tips of her rubber shoes. The soldier pocketed it and he and his group were about to move on when he saw the children standing silently about in the weedy field, the ball left idle between them.

"Go ahead and play," he said to them. His face was dirty and unshaven, his uniform caked with mud and dried blood.

None of them moved and he yelled, "Play! Play!"

One of the boys pushed the ball with his foot and another passed it on quickly to Hee-Sung, who awkwardly kicked at it. She had never played much soccer. The corporal muttered something and handed his rifle to another soldier and jumped down, talking about how there wasn't proper sports instruction in the schools. Two of his comrades stepped down with him. He motioned to Hee-Sung as he asked for the ball and commanded, "Watch me!" She'd tried to meld into the scatter of the other children but she was older and taller than all of them. He made the ball play back and forth quickly between his feet and then crisply booted it with his instep to one of the soldiers, who passed it to the other. It went back again to the corporal and he passed it on directly to Hee-Sung, who bent down and stopped it with her hands.

"What are you doing?" he said, exasperated. "Trap it and pass it back!" Hee-Sung hesitated and then did as he ordered but when the ball rolled to him he just let it deflect off his foot. His expression had stiffened. As he walked to her everyone stood still and June's mother began in desperation to call to him, though with an informal address, her voice sounding strangely youthful and demure, but he ignored her and when he reached Hee-Sung he pulled off her cap and took a long look at her short hair. He then held her by the neck and with his free hand pressed up between her legs. She crumpled to the ground, trying to push him away, while June's mother was shouting for him to leave her alone, begging him. He finally released her and for a moment it seemed he was going to strike her or perhaps kick her. But he simply turned to mount the road again. Hee-Sung had crawled away but then the two other soldiers stood her up on her feet, saying she made for a "pretty boy." The corporal told them they were moving on now but they kept pawing her, if not roughly, handling her short hair, her hips, and now her chest. One of them, a soldier whose eyes were set very close together, like an opossum's, tested her there again and then ordered her to take off her shirt. She refused. He slapped her and then tore violently at it, exposing the binding about her chest, as well as the hidden shapes within the layers. June's mother ran over to them, screaming, and the other soldier struck her with his fist and she fell heavily to the dirt. She was momentarily dazed and a front tooth was knocked out, her mouth and lip badly bleeding, and June rushed to her and dabbed at it with her sleeve, not knowing what else to do. She and the rest of the children were crying, as was Hee-Sung. She was terrified, her skinny shoulders quivering. The corporal was looking on from the road. The soldier told Hee-Sung to raise her arms and he pulled the binding loose, undoing it from her as if from a spool, and midway through, the packets of dried beef fell out.

"Well, look at this," he said, picking them up. He inspected the jerky, and the labels. "Where did you get this?"

She didn't answer.

"What are you, some kind of whore for the foreigners? This is American food."

"Please, I just found those."

"What did you do for them, to get such a present?"

"Nothing. I never did anything. Please, I'm telling the truth!"

"Sure you are."

"Let's see what else she has," the other one said.

There was nothing else, this was obvious, but the soldier undid her anyway, with a horrid, meticulous patience. Soon she was completely bare on top, her breasts as pale as milk. She tried to cover herself but he had her keep her arms high, and all she could do was hide her face in the nooks of her elbows as she sobbed.

"Now there's some sweet fruit," the other soldier said.

"She's mine," the opossum-eyed soldier told him, now grabbing her by the arm.

"Maybe yours first!"

She seemed to lose control of her legs and they practically had to carry her up to the road, where they flagged down a covered truck. The soldiers quickly came to some agreement with the driver, who motioned to the rear. Very few of the soldiers were lucky enough to ride in vehicles. But as they dragged her to the back, Hee-Sung began to resist, her feet digging at the dirt road. The soldier lifted her and slung her over his shoulder and took her to the rear of the truck. She was pummeling his back, kicking her legs. His partner jumped up inside and he handed her to him, and then got in himself. He shouted to the driver but the truck didn't move; it had stalled while idling. The driver turned over the engine several times before it caught. It was then that her mother, who'd scrabbled frantically up the embankment, reached it, and as it began to roll away she held on to the tailgate, suspended on its edge, Hee-Sung screaming from inside, *Uhm-ma! Uhm-ma!*, her mother screaming, *Hee-Sung-ah!* June was wailing, too, as were the twins, who stood frozen beside her, but she couldn't hear herself for the terrible shrieking, their cries as sharp as if they were being flayed alive.

But it was another sound that overwhelmed them: the roar of two silvery jet planes flashing by overhead. The planes flew in low, shaking the ground as they instantly spanned the length of the valley, then careened far in the distance in a long, banking ascent. They disappeared almost completely, but then June could see they were arcing back. Suddenly the column of soldiers and refugees broke up and dispersed. People sprinted for the fields. The truck had sped up for a distance but now stopped and June's mother climbed aboard while the two soldiers and a couple of others leaped out. But Hee-Sung and her mother did not. They were embracing, kissing, clothing each other in their arms, before the terrible onrush of sound and light.

When June opened her eyes the truck was gone. There had been a thunderous explosion; June and the twins had been knocked over by the force of the blast. There was an intense pressure in her ears and for several minutes she could not hear her own breathing. The planes had made only the one pass, firing a few rockets, and then flown away. She'd instinctively crouched over her siblings, and when she stood and looked back at the spot there was nothing but a burning half-chassis. She ordered her brother and sister to stay put and she ran there, in perfect silence, her heart feeling like it would burst out of her chest.

The rest of the truck was in small pieces, its parts on the road and blown for dozens of meters on either side. The section in flames lay at the rim of a blackened crater in the road that the explosion had dug two meters deep and many times as wide. But there was little else about. Later she would hear one of the soldiers say that the truck had been heavily loaded with munitions, and that one of the rockets had directly struck the covered bed of the truck. She searched the field below the road and saw the rent bodies of two soldiers on the periphery; the one with the pinched eyes had a large, jagged plate of metal lodged in his neck, his blood staining the ground in a small black patch. The other body was headless, but otherwise untouched. And she was ready for the most horrid discovery. But as long as she looked, circling back and forth, she could not find a single sign of her mother or sister. There was not a scrap of their clothing, not a lock of their hair. It was as if they had kited up into the sky, become the last wisps of the jet trails now diffusing with a southerly breeze, disappearing fast above her.

THE TRAIN HAD SETTLED into a steady pace, moving through the flat of the darkened valley at the speed of a fast horse trot, the locomotive's rhythm and the radiant warmth of her siblings' bodies finally ushering June into a state of virtual sleep. It was not wholly sleep because she did not yet dream—she never quite dreamed anymore. Instead, her mind rode alongside itself in a state of animal vigilance, such that she could see the three of them nested in the dull gray wrap of the blanket, their heads and feet tucked inside so that it looked like some huge spider's or moth's downy egg sac affixed on the boxcar, placed so that it might travel freely and survive. These last of their kind. If there were any purposeful thoughts bracing her now they simply marked the distances they were covering, the meter of the wheels upon the rails, the shriek of the turns, and the idea that if they could keep moving like this it would be their best chance of remaining together, staying sound. Her one resolve, just before falling sleep, was that they should stay on this train for as long as it would go, for as far as it might take them. There was almost no prospect of getting food on the train, as there would be at some camp; it was difficult to steal or beg anything inside the cars and all but impossible on top. But they were ground down by the road, and she calculated it might be worth eating nothing at all if they could stay cocooned like this and reach Pusan in the next couple of days. If she could administer a potion to make them sleep right through and so blunt the pangs in their bellies she would do so even if it meant them sliding dangerously close to death. For in every village there was a purveyor of herbal medicines who made teas for sleep—even the deepest sleep, if one wished, for the pained and dying.

But what would June in fact do if she had some of that tea now? She would not be afraid that they might drink too much. Maybe she would even steal some sugar or honey to make the drink delicious and sweet, have them gulp it and then lay them down just like this, clinging to her belly like they were her own children, and tell them a colorful story about the grand meal they'd soon enjoy with their cousins. She would give her life for them, but she had begun to understand that the other face of that will was that she could allow them to suffer only so much. They were in a grave condition. Their cheekbones, like her own, were sharply drawn now and jutting, but their bellies were unnaturally distended, the skin drum-tight and shiny. Ji-Young's hair was beginning to fall out and Hee-Soo had a weeping rash on her back that was festering as it spread. Both of them were listless, dull-eyed, growing quieter by the hour, and they'd even ceased to wonder about their mother and sister; after the attack by the planes they'd asked constantly about where they might have gone, as June had told them their truck had sped off before the planes swooped in and that they would make their way to Pusan soon, if they weren't there already. But in the last few days neither mentioned Hee-Sung or their mother, as if the privation had clarified their minds as much as their bodies, rendered away all infantile hope and wish and belief to leave only the unmysterious, the unmistakable, the real.

And yet June would not yet speak aloud what they already knew was the truth. It was not for them she delayed, but for herself. She cast a stony front to the world but in her sleep's throes it was for the moment vanquished and she was once again the child she had been on the eve of the war, a too-tall, soft-spoken girl of eleven who was content to play with much younger children, who was still too shy to look the village boys in the eyes, who wanted nothing more than to sit in her father's lap and hum along with his records while he drew on his corncob pipe, the smoke hanging fatly and sweetly about them. And the deep warmth she felt was not of her sleeping siblings but the heat of the *ondol* floor nearest the kitchen hearth, where in winter she often lay with a book, the housekeeper stoking the fire so hot that June was sure she'd be seared to the tiles if she read another page. In her sleep she could still believe that all of them would eventually reunite, for she hadn't actually witnessed her mother's and sister's deaths, or, for that matter, her father's. And then, for all she knew, her older brother, despite the surety of her instinct, might very well be hiking north through the hills with the Communists, beleaguered but alive. This was the waking picture in her mind. And even if she knew that all of this was illusory, perhaps the most perilous kind of self-lie, the kind that made one giddy and angry and desperate all at once, she might still choose to crawl inside of it anyway for as long as she could, let it have her breath if it wanted, let it extinguish her outright.

Her chest heaved at the close, used-up air beneath the tight dome of the blanket, and she involuntarily turned from her siblings and craned against the corner of the fabric so that the wind rushed over her eyes and nose. The air was frigid and tainted by the coally exhaust of the locomotive but she took it in and let it flood her lungs. She shivered terribly. The night sky was dying, brightening quickly with the light. She was awake but did not yet want to open her eyes. She wanted to sleep, to sleep a little bit again. But the train suddenly and violently bucked, sending her hurtling against the metal rib on the front side of the well. She struck it headfirst and was dazed for a second and when she opened her eyes she was half hanging off the edge between the cars. The train lurched forward once more and then finally stopped. Her nose felt as if it was smashed. It was only when she checked her own skin for blood that she realized they were gone. Her brother and her sister. She peered down and saw the blanket draped over the coupling, their satchel broken open beside the shiny rail, their few worthless possessions scattered in the dirt.

She screamed: *"Ji-Young-a! Hee-Soo-na!"*

She climbed down the ladder and jumped to the ground. But they weren't there, not on either side of the boxcars. They were in a wide, dusky valley, no buildings or houses or even a road within sight.

"Ji-Young-a! Where are you? Hee-Soo-*na!* Answer me! Answer me!"

She got on her knees and looked under the wheels but they weren't there. Other people had climbed down as well and were running toward the rear; the train had rolled a short distance before halting, perhaps the length of three or four cars. Some terrible shouting came now, and June followed it even though it was a grown man's voice, running in her bare feet—her shoes had come off—and when she came upon him he was grasping his arm in a funny way. He had been thrown off the train as well and had broken it, the lower part of his arm bent grotesquely backwards, as if he had an extra elbow. He asked her for help but she didn't answer because she heard the report of Ji-Young's voice weakly calling, *Noo-nah, noo-nah.*

He was two cars down, lying close to the train. A woman was kneeling before him. She didn't see Hee-Soo. At first it looked as if the woman were fitting her brother for a shoe, but when June got closer she saw what had happened and stopped a few paces short, unable to move on.

"*Noo-nah . . .*" Ji-Young said again.

"This is your little brother?" the woman said to June. June nodded.

"Then come here and help me! Well? Come on, girl, right now!"

June stepped forward and knelt down.

"When I say so, pinch his leg with your hands, here, just below the knee. As hard as you can."

June readied her hands.

"Now!"

Ji-Young moaned sharply with the pressure, crying miserably. The woman seemed to know what she had to do. She kept telling him not to look down, to keep his eyes closed, saying there was nothing to see. June would always think later that that was perversely right: for his foot was gone. The amputation was very clean. The stump was bleeding fitfully, the flow alternately staunched and then surging as the woman tried to bind his thin calf with a belt. The light was coming up now and the blood showed its pure color, while all else—the woman's clothes, the arid ground—was washed out, depleted. It was then that June looked away from the tracks and noticed a figure lying belly down near the weedy field. It was Hee-Soo; she could tell by her thick mop

28

of hair. For a moment June was sure that she was all right because her face was turned to her and her eyes were open, her mouth in a faint, if somewhat confused, smile. But she was dead. Both her legs were cut off. She had crawled all that way, and all her blood had run out.

The wheels of the train squealed and it began to inch forward, as though the locomotive was now pushing off the rails whatever obstacle it had struck. Then the train stopped for a moment before moving again. The woman's own children, who sat on top of the boxcar, yelled for her to get back on. But the woman couldn't cinch the belt tightly enough, and Ji-Young was bleeding freely again. The train kept moving, a little faster now, and the woman's children began to shriek for their mother, high panic in their wails. She looked June in the eye and said to her, "You should get back on, child."

"Please help us."

"I'm sorry . . . I'm sorry . . ." She got up, pausing ever so slightly, and then hustled to the car where her children were, climbing quickly aboard.

Ji-Young was quiet now, breathing shallowly, as though he wasn't very pained at all. June wound the belt around his leg and looped it through itself before pulling on it as hard as she could. Ji-Young screamed and momentarily fainted. But the bleeding stopped, and with all her strength she lifted her brother and cradled him. He was no heavier than kindling. And she began to run. One of the boxcar's doors was partly open and she could catch it and hand him up to the people packed inside. Some of them were waving her on, beckoning her. The train was speeding up, beginning to leave her behind. It was their only chance now. But it was then that the belt came loose from Ji-Young's leg and slipped off. The blood poured out as if from a spigot and she squeezed the stump as she ran, but one hand wasn't strong enough. She could not do it. So she halted and laid him on the ground, gripping the stump again with two hands. The cars were slowly rolling past them, only a third of the train remaining.

"How come you stopped?" he murmured.

"I can't run anymore."

"Oh." He was losing consciousness, the color draining from his face. "Will you come back for me?"

June nodded.

"You promise?"

She nodded again.

"It's okay. You don't have to."

She let go his still-warm hand, kissed his still-warm face. She stayed with him as long as she could. But when the last car of the train passed her she rose to her feet and steadied herself. And then she ran for her life.

TWO

New York, 1986

HERE WAS THE CITY of her solitude, set afire by the first autumn
light. Could a civilization ever be as peerlessly etched as this? The corner
windows of her apartment faced north and west onto the stone-and-
glass towers of Midtown, and through all the years she lived here she
had never quite seen this depth of gleaming or coloration, the low sun
sparking every niche of the building faces and lending shape to the sky
by lamping the high-floating ribbons of sheerest vapor.

June's work was all but done. How time had accelerated. The apartment was sold the very day it was put on the market, and here she was,
a mere six weeks later, peeling off rubber cleaning gloves and tossing
them into a black garbage bag. Earlier, the men she regularly employed
to deliver items from her antiques shop had carried out the last chair
and lamps from the apartment, and by now they were likely finished
with their rounds. Rather than hiring an estate service, she had done
the job herself, selling everything she owned in grouped lots to dealers
she knew around the city. She had practically given the stuff away,

strangely delighting in the knowledge that they would do very well with the pieces. One of them actually balked at paying the low price she proposed, insisting that there should be some honor, even among thieves. She told him he had better stop talking about honor or she'd reconsider, and soon enough he relented, to the point of inquiring, before he left, about a Late Federal desk he'd long admired. She undersold that one to him, too. The overwhelming balance, like the nonrare books and records, the kitchen- and cookware, the bath towels and bed linens, she bundled and gave free to a junk dealer friend on the Bowery.

For herself, she had set aside only two small suitcases packed with clothes and a zippered tote of toiletries. Just a few basic cosmetics. Vanity had never in the least ruled her. Mostly it was her nature, but there was also the fact that she had never needed to be concerned with her appearance. She had spent her life being not so beautiful as extraordinarily youthful, her wide, oval face ruddy and pure, her skin having an apricot smoothness, the lustrous sheets of her black hair shimmering and thick. To an undiscriminating eye, her sturdy figure might have appeared stocky, but her naturally bolt-straight posture, her shoulders set back like a dancer's, made her look taller, more athletic, as though she were just about to spring. Only a few months earlier, on her forty-seventh birthday, her favorite waiter at the corner diner brought her a huge slice of carrot cake with candles in the shape of 25 stuck in the white sea of the icing, though of course he could guess her approximate age. He was perhaps slightly younger than she, but he always called her his "lass," and like most men (and women) of every age who came into her shop or sat beside her on the subway, he was drawn to this freshness, this vitality, this odd but intractable sense that she was someone who might never grow old. Her late husband, David, who had passed unexpectedly two years ago, often said as much, jesting that her eternal youth would rub off on him, as though she were a charm against the dread pull of the years. He would say, "Come here and just lie on me."

"That's all you want?"

"That's all I need."

"Are you sure?"

"Well . . ."

How different things would be, if she had such powers. . . .

She twist-tied the garbage bag and hauled it out to the two others already slumped outside her door. There was one other apartment across the short hall, but June had never exchanged more than a hello with the occupants, so she hadn't bothered saying goodbye. They would have to learn of her departure from Habi, or from someone else in the building, or when the new owners moved in, and they likely wouldn't pause or think more than a second about it, which was perfectly fine by June. The apartment had been David's, but it suited her just as well; the building was on lower Madison Avenue and tended to attract those who didn't care that the area lacked services and was deserted at night, who didn't mind the traffic noise or lack of residential neighbors. They enjoyed the special brand of privacy that comes from living an exquisitely small, circumscribed existence, made exquisitely smaller and more private still when lived in the heart of the immense, bustling city.

The elevator bell rang and the door glided open; it was Habi, the young building superintendent. Earlier June had asked him to come up, and he assumed it was to help her with the garbage bags, and he grabbed two by the neck, but she waved him off.

"Please, Habi. Come inside. I want to show you something."

He let go of the bags and followed her inside the apartment, which was completely empty and swept clean. He had been in her apartment a half-dozen times, yet each time he entered he behaved as though it were the first, or perhaps he felt he shouldn't, and he lingered by the kitchen until she guided him to one of the back rooms.

Habi was from the Congo and she had come to know him best of anyone in the building, especially after David died. If he was around, he always helped carry her groceries upstairs (there was no doorman), and several times sat long enough to have a cup of tea with her. They didn't say very much, for whatever reason; she simply enjoyed his presence, which was a kind of perfect temperature, like tropical waters. She admired that he was intelligent and soft-spoken and polite and did his menial and mostly thankless job well and carried himself with unstinting dignity. He was always very respectful. He had a very pleasing and placid face, but for a long, raised scar that ran from the corner of his eye to his jaw. June had noticed that he had a scar on his left palm, too, which aligned exactly with the one on his face whenever he raised up his hand. Once she asked him about it, and rather than answer directly, he simply said he was orphaned when he was young. "It was a very difficult period," he said, in his heavy French accent. "A tribal conflict." He had walked for several weeks on his own, hiding out during the days and moving at night, covering hundreds of kilometers on his bare feet. It was then that he asked June what had happened to her hands. His question took her aback, but then she surprised herself by turning them over and showing them to him. Her hands were delicate and petite and perfectly normal in appearance except when she revealed her palms, which was something she shied from doing. The palms and pads of her fingers looked like they were somehow unfinished, being putty-smooth and only faintly lined, like the hands of a mannequin. One of them was more scarred than the other. She told him they were burned in an accident. He'd nodded somberly, but without the cloying concern that others might proffer, and said nothing more. Yet she would have told him (as she would never tell others) that they gave her discomfort sometimes, despite the fact that they were almost completely numb.

"There are some things I want you to look at," she said. They walked to the back bedroom, their footfalls echoing in the empty apartment, and for a moment June pictured them as a couple, shopping for their first home. "I've had this furniture for a while, and now that you are married I thought you might like to have it."

The furniture was a child's solid walnut desk and chair, as well as two matching chests of drawers and a bunk bed with rails and a ladder. All of it was in good condition, but June had spent a couple hours anyway filling and buffing the various scratches and dings, just as she might have in her shop. She then polished each piece until it looked brand new.

"But we do not have children," Habi said.

"You will someday, won't you? It's high-quality furniture, the kind they don't make anymore, at least not for children." She pulled open the desk drawers, showing him the joints, the bottoms, even stepping up one rung on the ladder to give a tug at the bedrails. "I was about to sell it with everything else, but then I realized how stupid I was. I would have shown you last week, but I've been so busy."

"I am certain I cannot pay you enough."

"Pay me? You'll pay me nothing. I'll have my deliverymen bring it to you tomorrow." Though she already knew it, she asked him to write down his address.

He nodded, offering, "Please, I can take it myself."

"Don't be silly. It's their job, and you probably don't even have a car."

"I do have one," he said. "But it is small. Two doors."

"It's a deal, then. But it has to be tomorrow, because that's the closing. Will your wife be home?"

He said yes, this was possible. His wife did alterations for a dry cleaner, work she could bring home. June didn't know much else about her, except that she was from Senegal, and that Habi had met her in a park in central Queens, where they lived. June wished that she could have met her so she could more easily imagine what their children might someday look like, but for now she simply pictured two skinny boys in their pajamas, climbing up and down the bunks, laughing together with wide, watchful eyes like Habi's.

"My wife will be sorry she could not thank you," he said, as if he had been able to read her thoughts.

"Tell her that she is most welcome."

"I will."

He gently pushed in the drawers to align them and said, "I did not know you and Mr. Singer had children."

"Oh, well, yes," she said, amazed at herself for not anticipating that Habi would of course wonder about who had used the furniture. Yet it was not at all disturbing to answer him. "But not Mr. Singer's child. Just mine. And only one. A boy."

"I see," Habi said softly. He was clearly hesitant to inquire further.

"Would you like to know his name?"

He nodded.

"It's Nicholas."

"Nicholas," he said, the sound of it mysterious and dashing in his accent. "That is a fine name."

"Yes," June said. "I've always thought so."

After she locked the apartment door she handed the keys to Habi. He was to let in the deliverymen the next morning, and once the new owners or their renters arrived he would give them the keys. She decided she wouldn't bring up again how her attorney would someday—and perhaps quite soon—contact him in regard to the bequest she had arranged. In the scheme of her finances, ten thousand dollars was not a huge gift, and was just enough, she figured, for him to put toward a down payment on a house, or to open a store, perhaps a dress shop his wife could run. Though it was unlikely that she would ever see him again she didn't want him to feel beholden to her because of some inordinate sum; she didn't want him to have to think of her always in gratitude, which turns, too often, to resentment. In fact, he might refuse the gift, when the day did come. He could never care about something like money in the same way she could never care about it; she knew they were alike that way, but she wanted to do something for him, to show him a kindness, and as there was no time left for a deepening friendship, there was little else for her to give him but the furniture, and this.

He placed the garbage bags into the elevator and rode down with her to the lobby. When they stepped out, three tenants were waiting for the car. On seeing Habi, they immediately peppered him with requests, June caught in the line of fire as they asked how soon he could unplug a drain, fix a dishwasher, call in the exterminator. While Habi patiently triaged their requests, June sidestepped through them, thinking that it would be best if she simply left right now, adieus never being easy for her. She was about to let herself out through the framed glass door when Habi called out somewhat sharply, "Mrs. Singer!" So she waited. When the tenants were satisfied they would be attended to and settled into the elevator, Habi turned to her and extended his hand. She shook it and let it go.

"It is possible that I may not see you here again, Mrs. Singer?"

"That's right."

"You will be going to where, Mrs. Singer? Another city?"

"Yes. But I'll be traveling. To Europe. To Italy."

"I have not been to that country," Habi said. "They say it is a beautiful place."

"I believe it is."

"You have not been there?"

"Not yet."

"You will be there for a long time?"

"I think so. Who knows. Maybe a very long time."

He nodded, with an uneasy smile, for she was smiling at him, but he wasn't looking at her as he always did with his clear-eyed directness. He clutched the ring of keys at his side. And all at once June felt that his interest in her plans masked a grave disappointment.

He said, "I am sorry that I could not help you more."

"You've always helped me plenty."

"I mean to say, during this difficult time."

"You shouldn't feel that way," she said. "And let's be honest, not everything can be helped."

He assented with a low hum in his throat. She felt a similar thrum in her chest and couldn't help but say: "I only wish you would let me help you. You must know how pleased I would be if you would accept something."

"Thank you, Mrs. Singer," he said. "I am doing fine on my own."

"I know you are. But it wouldn't hurt anyone. Especially me. You should remember that. I have more than I will ever need."

"I am fine, Mrs. Singer, thank you."

"All right. Goodbye, then, Habi. Good luck to you."

"Goodbye, Mrs. Singer."

They shook somewhat formally again until she surprised them both by pulling him in and hugging him. Habi momentarily stiffened but then he embraced her, too, his arms wiry and strong. He smelled faintly of machine oil and something spicy, like cinnamon, and though she breathed in deeply her heart suddenly sagged, as if the air was of great weight. She didn't want to cry. A loud knock on the heavy glass door separated them. A man stood outside with a white plastic bag in each hand, raising the bags up for them to see. Habi opened the door and a warm autumn draft rushed in along with the sweet, garlicky scent of Chinese food, and while the man kept repeating "10-B, 10-B," and Habi was buzzing the apartment, June slipped out the door and walked as fast as she could to the street to catch a stopped taxi, Habi's voice trailing her, his call of *Bon voyage* like a somber, gentle siren.

BON VOYAGE. For several days afterward June tossed about the notion, wondering if such a journey was truly possible for her. But why not? Certainly her affairs were in order: the apartment closing went smoothly, the last of the furniture was delivered to various dealers and to Habi, and the lease on her shop, renewed five years ago, was expiring in a week. The timing was miraculous. For the last month she had been steeling herself for the trip, consciously conserving her energy, and there was no reason it shouldn't prove to be a good one, kindly to her person, even fulfilling. She had just poured water from the electric kettle for roasted rice tea when there was a knocking at the glass-paneled door of the shop. She had covered the door, as well as the inside of the front window, with white butcher paper, and so she could make out only a large looming shadow against the fading light of the early evening. No doubt it was the investigator-for-hire; no one else would assume there was anyone inside. He had called the shop that morning, saying he had detailed news of her son. For a long moment she sat still in the rickety oak swivel chair, a part of her dreading the creak that would betray her presence: this was her last chance to let it all just be. But then a stouter knock rattled the glass and she rose with what seemed an external propulsion, as if she had been fitted with invisible wings that knew nothing else but to beat. She opened the door to a tall, broad-shouldered man wearing a dark suit and striped tie and gray overcoat and holding a bulky briefcase in one hand. He might have been a typical New York businessman were it not for the terrible roughness of the skin on his cheeks, the likely result of a childhood pox. The scarring was severe and, unfairly or not, it made him appear tensed, stricken.

"Mrs. Singer? I'm Clines."

She let him into the poorly lit shop. He appeared even taller when he stepped inside, and without being conscious of it she placed herself between him and the door. He had long pale hands and long legs, which ended in narrow, boatlike black shoes. He looked around the rectangular room of the shop, and she wondered if he was calculating the odds of her ability to pay him for his services. So far she'd only sent him a check for five hundred dollars as a retainer, and it was quite clear the sum value of what was left in the near-empty shop wasn't close to that figure: there was the oak desk chair with its rusty wheels and a chipped glass coffee table topped with prescription bottles that served as a nightstand for the twin-sized mattress and box spring placed on the floor next to it. There was a floor lamp on the other side of the bed and beside that a warped drop-leaf table with an electric hot plate on which the kettle was wheezing ever so softly as the heat of the coils died down. Her clothes were folded and simply stacked in two opened suitcases against the wall, which was unadorned except for the few picture hangers that had been left up and the more numerous holes made by former ones. She could have been a squatter in the store for all he knew, an unstable, destitute woman who had stolen in and invented a dire family scenario.

She offered him the desk chair. June herself sat down on the low bed. "I want you to know, Mr. Clines, that I live here because it's simplest for me, at this moment. This was my place of business."

"I'm not worried," he said, setting down his briefcase. He didn't remove his light overcoat. "I know you're more than solvent. I know that you've been liquidating your inventory. That you sold your apartment. I have to look into these things."

"I understand."

He nodded. "Now to why I'm here."

"Yes. Please."

"Before we start, I have to ask you whether you're set on wanting to find this person."

"He's my *son*," she replied, disliking his use of "this person."

"But are you sure you want to find him?" he said again. "I have to ask. Sometimes people think they want something when in fact they don't. We can stop now and all you'll be responsible to me for is a few hours."

"That's all right."

"You're certain?"

"Yes."

But June had in fact wondered, when she first contacted Clines, if she was indeed sure. It had been so long. The last time she had seen Nicholas in person was eight years ago, on the day of his high school graduation. He left that very night, for his own self-styled "grand tour." June was naturally under the impression that he was going to call her regularly from wherever he was. As he stuffed the last clothes and books into his backpack that evening, Nicholas couldn't tell her his itinerary because he said he didn't know it himself. He would fly the red-eye to London, as that was the cheapest flight, but then cross the Channel as soon as he could and roam through Europe on his way to Italy, where he would stay, he told her, until his money ran out. What she never imagined was that his tour would be continuous, that it would turn out to be a perpetual series of departures that would never quite lead him back home. For the first year he sent monthly postcards, addressed, oddly, not to the apartment but to the shop, the briefest scrawls about what he was seeing, a job he'd just taken, sometimes the only indication of place being the postmark. He never left an address where she could write him back. The monthlies became bimonthlies, and then seasonal, and by the time they appeared twice a year she had somehow quelled most of the confusion and hurt and rage their arrival brought on in her heart.

Eventually, at least during the waking hours, she rarely thought of him, and it was only in her dreams that she encountered him. He would appear to her as gaunt, even skinnier than he always was, wearing the same faded Led Zeppelin concert T-shirt and blue jeans he'd departed in, walking through the anonymous gray terminal of a train station or airport with nothing on his back. He wasn't hungry or lonely or lost, and for a brief, calming moment before she awoke, June could rest easy in how self-sufficient he appeared, how perfectly needless (if not perfectly contented), which she knew, even inside her dream, was a mirror of her own difficult character.

"Please show me what you have, Mr. Clines."

He opened his briefcase and removed a thick manila folder and handed it to her. Inside were faxes, copies of bureaucratic-looking documents with official seals on the letterheads, and then other handwritten or typed pages. Clines described what they were as she went through them; most of them were lists made out for local police, each page in a different language: Spanish, French, Dutch, Italian. The only one in English was from a prominent antiquities dealer in London, whose firm was well known to the New York trade; here again was a list of stolen items, a few small oil paintings, silverware, coins, jewelry, various objets d'art.

As he spoke she scanned the pages for mention of her son, but the name Nicholas Han (Han was her family surname) did not appear. The names on the pages rang familiar to her, like people she'd never known but might have read about, or had heard of through others, names varied on themes and notations that she alone could collate and make sense of. There were Stephan Lombardia, Leo Stevens, Leo De Nicole, among others, aliases that clearly came from things she'd once said to him. To know the derivations was almost heartbreaking; Leo had been his pet guinea pig who'd died a week after they brought him home; Stephan was what she'd blurted when Nicholas was old enough to ask about his father, having just noticed the name in the paper that morning. Naturally, he had asked other questions about his father, where he was from, what he had looked like, how he had died, and to all these she'd answer with whatever vague, half-true description or reason she could come up with, careful that they could never lead to an actual man.

"How can you be sure it's my son who's been doing this?" she said to Clines anyway, wishing none of it were true. There were no images on the faxes, including the cover from an Interpol office in Madrid, where a case agent, according to Clines, had just a few weeks earlier begun collecting and cross-referencing the materials. It was this file that he had received through a contact in Europe.

"One of the pages there indicates that the box number you gave me in Rome was rented by Stephan DiNicola."

"Who?"

"Stephan DiNicola. The person you last wired money to."

"Oh yes," she said. "I'm sorry. That's probably right." She'd been increasingly forgetful of late, at least of the recent past. She had indeed wired money, having received a typed letter from Nicholas, admittedly brief but marked by a renewed warmth, a casual intimacy that seemed to suggest he would soon be coming home. At the end, in a postscript, he asked if she could wire a thousand dollars to an S. DiNicola, a friend who would hold the funds for him until he reached Rome. It was the most he had ever asked for. Yet she had practically run to the nearest Western Union office, sending two thousand instead. She expected a quick reply, or even a phone call, but for a month now there had been nothing. Nothing at all.

"And are you obligated to tell any authorities what you know?"

"I'm working for you, Mrs. Singer."

"And if at some point you weren't?"

"I'm always working for someone. And I don't keep any records after I'm done."

She nodded. "What do you recommend we do?"

Clines cleared his throat. "I advise that we find him as soon as possible, before anyone else does. I can get a ticket to Rome for next week. So far he's committed just petty theft, if on a wide, serial scale. He hasn't stolen anything big yet. He hasn't physically assaulted anyone. If he did nothing else from this point on it's unlikely Interpol or anyone else would pursue him."

"Then we'll leave next week."

Clines shifted uncomfortably in the seat. He drew in his rough cheeks, eyeing her gravely. "I don't generally work *with* my clients, Mrs. Singer. It's not done."

"Then this will be different."

"He may have left Italy by now. He could have gone anywhere. To Eastern Europe, to Asia. I may have to move around very quickly."

"You'll move around as quickly as you need. If for some reason I can't keep up with you, I'll follow when I can. I don't want to be more than a half-day behind. It's not possible any other way. I'm sorry."

Clines scratched at his face. It was a sight she had seen countless times in the shop from buyers and consigners: the tight set of the mouth, the stare cast askance, and finally the yielding to her position, which was what made her business consistently, if never tremendously, profitable. Her talent, her gift, was an instantly patent resolve, so that both longtime acquaintances and strangers like Clines encountered an equally intransigent edifice, this deep-rooted stone. David had simply gone around, rather than attempt to dislodge her; for example, he was uncomfortable with her closing the shop herself, particularly in wintertime, when it was dark by five, and in the end he had simply hired a man to watch her from across the street to make sure she wasn't mugged. Had Nicholas done the same? Had he gone around her as well, but to an epic degree? He never appeared to be cowed by her, or demoralized. He always seemed happy enough. Aside from his scholarly ability, his teachers always told her in conferences that he was one of the more popular boys. But perhaps in the face of her, the sheer steep wall, he had receded like any child would, measure by imperceptible measure, until one day he must have seen the distance to be startling, and acceptable.

"Whenever we do catch up with him," Clines finally said, "you shouldn't expect he'll be pleased to see you."

"I won't."

"Or that he'll even agree to meet you. In fact, your being there might undo everything. There's a reason you've hired a third party like me. It's not only to find him. Sometimes you need an intermediary to settle someone down. Otherwise, he might just run faster."

"He's not running away from me, Mr. Clines."

Clines nodded severely. "As long as you understand what we're doing here."

"I do."

"Okay," he said, though clearly he was not satisfied. "Now, about your son."

She brought out the pictures of him Clines had asked her for, as well as the postcards, so he could have examples of Nicholas's handwriting. She actually didn't have very many of either. Over the years she had kept the small handful of postcards but had long ago discarded his old schoolwork, including most of the art projects he had made, the paintings and sketchbooks, for which she felt sharply regretful now. But what was shocking was the pathetically small collection of photographs she had of Nicholas. Most of them were the official yearly school portraits, the others being the few snapshots she'd taken through the years. She was never one to take pictures, and owned only the least expensive pocket camera. As Clines looked through the meager stack, she felt compelled to explain herself, to tell him about all the other things she had been doing instead, but she kept silent. Not taking pictures of Nicholas was neither a conscious nor an unconscious choice; it signified nothing, revealing only the fact that she rarely had much time back then for anything but the most basic parenting. She was a young single mother with a fledgling shop during a period in New York when the economy was dismal. She worked all the time, and rarely had the energy or inclination to cook or help him with his homework. She was always behind in doing the laundry and cleaning the apartment, which by his middle school years he did for them. For his efforts he got a very large allowance (for a preteen), which he was thrilled with, but they both knew he had to do it, as the basic chores would not otherwise get done. Toward his studies she took the attitude that since he was attending a good private school, on scholarship, his teachers would give him enough challenge and attention, and that as a single parent whose small business was their only means and lifeline she ought to trust their judgment and goodwill. Nicholas was naturally bright and was self-motivated enough, it seemed to June, that she could let him direct his own education. Little by little, though, he had chosen his own way in just about everything, things a boy probably shouldn't have to be responsible for, like buying his own clothes and ordering takeout. He had even neatly painted his bedroom one weekend while she was away for an auction in Philadelphia, though he chose a too-dark purple that seemed to suck all the light out of their small apartment, leaving everything gothically dimmed and crepuscular.

June didn't worry that she might be somehow depriving him. Like other mothers and sons, they had plenty of good times, for example when she brought him along on a furniture-buying trip when he was eleven and they stopped in Colonial Williamsburg. They churned butter together and made a long swath of rainbow-striped fabric on an old-fashioned loom, and one of the photographs in Clines's hands was of the two of them locked up in the stocks, both of them beaming with goofy grins, and that evening instead of driving home she decided to spend money she shouldn't have to stay at a decent motel with an indoor pool, so Nicholas could enjoy a swim before they ate their takeout dinner of burgers and fries. The next spring his class took a trip to Washington, D.C., and he had made her cry when he brought home a large vegetable-and-dip platter with seven interlocking porcelain trays illustrated with famous monuments. He'd bought it with the spending money she had given him, rather than buying his own souvenirs or snacks.

"But we don't throw parties," she said, her heart rent in her chest.

"Now we can!" he said.

She used the platter for his next few birthday parties, filling the trays with hard candies and chocolates and bubble gum. Every holiday saw it on their kitchen table. One by one the trays got broken, eventually only the Capitol Building and the Washington Monument remaining intact, and he finally told her he wouldn't be upset if she threw the platter away, as it looked silly with most of its trays missing.

Though she couldn't recall now, at some point she did.

"It seems your son liked the Roman times," Clines said, flipping through some pictures from various Halloweens.

"Yes, he always did," she said. "But he was drawn to Italy in general."

Clines showed her what he was looking at: there were shots of Nicholas, second grade, costumed in a centurion's outfit, complete with a plastic bronze breastplate and broom-top helmet. Another shot, a year older, had him as a gladiator, with a dirty, ripped shirt and a sword. Though there weren't pictures, she remembered him dressing up in middle school as a senator, in toga and sandals, a laurel on his head, and then one year in a beret and the loose, swarthy garb of a nineteenth-century bohemian. She'd asked him who he was and he told her, quite proudly, that he was Camille Corot. In her shop there was a shelf of old art books and one was full of color plates of the artist's Italian landscape paintings, which Nicholas often leafed through after school. He simply said he liked the soft colors of the houses and trees, so different from the city, but she wondered if it was because she had once falsely and stupidly suggested, after one of his random, out-of-the-blue queries, that she met and briefly lived with his father in Italy.

"Where exactly?" Nicholas asked. He was perhaps ten at the time.

"In the northern part."

"Show me," he said, quickly retrieving a large world atlas she also had on the shelf, and which he was always poring over. He certainly knew all of the national capitals, and most of the major cities.

"Here," she said, her finger tapping on a spot, with conviction. "Here, near Mantova."

She found that concrete facts would put him off for a while, even as she knew that such loose improvisations could only lead to trouble. So why had she persisted? She had wanted to keep their world as small as possible, for them to be simply a mother and son, as well as to circumscribe time, make only the present the time that was real. But of course Nicholas, an imaginative and artistic young boy, had begun to reconstruct what he wanted from whatever she said, to build up his own mythologies, until an irresistible mystery had naturally emerged.

During his senior year Nicholas told her that he would like to defer his college acceptance and go traveling, and at that point June had no objections, if that's what he desired. He had savings from his summer jobs and, of course, his household chores, and she didn't mind in the least offering him an extra thousand dollars so he could extend his travels. He said he didn't need it, that he preferred to work odd jobs wherever he was so he could actually live in the place, but she ended up stuffing an envelope of cash into his hand before he left. He thanked and kissed her—he had never minded kissing her, even in front of his friends—and scooted into the taxicab and then, to her disappointment, sat back without rolling down the window as the car roared off.

June did have worries, as any mother would, about his well-being, though her concern was less about the usual dangers of such a journey than it was about *him*. His sense of independence should have been reassuring to her, and yet she couldn't help but wonder if it was a quality of his that was already too evolved. Perhaps he didn't need to keep going it alone. As his teachers and others often said, he was well liked, and anyone could see he had plenty of friends, but she noticed that he never seemed interested in having a *best* friend, or even two or three buddies he would get together with regularly. He dated several girls in his junior and senior years, but June never would have said that he appeared to be in love with them, or even to be infatuated. He was enthusiastic with all of them, reliably available to anyone who called or invited him to a party, but June would have to say that he moved on too easily from one friend or set of friends to the next, sailing through the forest of them, from vine to vine like his hero Tarzan in the old movie series he loved to watch on Sunday mornings.

Over the years of his travels, the postcards he sent to the shop grew briefer in their messages, the ones he wrote out in pen somehow as cold as typescript, and then even more impersonal in nature, given the messages:

> *Doing fine.* N.
> *Okay here.* N.
> *Still kicking.* N.

Later he would simply type out his name, with no message at all. Once he'd neglected to do even that, compelling her to examine her own name and the address of the shop with the focus of a detective, trying to glean some significance in the press of the key strike, the freshness of the ink ribbon. The city or country postmark rarely matched the pictured site, and she thought he might well have bought a variety pack at an airport kiosk the very first day and posted them back to her whenever the idea struck him that his mother might think he was no longer alive.

In fact she had sometimes woken up in a panic, before and during the time she was living with David, certain that Nicholas was seriously injured, or ill, even dead, and David would calm her with an embrace and, at first, ask what was wrong, but she would never tell him. He knew she had a grown son, and, as with everything else in their quite happy but too brief union, he treated her with great solicitousness, never once pushing her to reveal the source of her distress, though he probably had guessed; David was a senior litigator at a prominent Midtown law firm and was as thorough in his work as anyone. Maybe it was because he knew how fragile his heart was from a previous heart attack, but once he came home in the evening he was wholly relieved to be with her, his weariness only softening his spirit, and the first thing he would do was sit her down from whatever she was cooking for them and ask her, like a good father might, what small pleasures had marked her day.

Her night panics had, strangely, subsided after David died, as if being alone again had firmed the resolve of her psyche. But they had started again with a phone call last year; the call had roused her well before dawn, an Englishwoman's voice on the other end, saying that her son was badly injured. June was still mostly asleep and terribly sick, perhaps out of her mind at the time with a third round of treatments, and she'd somehow blurted that she had no son and hung up. It was a monstrous thing to do, but the boy had not written her in more than a year and in her weakened state she couldn't help but give herself over to the sharpest, cruelest impulse. She felt immediately sickened and so called the operator right away to see if she could dial the caller back, but it was no use. She waited for her phone to ring again but it stayed quiet and she eventually fell asleep and by the morning it seemed it had all been a wicked and terrible nightmare.

A couple of weeks later she did in fact receive a postcard from him in the mail, saying that he was writing from a rural hospital because he had broken his leg, and quite badly, while riding a horse at a friend's country estate. *I'm going to be fine,* he wrote. *Maybe just a little crooked!* He didn't ask for money or anything else and she was happy that nothing had come of her hideous conduct on the phone, and the next time he wrote he didn't mention the accident, or his leg, only how he was going to continue his travels, now indulging in a slightly more expansive tone. The postcards didn't actually sound like him, but to her it was a signal that they'd turned a corner, that something new was beginning.

He hadn't asked her for money until recently, when suddenly he began to send postcards with requests for small sums to be wired to post offices in Amsterdam, then Frankfurt, then Nice. They were modest requests, $200 or $300, but that last one, for $1,000 (for which she sent $2,000 and mailed an enthusiastic note about his coming birthday), made her certain they would be reunited soon. She needed it to be soon. But then no word came. Each day afterward she awaited the arrival of the mailman, who soon enough knew what she was looking for and told her each day by the sorrowful hang of his eyes that he had nothing in his bag. It was through the mailman, in fact, that she got the idea of hiring Clines. The mailman was a chatty fellow with an oddly high voice who was a little off in the head, one of those reasonably functional people who was perhaps mildly mentally disabled. He didn't hesitate in telling her how he'd hired an investigator to follow his wife, as he suspected she was cheating on him. Clines eventually discovered that she was having an affair, but with the mailman's own brother. This is what Clines had meant when he asked if she truly wanted to find Nicholas: the truth is often more difficult than one might wish to believe.

But June was rarely hesitant in her life, and certainly would not be now. She said to Clines, "So it's good that you found Hector Brennan last week."

Clines nodded, clearing his throat. His face soured, as though he could not agree with her less.

"Where does he live, exactly?"

"In New Jersey. Fort Lee."

June's pulse suddenly spiked with the notion; all these years she'd assumed, for no reason, that Hector was still somewhere in the Northwest, or maybe in Canada or Mexico, or else gone back to his hometown somewhere in upstate New York. That he was so close, just across the George Washington Bridge, and oddly—or not so oddly—where many Korean immigrants were starting to settle and live, gave her a fresh bloom of optimism.

"How long has he been there?"

"Apparently, at least ten years," Clines said. "If not more." He took out another folder from his briefcase and handed it to her. It was all he had been able to gather on Hector, details of what he had already told her over the phone: a couple of faxed arrest sheets and a list of convictions that went back to soon after he left her, ranging widely from Washington to Texas to Pennsylvania and, in the last ten or so years, New Jersey. All were for minor offenses, possession of stolen goods, assault, resisting arrest. Typical drifter trouble, Clines told her. Hector apparently had no phone, no credit cards, no driver's license or car registrations, no bank accounts or loans. It had been pure chance that Clines had found an address for him; there was a recent judgment against him in small-claims court in Bergen County, where he was sued by his landlord for back rent and property damage. Clines had gone to the address, and though Hector was not living there anymore, a neighbor mentioned that he frequented a certain bar down by the river.

"What did he say?"

"Not much," Clines said. "He didn't want to talk."

"But you tried to persuade him?"

Clines nodded.

"Well?"

"He wasn't interested, Mrs. Singer."

"What do you mean?" she said sharply, using the voice she reserved for intransigent antiques dealers, or customers whose checks had bounced. "I don't understand you, Mr. Clines. You offered him money?"

"I did."

"And he still didn't agree?"

"We didn't get as far as that. Frankly, once he heard your name, he didn't say another word. He refused to speak to me. His friends told me I should leave."

Her eyes were half blinded with anger and she was about to berate the man but then a square dose of dread cooled her heart. For of course she understood she was perhaps the last person in the world Hector Brennan would choose to see, much less aid.

She said, however, "We'll have to try to convince him again."

"If that's what you wish," Clines said, frowning as if the skies had begun to pelt him with rain. "I'll arrange for a meeting when we return from Italy. If it happens that we're away longer than I expect, I'll have someone back here keep track of him."

"You misunderstand," June said. "I want you to take me to him. He must come with us."

Clines's brows knit sharply with alarm. "Your coming along is difficult enough. But I can't have him as well. Especially when he isn't interested. It can't work this way."

"I'm sorry. You'll have to manage."

"Some situations aren't manageable. This is not some guided tour." He considered her gravely. "Frankly, Mrs. Singer, you're much too ill for any of this."

She paused for a moment, hoping that somehow he might not have noticed; it was the reason she had kept the lights of the shop dimmed.

She said, "I'll be fine."

"What do you have? Is it cancer?"

"Listen," she said, gripping his arm. His flesh was malleable through the thin wool of his blazer and she could feel the soft plait of his musculature; she realized that he was quite a bit older than she thought, maybe even in his sixties, and could now see from the lightness near his scalp that he colored his hair. But rather than dishearten her, his lack of sturdiness only focused her, made her want to gain a better hold on the moment.

"Listen to me. I promise it won't be a hardship for you. You'll be able to do your job. You should know right now that it will be more than worth your time. And we won't get in your way. Hector can stay back with me, if I'm not feeling well."

"This is a terrible, terrible mistake," he said. "Especially if you want to find your son. I know you were briefly married to this man, but is he the boy's father? Is that why you want him to come with us?"

"It's how it has to be," she answered, explaining nothing else.

A little later, she saw Clines out into the street. The early-evening air held a residual warmth from the glorious day but now she clicked with bodily triggers that she had not known before, and they told her this endeavor had best be finished soon, before the autumn coolness descended for good. Would the cold bury her? She had given Clines another check to cover the next two weeks, and at triple his rate for taking on the extra difficulty. Naturally, she had planned to tell him that

Hector was the father of her son. But in that moment she suddenly thought otherwise, deciding that it was a matter between Nicholas and Hector and no one else. That Nicholas was his son would likely mean little to Hector. But she was hopeful it would be meaningful to Nicholas, so that someday, when perhaps he felt differently, he would know that he was not alone in the world. At this point in her life all she could do was to make a temporary bridge. Let them stand on it, if they wished; let them test its span; let them decide to bolster its footings, or else let it tumble.

She locked the door and shut off the lights save for the floor lamp beside the mattress. In the tiny bathroom in the back of the shop she brushed her teeth with lukewarm water. Any colder and it was like biting ice. She had to brush them very gently, as she remembered doing for Nicholas when he first got teeth, hers now feeling as if they were made of chalk. The next swipe might wear them right down to the nerve. She gargled and spit and then clipped up her hair to wash her face. It had grown back surprisingly quickly, if a shade grayer than before and not nearly as thick, and she had shocked her stylist by asking him to cut it in a boyish style. From afar, even across a room, she looked as youthful as ever, but up close the vigor was only in her eyes. Her face was more stilled than smooth, as though she had fought and fought and for the moment won but would never quite fight again.

Now she lay down on the bed and turned off the light. She felt her body unburden itself, shutting down in stages like an industrial complex. She could help it along: she had pills her doctor had dispatched an intern to deliver to her, including a special black kit fitted with the little syringes and vials, which the intern said she might eventually like to try; she'd even showed June how to do it, filling a syringe and demonstrating on a pillow. June had indeed tried it once already, and liked it plenty. But she refused to give in to the pain. Not tonight, at least. She had worked herself hard the last week, and look how much was accomplished. They were on their way. She wanted to feel her corpus. Her toes and fingers curled up first and then her joints contracted and the blood that had coursed with determination all through her returned to her heart depleted, nearly conquered, making her chest rheumy with its flood. All down her spine there was a serial drone of relief, each segment loosing itself from the next.

Only her belly couldn't rest, unceasing now as always, ever grinding about the original tumor in its futile attempt to consume it. But of course *she* was the one being consumed, from the inside out, being transformed into something else entirely. It was almost laughably ironic, that the cancer should be in her stomach. That she would die with her belly full. Hadn't she made that very pact a hundred times, a thousand times, when she was marching on the dismal road? *Let me eat until I can't, let me fill this infinite cave, and I'll die right here. I'll surrender.* And thus here she was, never to feel anything like hunger again. But she might take it on now, in trade for her life, that clenching weight of famishment. There was no more perverse fancy June could have.

She could easily remember the feeling. One afternoon long ago it had overcome her when she happened upon an American soldier. It was one of the final days of the war. She had been on her feet for three days and nights, having eaten nothing but chrysanthemum leaves and wild onions, sleeping a few anxious hours at most in a ruined, roofless cottage, and at the sight of the American down the road, a couple hundred meters away, she managed to leap down off the road and run into the gaseous knee-high muck of the rice fields where he wouldn't bother to pursue her. She was certainly delirious and half mad with thirst and her vision had been hinging and unhinging for a couple of days and when she looked back to the road he had transformed into a scouting party and turned toward her. The lone man raised his hands to show he was unarmed but she saw him instead as the herald of death, finally come to embrace her. She slipped then and fell and her mouth filled up instantly with the mud and as she tried to raise herself from the muck it only drew her in. She could not die. She was utterly, miserably wretched and her body was acceding to the darkness but she would not now let anyone else have dominion over her.

But then she could breathe; he'd plucked her up from the mud by her shirt, ripping a sleeve at the shoulder. She hit him in the chest and tried to scratch his eyes but in a flash he struck her back; when she came to she was lying in the shade of a rusted truck carcass that had been pushed off the road, some thirty meters from where they had been. The side of her face stung. But her shirt was still on, and her trousers were as well, and the American was sitting on the metal frame of the seats, torn out of the truck cab, chewing on a stalk of hay. She began to crawl away and was trying to get up on her feet when he rattled a yellow object in his hand; it was a pack of Chiclets. He tossed it at her feet and before she could open the end fold of the flat box, her mouth watered so fulsomely that she had to cough before she could stuff in all the pieces. Their hard shells cracked and then burst with sweetness.

"Take it easy, sister," he said. He told her his name, and asked hers.

She knew English well enough that she could have answered him, but the deliciousness of the mass was so overwhelming she couldn't help but swallow, the sticky strings of it catching at the back of her throat. She gagged, reaching into her mouth with her fingers, and then finally threw it up. When she picked up the shiny clot from the dirt to try to eat it again, he told her there was food where he was going. Other children, too. It was an orphanage, in fact, ten kilometers ahead. He had risen and stepped up onto the embanked road, his rucksack hitched over his shoulder. She could come with him if she liked.

She waited until he was well down the road, a full fifty meters ahead of her, before she began to trail him. She was chewing the gum again, now gristly with dirt. He turned and saw that she was following him and beckoned her forward with a wave as he walked slowly in reverse. She slowed as well to keep her distance, stopping when he stopped. He shook his head and resumed his march. But then a sudden swirling wind kicked up dust into the dry, hot air, swathing him in an obscuring cloud, and for a moment her heart skipped wildly with the fear that he was gone. Or wholly imaginary. But the dust cleared and his form became visible again, and she quickened her stride to follow him.

THREE

WAR IS A STERN TEACHER, his father would sometimes say to him, quoting Thucydides, the sodden, light-boned man slung over Hector's shoulder in their typical end-of-Friday-night lurch. Hector always helped him limp home from the workingman's pub in their town of Ilion, New York, the normally sweet Jackie Brennan having drunk too much and turned a late night bitter-sour. Hector, fifteen years old in 1945, was still as sober as a ghost, despite having drunk a half-dozen grown men into stammering idiots, sleepers on the barroom sawdust.

"What did I say?"

Hector would repeat it, flatly and dryly.

"Good. Never go to war, son. Please never do."

By the end of those evenings, with his father loaded up on the rye he had won on bets taken against Hector in drinking bouts, he would have to gird him all the way home, his father's breath earthy and spiced with the cheroots he smoked all night and the pickled pearl onions he popped like almonds, both of which he swore counteracted the liquor.

His father might sing a protest ballad like "The Dying Rebel," but on particularly long nights he grew sweaty and pain-faced and had to stop a couple times to retch into the gutter or the thickets of some Remington Arms Company manager's manicured boxwood hedge, and then in mumbles berate Hector for his "righteous silence," or for the "boyish piety" of his soberness. But by the time their footfalls played on the sagging plank steps of the Brennan family porch, the boy bearing most of his father's weight, he would sometimes say his son's name aloud, over and over, in a kind of monkish ecstasy: *Hector, my Hector.* And then, if consciousness still graced him after Hector let him fall upon the parlor room sofa, he would look up and ask if he wished to hear again why he'd named him so, to call him thus instead of, say, Achilles, a more glorious appellation?

"Okay, Da, tell me."

"Because a man wants a son for a son, and has no use for a champion."

After reading the epic in school, Hector pointed out to him that his namesake was killed, his city doomed to ruin, his father eventually slaughtered as well.

"No matter, boy," his father told him. "They tell us stories not to live by but to change. Make our own. Look at you. You'll live forever, anyone with eyes can see that. Just never go to war."

Jackie Brennan, of course, could never go to war; unlike Hector, he was a wisp of a man, and had a right foot turned permanently sideways at birth, his right hand unnaturally angled as well, while smallish and stunted besides, like that of a tiny, elderly woman. But he was cleverer than most, and had he been born to a family of greater means and aspiration he might have been a state's attorney or college professor, as he was well spoken and quick and had firm notions (for better or worse) of what people should hear. When World War II broke out and legions of Ilion's sons signed up, his was one of the few mutterings of skepticism, if not dissent, though at first Jackie mostly kept his feelings about the war to himself, or else lectured to his weary-eared wife and daughters, and to Hector, who in fact didn't mind listening to him make his roundabout arguments in his bright, resonant baritone. He loved him, but unlike most other boys whose love for their fathers was predicated on fear and misplaced idolatry, his was as for a favorite uncle, if deeper, a love that recognized the man's foibles and numerous failings and saw them as distinctive rather than sorry and pathetic.

But there was a limit to that view, and it came at the pub; after Jackie Brennan got his belly wash of beer and whiskey he grew overly voluble, his voice taking on a higher, more insistent pitch. The war was ever weighing on his spirits. In the pub, he might warmly address a group of young men in uniform, after not paying them any attention all night: "Permit me to buy you fellas another round of drafts, that I might hold up my head and know I did my part!"

The servicemen would raucously accept and make room for him while the regulars miserably eyed one another and Hector, wise to what would happen next. Hector would sit on the periphery until his father cajoled him to come in the circle when the mugs of beer went round, with Jackie serially playing prosperous gentleman, the boastful older brother, and, finally, the knowing comrade in arms. But he had other agendas.

"It's thirst-making work, defending our land. The noblest calling."

"You got that, mister!"

It was at this point that Hector would tug on his father's sleeve, though to no avail.

"But what I wish, my good lads, is that we'd do just that, instead of getting involved in every minor dispute on the far side of the planet."

"You calling Pearl Harbor a minor dispute?" one of the servicemen replied. "Last I checked, it was a dirty ambush by those rat Japs, where a couple thousand of our guys got it."

"Rat Japs indeed!" Jackie Brennan would cry. "But what conditions were in fact at play behind that horrid carnage?" his father would intone pedantically. At this point his father was already in the bag, but an audience of newcomers always inspired him, recasting his view of himself as a hardworking factory man into that of thinker, of wise man, someone whose main purpose was to bear light and truth to others, like the revered teacher he'd pictured himself becoming when he was young, before he'd entered the factory like everybody else.

"Precious few of us bother to look at the bigger picture. Did the Japanese intend to conquer us? Do they still? I very much doubt it. Look at our capacity for producing arms, right here in our small town, and then multiply that by thousands. They know they can't compete with us over the long run. So they attempt a single, stunning blow, to dissuade us from meddling further in their affairs. The scorpion and the lion. Pearl Harbor was about protecting their interests, in *their* part of the world, in *their* sphere of influence, and if we had sent them the appropriate signals beforehand, all those sailors—and now scores of thousands of others—would still be alive today."

"I've had enough of this," one of the men said, slamming down the beer Jackie had paid for on the scarred wooden table. "You're either one of those pacifists or appeasers, and I can't stand to listen to you another second."

"Do what you will," Jackie answered him, with an almost operatic tone of defiance. "But in fact I'm neither of those, young man. I'm an American, son, with no need for larger aims, which you will someday come to understand."

"Out of the way, mister."

"You can do me the respect of at least finishing your beer!"

"Go to hell."

"Don't you curse at me!" It was then, as a rule, that pandemonium broke loose, at least in his father's mind, a fierce, heroic scuffle that usually found Jackie Brennan tightly hugging a soldier around his torso so the fellow couldn't freely swing and punch. Hector jumped in and he would be beseeching the man to ignore his father's foul curses, the proprietor and a few regulars holding the other servicemen back until Hector could tug Jackie outside and hustle him quickly down the street and toward home. Nothing too serious ever happened, though after one night when the barkeep took a stray punch in the face, Jackie was ordered to stay away for a while, which he did, without even a private protest at home. Jackie knew he was liked well enough to be tolerated for such troubles, but not much more than that, and if he couldn't help but be a nuisance when he drank, he took great pains to make up for it, buying drinks for all the fellows on his return and not forgetting a box of candies for the barkeep to give to his wife.

One night, Hector left for home by himself, telling his father he was tired. It was a slow night at the pub, foggy and damp, with no newcomers about for Jackie to sermonize or bet with for drinks.

"I never heard you say you were tired," his father said to him, suspicion marking his voice. "Not a once in your life."

"Well, I am," Hector answered, lying to his father for the first and only time. "I just want to go home."

"Go on, then," Jackie said, waving Hector off from his customary place at the far end of the bar, clutching the handle of a mug of ale with his withered, child-sized hand. "And tell your mother not to wait up."

Hector grumbled in assent, both he and his father knowing of course that his mother would be long asleep, being accustomed to her husband's Friday-night foolery. Jackie only got sloshed this one night of the week, but never missed it, and his mother was glad that Hector went out with him.

As planned, though, Hector routed himself toward home by

Patricia Cahill's freshly painted bungalow and picket fence (done by his own hand), and seeing the parlor room light illuminated went directly to the back porch door, which she said she would leave unlocked if the twins were asleep. It was the spring of 1945 and the long war was still going and her husband was listed as MIA. She was a stunning raven-haired Black Irishwoman with sky-colored eyes and freckles on her little nose and a curve to her hips that made him think of a skillfully turned balustrade. He'd been fantasizing about her for days, and after school he'd stopped by to be paid but she was having a tea with a friend and told him to come after dark. He had known his father would never depart the pub so early, and that his mother would not be expecting him. The thought of lingering with her in her bed electrified him, the last block or so difficult for him to walk comfortably, his erection already straining his dungarees. He'd been with her once before (voraciously petting, if briefly, in her kitchen) but at that point she was the first mature woman he'd touched, and the give and savor of her body (not as firm as that of his sisters' friends, nor as blandly scentless) was a revelation; he was drawn to the moist tang of her skin, the scant animal note at the nape of her neck, between her breasts.

It had already begun to rain, and when he entered the darkened screen porch he was suddenly afraid that he'd mistaken what she'd said to him earlier, but then the parlor light went out and she descended and wound about him like a silken cloak. She was warm and naked beneath her thin bathrobe. She knelt and had hardly put him in her mouth when he helplessly came. In embarrassment he crumpled and made to get away but she gripped him and said it's okay as long as you do the same, and it was then, at her command, that he learned to swim the slant lightless depth, make his way instead by only treading.

Just before dawn he ran home in the steady rain to find a police cruiser parked in front of his house. All the lights were burning. He could see two of his sisters moving about upstairs. He went around back and heard his mother at the kitchen table telling the officers sipping the coffee she'd made that her husband and son had never not come home before. Could some drifters have rolled them and tied them up somewhere? Really, where could they have gone? It was too small a town. She didn't have to tell the officers that Jackie Brennan had no mistress, for everybody in Ilion well knew he was an uxorious man whose infinite gratitude to his pretty wife for accepting his deformations sometimes also made him crazy when he drank, his imaginings usually centering on her infidelities (which were none), or else he'd be mopey, glum, and self-pitying. One of the policemen caught sight of Hector peering around the hedge and called out, his mother turning to see him. When he went inside, they asked where his father was and where he'd been after he left the pub but he couldn't tell them about either thing, especially about Patricia Cahill, as one of the cops was her cousin. His mother kept asking him how he could leave his father to drink alone. Hector was silent, but was desperately worried now, too, and begged the officers that he might accompany them as they went to retrace his steps from the pub.

As he rode in the police car he felt a much purer shame than anything he might have felt with Patricia Cahill, and he began to cry; he knew he should have stayed with his father, as any decent son would, most of all if that father was Jackie Brennan. How many men craved such company of their sons, for whatever reason? With him gone missing, Hector suddenly understood what he in fact was for his father, and what he should always be: his ideal figure, a body supreme, his sturdiest hand, and foot, and liver. He would never leave him again. When they got to the pub, the officers and he walked in three directions, looking for any sign of him. Then he spotted his father's porkpie hat at the head of an alleyway between two warehouses; the alleyway led down to an old dock on the canal. The end of the dock had clearly just collapsed, the splintered edges fresh and jagged. The high water was swirling off muddily, heavy with a current; the locks had been opened upstream.

"Could he swim?" asked the policeman, Patricia Cahill's cousin.

Hector shook his head. Because of his handicaps his father had never learned how, and was otherwise naturally reluctant to show himself.

"I'll call the dredger," the other automatically said, his expression, on looking at Hector, one of instant regret.

"He's not dead," Hector said.

"We won't be calling anyone yet," Officer Cahill said. He was only slighter taller than Hector but he still patted him on the shoulder as if he were a young boy. "Don't fret yet, Hector. I bet your pop's just sleeping it off downstream."

The next day the dredger was called. His body wasn't found for nearly a week, and then not even by the riverman. It showed up finally in a canal lock miles away, clothesless and bloated and as shiny black as an inner tube, forever traumatizing some pleasure boaters down from Canada. Hector had to travel with local authorities and identify him for the family, his mother and sisters refusing to go. Hector was certain it was he, if only from the awesome gap between the corpse's two front teeth; his father would spit great arcing streams of beer at company picnics, these wonderfully downy, foamy rainbows, to the delight of at least the men and children. It was no doubt Jackie Brennan's finest talent. But at the undertaker's, that jesting font lay stiffly open and empty, and even in the chilly locker the stench emanating from it and the rest of the body gripped Hector with an otherworldly ferocity, as might some beast of the underworld, its invisible claws lifting him straight off his feet.

HIS POOR FATHER WAS RIGHT, of course: he should never have gone to war. For a long time after Jackie's death, Hector's mother could not speak to him for his leaving his father that night, could hardly even look at him, and though she eventually showed love for him again, for the quiet years between Hiroshima and the surprise attack by Communists on a hitherto unknown city called Seoul, Hector was hoping for another war to break out. He sought a war not for the sake of fighting or killing anyone or defending his country, but for the selfish cause of punishing himself, and so proving his father right.

How easily his wish was granted. It was a brief incident, involving a prisoner, that changed everything, a situation probably not too distinctive or unusual. But it would hold a firm place in his memory. It was in his first tour of duty, early spring, 1951. They were in the foothills of the Taebaek Mountains, 150 kilometers northeast of Seoul. After the chaotic opening to the war, the initial Communist invasion, and the headlong ROK retreat to the very southern tip of the peninsula, and then the breakneck American counteroffensive pushing back all the way north to the Yalu River, which was the border with China, both sides were now engaged in what was in essence trench warfare, if in the hills. The struggle was over any given (and supposedly) strategic section of high ground, the shifting of territory measured in hundreds of meters, each hill identified by only a number (and if bloody enough, eventually a nickname). The fighting was mostly night attacks, with small-scale raids by American and ROK units, and then operations by the Communists, who were now almost all Chinese, regulars in the People's Army, attacking often in mass, near-suicidal, waves, their aim to intimidate and overwhelm with seemingly inexhaustible numbers.

The prisoner was one of these. He was just a boy, in fact, fourteen or fifteen years old at most, his round moonface sprouted with only a few bristles of hair on his upper lip, his chin. Hector's platoon had taken him prisoner after repelling an attack the night before, when the whole facing hillside cranked alive before dawn with rattles and whistles and clanging cowbells and the rabid shrieks of several thousand soldiers rushing forward in a mad pell-mell push, their burp guns alive, the sound of their feet on the dry snow like locusts devouring a field of corn. Flares were shot to illuminate the battleground, revealing that perhaps only half of the enemy was actually armed with rifles, the others bearing bayonets and sticks and even toy drums like the kind given away as prizes at fairs, the ten-cent variety with two strings with balls on the ends that one rotated to make a noise.

Their first wave overwhelmed all the forward foxholes but was cut down before it breached the main line; the next ones were successively less effective, and by the fourth wave the Chinese hardly made any noise on attacking and quickly retreated after a barrage of American fire. It was all over after that. By daybreak there were many hundreds of bodies marking the hillside, mostly Chinese, the most unsettling thing being that a number of the American soldiers in the forward foxholes were missing, only the dead ones left to be retrieved. The survivors had been spirited away as prisoners by the retreating swarm to a fate that was known among the men (via report and rumor and fearful imaginings) to feature unspeakable tortures and deprivations and a life sentence of hard labor somewhere deep in the mines of China.

It was under this mind-set that the boy soldier had been taken prisoner by others in Hector's unit. Hector came upon them soon after he was captured. The boy was short, five foot four or so, and stalk-thin, not even a hundred pounds in his winter uniform, which had been stuffed tight with crumpled newspaper for insulation, ripped canvas tennis shoes on his sockless feet. He'd been found playing dead at the bottom of a foxhole and was beaten up badly by them, given an ugly shiner and a bloody nose and lip. One of his shoulders was dislocated. He had been found with a small brass horn, which a soldier named Zelenko now held in his gloved hand. The platoon leader, Lieutenant Bridger, was off being briefed at the field HQ. Zelenko and his buddies would have likely executed the prisoner right then, but an officer from another unit happened by and on seeing his condition reminded them that all prisoners were to be immediately processed for interrogation. They assented, but after the officer left, Zelenko said they should keep him a bit before transferring him up to field command; he was their first prisoner, after all. There were a handful of grunts from the platoon present, including Hector, who was off sitting on the icy ridge of the next foxhole. He disliked Zelenko, who was also from a small town in upstate New York, a carrot-haired loudmouth who was a dependable soldier but who had begun to subtly bully their tentative college-man lieutenant to send certain squads of men—Hector among them—on the night patrols. Hector didn't mind the more dangerous missions, for someone had to go and he'd begun to accept that by fate or nature he was strangely, miraculously, impervious, but he didn't like the idea that Zelenko's whim should determine anyone else's destiny.

With another soldier holding a rifle on the prisoner, Zelenko stepped up from behind him and placed the horn's end right next to his ear and blew as hard as he could on it. The prisoner dropped to the ground as if he'd been shot in the temple, screaming and holding his ear.

"That's for keeping us up every night with that crazy chink music," Zelenko said, he himself wincing from the sharp blast. The others were wide-eyed, chuckling. The Chinese often played an eerie, atonal oper-atic music as well as a suite of popular Western songs and slick propa-ganda through the night on loudspeakers. The boy was crying silently now with his mouth agape, squeezing on his ear. He was in terrible pain. Zelenko pulled the boy back up on his feet. He was covering his ear, but Zelenko slapped his hand away.

"You'd think all these lousy chinks would be half deaf already," Zelenko said, and then blew the horn hard into the same ear. "And that's for Gomez."

Gomez was his buddy, killed a week before. They'd found his body dumped on the bank of a frozen stream. He'd been tortured and then shot in the back of the head. Zelenko blew again. The boy crumpled to his knees, crying miserably, and Zelenko had his buddy, Morra, wire together his hands behind him so he couldn't shield himself. Then he blew the horn again. He did it three more times, and with such vehemence that his face grew flushed, as if he'd inflated a roomful of party balloons. But on the last one the boy hardly flinched. The ear was dead. This angered Zelenko, and he struck the boy sharply with his pistol. The boy fell like a tablet of stone. Fresh blood pocked the snow beside his head where he lay. His narrow eyes were open, his lips moving slowly and mechanically but making no sound. Zelenko was leaning over him with the horn to start on the other side, balling his chewing gum to plug his own ears, when Hector suddenly rushed him, knocking him over, sending him sliding on his back a dozen feet down the hill.

"What the fuck!" Zelenko cried.

Morra jumped him and Hector punched him once, hard, in the kidney, and the man fell to the ground. The others stood aside as Hector lifted the prisoner. The platoon knew him to be unhesitating in battle, vigilant and tireless, never cowed under fire, and no one made any move to stop him. He could lead a squad or even the platoon, if he weren't so laconic. The boy groaned heavily when Hector slung him over his shoulder, and then lost consciousness. Hector carried him up the path that curled around the hill to the reverse slope, where the field HQ and mobile hospital were set up. Zelenko cursed at him, shouting that he was a stupid mick, a dirty queer, a chink lover, but Hector ignored him.

After the prisoner's wounds were dressed and his arm relocated in its socket by a medic, Hector took him to the command post. The officer in charge had Hector search the prisoner again, and when he did he found something hidden in a rip in the lining of his jacket. It was a tiny notebook; a photograph was tucked inside. He gave it to the officer, who had the interpreter inspect it.

But it was nothing; just a personal diary. It was written in Korean, and apparently the boy contended he was a southerner, first conscripted by ROKs before being captured by Communists and reconscripted again, but the interpreter either didn't believe him or didn't care; he was a Communist now. The interpreter handed the diary and the photograph to the officer, who glanced at them quickly before tossing them back to Hector. While they interrogated him, Hector examined the writing, its lettering very neat and small, and then the photograph. It was clearly a portrait of the boy's family, his parents and himself and other siblings. What surprised him was how well dressed they were, respectable and attractive, and that they wore Western clothing, suits and dresses. They could easily be one of the Remington Arms Company managers' families, except that they were Oriental.

The boy was only very briefly interrogated. The intelligence officers had already collected enough information from some other prisoners and aerial reconnaissance over the last week about the strength of the enemy forces. The officer told Hector they had no use for him: he was just a bugler anyway, one of their many expendables. Normally, he would have been sent along with other prisoners to a rear holding area at battalion before being transferred to a POW camp, but there were very few enemy (only two others) taken alive from the assault, and with the promise of an even larger human-wave attack that night, and with no transport available or forward holding area or cell, no one could be interested in his final disposition.

"So where should I take him?" Hector asked. The intelligence officer didn't look up; the other officers in the tent ignored him, too. Hector didn't ask again. He knew this meant he should walk him back to the forward line and, at some point, shoot him. It happened all the time, and was practiced by them and the enemy alike. So he did walk him away, the kid trudging miserably ahead of him. He didn't look back or try to engage or beseech him, which Hector was glad for. He'd killed at least a half-dozen of the enemy in firefights, a couple at very close quarters, but it was always just the flash instinct or response, and he had never had to think the killing through mechanically. Where to stop to do it; whether to have him kneel or stand; whether to give him a moment to prepare or do it without warning; shoot him in the body or the head. The boy was skinny and short but his shoulders were quite broad and Hector tried to focus on this, the suggestion that he was a grown man, a genuine soldier. But it was no use; he looked like any boy wearily ambling home. The early April day was quickly warming and the temperature had risen to forty-five degrees and Hector became uncomfortably aware of the paired alternation of their schussing feet on the softened snow, a rhythm soon to be soloed. Maybe it would have been better (for himself) to have let Zelenko have his way; it would be over already and he would be in the dugout now, warming up his canned rations over a Sterno, maybe cleaning his rifle, writing his short weekly letter to his mother, in which he never said anything new or described much in detail but wrote anyway, in general terms, about the weather, the food, if only to get to signing his name, so she would know he was alive.

They reached the point where the path turned and led around a large, outcropped boulder. Hector told him to stop. The boy did so. He offered the diary and photograph to him, but the boy refused, shaking his head.

"Take it, okay? I don't want it."

The boy kept shaking his head, as if he understood that to do so would be his end. For it was his end. It was surely here that Hector ought to do it, if he was going to do it at all; there was something of a precipice as the path jutted out, below it a five-meter fall-off to a natural shallow bowl in the hillside. After he fell into it Hector could simply leave, would not have to drag the corpse someplace else, and it would be over. But he didn't want to do it. Why should he? Maybe he ought to let him go, let him run away and say that the prisoner had escaped.

But suddenly the boy turned from him and stepped closer to the edge. He wiped his eyes and then simply stared out into the valley, the bright, snowy hills starkly etched against the flat blue sky. It was as if the boy, too, now recognized the suitability of the spot. He must have long realized he wasn't meant to survive this war. He wasn't even meant to kill, bugler that he was. On the other side of the hills were his comrades, thousands upon thousands of them, regrouping and resting before another wave attack tonight, and Hector could almost hear the boy thinking about his fate, whether it was better to die like this, one-to-one, rather than sprinting forward in the darkness in a suicidal throng, with just a tin horn in his hand, screaming with a primal fear, his body tensed for the smash of bullets. Hector stepped closer to him. He leveled his rifle at the boy, the barrel nose a mere foot from his bloodied ear. He'd graded out as a sharpshooter but his hands felt numbed now, the gun hollow and light in his grip. The boy's shoulders tightened, anticipating the shot.

But there came voices on the path behind them. It was Morra and Zelenko. Zelenko's eyes lit up on seeing them in such a pose, but before he could say anything the boy recognized his tormentor and leaped from the spot. He landed down in the well, just as Hector had pictured he would. He began screaming like a child. One of his legs was clearly broken, the foot craned grotesquely back behind him.

"Man, you spooked him!" Morra shouted. "Just listen to him wail."

Zelenko said, "What you gonna do now, Brennan? He's your prisoner, isn't he?"

Hector pushed past him and hiked down, with Morra and Zelenko trailing him. When they reached the boy he wasn't crying out anymore, but rather breathing rapidly, wheezing through the spit and phlegm webbing his clenched mouth. The well was in fact a collection of fallen rocks; the snow had veiled the stones. Besides his leg, something had burst inside him.

Hector unslung the rifle from his back. He unlatched the safety. It was not a question anymore. The boy had shut tight his narrow eyes and was ready. But then a sudden pressure pinched at Hector's head and the world seemed to twist and when he opened his eyes he was lying on his side in the damp snow. Morra had his rifle. His helmet had been knocked off and had rolled a few turns down the hill. His head rang with a harsh note, but he felt almost silkily disembodied, too, like he was at last a little drunk. He sat up. The two soldiers were propping up the boy, who was crying miserably again, for they were taking turns prodding his broken leg.

"We're square now," said Zelenko to Hector, seeing him stir. "Hope it hurt. Now stay put."

"Yeah, right," Morra said. "Now, this, on the other hand, will hurt a lot." He stepped with his full weight near the break of the boy's leg. What came from him then startled all of them, clearing the foul cloud from Hector's head. It was a transcendent cry, the voice more piercing and pure than a mere body could have ever alone mustered. Then he fainted.

"Shit," Zelenko said.

Morra said, "I thought these damn gooks had staying power. But I got smelling salts."

They tried it and the boy startled as if he'd been roughly roused from sleep, half getting up like he wasn't injured at all. He'd collapse and they'd hold it under his nose until he jumped up again, though each time he jerked with less violence, until at last he flitted oddly, like a broken marionette. He was silent, too, in a state well beyond pain.

Zelenko tossed Hector a bayonet across the snow. "He's all yours now."

Morra protested, saying he wanted to finish it, but Zelenko made them go. They took up their weapons and hiked up the incline to the path. Hector heard them march off. Later, a couple of days on, in an informal contest of bare-fisted boxing that an unusually warm stretch of weather brought on, he would beat both men bloody, dispatching Morra quickly and easily, Zelenko with more effort, reshaping his features to near unrecognizable, only stopping when several others jumped him. Afterward the lieutenant asked him to transfer out, and Hector complied, requesting the Graves Registration Unit, for he didn't wish to commit or witness any more killing, figuring, too, that the dead were dead, and would always stay that way.

But death, he would come to learn, was in fact a tendency. Inevitably the dead came back. The boy, for one. For after Morra and Zelenko left, the boy began to talk to him. Of course Hector assumed he was speaking Korean or maybe Chinese but in fact it was English, broken and mumbled, heavily accented, but somehow Hector was certain he understood. *No live*, he was saying. *No live*. He didn't have much more than a few moments left, for he was going to die soon anyway, and yet he was insistent. Hector stood up and hefted the bayonet and the boy nodded to him, smiling weakly, snorting with the promise of final liberation. A new light shone from his eyes. A sheer living gleam. And though not wishing him more suffering, not wishing him more pain, mercy as simple as a nothing push on a blade, Hector could not make himself deliver him. He flung the bayonet down the hill. The boy began to cry. Hector retrieved his helmet, trying not to hear him. The boy was now saying something different, his voice barely above a whisper. Hector patted his pockets, for a piece of candy, food. He offered his water canteen.

The boy shook his head. He gestured with his eyes for Hector to come closer. Hector knelt and leaned in and the boy suddenly grabbed at his belt, snatching a grenade. Hector wheeled back away from him, but he was slipping on the side of the shallow well. The boy held the pin. To pull it would be to live a few more seconds. But he waited for Hector to get his footing, waited for him to hike up to the path. At the top he peered down and the boy was gazing skyward, perhaps waiting for him to gain distance, perhaps already blind with the nearing oblivion. Hector sprinted away, getting nearly all the way back to the rear line before he heard the distant, blunted blast.

F O U R

Fort Lee, 1986

HECTOR ROSE from the cup-sag of his bed.

It wasn't yet dawn. He stepped to the bathroom and pulled the chain on the light above the medicine cabinet. He didn't look much different, despite the fight with Tick in the street. His, it could be supposed, was the sentence of persistence. Was it an imposition from yonder? Or a dark talent that he couldn't help but invoke, whenever loomed his possible demise? His jaw and skull and knuckles were sore, his chest pinging with each breath, though it was not exactly the bodily pains that had roused him. The pains and even the scars would pass quickly, as always. But he felt lonesome in his wounds, and he awoke keenly grateful for the company of the woman in his bed.

Her name was Dora. He liked her but oddly had not yet actually seen her in the daytime. The bathroom light partly illuminated her as she slept. She didn't stir. She was a redhead from the bottle, by the look of her graying roots. She lay sprawled on her belly with a corner of the sheet flopped over her eyes and cheek, her mouth cracked open like a burrow hole. A molar was missing, something he hadn't noticed before, and though the picture was not wholly unattractive to him he clicked off the light so that he didn't have to see her mouth, being long uneasy with the sight of any insides.

He got back into bed. She groaned an unintentionally pleading note. He laid a hand on her cheek and pictured her face. And though of course he knew what she looked like he kept seeing a different woman instead, a woman he remembered from a book he'd read in his youth that had accompanying photographs of hard-used folk living in the wasted land of the dust bowl. The book affected him as a book sometimes can a young mind that is anticipating a story different from what it encounters but is taken up anyway; from the title—*Let Us Now Praise Famous Men*—he'd assumed accounts of heroes who'd endured great trials and tendered unequaled sacrifices to their gods and people and thereby won the glory of everlasting fame. From the time he could read he'd devoured those stories of ancient Athens and Sparta and Crete, of Alexander and Charlemagne. Yet what was it he encountered in the book but descriptions of penury and degradation that took on an awesome, almost mythical beauty; and the bleakness he saw in the eyes of one prematurely aged young woman made him think pitiably enough of his mother, who was a beauty in her youth but lost it after his father died and always seemed to be searching out an alternate destiny.

Dora had those same eyes, despite the surface of her easy levity she had them, and so was it this about her that had finally won him over? He hadn't even asked her to leave after their lovemaking, which was an iron habit of his. The rest of her now, her pale, sleeping nakedness, the smallish shoulders, the bland wide dune of her lower back, the cleft of the broad, stippled bottom enfolding into dark, struck him as fair and vulnerable, but he didn't disturb her, thinking he ought to let her sleep.

She was a regular at the bar, Smitty's Below the Bridge, or at least had been a regular for the better part of a year. All the fellows were glad for it. Dora was all right. She was what the place always needed: a good solid-looking woman who didn't take guff and liked to have a laugh or two and paid for her own drinks. She was smart, too, a book-keeper at the big furniture shop on Lemoine, and perhaps like a lot of them she might have accomplished a lot more in life had certain things gone her way and she hadn't been so enamored of wine. She wasn't a full-blown boozer, but she had, in significant part, ceased to care whether her nightly stint in the company of heavy-drinking folks meant she was likely becoming one of them, nor did she mind any longer that she was riding lower and lower in the water, steadily losing buoy-ancy, and that she might eventually be swallowed up.

As for the inevitable round of relations, she had gone out with some of the more presentable of them—Connolly, Big Jacks, once even with Sloan, who was a kind if somewhat simpleminded fellow with a narrow lamb's face and who took her to a fancy gilded French restaurant in the city with his monthly check from his ancient folks in Rochester—but nobody had yet called Dora a slut because it was plain to see she was a decent gal without airs or too special a self-view and because the rest of them probably still held out hope she might ask for an escort home after last call.

Hector had warmed up to her more slowly than did the others, though it was nothing she said or did. His nature precluded any easy rapport and even after all these years at Smitty's, the others knew to leave him alone for a while when he showed up at his usual midnight hour in the midst of their din and merriment. There always rose a hearty murmur for him when he came through the paint-chipped metal door, which he'd acknowledge with a nod, but then he would sit alone in the back booth with two double shots of Canadian whiskey that Smitty automatically poured for him. By the time he was at ease, they had maybe geared down a bit from their joking and quarrels and songs and were settling into the night's long, slow coast to some nether realm. On the nights he didn't want to be part of the company, Hector might still be wearing his janitor's coveralls and stinking not a little of ammonia and sourness and other human fetors, and on these occasions they knew to keep their distance; he'd be quieter than usual and down his drinks without a word and Smitty would know to double him again before he had to ask. If it happened some unwitting newcomers made a comment about his work clothes, or if a certain crew from Edgewater called the boys out from the street, then all hell could break loose, Hector and maybe Big Jacks out back by the Dumpsters hammering away at the interlopers until somebody up in the surrounding apartments called the cops and the whole lot of them got hauled in. The local precinct sergeant knew Hector's family from upstate New York and admired his fighting skills, and Hector would be let out first, a few hours later, once levied with the usual hundred-dollar fine for engaging the resources of the municipality, payable to the sergeant in cash.

Tonight there had been no expectation of fighting but instead a birthday party for Hector, which Smitty always threw for a small group of the regulars. None of them much liked marking such milestones—who needed reminding of the advancing years and, in their cases, the wayward trajectories, the diminished expectations?—but the beer flowed freely from the taps and Smitty poured plenty of shots on the house and more often than not everyone ended up shoulder to shoulder along the curved end of the bar, happily wrecking some sentimental song.

The evening, however, had started somewhat inauspiciously; early on, before Hector showed up, a stranger had come in asking after him. When Hector arrived, Smitty took him aside and pointed out the tall man in the dark suit sitting stiffly in the middle booth. The man wouldn't say what he wanted. Hector immediately figured it was about the gambling debts of his employer and friend, Jung; last week Hector had put himself between Jung and some baby-faced thug-in-training and without thinking it through grabbed the kid's throat when he threatened to maim Jung's kids. There were some things one should never say. The kid turned purplish and from the smell half-shat his pants and had practically crawled out of Jung's office in the mini-mall. Why the sports book would now dispatch an older accountant-looking fellow to accost him confused Hector, but he didn't hesitate when the stranger suddenly approached him, catching this one by his tie and collar, if only to get a better fix on things. The man gasped something through his contorted cheeks and when Hector relaxed his grip he was able to cough out "June Singer." At first it meant nothing, but then the man said, "She said to tell you, from the war. She wants to see you. June, from the war."

June, from the war.

As if he could forget from where.

Hector didn't really hear any of the rest, pushing away from the man as if he'd heard a dooming spell, and Big Jacks quickly stepped in and ushered the man out.

Hector asked for a drink and Smitty gave him a double and then another and anyone could see not to ask him any more about it. It was too still and Connolly asked aloud if there was going to be a party anytime soon and Hector said let's go and there was a shout of assent. Smitty then lined up on the scarred walnut top of the bar fifty-five jiggers of Canadian whiskey, one for each of Hector's years, and the whole gang and Dora and some underage rich kids come slumming from Alpine (whom they didn't actually mind) finished them in a relay, Smitty and then Dora especially insisting Hector step to and fro to take every fifth shot, which he did, as always, without word or sigh or gasp. Just sipping cool tea. Though tonight he was moving faster, as though he were filling a bucket poked with holes. He was locally famous for the ease with which he performed such feats. He was in prime form tonight. He kept hearing the stranger's words and he grew thirstier. And so he helped himself, as he'd done all his adult life, even as he couldn't really get drunk the way others got drunk. Unlike his father or cousins or anyone else in the Brennan line, Hector was a great drinker, maybe a historic drinker, he could drink as if his body were not a vessel but a miraculous device of filtration, a man layered inside with charcoal and sand.

Dora was not similarly constituted, and after a few shots of the whiskey she resumed drinking the jug wine Smitty stocked just for her and didn't seem unduly affected until later, when she said "Hey-ya" to Hector outside the john and leaned into his arms and blacked out for a good half-minute, her hair smelling to him of cigarette smoke and riverside nettles and the fish fry she'd surely had for dinner. There was no women's toilet at Smitty's and the one stall was where Dora and the few other women who wandered in had to go. He stood there, propping her up with his hands girding the soft flesh of her back, and to his comrades at the bar it must have looked as if he were fancying a dance. But it wasn't solely Dora he was thinking of, or even the many satisfactions of female grace. It was certainly not June, whom he had never wanted to lay his hands upon. In truth it was another woman, whom he had not pictured in what seemed a lifetime, a woman June could tell of and probably would, a recounting that would only bring him misery.

But he was done with misery, yes? It was his birthday, and here was sweet Dora in his arms, a faint smile breaking though her boozy fade-out. When she came to she righted herself and said, "Thanks for catching me."

"I was here."

She brushed her temple with the back of her hand. "That's never happened to me before."

Hector nodded, even though he was sure the statement was almost certainly untrue.

He said, "It's real late."

"Even for you?"

"I'm okay."

"You don't say that like you believe it."

He didn't reply, instead just leaning her against the wall where the pay phone used to be, the dirty pocked surface scrawled over with expletives and fake phone numbers and the hasty, anatomically exaggerated drawings that gave no quarter to anyone's sense of decency or beauty.

"I was wondering something," she said.

"What's that?"

"How come you've never asked me out?" Dora said, crossing her arms in mock offense. She might have been conscious again but she was still quite drunk, and while the coquettish pose would have normally turned him off, there was a melancholy thrum in her voice that made the question seem much weightier than simply whether he was interested in her or not.

"I don't know."

"Have those meatheads said stuff about me? Been talking big? Because I've never been serious with any of them, if you know what I mean."

"I know what you mean," Hector replied. The fellows had of course talked big, as fellows will, and with enough bluster and shine to make clear to him that Dora was something of an old-fashioned girl.

"You have a girlfriend at another bar?"

"I only drink in this lousy place."

"Then you must not think I'm pretty."

He did think she was pretty (she was at least as pretty as any man should hope for), and he told her this by meeting her eyes for a good long beat. And then he leaned in and kissed her, and she kissed him back, his whiskeyed lips sweetened by the cheap wine she'd been drinking.

"Will you escort me home now?" she said, almost brightly, as though she were starting a fresh conversation.

"I don't have a car. I can walk you, though."

"That's fine."

"I'm not about to carry anybody, just so you know."

"Don't be a wise-ass," she said. "I'm okay now. I just don't like walking around this neighborhood alone at this hour."

"Nobody does."

"Well, worse things can happen to me than you."

"That's what you think," he told her.

"Look, buster, do you want to argue the rest of the night or go?"

"I'll go."

They left the bar to the burbling music of his teasing chums and a toast from Smitty (who drank only ginger ale) and he followed her lead and they walked north past the immense concrete support blocks of the George Washington Bridge. It was past three in the morning but not at all quiet as they were buffeted by the *welt-welt-welt* of the traffic above them rolling over the expansion joints of the elevated roadway. They walked in the middle of the empty street; there was no provision for pedestrians because there was no reason for such provision. Hector liked this upward perspective on the great structure, preferring it to the vista from across the river along the West Side Highway, where one took in the postcard grandeur of the lighted span, this perfected example of human yearning and accomplishment. But he best understood the rather humbling view from below, here between its massive, inglorious feet, where one was just a minor creature skirting about its shadowed trunks.

As they climbed the street that rose and curled around the feet of the bridge, Dora's pace slowed and she confessed to him that she didn't want to go home just at the moment, that her apartment mate was a teetotaler and born-again and a too-light sleeper who would awake and harangue her with a sermon about her dissolute ways. He said he sympathized. Hector took her hand and hooked it onto his elbow, the rounds of birthday whiskey just now warming the back of his skull in such a manner as he could begin at last to feel that estimably sly speed: here was the sole effect he could fathom, the entire pleasure. Through the long career of his drinking he never came close to the sensation of oblivion but rather this small measure of an extra velocity, this slightest lifting.

The ripe scent of the river was like a two-day-old corpse and its fumes buoyed Hector all the more. Had an observer been up on the bridge's catwalk peering down he might have noticed a levity in the gait of both as they strolled in the cottony warm autumn atmosphere the way any pair grown to middle life together would, her head braced just slightly against his still-square shoulder as he guided them up through the twisting narrow streets of Old Fort Lee, not long ago Jewish and Irish and Italian and now lighted around the clock like any street in Seoul or Shanghai with its flashing neon scripts and ideograms. He'd settled here more than fifteen years earlier, after kicking around the country, and getting kicked plenty in return, finally tired of the serial misadventure and wreckage, and this place as much as any other had seemed a good locale to sequester himself for the duration, a mostly working-class town with neighborhoods that looked much like those in Ilion, where you could reach out the bedroom window of the weatherworn houses barely hanging on to tidiness and just touch the fingertips of the neighbor girl who was doing the same. Maybe he liked Dora because she could well be that neighbor girl, all grown up.

Dora had begun to lean heavily into him, though more out of

weariness than desire, but he didn't mind at all. He liked her fleshy weight. Though he was nothing if not catholic in his tastes, he'd come to esteem such women, not plump ones necessarily, though that was fine, too, but women with a fullness of body, a certain density when they pressed against him, pleasing him on a deep animal level. She was now cooing something, too, and he asked her to repeat herself but then she suddenly pushed away from him and stepped off the road, down into the thigh-high grasses and weeds.

"Keep going," she said, her words breathy and clipped. "I'll catch up."

He figured she needed to relieve herself and was impressed that she didn't care about propriety and so heeded her but soon enough he could hear her gagging in the distance and he turned back to help.

But before he could he registered a huff of breath from a man charging him from the shadows. He was knocked to the ground. The man struck him on the head and ear with a huge, rocklike fist. There was a fierce succession of blows, the pain lighting his face and skull like a hot fireplace poker. And yet all this quieted him, too, instantly evoking his most special talent; Hector watched his own body leave him and step aside and take the man's wrist and wrench it to an unnatural position. The big man then hit him with his free hand, hard, with a full and professional extension, the force pushing Hector back over the sidewalk and down the slope. Before he could get up the man hit him again, then again, the disciplined rhythm an unlikely anchor for Hector, and oddly catalyzing, for just as the man paused to catch his breath Hector got to his feet and began to return the blows, trading one for one and then soon enough only giving, until the hulking man was down on one knee as if he were on deck waiting for his turn at bat, which of course didn't come. Hector worked him with the perfect rhythm of a machine, losing himself in his own unrelenting pace, the hard plate of the man's face going to clay, and the thought crossed his mind that transmogrification was less a process magical than something geologic, pressure and heat still the most mystical forges of the realm.

Thus the flesh descends, back to simple terra.

"What do you want?" Hector rasped into the bloodied face, made unrecognizable by the gruesome sheen and the darkness. "What do you want?"

The fellow groaned miserably, unable to speak, his mouth full of spit and blood. Hector raised his fist again and the man trembled, covering his head as he lay curled up on the ground like a gargantuan shrimp. Hector recognized him now. It was Tick Martone, a former club boxer who was sometimes employed by the usual malign people to collect debts, et cetera, but who in fact was not a bad man at all. Toward the end of his fighting career, Tick became punch-drunk (he was only forty or so now) and got confused easily and sometimes even forgot where he was. In the weak moonlight his puffed-out, gourdlike cheeks looked alarmingly innocent, even adolescent, the sight enough to make Hector's heart pause for a moment, resurrecting as it did the ugly memory from the Korean War, a war in which, for a long stretch afterward, he wished he had met his end.

Hector made him sit up. Tick wiped his bulbous nose and face with his shirtsleeve.

"What are you doing here, Tick? Why are you out making trouble for me tonight? It's my birthday, you know."

"Gee, I'm real sorry, Hector," Tick said with genuine remorse, in his distinctively shrunken way. He had a miniaturized, lispy, birdlike voice. He had been a tough fighter in his prime, able to take a load of punishment and still hang on until his opponent tired, then step in close and deliver. His opponents couldn't shake him off. Hence the name.

"I didn't want to, because it was you, but I owe money to Old Rudy, just like that crazy gook, Jung."

"Don't call him that. He's a pal."

"Sorry, Hector. You know I don't mean nothin'.""

"I know."

Among other things, Old Rudy ran a sports book, one of the biggest ones in North Jersey. Physically he was still imposing and when younger had been known for his easy, almost casual, brutality. But it was his hooded, gray-eyed gaze that always spooked Hector, his long-fingered, sheet-white hands, as if the man were a bloodless ghoul, a reaper of low-life souls. He was in his seventies now, failing in body, but word was he was losing his mind, too.

"How bad were you supposed to hurt me?"

Tick was pinching the bridge of his nose to stanch the flow of blood and still could have talked but he wouldn't answer, which to Hector meant on the serious end of things.

"Come on. Just because his errand boy soiled himself?"

"All I know is, Old Rudy wants it to come out of your hide. You're supposed to pay Jung's debt for getting in the way."

"And if I don't? Or can't?"

"I dunno know, Hector. Nobody tells Tick nothin'. But, hey, don't everybody know you two go back a ways?"

Indeed, they did. Like Tick and Jung, Hector owed Old Rudy, but it wasn't money. It was a debt that he assumed he had more than paid off with the last fifteen years of working menial jobs like the one he had now; he was unable to get auto body or carpentry work on the big construction jobs in the nearby counties because of Old Rudy's longtime ties to the mob. After a week or two on a job, Hector would be pulled off the site, no explanations, just a couple of days' severance in cash and advice to not make a peep. Hector easily could have moved on, of course, to another region or state, started fresh, but didn't a certain part of him want to punish himself, too, for the miserable fate he had brought on Old Rudy's beautiful daughter, Winnie? She was yet another woman who had come to disaster by having relations with Hector, and he'd promised himself then that she would surely be the last.

"Hey, Hector, can I get up now?"

"Okay, Tick. Just don't try anything."

"I won't."

As Hector helped Tick to his feet, Dora approached them in the street, her gait somewhat steadier now but still careful, slow. She was about to say something but stayed quiet when she saw Hector and the unfamiliar man with his messed-up face. She'd been around Smitty's long enough to know things like this happened around Hector and the crew, and she simply went to his side and clasped his hand and asked if they could get going now.

Tick said, "Hector?"

"What?"

"Are you gonna try to get even with Old Rudy?"

"I don't know. I guess I can't just wait around to get jumped. Does he still live in the same house in Teaneck?"

"I think so," Tick said. "Listen, Hector. If you do go over to see him, could you let him know I roughed you up all right? If he asks, I mean. I'm still working down my account."

"Yeah, Tick, sure."

With a wobbly step Tick lowered himself into his car, and even offered Hector and Dora a birthday lift. But Hector waved him away, bidding him good night. Though the back of his skull still sharply ached, and the bones of his knuckles felt fused, Hector could generate no real enmity for the man. He couldn't help but see Tick as the kind of fellow who had earnestly labored all his days for self-interested others (fight promoters, managers, shady businessmen, quasi- and outright criminals) for the end sum of what he had at the very start of his humble existence: a long-odds line on a barely worthwhile life, and not a smidgen more. Maybe Hector was caught in the first onset of that sticky middle-aged empathy, which would now cause his throat to tighten and his eyes to well up at the merest suggestion of thwarted dreams (like the other day, when he walked past a bent-backed, toothless Eastern European couple peddling used clothing and shoes on the sidewalk), empathy meaning connection, connection meaning solidarity, if a solidarity he might never act upon. Or maybe it was plain sentimentalism on his part, a soft form of self-pity for his own long-discarded dreams, though he had no doubt his failings were ultimately self-inflicted, one and all. And what were Hector Brennan's dreams? Once clarified, surely no different from anybody else's, in this too often lonely-making world: the haven of a simple, decent love.

After a block Dora slowed almost to a stop, holding on tightly to his arm, his waist.

"We should have taken that ride," he said.

"I'm fine. I'm glad we didn't," she said. "I don't want to think about you fighting that man. Or anybody else. Look, you're bleeding." She reached up and swabbed the corner of his lip with her thumb. But it wasn't his blood. He had some scrapes and bruises, but they would disappear by morning, along with the aches, just as they always did, with a miraculous, almost furious, speed. As though his own body were mocking him, with its incessant, strange perfection. "Why do you want to get hurt?"

"Who said I wanted to get hurt?"

"Then why fight?"

"Why not?"

"Did your father like to fight, too?"

"That's a funny question."

"Is it? Fathers and sons, you know."

"I don't know."

"Legacies, expectations. All that stuff."

"You're losing me," he said, though she in fact wasn't.

"Oh, just forget it, Hector. Don't listen to me. I'm a drunk, silly woman."

"You're not silly."

"Don't be fresh now."

"Sorry."

"Okay, then. I'm serious. I want to know. Is it so fun? To be at war all the time?"

"No," he said, his mind searching a thousand instances, if one. "Not at all."

"But it just happens."

"Yeah."

"Then maybe I ought to stick close to you. Nobody would harm a weak person like me."

"Not if they had a shred of feeling they wouldn't. But you're not weak."

"I am. You'll see." They walked a few more blocks. At a curb she tripped and faltered, and he luckily caught her before she fell. "I think I need some air."

"We're outside already," he said.

"I mean I need to rest," she answered.

He didn't know if she meant to sit or lie down (there was no place to do so) and when she teetered he grabbed her and she immediately kissed him, her mouth tasting sappy and fermented with the hard butterscotch candy she'd been sucking to cover the smell of having thrown up. But who was Hector to mind? He was fouled but not sweet and she was no doubt suffering his own ruined flavor as he kissed her in return, embracing her with his full strength, the tender flesh of her waist pushing up between his fingers. The air then truly seemed to go out of her and it was fortunate that his apartment was only a few blocks away. By the time he had the key in the lock she was practically shaking and he lifted her up so that her legs wound around the backs of his thighs and he could feel the sharp but weak dig of her shoe heels.

He carefully walked them through the darkened two-room flat and when he was at the foot of the bed he believed she was out but she began to kiss him with a new force and craving. They fell into the sorry thrift-shop mattress and soon enough she had pulled his T-shirt off and had unbuttoned her own blouse and was atop him, lowering a still-soft nipple into his mouth. It bloomed in a taste of salt and funk and iron. He hefted her other breast and with his free hand he hiked up the willowy crepe skirt and cupped the heat between her legs until she began moving against him in a cadence that marked her breathing. It was terribly stifling in the room all of a sudden and he rose to slide open the glass door onto the weedy uneven patio he shared with a neighbor he'd hardly spoken to. She followed him, dropping her skirt and wilted panties to the floor, the two of them now attracted outside by a cooling breeze, and in the white-green light of the sodium lamps of the apartment's inner courtyard it appeared as if she might have just ascended from some forsaken underworld, her naked form at once strangely aglow and lifeless. To another man this vision might have been troubling, but to Hector it was an irresistible invitation, and he pressed her up perhaps too hard against the pane of the sliding door. If she gasped with fear it was for but a second, and they stayed there, moving against each other, until it was clear they were too spent to finish, and he carried her already asleep to the bed.

WHEN THE DAWN BROKE Dora was still fast asleep and he left her a note about locking the door behind her, though nothing about whether he would see her tonight. No doubt he would, whether he wished to or not. But he was quite sure he did. He made his way to work through the scatter of the Sunday-morning streets, already caught by a keen urge to turn back and not so gently rouse Dora from her slumber. A surprisingly clean, waxen scent from her wreathed him, a pleasing note in itself but also a contrast to his own aroma, long indiscernible to him but which he was suddenly aware of now in the already bolting warmth of the late-September day, this stubborn rime of lye and bad meat, a consequence of his job, no doubt, though by any measure it was in fact a much deeper insinuation. He wondered if Dora had noticed anything. He was thinking, too, that if he was going to have the regular company of a woman again, maybe it ought to be one like her, even if it meant a more scrupulous regimen of self-hygiene. In a store window he caught a glimpse of himself and paused; he looked murky, watery, either half eroded or half formed. The image aligned with what he had been thinking of himself even before the birthday celebration at the bar, the crux of the matter being that he was a man not yet fixed into his own life.

Jackie Brennan would always say that that was the mark of success, not how large a house a man owned or the model of car he drove but how firmly one was rooted in his family, his neighborhood, his work. Hector had arrived at this point in his life by his own design, and anyone could marvel now at the extent of his feat: he had neither money nor status nor prospects, which was okay by him, even if respectable people might classify him to be a lowlife. But in truth he knew his near-indigence was also easy cover, a way to hide and be freed from responsibility for anything in the least vital or important, which in effect was to be freed from the present, and the foreseeable future, if never quite the past.

For with the bright daylight the past reared up, the name of June its unexpected summons. *June, from the war.* He almost wished now that Tick had gotten the best of him, put him in the emergency room at Hackensack. He'd have to forget all over again. The last time he'd seen June she was only nineteen years old, this fierce, sharp-cornered girl he'd married for her convenience only, despite how miserable and guilty her presence made him. He brought her over to the States and they had lived together (if not as husband and wife) for five months, until it seemed clear enough she could make her own way, and for what seemed an eternity he'd not heard a word of her, neither of them much caring whether the other was even alive.

He walked faster now, as if he might outpace the visitation. A sweat broke out on his back and chest and he was glad that the good aura of Dora was still clinging to him; he breathed it in, to etherize himself. He was thirsty. He knew there was a pub around the corner, and luckily the owner was just opening up, nine o'clock on a Sunday morning. It was his kind of place (or, more aptly, a place for his kind), and amid the stools still perched upside down on top of the bar he stood and quickly drank three draft beers and by the end of the fourth he felt cooled enough to get going again, his thoughts quelled and lingering once more on Dora.

He should think only of Dora. He was honestly looking forward to seeing her tonight. The last time he was with a woman—a long while now, as it had been cold and wet, March or April—he had encountered that most alarming of troubles and despite the woman's patience and valiant efforts he had remained as inert as a day-old balloon. He could not be coaxed. It had never happened before but it didn't surprise him—for some years now he had been sensing a steady depletion in that area, the feeling that what had always seemed his vast reserves of desire were being drawn down at a rate too quick for anything save an eventual exhaustion.

Sometimes he thought maybe he was spent because he had been sexual too early, just as he reached puberty: he was not quite twelve years old when two crazy girlfriends of his crazy older sister took him down to an abandoned boathouse on the Erie Canal and showed him how to play doctor and probe every facet and fold of their wild-blooming bodies and they'd do magical things to him with their tongues and soon enough they would be trysting in all manners like the hobo couples they sometimes spied on in the reeds. When his mother over-heard him tell his friends what the three of them were doing she banned the older girls from visiting his sister and threatened to drag them to the police station, but even back then Hector could not imagine any better initiation, Jeanne and Jenny and him playing with one another with the same pure delight as if they were at the big carnival fair in Herkimer, where, naturally, they'd done fanciful stuff, too, high up in the Ferris wheel gondola.

In Ilion, people would tell him he ought to be a film actor, and during World War II a local committee asked him to model for a war-bonds poster that would feature a handsome family, he being the boy bursting with pride as he gazed up at his uniformed older brother. For the poster the artist had to render him a bit more wholesome than he was, recasting the set of his eyes and diminishing his full mouth in a mold less shadowed and sexualized. The poster went out all across the country and was seen locally as well, though in Ilion it was perhaps unnecessary, for the town had already been awarded the "T Flag" from the Treasury office in Washington for having one of the highest par-ticipation rates of war-bond buying in the country; its sons would enlist in the services in record measures as well, returning home maimed or dead in corresponding proportions, a mostly uncomplicated point of pride in the city that was the birthplace of Remington Arms, manufacturer of the famed Berthier, Enfield, and Springfield rifles, car-ried on killing fields from the Marne to Iwo Jima. *History is made by what is made in Ilion,* Hector's father used to croon darkly, most all of Hector's uncles and cousins either in the employ of the company or bearing its arms into battle, or both. Hector turned sixteen a week before Hiroshima was leveled and like most of his friends he was ready to take the bus to Albany where no one knew them and enlist, of course by lying about his age. He'd had to wait until a place called Korea erupted in war five years later to take his turn.

Certain grown women were always asking him if he would do some yard work or painting for them, and when he was a sophomore in high school he took to the forlorn beds of young wives in the neighborhood whose husbands were away in the Pacific. Of course, given the smallness of his neighborhood, of his town, he well knew the young men, a few of whom would never return. Among those was James Cahill, a Navy lieutenant, who had been an all-county halfback and track star and the youngest floor boss ever at Remington Arms, his wife, Patricia, of the ebony tresses and the hueless glowing skin the one who, that fateful night, shamefully and miserably wept after she and Hector finally coupled. But she had not let him leave right afterward, instead reaching down while she was straddling him and tightly squeezing the weary root of him to sustain another congress until she was almost faint with soreness. She had uttered his name as though he were harming her and he tried to twist away but she held him down by pressing on his shoulders with all her weight. When she finally released her grip, he was unsure if she had come but he let himself go in a violent, near-blinding acceleration that he would rarely achieve afterward, that hot push behind the eyes.

He now wondered if he could have that same push with Dora, but, really, what would he do if he ever felt so vibrantly alive again? Maybe it would be better to count himself as among the creeping, living dead. His worry now was whether Dora might suddenly be inspired beyond his ability to please her; he imagined her now padding about the two dim rooms of his existence in her pale, florid nakedness and thinking that he was not such a dreadful sort at all, certainly sufferable, even suitable, a man with whom she might do things other than drink and share a tumble in the bed. Of course he was not a suitable man, and if in the past he never bothered to alert the relevant parties of said truth, he thought he should do so for Dora, in case she was similarly mistaken.

He had been around enough places like Smitty's to know that a woman of Dora's age and station had perhaps one remaining chance at a generally undamaging union. No one at Smitty's was any use, but maybe someone would walk in one night by accident and save her, a traveling salesman, a retired cop or firefighter. Even (and, maybe, best) another woman. Or perhaps Dora had no chance, being already lost, a scenario in which he would thus serve as none other than the precipitating element in her life's final downdraft.

He made his way east on Whiteman Street and then walked the half-block south on Lemoine Avenue to where he worked, a small two-story Korean mini-mall wedged between Lemoine and Palisade avenues. Hector was the night and weekend custodian of the property, and more often than not he did the work of the day custodian as well, given that the day custodian—his boss, Jung—only periodically showed up.

This morning he found Jung as he sometimes did on Sundays, the thin, deeply tanned man curled up in the ratty vinyl love seat in the ground-floor custodian's office, snoring loudly with a mesh golf cap pulled down over his eyes. Hector could smell the familiar stale reek of Jung's busy night, the sugary charcoal of Korean barbecue and the funky gas of his sleep breath sharply perfumed by garlic and Marlboros and Chivas Regal. An empty bottle of the whiskey lay on its side on the floor. Today was unusual only because Jung was still wearing golf clothes, wearing even his black-and-white saddle golf shoes, tufts of grass and dried mud stuck in constellations about the spikes.

As Hector changed into coveralls, Jung grunted, eyeing him, rooting around in his trousers to scratch and rearrange. He let out a sharp fart before turning over and going back to sleep. He was already snoring when Hector opened the janitor's closet where he kept the tools of his trade. The man was a lower god of indolence. Hector noisily hefted the heavy commercial vacuum (Jung didn't stir) and rode up the elevator to the second floor. It was just after nine in the morning and the place was empty of activity save in the Korean restaurant on the mezzanine, which was open twenty-four hours; a lone diner spooned methodically at a half-dozen small plates of vegetables and a stoneware casserole of steaming soup. A waitress sat two tables away, robotically folding utensils within cloth napkins. When she looked up and saw him, her body relaxed and she smiled, waving him in. Hector suddenly realized he hadn't eaten—not since yesterday's lunch—but he wasn't hungry yet and made a gesture to her to say that he would work first.

He set himself to vacuuming, pushing the machine back and forth on the mezzanine where the carpeting wasn't frayed and could get caught up. In most spots it was worn down to the webbing; one could see the poured-concrete floor beneath it. The mall itself was similarly decrepit, the linoleum overlay by the entrance scratched and buckling, and the central elevator rickety-sounding and dangerously temperamental, its doors sometimes opening just before reaching the right level. The entire inside was painted in cheap off-white paint, save for the ceiling above the central open well, which was a slightly different shade of the old color, somewhat duller, where the painters couldn't (or hadn't bothered trying to) reach. The owner didn't care if the place was in presentable, or even half-presentable, shape, as the tenants clearly valued most the modest rents. Nor did the poor condition of the building seem to dissuade the steady foot traffic of the Koreans and Chinese and the few non-Asians who shopped there and ate at the restaurants. Despite the state of the mall, most of the goods in the shops weren't inexpensive, certainly nothing Hector could ever afford— knockoff designer clothing and shoes and home and car audio equipment with brand names he didn't recognize. There was also a hair salon, an Asian video store, a toy shop, a bakery, a copy shop, a dentist who was also an acupuncturist, and a tae kwon do studio, as well as the karaoke bar and the restaurant.

In the time that Hector had worked in the mall, there had been what seemed to him an extremely high turnover of tenants, none except the restaurant remaining open for very long, and then even the restaurant changed ownership twice in the last few years. Jung had told him that it was because the tenants were often inexperienced business-people, immigrants who got onto a notion of selling some product they could import cheaply and easily, but rarely, it would turn out, cheaply and easily enough to compete with the stores at the large malls nearby. The dentist did reasonably well, as did the bakery, which sold sweet, buttery breads and pastries filled with custards and sweet bean paste the customers couldn't get anywhere else. But mostly the stores here were poorly planned, overhopeful, hastily opened ventures that were preordained to fail, or, even worse, to fail ever so slowly, in an unremitting, soul-grinding diminishment that was invisible by the hour and the day but by season's end could be seen in the wilted posture of a store owner as she hand-lettered signs for a clearance table of hand-bags and scarves. Except for Sang-Mee, the waitress at the restaurant, Hector kept his distance from the tenants so as not to have to deal with their potential difficulties and failures, which might stir up in him an even more insidious disturbance than his suddenly charged empathy, something that he could not so easily drink into oblivion or brawl his way through.

Before the incident with the boy soldier he had been a willing enough soldier in their war. Or maybe not their war exactly, but Mao's war, or Truman's, or someone else's; it was a war that from the beginning had been nobody's cross, inciting only mild attacks of patriotism and protest, jingoism and pacifism, a war both too cold and too hot and that managed to erase fifty thousand of his kind and over a million of theirs. Hector had enlisted immediately after hostilities broke out and so was among the first to be shipped to Japan before landing in Inchon, among MacArthur's forces. He was twenty years old and of course carnally educated but knew little of much else. He had a healthy native intelligence but it was never more than lightly worked, due to his patent beauty and his prowess on the playing fields and in school-yard fisticuffs. If the North Koreans hadn't invaded their brethren in the South, he would simply have worked at Remington, if not in arms, then in typewriters, adding machines, whatever else. He would have been a husband and a father and played baseball on summer Saturdays with his buddies and inevitably slept with some of their wives, but at least it wouldn't have been at his invitation, never his initial doing. In his alternate life there would have been the customary troubles, his own wife maybe leaving him and coming back and leaving him again in a serial drama that had as its greatest satisfaction the comfort of familiarity, of reprise, his days played out in a circle no larger than the carry of a human shout. He sometimes wondered what his life would be like for him now, as a middle-aged son of Ilion; by now he'd be drawing a small pension and playing with his grandchildren on the porch of a row house on a street thick with other Brennans and won-dering what it would have been like to have ventured out and seen the wider world.

With the war he saw it fully wide and dark and deep. But it wasn't the usual rough awakening: he'd never been in thrall to the notion of hero. As a soldier he'd pictured himself not a savior, or some killing machine, but rather one of countless figures on the battlefield, just like the toy soldiers he played with all through his youth; each mini-statuette was formed in one of several poses, as either a prone shooter or a bayonet-wielding assaulter or a marcher, Hector seeing himself as the last of these, the ones the other boys didn't care for and would trade to him at ten to one for the others. He was captivated by the swarm of great numbers, the feel of them bunched in his hands like a

massing of tiny bones. On the chipped, painted porch of his parents'
house he'd line them up in neat rows, the marchers, gritty-faced, pushing on, their rifles shouldered, and though many in the front would
perish before the shooters and bayonets, he knew their flood would
prevail.

Now, as he put the vacuum back in the closet and began filling the
rolling bucket, Jung woke up and stood and stretched, yawning wide
as a lion before sitting back down. As if he'd slept with a lighter and
cigarette in his hand, he instantly lit one up. Hector well knew the
pattern of the man's Saturdays; Jung would play a heavily wagered
round at the municipal golf course at Overpeck and then eat and drink
and gamble the rest of the night with his playing partners and maybe
visit some bar girls at one of the Korean nightclubs in town. In between, when he could get to a phone, he'd bet on football games,
baseball games, basketball in the winter. He was in his mid-thirties and
married and had young children, but a few weeks ago his wife had
kicked him out of their apartment in Palisades Park, fed up with his
womanizing and chronic absence and gambling and his unrepentant
laziness, which was in fact his core charm. There was an admirable
self-comfort in Jung's manner, like he'd evolved himself so completely
that anything but utter acceptance of his ways would be absurd, akin
to thinking less of hippos for wallowing in mud, or of flies for seeking
dung. Jung never actually worked as a custodian, sub-hiring a day la-
borer or two off a street corner in Little Ferry to fill in for him; the
most he did was light carpentry for the tenants or replace burned-out
fluorescent tubes, and of course collect the rent.

"Starting late today, huh, GI?" Jung murmured, checking his fat
gold diver's watch, his eyes squinting against the stream of the
smoke.

"Want to know why?"

"What, you have big date last night?"

"In a manner of speaking."

"She fat lady?"

"He."

"No fucking way," Jung guffawed, the cigarette tilted down loosely in his mouth. "Don't tell me this, GI!"

"Relax. He wasn't there to be nice to me."

"Oh shit," Jung said, sitting up in the couch. "You okay? You look okay."

"I'm all right. But do me a favor. Don't mess around with this any longer. Pay what you owe. For my sake as well as yours. I might not be around when the next guy comes, and even if I were . . ."

"Okay," Jung said, smoking slowly now. "Okay."

"You don't have the money, do you?"

"I'll get it."

"I hope you win big this weekend, chief."

"Me too, GI."

Jung had been calling him GI since learning that Hector had been in the Korean War, or else called him Joe, or Rambo, something else Hector would have never suffered from anyone else but didn't mind from Jung. In fact he took a small pleasure in the idea that more than thirty years of tumultuous world history should presently lead to a moment like this, for him to be dressed in cheap coveralls, mop in hand, preparing to clean the toilets of a grubby Korean mall in New Jersey for this most slothful of their kind, a man who was, literally, born in a roadside ditch during the war but didn't remotely know or care a thing about it now.

"But hey, Rambo, you got hot sex last night, too, huh?"

"Why do you say that?"

"Otherwise you'd be real mad at me."

"I wouldn't tell you if I did."

"See, I'm right," Jung said, leaning back on the couch. He had already forgotten about his betting debts. "I'm glad. I'm afraid you some homo."

"Dream on."

"Maybe, brother. You never know. Maybe I'm sick of women. Sick of all their bullshit. You not?"

"Not near as much as they're probably sick of mine."

"See what I mean? Listen to you! We getting trained, like this! Fucking bullshit. My wife make me jump up and down whenever she want. Go to work early, go back home early, don't see my friends, feed baby, fix shower door, fix car. Don't touch, no sex now. Or, wake up, wake up, sex right now. Now she kick me out and I get same kind bullshit, but from God damn waitress!"

"You should leave Sang-Mee alone."

"Tell me about it! Whole night she was crying, her face a fucking mess, saying where I been? Why golf take so long? Why poker take all night? How come no more present, no more ring and necklace? How come I don't love her anymore? I want to say, 'When did I ever love you, fucking bitch?'"

"But you didn't."

"Hey, I was tired. Then she got very mad, when I fell asleep. Then she cry some more. She was here for a while but I guess she's gone." He immediately checked his wallet, expecting it to be emptied, but there was still a decent slab of bills inside. Being skilled at golf and cards, Jung made his pocket money off his friends; but, after the custom, he spent most of the winnings on their eating and drinking afterward, and whatever was left on his mistresses.

"I'm hungry. Hey, you want to eat? I pay."

"I got work to do."

"No problem. I give you morning off."

"You know I'll just have to work twice as long tomorrow. Besides, the head's probably a mess. Mrs. Kim will just complain." Mrs. Kim owned the Korean restaurant on the mezzanine, and because her customers had to use the mall bathrooms she was often harping on Hector, though more to get him to speak to Jung than anything else. She despised Jung because he never did anything he promised in the way of improvements, but she let him eat gratis anyway (even if he ordered extravagantly), for he convinced his uncle, the mall owner, who lived in Long Island, to keep extending her lease every six months, at a very reasonable rent. She had the cook make the food too salty or sweet whenever he came in with his buddies, so they would think twice about eating there when he next suggested it in the hope of saving himself the tab.

"Okay, you work, and when I wake up again we can eat."

"Sang-Mee's working today," Hector told him.

"You think I give a damn? I'm not afraid of her."

Last week Sang-Mee spilled a pitcher of water onto Jung's back, saying it was an accident. Jung had jumped up and might have struck her but Hector had held him back. Sang-Mee mused aloud how fortunate it was that it wasn't hot soup. This made Jung angrier and he berated her viciously in Korean but she just smiled and went into the kitchen. Jung deserved it; he had been seeing her off and on for the past couple of years, but had dumped her right after his wife booted him, presumably because he had no more excuses about having to stay in his marriage. Hector liked Sang-Mee, for she was always quick with a kind word and had a spark in her eyes that made her prettier than she was otherwise, but then he pitied her, too, for her sticking by Jung for so long.

"I'll eat with you if we eat somewhere else."

Jung cried, "What? Now you on her side?"

"I just think you ought to leave her alone."

"Me? She better leave *me* alone! She *harass* me. Last week she spit in my tea! I get her fired real easy, you know."

"No you won't."

"Okay, Rambo, okay!" he said, holding up his hands. "See, you on her side."

"You want to eat or not?"

"Okay. But I want to eat here. I leave her alone. Been too long, and Mrs. Kim getting off easy. Plus, I need cash. My wife taking all my money, say it's for kids but I know she lying."

"She's using it for booze and gambling and boys?"

"You hilarious guy, Joe. Maybe I'm not so hungry anymore."

"Suit yourself. I still have the bathrooms to do."

"Okay, okay, let's go up."

"I filled the pail already. I'll meet you in an hour."

"I'm starving, Joe!"

"Go by yourself, then," Hector answered, turning to leave.

"You better work first," Jung grumbled, tapping out another cigarette. He lit it and flitted his hand at Hector. "Go, go. I can wait, God damn."

Hector wheeled the full rolling pail of hot water and ammonia to the elevator and keyed it to STOP while he swabbed the floor and then wiped down the walls and button panel with a dampened rag. Like everything else in the mall, the elevator car was in a sorry condition, the wooden floorboards buckled and the metal walls dented and scratched and scrawled over with permanent marker in several languages. As he rode it up to the second level, the car lurched and seemed to slip off its catches as if due to a worn clutch and he imagined the cable above him finally fraying and sending him hurtling to the bottom. And it would be fine, if his end should happen here; there was no better place, if certain dark gods should be served. But the fall might not be quite far enough (there was just one underground parking level) and he knew his fate would likely be that he'd emerge as usual from a heap of sure mayhem with nothing deeper than the usual transitory wound.

The bathrooms he saved for last, for if he started there he'd have to change again before vacuuming the carpets amid customers. It always smelled like a stable, but then worse for the carelessness of people. People could only wish that they lived like animals. Hector could clean them up well enough, but the general condition of the facilities was past maintaining, the stall doors long missing, the walls covered in graffiti, the sinks cracked, most of the panels of the drop ceiling water-stained and ajar. When some of the panels finally rotted through enough to fall down, he mentioned it to Jung, but nothing was ever fixed or replaced and Hector felt no need to mention it again.

As usual the bathrooms were a disaster, the toilets plugged, the basins and floors rankly fouled as they always were on weekend mornings, but especially so ever since the karaoke bar opened, several months ago. The women's room required extra attention, as someone had vomited in the sink but mostly missed the mark. Hector swabbed it first with the mop before spraying it with ammonia and then took a sponge in his hands to wipe down the worn porcelain and rusting faucet and handles. He didn't use gloves. His hands were perennially red from the cleansers but no longer felt the sting of the caustic solvents, being scalded into numbness; as such they were also oddly smooth to the touch, as Dora had once noted in the bar. The mirror above the sink had long been smashed and instead of glass Jung had screwed a thin panel of stainless steel to the wall. Hector took a plunger to the toilets and worked each steadily until all manner of detritus welled up and after flushing each several times he mopped the floor and then had to mop it again with a freshly filled pail from downstairs in the janitor's closet.

On the way back up he saw Jung and Sang-Mee across the mezzanine, standing very close to each other outside the restaurant. She was softly pummeling Jung in the chest as he was trying to pull her against him. They were both slight of frame and not tall, and if he hadn't known them he could have mistaken them for youths in thrall of a complicated and passionate first love. Then they were kissing, quite tenderly, and Hector was reminded that while rife disorder ruled this world, there was also human tendency and need (however misguided, however wrong) forever tilting against it. Love was the prime defiance, of course, most every story told of that, though well short of love there was the simple law of association, just nearness and contact, which Sang-Mee and Jung were reenacting, and which Hector was perhaps about to broach more deeply with Dora. He was rootless and unstrung as always but something in his gut felt at ease with the notion that she might be in his apartment when he returned.

He cleaned the men's room in the same manner, and by the time he finished, his hands and arms and the front of his coveralls were splattered with muck and dirty water, dressing him in a feculence that was at once vile and familiar, this coat of waste and rot.

He was long past being repulsed by such things. After the trouble with Zelenko in his regular platoon, he was assigned to a Graves Registration Unit. Hector ended up serving in it for the largest part of his active duty; like many of the Graves Units it was a colored one, and as such the assignment itself was meant to be an equal part of his sentence, apart from the work of having to handle bodies in every state of mutilation and decay. It was unsettling at the beginning for him to work side by side with the black GIs, for he'd never known or even been in close proximity to any blacks except when he was in Albany once with his parents and they got momentarily lost at night in the streets of Sheridan Hollow, finally venturing into a church to get directions out. The Negro soldiers were estimable and relaxed among themselves, and though he kept his distance as he did with everyone else, none of them had a need to call him out or taunt him for his movie-idol looks. They avoided trouble because there were other troubles to be had equal to or worse than the misery of body handling, like un-loading munitions, or fighting on the line. Better to do the ghoul's work of cleanup and retrieval, which was dangerous enough with the booby traps and land mines.

But it was like anything else, for as disgusting as the tasks were, one grew accustomed to the abominable sights and smells and pro-cesses of the necessary operations: the way you'd have to tug just enough on a corpse's arms, say, if the rest of him was stuck in the dirt and a bit too ripened, so as not to pull them off completely; or how you'd pour hot water from a kettle and chip away carefully with a bayonet to release a poor bastard who was frozen facedown in snow and ice, the flesh falling off sometimes like shredded meat, and other times remaining absolutely preserved and perfect if he'd been there only a night or two. Or in the first days of the spring thaw how they'd find a mess of bodies in a ditch and could tell only from the uniforms if they were enemies or friendlies, and if friendlies maybe only from the hair whether they were white or black, because all of them had turned the color and sheen of licorice by then, the skin finely lacquered by the elements. Every man is a black man in the end, was the joke among them, which made for a bitter laugh and a moment's introspec-tion before they'd continue traversing the slushy snowpack of the hill-sides in search of newly exposed bodies. That is, when the front line had moved far enough forward; but even then there was the threat of sniper fire or an opportunistic mortar round, Davison and Jeffords get-ting it that way one day in early April, a single round landing on the exposed slope of the next hill and leaving a scatter of red on white. The Chinese mortar position was instantly wiped out of existence by both rear and forward artillery batteries, and then Hector and his part-ner and a pair of medics didn't wait for the regular grunts to go up but hiked up to help them, though it quickly became apparent when they reached the spot that it was retrieval duty for them now, Hector immediately heading back down and then up again with body bags, their uniforms and boots getting more bloodied than usual from handling the freshly dead.

Hector could never quite inoculate himself against the sight of blood, and he readily volunteered to do the very worst tasks, gaining the respect and appreciation of the other men, though it was secretly to avoid that certain hue, that crimson brightness. They called him the Prim Reaper, though chummily, judging him to be a little crazy as he knelt over some headless, legless, armless torso, probing with chopsticks or needle-nosed pliers or with his fingers to see if the dog tags had somehow descended into the flesh. They couldn't know that he'd rather deal with the horror of a rotting body visibly shifting and radiating a sickening warmth from its hold of maggots than with that clean red proxy of life. It was that blush still in the skin, in the eyes, that residual vitality of someone just dead or killed, that always shook him to his bones. Life was too fearsome. At least the long dead were dead, if fouled and base, their forms a mere figuration of the inevitable, just flesh collapsing, denaturing into nothing but unsung mud and dirt. It was mud and dirt he was lifting, bagging, collecting with his bare hands, and he could simply wash it off afterward, though having to clean carefully under his fingernails, scour them with a tuft of steel wool dipped in kerosene to rid the most resistant notes.

He unconsciously brought his fingers to his nose now, as was his habit ever since those days, and while they stunk for sure he couldn't make out any of that unsavory, fecund redolence. And yet, something else had been revived. Was it the smell of smoke, of ash? He had long thought that was finally dissipated, gone for good, but then he was someone who was too often mistaken.

FIVE

Yongin, South Korea, 1953

HECTOR BEGAN WORKING at the orphanage soon after the armistice, in June. He had been given his separation from the army for "a pattern of discreditable conduct" that included charges of chronic fighting, trading in contraband, and assaulting an officer. The fighting he was certainly guilty of, but the other charges were debatable, the black-market dealing a case of his being an unwitting courier for a friend, and then the one of striking an officer outside a bar in Itaewon completely bogus; there was a wild scrum of drunken servicemen and Hector pushed a lieutenant who was kicking an already passed-out grunt and the officer tripped back over someone else, his face clanging against the rim of an empty fuel drum. The officer was badly gashed and nearly lost his ear, and it was only due to the resolve of his idealistic army lawyer that Hector received a bad-conduct discharge and not six months in the brig.

Hector decided to look up a Korean preacher he knew, a Reverend Hong, who eventually arranged his papers so that he could stay on in the country. Hong ran an orphanage an hour's drive south of Seoul and had once offered Hector a job there as a general handyman. They'd met, by chance, when Hector had defended him, coming upon the reverend being mugged in an alleyway of Seoul. Some street kids had beaten him with their fists and bamboo sticks, one of them trying to strip him of his briefcase, his billfold, even his shoes. Hector had to punch the biggest kid when he waved a knife before they would all scatter. After the reverend gathered and composed himself he asked if Hector wanted a job, which Hector immediately declined. But after the discharge Hector remembered the orphanage's name, New Hope. He hitched a ride part of the way but walked the last half with just a satchel of his things and the clothes on his back and, of course, a starving girl named June marking him in the near distance like a dusty little moon. They had arrived at the orphanage like this, in tandem but separate, and soon enough both found a place there. They would have likely remained in their respective orbits and never drawn closer to each other had an American couple not arrived in late summer, a reverend and his wife.

When the Tanners first arrived, Hector was out gathering firewood with a crew of boys. He liked working at the orphanage, being in the clean, sweet air of the valley and fixing and making things with his hands. The grounds of the orphanage were set on a low and wide plateau amid steeper, higher hills and mountains that ranged across much of the country. The land was a lesson in hills, one right after the next. The orphanage itself comprised two old, long dormitory buildings (a former stable, a granary), a cottage, and a new building that had been built by an army unit that held a kitchen and classrooms that doubled as mess halls. The structures, laid out in an L, bounded a dirt field where the children played soccer and other games. Reverend Hong played with them all the time, but Hector knew only American football and always declined. In truth, he tried not to spend much time with the orphanage children, even though he enjoyed their company; he admired these children especially but he was wary of getting to know any one of them too well, to get close to them, to be relied upon as a friend. By definition they were hard-luck cases (and often worse) and in the time that he was in Korea he had witnessed enough acute examples of wartime suffering and misery on the roadside and in the villages and in the red-lanterned parlors that he couldn't help but see cast over them an altogether different shadow, with the conflict being over: for who could bear the idea of any misfortune befalling them now?

The hills of the valley had been nearly cleared during the war for fire fuel, or else blasted clean, and once a week he led a group of boys to collect loose kindling and branches. Each time they had to go farther to get the same load. That day was seasonably hot but there was a drying breeze coming from the north and the boys were especially playful and energetic as they combed the hillsides. As usual there was little wood to be gathered to start but before hiking the steep hill to the next valley he let the older ones organize a game of Capture the Flag. They had enough wood back at the orphanage anyway, not even counting a recent shipment of coal, and as winter was still a long way off, it didn't much matter what they gathered now.

Hector watched them for a while, and when the boys of one side kept losing and cried for him to help them, he finally joined in. To be fair to the other team, he carried the smallest boy, Min, on his back and ran about that way. Min was not the youngest but he was under-sized from severe malnourishment during the war. Reverend Hong had found him sitting slumped in an alleyway of Seoul, barely conscious, near skeletal, pocked with insect stings and rat bites. With a month of regular eating he was growing again, but the other boys still made fun of him for being tiny and weak, and then because he was smart. With Min on his back, Hector ran easily, and after a few furious end rushes they won, Min shouting and waving the rag that was the other team's flag. Hector made sure to win the next game again, the boys crying foul, Min chattering at them from his perch. A small, rocky stream cut through the ground of their play, and afterward they all knelt and drank from it, splashing the cool water on their necks and faces, the boys recounting how the game had gone, teasing and taunting one another with grown-up bravado and bluster. It could have been any summer afternoon back in Ilion, and for a moment Hector forgot who they were and where he was, until he noticed Min idly upturning stones along the bank. The boy was hunting for insects and worms, and when he caught a large water bug in his fingers he seemed to inspect it, not with curiosity but a long, knowing gaze. Hector watched as he brought it to his lips but then stopped just short, quelling a certain habit. Hector called them all then and got them up and moving again.

In the next valley they found a stand of trees tucked back in a shady ravine and Hector was glad that he'd brought along an ax. He set the boys to gathering kindling while he worked on a dead tree. Its thick trunk had been cleaved by lightning. He chopped at it steadily but the ax head was dulled and whenever he struck a dense spot or knot it jumped back at him violently. The tree still had most of its limbs and as he got closer to felling it he kept ordering the boys to move back, which they did, but soon enough they had gathered around him again and were begging for a try. He let some of the older boys take a few swings each and then he took up the ax again and worked steadily, gradually losing himself in the exertion, in the rhythm, the muted *chucks* of the blows, and by the time he was near done he was sweating like a draft horse, his hands raw and abraded but alive. Finally he dropped the ax and pushed; the tree groaned once and then cracked and fell in a sudden threshing of dry leaves and dust. The boys cheered him and themselves, clambering upon it as if they'd brought down big game, raising their arms in triumph, with even Hector chiming in.

No one noticed that Min had picked up the ax and was swinging at a root; Min gave it a couple of good hits, but on the third try he slipped and lost his balance and missed and the blade came down on his foot. He screamed as if he were dying. Hector was immediately on him, his own heart bolting, but he couldn't get Min to move: the heavy blade had gone straight through his foot and was stuck in the wide root below. Hector took the boy's face in his hands and told him he would count to three but immediately pinched the boy's ear as hard as he could while pulling out the ax head. Min cried out once more and fainted. The worn canvas sneaker welled instantly with blood. Hector took off his T-shirt but was afraid of removing the sneaker and so bound it all up as tightly as he could. He put Min on his back and ran, trying not to jostle the boy too much, ordering all the boys to sprint ahead and alert Reverend Hong to what had happened. But they had marched a half hour here and he knew he would have hills to cross on the return. Soon Min was awake again and moaning and crying softly, and to his own surprise Hector began singing the chorus of a song that his mother often sang to try to put him to sleep, an Irish famine-era ballad called "The Fields of Athenry":

> Low lie the fields of Athenry,
> Where once we watched the small free birds fly.
> Our love was on the wing.
> We had dreams and songs to sing.
> It's so lonely round the fields of Athenry.

He got Min to hum along and for a while it was as though they were a young father and son on a Sunday hike as they ascended the hillside, making music together in a sentimental key. But it was warm, and with Hector sweating and shirtless the boy began to lose his grip; twice he nearly fell off and Hector had to slow down. Soon he was crying and the sopped bandage was dripping blood again and after a while the boy's frame went limp around him and Hector realized he was drifting in and out. He was losing too much blood. Hector laid him down and tried to rebind the bandage, but when he loosened it the blood only seeped out faster, so he tied it up as tightly as Min could bear.

"Ah, ah!" he moaned sharply, the pain sapping him. He began to cry weakly again. "It hurts, Hector. It hurts."

"I'm sorry," Hector replied, breathless, "I know."

But Hector didn't know. It was amazing, but through all the battles and firefights and skirmishes, he'd never been seriously injured: he'd been knifed and shot, even hit by shrapnel, but they were always superficial strikes, glancing off him as if he were shielded by the harder steel of some mysterious fortune, the only drafts of his blood drawn by the nurses for the blood and plasma reserves, or else coming from his bloodied noses after the tussles outside bars and whorehouses. Then his wounds always healed with miraculous swiftness, as if his corporal self existed apart from everything else in a bounding, lapsing time. And in the same way that he could not feel true drunkenness he felt no true pain, either, just the cold report of impact, his nerves disconnected from the necessary region of his mind, if never quite his heart. Looking at Min, he felt a dense, sharp lump knocking in his chest; he knew if he didn't get him to a hospital soon the boy might die. So he lifted him over his shoulder and set his head low and started to run, run as fast as he could bearing fifty pounds of child, trying not to remember how he'd futilely done the same for a soldier with his foot blown off by an errant friendly shell, applying a tourniquet and ferrying him back to the HQ only for the medic to declare him dead after discovering a perfect half-dollar-sized hole in the back of his head.

When he appeared in the central yard the entire orphanage descended on him, Reverend Hong and the kitchen aunties and all forty or so children, even June, who like Hector typically kept her own company, leaning against the corner of the dormitory building, watching all with her sullen glare. But she was right up front now. Hector put Min down gently, the boy's eyes half open, his mouth slack. His foot was a bright, sopping mass. Hector was shirtless and slick with sweat and smeared blood, one pant leg soaked crimson all the way down to the cuff. Reverend Hong, ever-suffering Hector, made a great pained face of resignation but said nothing. Sterner of expression was the thin, bespectacled American kneeling beside him, square of jaw and formally dressed in a black woolen suit. He was in his mid-forties, the minister from the States they'd been expecting for several days now. The man immediately began working on the boy, carefully removing the bloody bandage of the shirt and the sneaker to reveal that the ax blade had cleaved off his smallest three toes. He picked the little nubs out as if they were stones and gave them to Hong, who gingerly wrapped them in a handkerchief. But Min was awake now, wailing on seeing his own foot and the horror in the onlookers' eyes.

"Have you got it yet?" Tanner called sharply up into the air. "We need it now!"

"Here it is," a woman's voice answered. "It was in my bag."

It was Tanner's wife. She appeared above the gathered mass and passed him a first-aid kit over the children crowded about him. In the strong sun her wheat-colored hair and pale skin shone almost too fiercely for Hector's eyes, her face obscured by the brightness. Tanner opened the kit and from a smaller metal case lined with slotted rubber he removed a syrette of morphine and without warning stuck the boy behind the knee, leaving it in for less than a full second; the boy's size apparently made the anesthesia dangerous. Min gasped but then went slack in his limbs, his fists slowly opening. Meanwhile Tanner was completely focused on the task, sweating heavily in his tie and suit jacket but not bothering to remove them while he re-dressed the foot. His hands were unhesitating and this seemed to calm the boy and everyone else. While Tanner attended to Min, Reverend Hong directed the taxi driver who had just brought the Tanners to retrieve his own bags from his cottage and load them into the car. The Tanners had come to take over for Reverend Hong, who was tasked by the church offices in Seoul to go to America to begin making contacts for future adoptions of the children.

Hong motioned to Hector, for a word. Hong was ten years older than he, in his mid-thirties, but with his slight, short frame he appeared almost adolescent beside Hector's broad bulk. And yet Hector seemed callow and shrunken before him now, his head dipped down as Hong spoke quietly to him in his fluent, quite formal English. Hong knew Hector had been considering leaving as well, but he reminded him again how much the orphanage needed his labors, asking him to promise to stay on until he returned from his trip to the States.

"Will you do so?"

"I don't know."

"No one blames you for this. I am sure the boy will be all right. Reverend Tanner and I will take him to the hospital at the base, and then I must go on directly to the airport. Reverend Tanner will return and administrate the orphanage. You will help him and his wife, Hector, the same way you help me. Agreed?"

Hector didn't answer. Hong clapped him on the arm and said he hoped he would do the right thing. Hector didn't want to lie to him, for the reverend had always treated him with an everyday decency. He'd wait until they were gone and go back to Seoul tomorrow, to one of the rooming houses in Itaewon, where he could blend back in again among his kind, to whom he could do only superficial harm. Meanwhile, Tanner had lifted Min in his arms and laid him out on the backseat of the taxi. He told his wife he would likely be back later tonight, and said he was sure she would be all right; there was no room for her in the car. She answered there was nothing for him to worry about, that he should just take care of the boy, waving him off with a smile.

Tanner got in beside Min, and Hong went around to sit up front. Reverend Hong waved goodbye to everyone and shouted, "I shall return!" and the whole camp bid them off as the driver accelerated down the dirt road, kicking up a dusty reddish cloud.

Hector immediately went to his quarters at the far end of the orphanage's supply building. Soon after he came to the orphanage Hong let him convert part of the storage room for his quarters, framing out a door on the rear, hillside face of the building, but not bothering with a window. Inside it was still and hot, with the only light coming through splits and cracks in the single-sheath panels of the walls. He stripped off his bloodied trousers and found his hands were caked with dirt and blood. Outside he'd rigged a simple gravity shower, a round tin washtub that he had affixed to the roof eave and fitted with a short length of pipe and a hose bib. Of course it would be useless in freezing weather, but he had no other private spot to wash himself. He washed only his hands at first, but then decided to clean the rest of himself. The water was tepid but fresh, for he'd filled it that morning, and he let it run freely, not bothering to save it for another day.

As he scrubbed his forearms and chest and legs with the bar of green laundry soap he wondered if Min was crying again in pain in the back of the taxi, or else gone that ill shade of gray. The thought of a small coffin being lowered into a hole at the orphanage graveyard made him shiver. It was a grave that he should have to dig, but he was sure he couldn't do it; he'd dug scores of graves during the war, and a few afterward, but he couldn't bear to dig this one. His flanks were smudged with dried blood and he scrubbed them harshly until they were raw, doing the same everywhere else the boy had marked him with blood, now using an old hairbrush (as he had learned to do after a long day of handling bodies after a battle) against his skin until the last of the water ran out. As he reached for the towel he caught a flash of reflected light disappearing around the corner. He thought at first it had been a falling leaf or a bird but there on the ground was his torn, blood-soaked shirt. He peered around the building and saw the children running and playing in the central yard of the compound and the aunties observing them from the shade of their lean-to but then just beyond them the new reverend's wife stepping quickly up the stoop of Hong's cottage.

The rest of the afternoon he worked, waiting for Reverend Tanner to return with Min. He stacked the kindling and filled five-gallon water cans from the well and ferried them in twos to the dormitories and the women in the kitchen; from around the buildings he cleared high weeds and dead leaves and brush, to lessen the fire danger; he patched a leaky spot in the dormitory roof; and he began digging a deep, narrow trench for a permanent run of pipe that would finally connect the outhouse to a small pond-sized cesspool he'd been digging for the last month. The water plumbing was already in. By the time dusk fell he had trenched five meters (it was in fact a lot, given the hard-packed, rocky soil), and the children were eating their supper at the tables outside with the kitchen aunties. He asked one of the aunties if the new reverend's wife had come out yet from the cottage and she shook her head and mumbled something that he didn't understand. He had learned enough Korean for basic communication but could rarely comprehend past the first phrase. He asked her to repeat herself and she said it was no matter, saying the woman was probably tired and that he should not bother her. He said he wouldn't bother her, but the auntie drifted away without hearing him. She and the other aunties liked him well enough and certainly appreciated his help fetching firewood and water, but he'd always sensed that their enthusiasm for him was limited, that they'd learned certain lessons from the war and that he, as a former GI, could only ever be provisionally trusted. If anything, they'd warmed to him because of Reverend Hong's obviously sanguine feelings for him, which was another reason why he thought he should be leaving now. But he never finished packing his satchel, instead emptying it and hanging it up over the exposed rafter, his guilt over Min at least the primary reason, though he kept checking the cottage door from wherever he was working for any sign of her.

When night fell, candlelight briefly illuminated the front window of the cottage. Hector was sitting out front of the supply room, leaning back against the support post on a cut-down stool, drinking steadily from a bottle of warm whiskey. Reverend Tanner and Min had still not returned. The candlelight went out and for the rest of the bottle he waited for the panes to be lit again, to catch a glimpse of her moving through the rooms. But there was nothing. The more he drank the more restless he grew, his limbs bristling with the inaction, aching to push back against the calm. He got the Willys to start and drove it fast into Itaewon, his knuckles alive with anticipation. He went to a bar where no one would know him and proceeded on his typical late-night program, his *modus bibendi* (as his father, Jackie, liked to say), casually winning enough money in drinking contests (the first always leading to another, and another) to more than pay for his tab at night's end. But one of his earlier opponents, a thick-lipped, sour-faced sergeant who watched him submerge all comers, decided he was a trickster or a hustler and called him out as he left, and Hector, wide-eyed as a full moon, let the drunken, angry sergeant swing wildly at him before stepping in close to trade blows. Without any grappling or pushing they struck each other, locked toe to toe, for a good three minutes. The man had surprising strength but he soon flagged, and then the contest tipped, as it always did. It was cruel of Hector, surely, for he knew it would have to come to this, the sergeant soon just another ambulant dreamer, held up only by the alley wall, his thick lips split top and bottom and petaled out horribly into four. Hector's last blow was simply to nudge him sideways, the man crumpling down slowly to the gutter, set forth now on that bruised, booze-soaked slumber that never quite mollifies.

Hector went on to a rooming house where the proprietress knew to have two women from the adjoining brothel sent to his room. It was how he preferred it, never hiring just one if he could afford two, a satisfaction and habit that had grown out of those first ministrations with his older sister's girlfriends, though on this night it was a craving not so much libidinous as a want of continuous labors, an intense need for usage on his body. But when they stripped for him he could see they were girls, and young ones—hardly sixteen, if that—and rather than send them back down to someone else, he just had them lie with him in the bed. It was four a.m. and they were tired, too. He had not been so valiant in the past but his heart was sodden with the unhappy sights of the day, and though he had no desire to go home to the States he realized he ought to leave Korea soon. It was true he had little sentiment left for his ex-comrades—he could bait any poor bastard like the sergeant into a harsh and probably undeserved realm of pain—but seeing for three long years these destitute people and their children serve as handmaidens in their own wrecked house had finally begun to vanquish him. It had not seemed a problem at first, for it was nothing compared to what he had witnessed in the war, but he sensed that he was being replaced, cell by cell, with bits of stone. Even in regard to Min his guilt was as much conception as feeling. And he still wanted that feeling, at least for the natives. In the morning the girls stood above him in their too-colorful dresses and the older one politely asked him if he would pay them extra for staying the night, which he did, knowing that they would otherwise get docked of their pay, or even beaten.

When Hector got back to the orphanage in mid-morning, Reverend Tanner was conducting the Sunday service beneath the pavilion in the central yard; it was where everyone gathered and ate in the warm weather. He parked the Willys in its spot just inside the arched gate and walked in. They were singing a minor-key hymn and his heart sank in fear that they were doing so for Min, but then he spotted a pair of crutches at the end of the front row, Min sitting up straight and bright-faced, his mouth wide with song. His foot was heavily bandaged. Tanner's wife sat next to him, focused intently on her husband at the head of the congregation, singing, too, with the enthusiasm of a preacher's wife.

When they were done, Tanner addressed them. He was very much at ease and spoke Korean quite well, as he'd worked in Pusan the last year of the war. He had told them, as Hong had before, how he had come to oversee the orphanage as well as tour the many other church-affiliated orphanages around the country, to observe conditions and allocate resources as well as to teach classes, and also, of course, arrange for adoptions. But then he was humorous in recounting what had happened on coming back from the hospital, telling how Min somehow convinced the taxi driver to let him take the wheel for a little bit, which nearly led to their skidding off the road. There was a hearty laugh and Tanner prompted Min, who hopped up on his crutches, grinning and waving his hands, and then took a deep bow. There was rousing applause and shouting and anyone could see that Tanner had already begun to win them over. He continued, not with a Bible lesson but with a talk about his background as a physician and how he had come to his faith after his own miraculous recovery from an otherwise fatal blood poisoning.

"It happened soon after Mrs. Tanner and I were married." He spoke to them as if in confidence, as though they were all his intimates and he was confessing to them. "Our life together was just beginning. But after I became deathly ill, I felt powerless and insignificant. I was afraid. I was no longer the arrogant doctor who had always believed in the boundless possibility and reach of the human mind. I realized my conceits and accepted at that moment not only death but the grace of an Almighty Spirit. I refused further treatment and bid my parents and my dear wife, Sylvie, goodbye. I was no longer fearful, only sad for leaving my beloved wife and parents and for being so willfully blind. I shut my eyes and fell into what all believed was my final sleep, but two days later I awoke, my fever broken. My limbs were weak, but gone were the terrible shaking and pain. But this was not what struck me. It was my mind, yes, but altogether recast, my thoughts suddenly as clear as the water of the deepest, purest spring. I knew then that I had been living only half a life, and thus not a life at all, that all of my worldly knowledge and expertise and efforts were useful and valuable but only as a living devotion to the mercy of God and His Eternal Love. I had been delivered, as I hope you will be delivered, into a glorious new life."

As he spoke, Hector caught his wife's eye a few times but she looked away whenever he did, her gaze returning straight to her husband as if to a beacon shining out from a dark shoreline. Tanner clearly was aware of him as well but didn't break at all in his speaking or gestures, even after Hector turned to go to his room. He had been a vessel for plenty of religious talk throughout his life, and in recent months from Hong as well (the good reverend would come and share a whiskey with him and read the Gospels aloud), and although he was not yet a believer, he was becoming a willing subject himself, someone who had indeed begun ceding his life, too, if arranging a very different surrender.

For the first week, Hector steered clear of the new reverend and his wife; he worked on the immediate grounds in the early mornings and during congregations and meals, saving any fieldwork for when they might be about. He couldn't help but pause, as everyone did, whenever he caught a glimpse of Sylvie Tanner, her hair as it fell against the grave paleness of her shoulders glowing as vibrantly as anything he had seen since being in this desolated country. She was near forty, the creases at her eyes and mouth just now insinuating themselves for good, the first white wisps ashing the hair at her temples. There was the tiniest downward lag at the corners of her eyes, which he thought gave her an almost Egyptian sadness. The children adored her, the girls especially, floating about her like hungry bees around a tall, straight flower. She had introduced herself briefly to him as he ate alone after everyone else had finished, but he felt Tanner's obvious disdain and didn't allow himself to approach or speak to her. She seemed too mature and complete and happy, and this easy perfection, besides her loveliness, made him all the more shy and grimy-feeling and compelled him to drive the Willys into Seoul each night and enact the depravities Tanner saw in him.

One morning Hector was scraping old paint from the side of the main dormitory to ready it for a new coat when Reverend Tanner suddenly appeared and surprised him, asking if he could help. Hector nodded and handed him a scraper and they worked together for an hour. Tanner had spoken to him several times about work projects and such but it was the first instance that they'd stood this close to each other for more than a brief moment. Tanner didn't pretend that he was solely there to work, immediately asking Hector when he had arrived in Korea and where he had been during the war. He asked if he'd seen action and Hector told him only that he'd been in Graves Registration. Without prompting, Tanner spoke about himself, saying he was from Buffalo but had studied medicine and later divinity in Chicago and was now based in the Seattle offices of the Northwestern Synod of the Presbyterian Church. When he found out where Hector was from, his eyes lit up.

"I was actually near there once, as a boy. I swam with my cousins in the Erie Canal. When they opened a lock upstream we jumped off one of the bridges and rode the current down and then hitched a ride on whatever boat was heading back. You must have done that a thousand times."

"I didn't swim much," Hector said. "I never liked the water."

"I remember now. That was some of the foulest water I've ever seen. All sorts of things floating in it."

"Yeah," Hector said, seeing again the blackness inside his father's gaping mouth. "That's right."

"Will you be going back?"

"To Ilion? No."

"Then to somewhere else in the States?"

"I don't know."

"You must be having a time of it here in Korea," Tanner said. "Like most of the servicemen."

"I'm not in the service anymore."

"Yes, I know that. I suppose I meant all you young men."

Hector didn't respond, keeping focused on the task. Tanner didn't press him and they worked steadily with their scrapers on the long section of wall, working from opposite ends and moving toward the center. Soon enough flecks of white paint dusted them from head to toe, the two men looking as if they'd shoveled out an ash pit. Tanner took to the work with ease. He was still wearing his minister's gray shirt and white collar and in the gaining heat he perspired heavily. But he wasn't laboring. He was athletic and rangy and he clearly welcomed the renewed physical activity after his extended travels; back in Seattle he sculled his one-man shell every morning on Lake Union. He was twenty years older than Hector—some thinning showed in an otherwise full head of hair—but there was otherwise an animation and sturdiness about his constitution that was not unlike the younger man's, though unlike Hector's, Tanner's was drawn as much from the force of his will as from an innate, brute vigor: his obviously steel self-belief primary still, despite the story of his miraculous recovery.

Tanner reached the midpoint of the wall even before Hector, whose efforts ticked by as always at a constant, unremitting meter. Tanner stepped back, removing his wire spectacles and wiping his brow with his sleeve.

"From your surname I assume your family is Catholic?"

"My dad. My mother was lapsed. They're both gone now."

"I'm sorry to hear that."

"Yeah."

"And what about you? Do you consider yourself Catholic?"

"I'm nothing."

"Surely you must have been christened."

Hector nodded.

"I was just curious. It's not important, but I suppose I was wondering how much time you'd spent in church."

"Why's that?"

"Again, it's not material, but I want to ask if you would be able to construct a chapel for us. The outdoor pavilion is perfectly fine now, but I don't see how it will be useful come winter. Had Reverend Hong any such plans, about what to do?"

"If he did, he didn't tell me about them."

"I'm glad we're talking about it, then. I was thinking that perhaps you could build a small chapel, just one big enough to house all of us."

"I doubt I could get the lumber to build anything but a shed."

"What about converting a space?"

"There's really nothing that would work, except maybe the main classroom."

"No, that won't do," Tanner said. "I feel strongly that if possible we should have a chapel that's just a chapel. Where we solely hold prayer services and read Scripture and sing our hymns. Nothing else, no classes or eating. It doesn't have to look churchlike. A room with benches is all we would require. Nothing large. The closer we are, the better."

Hector pictured the big Catholic church in Albany where they went for Easter, and then the one on West Street in Ilion where his father would regularly take him and his sisters on Sunday mornings, and sometimes for the Vigil on Saturday afternoons. It was massive and impressive to his boy's eyes, built from blocks of granite and with a medieval-style tower, and within its soaring buttressed wooden ceiling above the nave, the supports and walls were clad in a limestone that shone brilliantly in the daytime from the light that streamed in through three high, narrow stained-glass windows over the main entrance. It was a very long structure with dozens of rows of burnished mahogany pews. On certain stifling summer days the air would be unbearable and his father would often doze off for a while, and if they were sitting toward the back Hector could slip beneath the pew in front and lie down on the cool stone floor until just before the sermon was over. There was a separate small chapel off the nave, devoted to the Annunciation, and Hector was surprised how well he could recall it now, the narrow space like a miniaturized chapel with its smaller altar and cross and off to the side a statue of a remarkably beautiful Irish-faced Mary, who could have been one of his wild sisters.

"There's the vestibule between the girls' and boys' sleeping rooms," he told Tanner. "I think it was open space between the buildings that was enclosed at some point. I wouldn't have to do much except maybe install a woodstove, if I can find one. I suppose I could salvage enough boards from the base for some pews."

"Yes, that sounds fine. That might just hold all of us."

"Not me."

"Have you not attended any of the services here?"

"No."

"And Reverend Hong never minded?"

"I do jobs here. He knew that."

"Well, you should know it's likely he won't be returning in three months. He's done a good job and the Church will be asking him to go to Minnesota after his time in Seattle, to help begin a new ministry.

He doesn't know this yet. A good number of the children, from all our orphanages around Korea, will be adopted into families there."

"Are you telling me I ought to get going? Because I'll move on whenever you like."

"I wasn't suggesting that." Tanner said. "Of course, it's up to you. However, I would ask you to stay on for a while. There's clearly much work to be done around the property before the weather turns. Reverend Hong went over it with me, particularly the refurbishing of the kitchen and the new septic tank, as well as patching the roofs of all the structures. And now this chapel. I'd ask you to see these projects through, if not for me, then for Reverend Hong. For the children."

He looked directly into Hector's eyes. "May I be frank with you? All right, then. Although I've only been here a week I will tell you directly that I think your presence otherwise is detrimental to the children. I took the liberty of interviewing some of the staff aunties. Please don't blame them, but I was quite forceful in my queries. Again, I have nothing against you, personally. Your life is your own, and I didn't come to Korea to mold your habits or your character. But I am certain that the children don't need to see you return every morning after long nights in town. Or be so aware of your public drinking. Or your obvious indifference to our assembly and worship. So I disagree with Reverend Hong when he says that because the children are accustomed to you there should be no concern. They are rootless in every regard, and this may be their last chance for a new beginning, and so why would I wish any influences on them that weren't wholly benevolent? Do you think I should?"

"No."

"So you can understand. You agree."

Hector didn't disagree.

"Good. I want to say now, too, that in my view everything is conditional. My hope is that from this point on I'll be persuaded otherwise.

You're a very young man, with your entire life ahead of you. I don't know what happened to you before or during the war, or what you think this life now holds for you. But I would say you have the posture of someone awaiting the inevitable. Or even inviting it. I am sure that there is no worse sin than the one a man can perpetrate on himself."

For the next few weeks Hector kept fast to his work. It wasn't to try to impress Tanner or alter any of his views. He didn't like the last thing the reverend had said about him, but there, too, he couldn't quite do anything but agree: indeed, he was waiting for the inevitable. He was looking for something to befall him, to strike him down; he was a man clambering to the top of a hill in a lightning storm, waving an iron rod. But for Hector the skies blew always empty, broke open vast and blue. So he threw himself into the labor. He wanted the rack of heavy toil, not as discipline or punishment but as cover, a way to erase himself. He patched the older roofs in the afternoons. Only the small schoolhouse roof was solid and sturdy, having been constructed by an army ordinance battalion a year earlier, at the end of the war, but the rest of the buildings dated from the 1920s and were converted farming structures, rickety swaybacked buildings meant for housing livestock and chickens. He spent the hottest part of the day on the clay tiles, clearing everyone out from beneath the roof he was working on, in case of collapse. In the intense late-August heat the orphanage grounds were deserted, the rest of the populace staying inside for their studies, or else resting or doing chores under the tent or the meager tree shade on the edges of the compound. The sun was relentless, its rays like sheets of fiery glass cascading down to shred him, but he welcomed the burn on his shoulders and back as he stepped about on the creaky structure. He felt nimble and insignificant, an ant at labor, but an ant alone, drifted far off from its brethren.

At meals he took his bowl of rice and soup back to his quarters, drinking his PX whiskey in private as well. He had stopped going into

Seoul. He mostly avoided the children. With the excuse of what had happened to Min he disbanded the firewood detail, doing the gathering himself. It was not that he felt chastised or shamed by what Tanner had said so much as alerted to an idea about himself that had begun to haunt him: that he was a bane on otherwise decent people, somehow instantly embodying the exact cast of their most profane weakness. He inspired only homely acts of Eros. Hadn't it been that way with Patricia Cahill, voracious for his physicality as she was going mad over the lost corpse of her husband? And with his good-hearted but ever-needful father, Jackie, whose sodden drift down the Erie Canal found its source from the same? And so in regard to the children Tanner was of course right: there was no good reason to allow a figure like him within their view. Each one had surely witnessed enough depravity and death to last all their days. And while most of them were now gleeful and antic like any other children, kidding with him more easily than he did with them, he sensed that a few of the quieter ones, like June, the girl who had followed him here from the road, could see through his surface to the potential disaster lodged in every cell of him.

At the army base he was able to find an old stove and collect enough boards and plywood to make four benches for the space between the dorm rooms. He would have to wait to make the four others they would need. It was too narrow for a middle aisle, so the benches would have to stretch almost to the side walls to be able to seat all the children. Unlike the roof work, it was more meticulous than strenuous, but he found himself drawn to it anyway, saving the very end of each day for the job. With a hacksaw he cut out from the plywood sheets that would form the ends, at first plain square supports for the long boards of the benches. But after the first one, he decided to cut a simple curve along the top edge; the squared-off ones, veneered in a light-hued pine, looked too much like the ends of little coffin boxes for his comfort. Because it was plywood it was difficult to plane the edge without badly splintering the sheet, so he used a sanding block instead to null the roughness. He would sit outside his quarters working the edges in the twilight, the smell of the wood a little miracle of freshness, of released former life, and he didn't care if some of its dust drifted into his tin mug of whiskey. Even though all this was due to Reverend Tanner's wishes, and he could never care in the least about anyone's worship or God, Hector didn't like the idea of the children having to sit outside in the cold during services, which were far lengthier with Tanner than with Reverend Hong. He knew the cold in Korea, at least in the mountains in the far north, how it seeped into you and then resided with an unrelenting grip so that you felt colder than even the frigid air of the foxhole or dugout, like a chunk of ice at the bottom. During a slow retreat the first winter of the war he had seen two girls curled up and nested by the side of the road, their unblemished faces and bare hands and feet the color of ash. No doubt someone had taken their shoes. He'd waved another GI from the Graves Unit over and they had to pry them up from the frozen mud with shovels, bearing them in one piece to a spot behind some sagebrush like museum workers moving a sculpture. But the ground was rock hard, and so instead of a burial they draped them with a blanket, the edges pinned with stones. Of course it was useless—the blanket would soon be taken, the bodies scavenged by birds and animals—but he thought they ought to be covered and allowed, at least for a while, to sleep a dignified measure in private, undisturbed.

After he finished all the end pieces, he cut out notches for the long boards, which he had sanded as well, and then nailed two-by-fours underneath for the cross-bracing to support blocks in the middle. The backless benches were somewhat crude, for he was no artisan, but he had skill enough from a summer job as a carpenter's assistant to construct them to sit sturdily and in balance. He had intended to stain them, but he could get only free paint (no primer) from the base quartermaster and the paint came only in gray, flat, mute gray, and after the first swath the lifeless hue stopped his hand.

"It looks all right to me," he heard behind him. It was Sylvie Tanner. She wore a billowy cotton dress, the points of her shoulders shiny in the sun. Like everyone else, she had seen him outside building the pews but until now was one of the few people at the orphanage who had yet to come up and make some comment about his work. "I think it's a good color."

"You must like rain clouds," he mumbled. "Or battleships."

"Maybe rain clouds," she said, taking the wide brush from him. She dipped it into the can and dabbed the excess from both sides on the inside rim and added three strokes to his, painting a section the width of the board. Her motions were lengthy, voluminous, almost flamboyant. "There. You see, it's not so bad."

"I doubt your husband will like it."

"Why do you say that?"

"He's not a fan of me. I don't care, but I'm just saying."

"I know you don't care," she said, surprising him. Her eyes, which she visored with her hand, were remarkably large and dark, even in the daylight, her pupils seeming to push out nearly all the sea green around them. He was trying not to look at her, but he kept failing. "Besides, I wouldn't be so sure. He admires all the work you've been doing, this project especially. As do I."

"You want to paint some more?"

"Would you mind?"

He told her to keep the brush. He went to find another in the storeroom, and when he finally returned with one she was nearly finished with a first coat. They moved on to the others, and soon they were done and ready to go back to the first bench she'd painted. But it wasn't yet dry enough for its second coat, so she asked if she could see the work he'd done so far in the vestibule. He had already brought in the salvaged stove, now situated in the rear corner, and shifted and reframed the facing doors of the girls' and boys' rooms to be closer to the main entrance so that they wouldn't be impeded by the benches once they were installed. He had taken apart a pair of broom closets to make as much room as possible and the space was starkly bare. The wooden walls, formerly the exterior of the separate structures, had been long weathered to a dark, silvery sheen.

"It's dark in here even with the door open," Sylvie said. "If we were to hold a service now we'd have to use oil lamps, or candles."

"This wasn't meant to be anything but another storage room. And a windbreak."

"What do you think we should do?"

He didn't know, but he felt as though he suddenly did care, if only because she was here, away from everyone else, within his reach.

She said, still holding her brush, "How much paint do you have?"

"There's plenty. But it's all that same color."

She looked about for a moment, then took some broad swipes at the wall, down and then up. She stepped back. "You know, I think that will be fine."

"It's going to look like a concrete box in here."

"Maybe not," she said. "We'll see. But do you mind? It's a lot more work for you. I can help, if you like. In fact I should, since I'm putting you up to it."

"It doesn't matter," he said. "You can do what you want."

"Then I'll help," she said brightly. They were standing near where the altar would be. Painted or not, this would be like no other house of God he'd ever seen. Above them there was no ceiling, and the bare rafters were strung with cobwebs and pocked by old hornet's nests. It was quite warm inside and though they were both marked with the pungent oil paint he could still glean faint notes of her, her sweet sweat, the soft, palmy oil of her hair. He could smell himself, too, and it was not good, this dried animal reek, this lower-order tone, but she didn't seem to mind being this close to him. He had the strange compulsion of wanting to pick her up, to see her high in the cathedral; maybe he was a Catholic after all. But the little light there was flickered and the lanky silhouette of Reverend Tanner appeared in the frame of the main doorway.

"There you are," Tanner pronounced, though not quite sounding as if he was surprised. "I saw the benches out by the storeroom."

"Don't they look good to you?" Sylvie asked.

"Indeed, they do," Tanner said. He cuffed her waist and leaned to kiss her but she warded him off by flaring her brush, her paint-splotched hands.

"We've decided we'll be painting in here, too."

"Is that right?" he answered her, though he was looking at Hector.

"Yes," she said. "We think the same color as the benches."

"Well, I'm sure that will be fine," he said. "Perhaps I'll lend a hand as well."

"Yes," Sylvie added enthusiastically. "We can all work together."

"Listen," Hector said. "I really don't need any help."

"It's a lot more than painting a few benches," Tanner said.

"It's still not a big job."

"Don't be silly," Sylvie said. "Anyway, that's not the point."

"I'm not being silly," he told her, with an edge that seemed to deflate her. "It's not a big job, and if you want me to do it, I will. Look, I better get a second coat on those now." He held out his hand to Sylvie and she handed him the brush. Outside, the benches were dry and he pried open a fresh can of paint and stirred it and began applying a second coat, not looking up. He didn't see when the Tanners left the vestibule. It bothered him that her enthusiasm didn't seem to wane when her husband appeared. But who was he, to care about such a thing? He was being a child. As he painted he was surprised at how tense his hands were, not realizing until it was too late how fiercely he was pushing the brush against the surface, enough so that he marred the first coat beneath. He had ruined all of the first pew, and a good part of the second, before painting the others properly. He had to wait until the first two were completely dried before stripping them down and starting all over again.

FOR A COUPLE OF WEEKS he tried to steer clear of her. It was easy to avoid Tanner, who was busy giving sermons and teaching history and math and regularly leaving on day trips to tour and inspect other orphanages. Sylvie was busy herself, teaching English and sewing and sometimes helping the aunties with the cooking. She worked along with the children in the large gardens of the orphanage, harvesting the last of the summer peppers and tomatoes and preparing the plots for lettuces and cabbage. But she would appear in the most casual of manners, coming around to where he was working bearing a glass of iced barley tea or skillet corn bread, invite him to come down from the searing rooftop and try what she'd made. He hadn't yet started painting the chapel. Or at dusk, if he had forgotten because of working straight since dawn, she might knock on his door with a supper tray. She never came to him alone, for June accompanied her now almost everywhere. He'd hardly meet Sylvie's eyes and nod and take the tray inside. She'd go away with the girl's hand in her own, arms swinging easefully as if they were sisters.

Sylvie had originally taken her up because June could not play with the other children without a resulting argument or fight, her counterpart invariably ending up the more injured party. June was moody and aggressive and when she wished could be unrelentingly cruel, as harsh to the youngest ones as she was to those nearer her age. Her main chore at the orphanage was to help the aunties with the laundry, and she once made a boy who chronically wet himself take off his underpants after an accident and wear them on his head. She would often bully other girls when she found them too girlish or weak, especially when it came to standing up to the boys. Hector himself had broken up several of her fights—the last one found her crouched in the middle of a gang of the oldest boys, who were taking turns punching and kicking her, shouting at her to go away, that she was ruining the orphanage. She was trouble enough that Reverend Hong had quietly attempted to place her in another orphanage, or in a job-training program. And yet because he knew there was only misery and degradation in store for most family-less girls, he had at last decided he must try to keep her on even after she turned sixteen, to delay her entry back into the world for as long as possible.

But after Sylvie took an interest in her, she visibly softened; before, she was always quiet and kept to herself when not fighting, but now she sometimes helped the smaller girls carry the clean folded laundry back to the dormitories, or worked extra hours in the garden, and was particularly helpful in translating for Sylvie and the students during English classes, where she was easily the best speaker. Soon she was working a couple of hours each day in the Tanners' quarters, sweeping and dusting and making the beds. There was always some group of children naturally clinging about Sylvie, but in the off-hours, well after supper or very early in the morning, when only Hector might catch sight of them, it was always just June who was with her, the two of them sitting on the stoop gently brushing each other's hair, or else coolly whispering to each other like a pair of thieves.

One afternoon he saw Sylvie reading a book while he was clearing the underbrush as preparation to trench the new sewage pipe. She sat on a large rock that overlooked the lowland where he would install the septic piping and field. June was not with her. Reverend Tanner and the aunties had taken most all of the children, including June, on a trip to a waterfall and swimming hole. They had been gone all morning. When Sylvie saw him pause in his work she quickly waved to him, but then returned to her reading. He had no pretext for doing so and didn't know what he would say, but he dropped the machete and hiked up to her. When he said hello she stood up and simply replied, "Hello there," and to his relief didn't ask what he wanted. She simply shut her book without marking the page and put it down on the rock. It was a slim blue volume that he'd seen her often reading and not always sequentially, as though she had read it many times over and could pick it up anywhere.

"I see you've started to dig for the pipe," she said. She peered down the line he'd freshly cleared of brush, which easily ran over fifty meters. "Are you actually going to do the whole job by hand? Isn't there a machine Ames can get to help you with it?"

"Not out here. It would cost too much, besides."

"I'm sure you're right."

"You could help me."

"I thought you never needed help with anything."

He didn't answer.

"Well, I'm glad you changed your mind."

"It's not going to be easy work. Not like the painting. The ground is mostly stone, and where it's not stone, it's hard-packed clay. Or maybe it's all the same thing."

"That almost sounds like a koan."

"A what?"

"A koan. It's a kind of a riddle, but one you keep saying to yourself. Buddhists use them to focus the mind."

"You won't want to focus, for work like this."

She smiled at him. "I do feel like doing something difficult. Something strenuous. It's been awfully quiet today. And, frankly, you look kind of lonely down there."

"I'm all right," he said.

"I'm sure you are. Shall we try it, then?"

"Okay."

They went down to the head of the trench that he'd begun earlier. He had a pickax and shovel with him and held them out to her.

"Your choice." She took the shovel and followed him down to the mouth of the trench; they would work from the empty new cesspool back up the slope. He hopped down into it and gestured for her to step clear, and he began working it, raising the pickax directly over his head and hammering it down on the dry, rocky ground. Once he warmed up he kept a steady cadence, the muted tremors of the blows lifting them imperceptibly off their feet. After he'd broken up a meter or so Sylvie stepped down and shoveled out the loosened earth and rock. The pile was denser than she expected and she had some trouble at first. Hector went to help but she told him she was fine and she speared furiously at the gravelly dirt. After she cleared it they switched, alternating several times until during her turn she suddenly stopped shoveling. She turned up her hands; several blisters had welled up on the pads of her palms and on one hand an especially large, angry blister bridged the space between her thumb and index finger. Hector told her she should stop and she nodded, but instead of going back to her cottage for a bandage she simply pinched the mass until it broke. She picked up the shovel again, wincing as she hefted it, and attacked the pile as before. She didn't complain or hold back.

They worked for the better part of an hour in the high afternoon heat, the sweat completely soaking through Hector's denim work shirt. Sylvie was flushed about the neck and cheeks, the delicate tendrils of her hair matted to her temples. The fabric of her blouse was a gauzy linen and with the angle of the sun he could see clearly her tan-colored brassiere and the dark nook of her arm and the smooth line of her torso as it led down to the spur of her high hip. She cleared as much as he loosened and they would each unconsciously extend their turn slightly and Hector finally had to tell her she should quit for the day when he saw the condition of her hands, several new blisters split open on each, the loose skin shredded and curled back to reveal the raw underlayers of her palms. She might not have agreed, but they heard the heaving clatter of a big diesel motor in the distance; it was the old transport truck the children had piled into this morning.

"I should go," she said, pushing him the handle of the shovel. For a second he was sure she was going to lean up and kiss him on the cheek, but she simply touched his arm and then hurried up the gentle slope. When she just reached the top he saw that in her haste she had left her book on a nearby rock, but he didn't call out, letting her disappear past the buildings to greet the children and her husband.

Sylvie worked herself hard every day. Reverend Tanner was on the road for a good part of each day, making visits to Seoul and other orphanages, and she was tireless in his stead, teaching and leading services and gardening and playing with the children until suppertime, when she'd disappear into the cottage without having eaten. The kitchen aunties whispered comments to one another about how she was losing weight and looking ragged. *She's going to get sick*, one said. *He expects too much of her*, another replied.

But there's so much to do! Can you blame him if he has a big heart?

His heart is big enough for everyone but his wife.

It was a hard-edged statement but once said it seemed true enough: Tanner was by any definition an admirable man, but one could see how his utter devotion to his missions—which obviously Sylvie had given herself over to completely—might leave none of their passions unspent. He wondered if this was the reason they didn't have their own children, or if they now slept together at all. She had indeed grown thinner with the change in diet and the constant work, but it had seemed to Hector that there was a certain weathering in her eyes from the very first day, this eroded sheen. Hector had begun to linger outside his quarters, waiting for her to come out for a while before her husband returned in the mid-evenings. But she didn't, never emerging until dawn. Whenever he worked on the trenching he kept checking the crest of the hillside for her. He kept on with the digging now, alternating between the pick and the shovel himself, loosening as much of the rocky earth as possible so that for long stretches he could toil in the belief that there was something of her sloughing off on him, this phantom print of her hand.

Before bringing it back to her that evening he had done the same with her book, pressing its rough pages against his cheek, smelling the tattered cloth cover, the nook of the spine. It was titled *A Memory of Solferino*, a translation from the original French. The author was a man named J. H. Dunant, a young French-Swiss banker who was traveling in northern Italy, a "mere tourist," as he described himself, when he happened upon a massive conflict fought near a tiny hill town called Solferino. Hector flipped through the volume but it was dry and airless in the beginning, thick with names of foreign places and generals, and he was going to put it down when he came upon a passage well inside the book. It was the author's account of the aftermath of a battle between two immense armies totaling 300,000 men, fought on the 24th of June, 1859, one army comprising the allies of France and the other the allies of Austria; the scene was a description of the wounded, crowded among scores of others in a church:

> With faces black with the flies that swarmed about their wounds, men gazed around them, wild-eyed and helpless. Others were no more than a worm-ridden, inextricable compound of coat and shirt

and flesh and blood. Many were shuddering at the thought of being devoured by the worms, which they thought they could see coming out of their bodies (whereas they really came from the myriads of flies which infested the air). There was one poor man, completely disfigured, with a broken jaw and his swollen tongue hanging out of his mouth. He was tossing and trying to get up. I moistened his dry lips and hardened tongue, took a handful of lint and dipped it in the bucket they were carrying behind me, and squeezed the water from this improvised sponge into the deformed opening that had been his mouth. Another wretched man had had a part of his face—nose, lips, and chin—taken off by a sabre cut. He could not speak, and lay, half-blind, making heart-rending signs with his hands and uttering guttural sounds to attract attention. I gave him a drink and poured a little fresh water on his bleeding face. A third, with his skull gaping wide open, was dying, spitting out his brains on the stone floor. His companions in suffering kicked him out of their way, as he blocked the passage. I was able to shelter him for the last moments of his life, and I laid a handkerchief over his poor head, which still just moved.

Hector stopped reading, placing the book on the footlocker that served as his bedside table; he would not look at it again before returning it. He poured himself a teacup of whiskey, though ended up not drinking it. The descriptions matched any number of his memories from the war, and as much as they pained him—an icy clawing at his lungs, puncturing his breath—the feeling soon gave way to a numbing pause. It was a pause not of reflection or reckoning but of a pure self-erasure in which he felt that he had died, or, better, had never existed; that as such he had not had an effect on anything or anyone, going either forward or back; that he had, for a moment, completely disappeared. The solace of this state might have compelled him to read further if not for his deepening curiosity about the book's owner, this stubborn, jade-eyed woman, quietly fierce and persistent and yet also clearly fragile. Perhaps even infirm. A book was a book, but it was another thing to keep a particular one close, and then one such as this, and he couldn't help but wonder what private rigor or calamity of hers this tale of woe was shadowing, keeping vigil over.

He waited until Tanner had departed again to return it; the reverend had gone off to Seoul, for a dinner meeting with some other clergy. Just after Sylvie left the children for the aunties to take care of for the rest of the evening he went to the cottage. He knocked on the door and called inside. He knocked again. When there was no response he stepped inside, calling "Mrs. Tanner." The cottage was a three-room railroad flat, with a front sitting room and a rudimentary kitchen with a washbasin and tub in the middle and at the rear a small bedroom with a window and back door. He had often sat with Reverend Hong in the front room and he was surprised to see that a single cot had been brought in and jammed in the corner, with a proper double bed in the bedroom. The rear door was slightly ajar and when he pulled it in he saw her sitting in a chair in the tiny weed-choked plot with her head down in her lap, like she'd been ill. The sky was a curdled mass of high clouds lit in their bellies by the dusky light, the top of her white blouse aglow like dying coals, cooler blue beneath. She was wearing khaki trousers, but she was oddly barefoot.

"Are you okay?" he said.

She startled with the sound of his voice. "My goodness, you scared me."

"Sorry."

"It's all right," she said, catching her breath. Her eyes were glassy, shimmering as she looked up at him. But she hadn't been crying. In fact she now smiled, with a strangely easy languor. "You have my book."

He gave it to her. She pressed it in her lap and thanked him. It was somehow difficult for him to meet her eyes. Her pupils were so small that the gray-green of her irises seemed as large as coat buttons.

"You left very quickly."

"Did I?" she said absently. She was now leaning back in the chair like she was near-paralyzed, her wide, pretty mouth slightly hanging open. "Maybe I did. I don't know why I feel I should be ready and present whenever he comes back. Ames isn't at all needy, that way, but I want him to see me when he returns, even if he doesn't care and he's constantly coming and going anyway. I didn't even know he was going into Seoul for dinner."

"Is he coming back tonight?"

"Later, yes," she said. "Did you look at the book?"

"No," he answered, though not exactly sure why.

"I'm glad. There's no reason for you to read it," she said.

"Why's that?"

"It's about a battle. Someone who was a soldier doesn't need to know any more about that."

"And you do?"

She was silent for a moment, running her hand over the book's cover. "Maybe, yes. Like most people, I have my own problems and get wrapped up in things. Everything seems so important. But despite the signs, sometimes I forget what's happened all around us here. The enormity of it. The cause of all this."

"You should have been a soldier," he said to her. "Then you'd be dying to forget."

Her eyes flashed at him, which at first he took as edged with anger but then realized instead was a disarmed recognition, as if he'd poked through some hard wall. But then she went back to the way she was before, slack again, and she seemed to be washed over by a wave of dizziness and nausea. He asked if she needed to lie down.

"Okay."

He had to help her to her feet, pulling on both hands, and for a moment she teetered and leaned into him as they went inside. She walked as if the floor were pliant. She passed the bed in the bedroom and when they reached the front room she lay down on her side on the cot in the corner.

"I left the book out there. Again."

"I'll get it."

"Listen, Hector," she said. He liked the way she said his name, with a faintly Spanish inflection. Not so hard, or Aegean. "I'm so terribly thirsty. Would you get me some water, too?"

Out in the back there was a pump and he let the water run until it was very cold before filling the mug. He picked up the book on the way and when he got back to the front her arms were turbaned about her eyes. He watched her for a long moment.

"Mrs. Tanner," he finally said, if too softly. She didn't stir.

He didn't try to rouse her. He understood now what was the matter with her; he'd seen her kind back in Seoul. Most all of the servicemen and ex-servicemen like himself, and the aid workers and newly arriving businessmen, preferred the scores of lounges and bars, but there were a few places for those who had acquired a special taste, from a stint, say, in Shanghai or Rangoon, or from the treatment of an injury. He examined her closely now, her wrists and her arms, and was surprised to see them unblemished. Perhaps he was wrong. But her leg slipped over the edge of the cot and when he lifted her cool ankle to set it right he could see them, a perfect line, a dozen tiny healed marks tattooing the nook of her heel, the last one still weeping a pin-dot of red.

THE NEXT DAY at the morning meal the Tanners ate among the children, as always, Sylvie's heel tucked inside her blue canvas sneaker. Hector sat by himself at the far corner of the pavilion. She was animated and laughing and joking with the children and didn't look over at him, but Tanner acknowledged him with a typically direct, if bloodless, nod. Hector wondered if he even knew about her habit. Maybe she hardly knew herself.

She could certainly believe all was in order. The atmosphere had changed since their arrival. The orphanage was named New Hope, for obvious reasons, and it surely was that for these children, but there had always been certain reminders of a natural limit to the notion, maybe found in the spartan meagerness of the surroundings, the children's worn, ill-fitting clothes, but now the air in the play yard seemed eminently clearer and fresher, as if a vibrant, sturdy fir had suddenly taken root in their midst, its limbs heavy with sticky needles. The children were orbiting about Sylvie in ever-denser clusters, following her lead to the last letter and note as she taught them old camp songs and games like Red Rover and Telephone. She had also bought a brand-new soccer ball when she was last in Seoul, and after classes and chores (Tanner would always retire to the cottage, to read or go over plans), she'd often run around with them until suppertime and have to switch teams in the middle to prevent arguments, and it wasn't hard to see how any of them could begin to forget that she hadn't always been a part of the orphanage, and wouldn't always be so in the future.

They began their play in the late afternoon. Hector never tried the game and this was his excuse for not joining in but often now he'd pause at his work and watch the action, the more sporting boys quicker than everyone except for Sylvie, who wasn't so much skilled as determined; she seemed intent on keeping the contest fair and getting everyone involved, and with her long legs she could protect the ball and keep them at bay so that the more tentative boys and girls could get touches and shots at the goal. She wore light cotton men's trousers, which she cinched tight with a doubled length of rope; by the end, her knees and flanks would be dusted brick-red from the clayey dirt of the yard. When she took a break she led the rest of them on the sidelines in chants and cheers, and here, too, there'd be a competition among them to see who could sing the loudest, not for their own esteem of course but for the sake of gaining Sylvie's, and for brief moments Hector almost felt as though he were a young boy again in Ilion, sitting in the high school field bleachers with his father, the crisp autumn air thrumming with hoarse, happy voices.

The only child who never played or cheered was June. Hector sometimes saw her slip into the high brush of the valley, or into the dormitory, making a point of disappearing for the entire time. It was as if June couldn't bear the sight of the others enjoying Sylvie's company, even as it was evident to all how special her own position was. But one afternoon she emerged from the brush behind Hector's quarters and stood leaning against the corner of the building as he cleaned rust from some tools with a scraper and a rag soaked in kerosene. The game now was especially spirited, for it was the boys against the girls and Sylvie, and he could see in her tensed chin that June was wanting to join the action.

"Go ahead, why don't you."

"I don't want to," she told him. "The boys are losing. They need you."

"I have work to do."

"You always have work." She spoke to him in the declarative tone she employed with everyone except Sylvie Tanner.

He replied, "I like work."

"No, you don't. You do it for another reason."

"Yeah? What's that?"

"Because you don't want to have fun." She said it seriously but was smiling at him, slyly but almost broadly, at least for her. It was the first time she'd ever smiled at him (and maybe at anyone else) since he'd met her on the road, and he was surprised by how fetching and kindly her face could become.

"Maybe you're right," he said, wiping the rusty leavings from the spade with a cloth. "What's your excuse?"

She was watching the game intently now, as one of the older girls, a very pretty, very round-faced girl named Mi-Young, was celebrating a goal with Sylvie, hugging and laughing.

"Same," June said, with sudden seriousness.

"I guess that makes us birds of a feather."

"I don't understand."

"Flocking together. Enjoying our no fun."

"I don't understand."

"Forget it. You want to scrape that shovel head for me?"

She glanced at the game and then diffidently nodded and he tossed her the wire brush. She held the wooden handle and went at it hard, as though she were playing a cello but trying to break the strings.

"Take it easy," he told her.

"Why?"

"You're going to breathe in the rust."

"So?"

"It can't be good for you."

"It's okay."

"You want to live a long life?"

"Yes," she answered, with near defiance, as if he were somehow threatening her.

"All right, then."

She didn't answer him but soon she slowed her scraping, carefully blowing away the dark orange dust after every half-dozen or so passes with the brush. The game grew more raucous and vocal, the aunties and children on the sidelines guffawing and cheering whenever there was a nifty pass or a good shot, but he and June simply tossed the damp rag back and forth, both subconsciously trying to show their lack of interest in the game, which would have been easy had Sylvie Tanner not been at the center of the action, the girls constantly passing the ball to her, the boys checking her closely or else trying to dribble right through her. But she was more agile than her tall frame suggested and had clearly played the game before and she set up two quick goals and kicked in one herself, while the boys were held scoreless. They all seemed deflated by this last goal and one of the most skilled boys, Hyun, even sat in the dirt in disgust, wearily rubbing his scalp, and soon some of the others began to sit down as well. Sylvie went about their side, clapping her hands, shouting, "Hey, hey, we'll have none of that, boys," and though they were listening to her they didn't rise to their feet until June appeared in their midst. She had simply handed Hector the cleaned spade and trotted out to them.

"May I play now?" she asked Sylvie.

"Of course!"

"I'll play with them," she said, pointing to the boys.

"Even better!"

The boys protested but Sylvie would have none of it. She whistled through her fingers and put the ball into play by nudging it to June, who without hesitance bolted by her and then passed it to Hyun, who had broken toward the goal. He scored easily. The boys whooped and hollered as the girls cried foul that they weren't yet ready.

"Let them play like that, girls," Sylvie exhorted them, lining up the ball at midfield again. She was beaming at June, obviously pleased by her unexpected involvement, though crouched in an athletic, ready stance. "We'll win our way."

The game was a tight contest from that point on. Mi-Young scored next, but then the boys' team put in three in a row to tie the score. Everyone could see that the difference was June. She was adept enough at dribbling and passing, but it was her tireless, almost furious play on defense that changed the flow of the game. The boys had been holding back somewhat in checking the girls, but this was not the case with June; she threw herself at whoever had the ball, and covered Sylvie closely so they couldn't pass to her, and then relentlessly hounded Mi-Young, who was their best player. They were the same size and age and perhaps rivals in that Mi-Young was well liked by all the girls and seen as a mentoring big sister (the girls would crowd around her cot in the dormitory), whereas June was June, someone to avoid, or at least to give a wide berth to. But now June was bringing the action right to her. If Mi-Young was near, June would bump her, and whenever she had the ball June would lean into her roughly and fiercely kick at the ball. Mi-Young would push back with equal force and kick at June as well, neither girl wearing anything on her feet, and by the end of the match they had gouged jagged little cuts into each other's ankles and calves with their toenails. Sensing that their mutual malice was now detracting from the friendly mood of the game, Sylvie announced that the next goal would be the winner. By this point Hector had ceased cleaning the tools, caught up, too, in the action. In the final moments Hyun attempted a crossing pass to June but it was intercepted by Sylvie, who fed the ball to Mi-Young as she streaked alone the opposite way. It was surely the end of the game. But June then seemed to fly downfield, passing everyone as though they were rooted, and before Mi-Young could take a shot June tackled her so hard that she upended her.

Mi-Young came up swinging; she madly pounced on June, all fists and fingernails, and for a moment no one did anything, paralyzed by her uncharacteristic, explosive rage. Hector actually confused the two of them, sure that only June could be as furious as that. He was the first to reach them, and as he pried Mi-Young from her he was struck by how June left herself wide open as Mi-Young wildly rained down blows, not even curling up in a ball, not even shielding her face. When Sylvie got there she instinctively fell upon June to cover her and it was only then that June began to cry. It was like any girl's weeping, the sobs breathy and plangent, but no one had ever seen June cry before and the sight and sound of it was oddly awesome, everyone (including Mi-Young) standing by silently. Then Sylvie spoke, murmuring to her that she would be all right. But June didn't look all right; there were ugly scratches on her cheeks and nose and her lip was bleeding and one eye was already turning purplish and inky with a bruise. It was wholly her own fault, yet she was the injured one, and Sylvie helped her up and the two of them walked back to the Tanners' cottage, June's bloodied face staining the fabric of Sylvie's blouse.

After that, June didn't play in any of the games. Whenever Hector saw her outside in the yard or at the dining tables under the pavilion she appeared to keep herself at a distance from Sylvie and the other

children. She continued working in the Tanners' cottage, and for longer
stretches than before; from his chair outside his quarters Hector would
catch sight of her coming and going whenever Reverend Tanner
traveled. It was as if they had entered into some kind of agreement,
one in which June would respect the right of the others to be with
Sylvie in exchange for more hours together. He couldn't help wondering, as surely everyone was, what they did in private, picturing how
they were knitting (Sylvie was having the older girls make all the children mittens for the approaching winter), or reading books, or simply
sitting together talking (though about what? the wondrous future? the
awful past?). He thought he knew what any orphan would desperately
seek in a woman like Sylvie, but what Sylvie was doing, what she was
actually intending, he couldn't fathom. Reverend Tanner had made
announcements about adoptions, that they might be chosen in the next
period and should be prepared, but he would always note that he and
his wife would be continuing their work only here, knowing every last
one of the children was surely wishing it would be he or she the Tanners themselves might eventually take to America.

It was strange, but sometimes he felt he might like to be adopted
away, too. Welcomed back but by an unfamiliar set of people and in a
circumstance in which he would have no responsibilities except for
some strenuous job or chores. His mother was gone now, too, from a
massive stroke during the last month of the war, and though he still
had his sisters, he didn't want to return to Ilion or any place like it and
he even surprised himself with the ridiculous fantasy of being the Tanners' handyman, lodged in a shack he imagined would be damp and
cool for being set on a property on a bay of Seattle, waiting for Sylvie
Tanner to come bring him a slice of cake, a mug of tea.

The kitchen aunties had opinions about everything and held forth
in their hardscrabble voices, and while cleaning out the garbage cans
he heard their baseless conjectures about why the Tanners were

childless ("She's too thin to become pregnant"; "She must not want *his* children"; "They lost the one they had"), and why she gave special attention to June ("She needs the most mothering"; "The girl reminds her of herself"), but none of these remarks quite described the cloister Sylvie was willing to make for them, despite Reverend Tanner's obvious displeasure and the growing puzzlement of the other children. Did the marks on her heels explain it any better? Was any addiction or compulsion (like his own jags of drinking and fighting) really worth looking into, for explanation or cause? Those pin-dots—and all his own perfectly healed scars—went forward and back, and they were now their own reason and consequence.

As the weather cooled with the onset of autumn, the schedule of Sylvie's day began to change; she would teach the English class and take the midday meal with the children, but instead of communing with them in work or play the rest of the afternoon she began to retire to the cottage, at first excusing herself in the late afternoon but then going off sooner and sooner until finally she would slip off right after lunch, sometimes for the rest of the day. Whenever she went inside, June would go with her and leave only just before eight o'clock, when Hector shut down the compound's generator and the entire orphanage went dark. There was talk that Mrs. Tanner was ill—even her usual paleness seemed diluted, as if water had been added to her blood—but she didn't complain of anything or travel to any hospital, and no doctors visited her. Of course Hector saw her differently, noticing only how she would keep scratching at her arms, her throat, how she would momentarily disappear within herself while the children or aunties were talking to her, coming back only when they raised their voices. He assumed she had a stash of vials hidden somewhere, but what would she do when she ran out? He could get her more, for sure, from the base in town, or some bar in the red-light district. Was that where she really went, when she took her weekly trips into town? Maybe she had already depleted her supply; for a while now everyone else had believed she was suffering from what appeared an intransigent head cold, her eyes rheumy, puffed; she sniffled and blew her nose constantly. She hardly seemed to eat at meals, always just sipping from the roasted barley tea the aunties made for her daily. She didn't look thinner so much as hollowed out, in certain bright morning light her skin seeming practically diaphanous, the veins of her throat run through with such a deep, dyed blue that Hector kept ready to press his hand against her neck, to warm her in case she fainted. She was paying no more or less attention to him, paying him the usual small kindnesses of a sandwich or a roll of Spam kimbap delivered by June to where he was working, or leaving a pint of bourbon or scotch by his door if she'd been into Seoul for supplies. The regular attention led him to believe she was thinking of him daily but it was still only June who came around, Sylvie no longer stopping by even to watch him work the trench or the roofs. Soon he was alternating between irritation for this surely pitiable person and a feeling as if he were completely parched inside, crackled with a web of fault lines that ran from his insides outward and showed to everyone who looked at him. He felt somehow wounded and ashamed.

One morning, before first light, he set himself to the trench work, carving out a few meters of earth, thigh deep and twice as wide as he. He welcomed the toil; the only time he felt remotely righteous was as an instrument. In the afternoon he ascended yet another badly leaking roof and pried up the broken tiles and peeled away the rotted layers beneath, reframing the section with fresh planks and sheathing, sometimes working right through dinner. By the end of the day he could hardly lift his arms to strip himself bare behind his living quarters, where he washed his mucked clothes beneath the shower he had rigged. He knelt and scrubbed them with the harsh oil soap, kneading each against a piece of flat stone like the aunties did. After draping them on the bushes he turned to himself and worked the large soap block severely against his arms and flanks in order to get up any suds in the hard well water. Early one evening Sylvie came around the back corner and before he could say anything or cover himself she simply left the supper tray on the ground and was gone. The next day he didn't see her at all but on the following one she appeared with June at her side where he was digging and offered him a drink of cool plum tea, the two of them departing immediately after he handed over the empty glass, only June looking back at him, twice, three times, as if making certain he would keep his distance.

After that, during the nights, in his cot, he couldn't help but keep thinking of her. At first he pictured her chastely, as he might recall a striking woman he'd seen on the street. Was it the beauty of her particular age? She was the age he most often remembered his mother being, still youthful and beautiful enough to draw catcalls from laborers, servicemen. But then his thoughts would turn hazardous. He imagined her beside him in darkest silhouette, only the burnt flax of her hair visible, its brush alighting upon his body in scattered, sweeping sheets, a blowing rain. Or she came to him clothed only by a wide emerald ribbon, and he had to walk around her, undoing her until she was bare. But sometimes June would appear and encroach upon his reveries, as if he had no control of her whatsoever, haunting the shadows behind Sylvie. He screened the image of them bathing together, if innocently, patiently taking turns sitting in the tub in the middle room of the cottage, pouring water on each other's back and shoulders, pleased in the thought that no one would disturb them, all this ironic in light of Reverend Tanner's changed attitude toward him. He had surely grown more tolerant of Hector over the past month, was sometimes even friendly when he stopped to ask about the progress of the work projects, as if he, too, understood that this smaller, tighter universe which had coalesced amid them was self-sufficient and complete.

Reverend Tanner went about his duties with his typical intensity and rigor but there seemed to Hector a different scale to his prayers and his ministrations, an urgency and heat to his teaching and sermons that in another preacher might hardly be noticed but in Tanner seemed the spur of a revitalized faith. He had happiness, as well as zeal. He had lost weight with his traveling and the change in diet, his long face grown gaunt, his dark minister's suit jacket hanging off his shoulders in mournful gathers such that he looked like a gangly youth donning his father's clothes. But despite the awkwardness of his appearance he had become more approachable as the weeks passed, his manner when he was addressing the children, at least informally, softened by a newly lingering gaze: when they lined up in the mornings they were no longer to him just rows of moral projects and obligations, but each a hardened kernel of memory, this mystery of survival. If anything, his view was more akin to Hector's than to his wife's, that in recognizing the awful turn of their experiences they should now (with his aid) move past them, and quickly, by whatever means might work best: education, the love of God, lessons in discipline, self-reliance. Of course Hector knew his own ways to trounce the past. Sylvie had come to see them differently still. Perhaps she would not have wanted to, would have rather subscribed to the modality of forgetting, but during the brief interviews she was conducting with every child—she was writing an adoption file on each, with biographical information and a description of character ("She is a delightful and bubbly girl with a talent for singing")—one of the older girls suddenly broke down and as Sylvie comforted her she began, unbidden, to tell what had happened to her family during the war. Word must have gone around, as many of the others did the same, even some of the toughest boys unwinding upon her the circumstances that had brought them to this place.

But over the last few weeks, with Sylvie gradually receding, the rest of the children began to warm to Tanner, and it wasn't unusual for

Hector to see him heading up through the now gold and rust-flecked bushes of the hills with a long file of children behind him, or leading a round of vigorous calisthenics in the play yard.

"Let's raise up our knees," Tanner said brightly to them, all of them running in place. "Higher, boys and girls, higher. Let's reach up to the sky." He did this wearing woolen trousers and a dress shirt and tie, his sleeves rolled up, his height and thinness and pointy elbows and knees making him appear distinctly marionette-like, the silliness of which he seemed quite aware. Soon he made fun of himself by pretending to hit his chin with each high pump of his knees, his head knocking back in time. The children began to mimic him, some of them falling down laughing when he switched to double time, then triple, before he finally broke down himself, lying flat on his back on the reddish ground. The children all did the same and one of the aunties ambled out from the kitchen with scoldings for all of them, complaining that they were making unnecessary laundry.

Tanner promised they would all lend extra help with the week's wash. Though he was no less serious than before in his sermons and lessons, he was clearly enjoying his relations with the children and new place in their regard, and sometimes he even cut short a lesson to let them play the games they'd learned from Sylvie. But the instance in which Hector saw the starkest change was when Tanner and Sylvie prepared the children to have new photographs taken for their adoption files. Five children—all young ones, between the ages of three and five—had been sent to America a few weeks earlier to be placed with families in Washington and Oregon.

Tanner wanted new photographs; the existing ones in the files were lugubrious, stern portraits, joyless and hard, and didn't show off a single one of the children well. These new shots would be developed and printed in Seoul the next day and air-mailed to the church offices in Seattle, where prospective families would soon view them and make their choices. Hector couldn't quite tell if the children, at least those who were old enough, were truly eager to be adopted, even when they professed as much and talked excitedly of the rumors of living in a big house where the dinner table was laden with meats and fruits and cakes. For it was obvious that they were fearful, too, and hiding it well, for nothing could be more terrifying than being passed over time and again and eventually being let back out into the ruined streets of Seoul, where there was little to earn in any legitimate trade.

The new photographs would get them all placed. A chair was set up against the external wall of Hector's quarters, which was sided with rough-hewn clapboards that were in the worst condition in the compound—Tanner insisted that it serve as the background of the portrait, to present the children as lively and happy but in the grip of privation—and all the children lined up to sit before the old Leica Sylvie had set up on a tripod. One could tell the children were accustomed to the serious portraits they'd seen or sat for with their families, stern pictures of stone-faced adults and children in their best suits and dresses—like the one he'd taken from the boy soldier he was supposed to execute—and Sylvie was having a hard time getting them to relax their mouths, their shoulders. They had only two rolls of film, enough for a single shot of each child and maybe a half-dozen redos. She kept asking the first few to smile but mostly what would come was a strained, stunted grin that made them appear cowed and wary, and so Tanner told her to wait before taking the next picture.

"For what?"

"You'll know," he said to Sylvie, who looked at him quizzically. "Just be ready."

He caught the eye of the next child in the chair. Tanner grunted strangely, then hunched his shoulders and began hopping from one foot to the other. The boy started giggling and Tanner stepped behind Sylvie and the camera and then made ape-lips and began scratching himself and sniffing at Sylvie's hair, which was when she clicked the shutter. He did this with each child, whooping and beating his chest until it no longer worked, moving on to being an elephant, a rooster, a pig, a sheep, only giving up when it came to June, who was the last to sit for her photograph (after the first three children to go were re-shot). She wouldn't budge for him, not even offering the slightest smile, any break of the lips, and it struck Hector as odd that Sylvie didn't try to convince her more heartily to look happy and friendly for her file. She ended up taking the image of June that any of them who cared to remember her might someday see in his mind, that iron gaze that was hers alone.

Afterward, Sylvie again shrank from view for a few days, staying inside when she wasn't teaching her class. Her mood had seemed to darken after the taking of the photographs and she wasn't coming around with June to wherever Hector might be working, the aunties saying she had a bad cold. But he knew it was because she was helping herself too much to the needle, or else not enough. He'd seen it plenty back in the GI towns, former "old soldiers" barely older than he, gaunt and pale from their long weeks inside the dens, their expressions vacant, shattered; there was no worse loneliness than having to take mercy on oneself.

He felt a new loneliness, too, digging alone in the valley, and he found himself looking up every few minutes from his work, hoping to see her perched on the flattish rock on top of the hill, whether June was by her side or not. But she had ceased to show. A late-summer storm rolled in from the south and made the digging near impossible, its heavy rains undermining his footing; he kept slipping whenever he swung the pickax. So instead he decided to paint the would-be chapel, which he'd been putting off to make progress on the trench-ing. First he wiped down and dusted every surface, running an oiled rag over the walls and floors (the painted benches were being used for now in the main classroom). He hadn't planned on painting the exposed beams of the roof or its underside, but he saw how dark it would be if he didn't and so he set a stepladder atop a table to reach the rafters. He nearly fell a couple of times, once even hanging on to a crossbeam as the ladder beneath him toppled over, letting himself drop to the floor with a great thud. As they couldn't play outside, the children silently watched him work, pointing out to him the spots he had missed or coated too thinly. Neither Tanner nor Sylvie came around. When he completed the roof and walls the children had to step back into their rooms so he could paint the floor. It was dark outside and even darker within and he lighted an oil lamp, dragging it as he slid back and forth on his knees. The fumes from the paint dizzied him but he felt he was being resurrected, too, with each breath, raised up above the floor as he lost himself in the work, and he thought he could see colors in the broad wash of gray, subtle shimmers of gold and green that made him think of her hair, her eyes. He painted the floor to a line up to the dormitory doors (so the children could get in and out without trampling the fresh paint) and then brushed another coat on everything the next day. The thunderstorms had blown through and the sky was clear and bright but when he stepped back to appraise the room he was disheartened to see how shadowy and grim it still was, even with the front door wide open. It was far worse than what'd he said to Sylvie, the room looking not just like a concrete box but a weird, improvised dungeon, this slapped-together catacomb with painted rafters and a black potbelly stove. A tomb for the living. He'd already sent word to Sylvie via Min that she should look at it tomorrow, and he wished now that he had never begun the project; he entertained the thought of tearing it all down. But Min returned, saying that Mrs. Tanner was still sick and that he hadn't spoken to her, and while standing there unevenly with his good foot pointed at the rear wall of the room the boy muttered *chahng-mun*, the word for window.

Hector couldn't believe he hadn't thought of it himself. For he had windows, a half-dozen of them in fact, none of them very big (they stood, propped up, in the storage shed, leftovers from various bygone outbuildings), and he mentally constructed the supporting studs and headers for the largest of them in the center of the wall. But when he actually inspected them he found them to be even smaller than he remembered, the biggest the size of a large square tray, some of the others narrow and elongated. He spread them out on the floor of the storeroom to choose which he'd install. There was plenty of lumber for the supports and framing and soon enough he was combining them to try to shape a single large window. But he couldn't quite make it work and realized he ought to abandon any hope of balance or symmetry. Nothing else in the orphanage was so graced, and he had no feel for such things anyway, and so he simply settled on what he thought might please her. Several days later when she reappeared and was feeling better he caught up to her while she was gardening with the children and informed her the work was done. Tanner was teaching, and although Hector could easily have shown him the chapel he wanted Sylvie to see it first. He was afraid of what she might think (he couldn't care less what Tanner's opinion might be), and he had even waited until a wide bank of clouds had drifted past and there was nothing else on the horizon, to make certain there would be maximum light in the room. She rose from weeding on her bare knees, now smudged with soil, and her hair was stuck to her temples, her neck mottled and flushed, and she seemed as lovely to him as a bride awaking on the first dewy morning of marriage, her skin alive with vital, pumping color. Suddenly a bolt of panic bored into his chest, at the realization of the dread flavor of his project, its absurd aspirations, its dire, smashing homeliness. How ridiculous it was, he was. He wanted to crawl away now but the children working with her were staring at him and he could hardly call forth enough breath to murmur that he didn't mean to interrupt her, that she ought not stop her gardening.

"Don't be silly," she said, dusting off her hands on her work shorts, cutoffs from surplus army-issue trousers. "I can't wait to see it. The children were just telling me you tacked up a curtain and were sawing and hammering behind there in secret."

"It's all nothing," he said. "None of it is any good."

"What did my husband think?"

"He hasn't seen it."

"I'm lucky," she said, walking past him toward the dormitories. "I'll be the very first."

When they were inside the vestibule the tarp he used for a dust curtain was still up and she told him she was ready and he pulled it down all at once.

"Oh, Hector."

She stayed in the back for a while, not moving at all. Every surface was gray, as he had painted the pews, the floor, the walls, the roof beams, the old picnic table he converted to an altar, even the large, simple cross he fashioned by notching two two-by-fours and suspended by wire from the rafters. He'd left only the stove its color. But it all shined fiercely in the sunlight streaming in through the three narrow windows in the far wall, which he'd set intentionally unevenly, because of their difference in size. And then the light came through the square window he'd put in the roof, directly above the floating cross. She made her way forward along the wall, touching the side of each pew, and when she stood beside the altar and peered upward the glow of her face and hair radiated a burning, white firelight.

"How did you ever put that in?"

"I got up on the roof and built out a frame. I sealed the edges with pitch, but we'll see if it leaks when it rains."

"It won't matter if it does," she said.

"I was going to try to paint the insides of the windows with finger paints, to make them look like stained glass, but I couldn't find any. I can still try to get some when I go to the base next."

"Please don't," she said. "It's just right, as it is."

"You don't think it's colorless?"

"It is," she said, gently nudging the cross. "But that's what makes it perfect. It's so ghostly and serene."

"You don't make it sound too good."

"But it is, Hector. You've made me remember now. You couldn't have known it would, but you have. This is how every church should be."

When he looked down at his feet, like a boy greatly relieved, she surprised him with an embrace. He felt his heart might collapse. He instantly took her up and held her against him. Her face was turned but his mouth and eyes were pressed against her ear, the soft plate of her cheek, and the more tightly he held on to her the more she seemed to give way, to cave, as if she were made of loose, dry dirt. He wanted to pick every piece of her up. Fill his mouth with her hair. But they heard voices and she came alive and pushed away from him just before a boisterous troop of girls came bounding into the room. They were suddenly quiet but their eyes widened and they started chattering excitedly about the chapel, all the windows, the big cross in the air, the strange color of the room. Soon he and Sylvie were up to their belts with their bristling number, he lifting the littlest ones so they could make the cross sway and swing, Sylvie explaining to the others that the three windows he'd put in were meant to suggest those in a Western church, and for the first instant in his adult life, in this ease of happy bodies, Hector could imagine himself in willing tow of such a brood, to be always trailed by its shouts and flows.

. . .

BUT WOULDN'T SUCH A TRAIL have to include June? Perhaps like any of the children in the orphanage he, too, was fantasizing some ongoing life with Sylvie, and assumed that June would always be in the picture. But the next evening, as Hector was crossing in front of the Tanners' cottage after shutting down the generator, June ran past him in a moonlit flash. She quickly disappeared into the dormitory. He would have kept going on to his quarters but the cottage door was ajar and he could hear Tanner's voice. Something possessed him to crouch down and he leaned with his back to the cottage, his head turned so that his ear pressed against the wood. There was nothing but clapboards and a thin sheathing covering the structure and he could hear them as clearly as if he were sitting beside them in the room.

"I'm sorry I had to say that to her," Tanner said, though he didn't sound sorry at all. "I lost control. But I can't stand her speaking to us like that."

"She's only a child, Ames," Sylvie answered. "She doesn't know what she's saying."

"Oh please, darling! She's smart as a whip. Nothing is an accident with her. When she said she would be sure to 'take care' of us it made me crazy. Her arrogance is astounding."

"But you couldn't have been meaner," she said to him, her voice low and hard. "To tell her that we would *never* need her."

"I'm sorry. I am. I shouldn't have said it. But here's the truth, the truth I've known since the day you took her up. I don't want you to spend any more extra time with her. She can work here in the house for her chores, but that's all. It's unfair to let her believe she has a future with us. Can't you see that? You're simply being cruel. You obviously can't believe it, but you are. You're going to devastate her."

She didn't answer him. Finally she said: "I think it's you who's cruel."

There were steps across the floor and a creaking sound, as if he just sat down beside her on the daybed.

"Do you truly think that of me?" he said to her.

"No, no," she said, her voice full of misery. It was quiet and then after a moment she began to cry, her gasps coming in soft heaves. "I don't. You've been nothing but wonderful to the children. More so every day."

"Then you must believe me when I say this can't come to any good. I'm sorry for what I said to her and I'll apologize to her tomorrow. But you must be realistic. The three infants in Seoul we signed on to adopt, have you completely forgotten about them?"

"No . . . of course not. . . ."

"So what does she think is going to happen? What have you promised her?"

"Nothing. I've promised her nothing."

"Then what are you hoping for?"

"I was hoping we could take her, too. I know it'll be difficult with the embassy, but you know that one consulate officer well and I thought you might ask if he could make an exception for us, so we could take one more. Besides, I thought June could help me with the children. I don't know if I can handle them all myself."

"First off, I'll help you. And your aunt will help out, too, I'm sure. But do you for a second believe that June will make things easier? For you, perhaps, because she obviously loves you. But for us? For our other children? Do you truly believe that June would be kind to them? That she would show them love and care? Do you think she would treat them well when you weren't around? Come on, tell me the truth."

"I don't know," she said softly. "I don't know how she'll be."

"Of course you do, dear. How can you imagine otherwise, with the way she's behaved herself here? The fact is, the girl has already grown up. She's who she is now, through and through. She's not going to change."

"Why couldn't she?"

"Because she's not a nice girl. She's not a kind girl. Maybe she was once, but she isn't anymore. I hate to be so hard, but I don't know any other way to say it."

"You have no idea what's happened to her, Ames. You don't know what she's been through. If you did you wouldn't talk like this."

"I don't know what happened to her," he said. "That's true. But I know plenty about some of the others, as do you. None them has a more profound story than any of the rest. Not in sum, at least. They all have nothing, and we agreed that we would start with them from this point on. It's all we can do. There are thousands of needy children in this country. Maybe tens of thousands. And we're only helping the orphans! We were warned by our colleagues, remember? What was their saying? 'So many pretty stones in the river, but you can't pick them all up'? How right they were—so many of them, right here with us. But you chose the stone that's razor sharp."

"She chose me, Ames."

"But you encouraged her over all the others. Everyone saw that."

"No one else is going to adopt her," she said, defeated. "They won't, and you know it."

He didn't answer her. Soon Hector heard her crying again, if very softly. Weak beams of candlelight showed through cracks in the door-jamb and when he put his eye before it he saw Tanner embracing her as she sat. She was wearing a thin cotton nightgown, dark knee socks. Hector could see the silhouette of her breast inside the loose fabric. Tanner cupped her there and tried to kiss her but her posture was unmoving and after a moment he gave up.

"You've been terribly low, darling. For so long now. It can't be all about that girl. I've done nothing different since we've come here. I've done nothing wrong. Have I?"

She shook her head.

"Maybe I have but can't see it," he said anyway, exasperation pitching his voice higher. His face looked as desperate and broken as hers. "Please tell me. Tell me if I have."

But Sylvie didn't say any more or look up at him and Tanner finally rose and picked up a tea mug and reared back as though he were going to hurl it against the wall. But he stopped himself, then set it heavily on the desk. He walked back to the bedroom. She pulled her knees up to her chest and covered her head with her arms, her hands. Hector watched her for a while longer, searching her, until the point at which the votive candle burned down, flickered out, flared alive again, then finally died. It was pure black and nothing moved in the dark. He was going to wait her out, but two aunties were heading his way to leave by the back path to their village at the other end of the valley, so he got up before they caught sight of him pressed strangely against the cottage and ambled back to his room. He could have crouched there until morning. Instead, he found himself, in the middle of the night, mirroring her shape in his own bed, rubbing his face against his forearm, his knee, to try to taste anything of flesh, wondering how long she would remain that way, if she could spend the entire night in that self-bound coil, or would wait until her husband was dead asleep and then spring herself back to life.

That week the Tanners had planned to leave for ten days to visit other church-associated orphanages, a trip that would have taken them south to Pusan through Andong, then up along the western coast, from the city of Kwangju. But on the morning they were to leave it was Tanner alone bidding everyone goodbye, the children and aunties bowing deeply as his car departed. Hector was fixing the fallen rails of the wooden gate of the entrance when Tanner had the car stop. He stepped out of the car and lifted the other end of a rail as Hector fitted his end into the post he had just reanchored. Hector asked him what he wanted. Tanner took them a few more steps away from the car. He spoke softly, as if not wishing the driver to hear them, though there was little chance the man spoke much English.

"I'm going on a trip now."

"I know."

"Mrs. Tanner is staying behind. Another minister from Seoul will come for part of each day while I'm gone, to supervise. But I would ask if you could remain close to the compound while I'm away. Will you do that for me, Hector?"

"I haven't been anywhere else, for a while."

"Yes, I know, and I appreciate it. That and your hard work. You're making excellent progress on the projects. But while I'm gone I'd feel more comfortable if you'd be sure to stay on the grounds. Or at least nearby. My wife hasn't been feeling well for some time now. Perhaps you've noticed something."

"She's been sick."

"It's not only a physical illness," Tanner said. He cleared his throat. "I'm only telling you this because I'm afraid something might happen while I'm away."

"Like what?"

"I don't know," he answered gravely. "I'm afraid that she'll somehow hurt herself."

"Why don't you take her with you, then?"

"She won't come. She wants to stay here." A column of wind whipped up dust from the road and Tanner had to hold on to the brim of his hat. The car rolled up and the driver reminded Tanner in Korean that they still had to drive in the opposite direction, toward Inchon, to pick up the other American minister who was accompanying him.

"I have to go. Will you do this for me?"

"I don't know what I'm doing."

"You'll please just look in on her. Knock on her door, if you like."

For the rest of the day Hector rehearsed in his mind how he would do so. But for the first few days of Tanner's absence Hector simply avoided her. There was little reason for anything else, as Sylvie was regularly teaching her classes and taking meals with the children under the newly patched roof of the mess hall. She was even playing tag in the yard after the Korean minister from Seoul departed in the early afternoon. The minister, Reverend Kim, was a rail-thin, bookish young man who arrived each morning by nine and led prayers and Bible study and then ate with a ravenous vigor at lunch, even as he was nose deep in his volumes, taking second and third helpings of rice and vegetables and downing his soup in long slurps that echoed in the hall like the sound of a great, sucking drain. The children slyly mocked him by doing the same, and even Sylvie did as well—the man was almost completely oblivious—and whether it was because her husband was gone or she was left alone to play with the children she seemed mostly at ease again, lighthearted and girlish.

The one obvious difference was that June was no longer at Sylvie's side as she went about the camp; Sylvie walked by herself or with a phalanx of various others, favoring no one, and perhaps it was now only June who wouldn't take her turn. Hector didn't know if Sylvie had spoken to her. He and everyone else was waiting for June to do something, push someone down and start a fight. But she simply kept to the periphery, marking Sylvie from a near distance, watching and listening like some secondary conscience; and if the girl was broken inside or in a rage, one couldn't tell from the way she wordlessly completed her chores and attended classes. She conducted herself like a more typical orphan, a child vigilant and laconic and careful, as if her temper had completely disappeared.

In truth it was Hector who most clearly felt the burden of the

period. Or at least showed the strains. The reverend's absence was op-
pressing him. He had not counted the days at first but now he was
counting them down. Soon Tanner would be back; from Pusan he'd
phoned the ministries' administrative office in Seoul, the young Reverend Kim's home base, and the fellow announced word of it before
the service, adding at the end of his prayer an entreaty for Tanner's
safe travels and return, which drew a melodious, resonant amen from
the children and the aunties. He thought he heard Sylvie singing it.
All this made him moody and preoccupied, at night even more sleepless
than usual despite the fact that he was working constantly, his body
driving hard to try to exhaust itself, self-bury. He ranged far to collect
firewood, affixed yet another stretch of roof tiles. But he would run
out of nails, or his ax dulled and too often bounced off the wood, and
the night would descend quickly and he'd have to walk with his hands
stretched out before him to make his way back to the darkened compound. There was always more sewer trenching to be done, so he returned to that with fury, but this, too, was beginning to thwart him; a
spate of rain came and he was becoming slowly sickened by the smell
of damp earth, the half-alive taste it left in his mouth, in his gut, the
feeling that he was not burrowing into it but that it was instead coursing through his body as if he were an earthworm, veining him with
seams of slow-rotting grit.

On the way back from the digging he stopped when he saw a glow
from the rear of the cottage. By tomorrow Tanner would have likely
returned. The night sky was clear and the clouds of his breath lingered
in the crisp air. He stood at the edge of the small back plot, in full view
of the house. He was still running hot from the work and wearing only
a light shirt and dungarees and the sensation of difference against the
chill was a kind of welcomed fever. The bedroom window was cur-
tained with a thin lace fabric and he could clearly see she was reading
by candlelight. He must have counted a dozen turns of page, deciding

each time she lifted her hand to await yet another before he would let his shovel drop and go to her. When at last she put down the book he was resolved, but she rose abruptly and left the frame of the window, as if she realized she was being watched. He froze and braced himself for her to come out and confront him. But now she simply reappeared in the window. She had already taken off her sweater. Without hurry she slipped off her blouse and underclothes, exposing the long smooth shell of her back, the spur of her hip. She shivered visibly but did not clutch herself. Then she pulled on the frock of the nightgown, pushing up her arms, shaking loose the folds gathered at her waist. She extinguished the candle flame. He searched the window, the panes black and glintless, and although he had just glimpsed her in full it was the slow, measured covering of her nakedness that caught his breath. He turned to go, but then he heard the sound of a creaking. And in the starlight he saw the reflected sway of her gown as her long pale hand pulled open the door.

SEVEN

Manchuria, Lunar New Year's Day, 1934

"WHAT A GRAND FEAST THIS IS," Sylvie's father said. "Let us pray." Everyone at the long table clasped hands and her father led them in their praises and thanksgiving. Her mother had sewn two old draperies together to make a pretty tablecloth and the Chinese minister's wife had prepared the midday dinner with local helpers who worked at the missionary school. It was a true feast, especially in light of the times. There was brown rice and sour pickled cabbage and preserved duck eggs and candied black beans. Some moon cakes for dessert. But the dish everyone was waiting for was the stewed pork ribs Reverend Lum's wife had just brought to the table in a large earthenware casserole. She had the village butcher slaughter their last pig and had every other part of it salt-packed as a provision for the winter but had decided to make a special New Year's dish with the ribs, vowing that the Japanese would never taste them. A battalion fighting the Communist Chinese forces had swept through this part of the province months before but some elements were now filtering back through the territory, ransacking and sometimes taking over farms and houses and killing anyone who resisted. Some officers on horseback had come inside the gates last week to inspect the school and its grounds, questioning each of the men separately about his background and purpose here. They left, assuring them no interference, but everyone knew it was only a matter of time before they returned.

It was a crowded table: Sylvie and her parents, the Binets, Francis and Jane; the Lums; a visiting aid-worker couple named Harris; and sitting beside her a young bachelor named Li, who had arrived in the summer soon after the Binets and who taught Latin and mathematics. He was a Chinese from Hong Kong but had studied classics at the university in Manchester. He held a British passport. Jammed in at the far end of the table were a few local families whose mothers worked as helpers at the school, and two orphaned children. Normally the helpers didn't eat with the missionaries, but their families were father-less (the men either conscripted or killed in action) and Francis Binet had insisted that they be included for the New Year's meal. They passed around the other dishes but Mrs. Lum doled out the ribs, everyone receiving exactly five bite-sized sections. Conditions at the school were normally spartan, but with the constant state of war (though it was not formally a war yet, despite having begun in 1931), there was less and less to purchase from the purveyors in Changchung, and for a month now they were surely undernourished, though never close to starving.

The most pressing problem, however, was not hunger but the cold. Even as they ate, elbow to elbow on the benches of the small dining room, it was as if they were outside in the weather. They were certainly dressed so, with overcoats and hats and even gloves. It had snowed furiously earlier in the month but since then the skies had been swept clear by a piercing arctic wind that left everything frozen and desic-cated. Although it was just past noon now, and the sun was shining from its low perch in the sky, it was barely fifteen degrees Fahrenheit and perhaps just above freezing inside. There was a small coal stove in the room but Reverend Lum and Francis Binet decided not to light it, hoping all the bodies in the small room would produce enough comforting warmth. They had to conserve what little coal they had left, as both Chinese factions and the Japanese colonial forces were depleting most of the available supply; it was still the heart of the winter, nearly two whole months left of it at least, and no one had spoken a word about how they would make it through without some profound happening or change.

As the diners ate, puffs of steam rose up from their mouths. People weren't talking very much as they sat hunched over their small plates, trying to keep warm. Everyone ate the ribs first, for they cooled almost instantly on the frigid plates, the drops of fat congealing into opaque disks that floated on the thin dark sauce. Not a drop of it went to waste. Sylvie didn't favor pork, but the fatty, gristly meat made her mouth gush so much her tongue almost ached and she had to quell the urge to try to swallow a section of bone whole, for how delicious it was. Instead she chewed off any nubs of soft cartilage from the ends and when she was done placed the bones on a plate being passed back around to Mrs. Lum, who said she was going to make a soup out of them for the next day.

Sylvie's father nodded to her from across the table when he saw her ribs were as scoured clean as the rest. She had worried her parents for as long as she could recall because she rarely ate very much, but lately she was feeling hungry, even famished, and not simply due to the diminishing rations. She was almost fourteen and her body was at last changing, even if she was still too slim. Her hips had widened and her chest was welling out and there was a rougher hand to the surface of her skin, *Like chamois instead of silk*, her mother pronounced, in her typically clear-eyed style. As she took after her mother, Sylvie wasn't ashamed or embarrassed, not even by the less pleasing difference in her hair, especially the tufts others couldn't see, the new coarseness and musk beneath her arms and elsewhere. Maybe she did not fully feel like a woman because she wasn't yet sure what being one was, or meant, but she was certain that her girlhood had passed, or if it hadn't passed, that it was something only barely remaining, like a baby's blanket finally worn through to a web of threads.

Besides, Sylvie knew she could not afford to be a child anymore. With the fighting, their life was becoming too dangerous and real. Her parents had been talking about her leaving with the Harrises, who were departing in several days for Shanghai, and then going on to Hong Kong, from there embarking on the long sea journey to Honolulu and finally Seattle, where they and the Binets were from. Sylvie's aunt lived there, too, and offered a place for her to stay until her parents returned in the spring. They had each tried to speak to her about it in an idle, casual way, bringing up the idea as if it were merely a choice between summer camps, but Sylvie was old enough to know that her parents were not in the least casual or idle about anything. They were people who took seriously every action and effort, brooking high risks if necessary, for it was all in the service of what they saw as the most urgent calling in this life: educating children, feeding the poor, ameliorating suffering. Throughout her childhood they traveled from destitute place to destitute place, from the Amazon to West Africa and now to Asia, and although she always felt their love for her, she could feel cast apart from them as well, set just outside the tight centripetal force of their labors, the impassioned orbit of their work. She was rarely if ever out of their sight but she often felt eclipsed by the boundless, grinding need of the foreground, and in certain moments she was sure that she was the loneliest child on earth.

And yet her admiration for them never waned. If anything, it had only deepened as she had grown older, as her shame at her own selfishness and self-pity seemed monstrously childish in the face of her parents' unstinting efforts. They had come to this village twenty-five kilometers outside of Changchung to revitalize an old church school, which, like every other mission they had helped run, was also becoming a de facto health clinic and agricultural center and, of course, soup kitchen. In five months the enrollment had doubled, even some well-to-do merchant families from the city now sending their children daily for schooling. Yet as the fighting escalated, it was also becoming a sanctuary; just a few days earlier her father—against the protests of Reverend Lum—had taken in and treated a pair of haggard, lightly wounded Chinese soldiers who said they were being pursued by the Japanese but might well have been deserters. Either way, it could bring trouble to them, Lum argued, but her father was nothing if not calmly pragmatic in such moments. He saw everything in its most essential human terms. "They're simply scared and hungry," he said to Lum and the rest. "And ultimately, we know, through no cause of their own. So how can we turn them away?"

Nothing had happened, neither side coming to search for them, and the two soldiers had slipped away the next evening under cover of darkness, each given a two-day bundle of rations. But Reverend Lum and Tom Harris were still concerned that such occurrences would only become more frequent and more dangerous, aside from taxing their dwindling resources, and after the helpers and their children finished eating and were excused the discussion around the table was about how the school should continue if and when full-scale war broke out. Reverend Lum and Harris were in favor of closing the gates to any combatants. They wanted to negotiate with both Japanese and Chinese officials to get them to recognize the school as a neutral zone.

"It'll be safer if you can stay out of this thing completely," Tom Harris said, his large hands wrapped around a cup of hot tea. He was about the same age as Francis, in his early fifties, not a minister but a second-career aid worker who was an expert in agricultural practices and irrigation. His wife, Betty, was a nurse practitioner, and during the last few months they had traveled northern Asia, immunizing children in remote villages against smallpox. "Or else, if they won't let you be, then just close the school and all get out now. Don't you remember what happened to that Lutheran missionary school in the Congo in 'twenty-nine? It was right smack in the middle of a brutal tribal war, and ended up being used by both factions. The head of the mission wanted the place to be an open refuge but in the end he was distrusted by all and they tore everything to pieces."

"What happened to the head of the mission?" Reverend Lum asked.

"Please, Tom," his wife said to him. "Sylvie's parents don't want her to hear about such things."

"That's all right, Betty," her father said. "We don't try to shield her from what goes on. Anyway, she's old enough now. Aren't you, sweetie?"

"Yes, I am."

"Nobody was spared," Harris said, looking away from Sylvie. "And they don't use guns in the Congo. They don't just shoot people. I'll leave it at that, for everyone's sake."

"This isn't Africa," Mrs. Lum said.

"Oh no? I keep hearing about certain things up north. How the Japanese wiped a few villages off the map. Eradicated every last soul."

"That's a rumor they themselves spread to scare us," she answered. "I heard it was just one remote village the Japanese wanted for a base, and that all the people agreed to be relocated and work in a boot factory near Harbin. So what's the truth? What should we believe?"

"That this is effectively a war zone," Harris replied. "Whether declared or not. Something is different now. What I see and hear is that there's no protection here for anyone. Including foreigners."

There was a moment of silence before Jane Binet spoke up. Sylvie caught a certain glimmer in her eyes and she could anticipate what her mother was going to say. "I think if you're right, Tom, then we need to keep the mission and school open for as long as we can. I don't know if that means coming to some agreement with a certain side or not. You and Francis and Reverend Lum must decide on that. But whatever it is, it has to allow us to stay on here until the very last possible hour. The last possible minute. Because all of us can imagine what it will be like for these children and their families when the war does come."

"The problem is determining what that last minute is," Tom Harris said, but not forcefully, for of course he knew it was pointless to argue. He and his wife had been stationed in the same place or area with Sylvie's parents several times, and like all the other aid workers and missionaries who had worked with them, they came to understand that the Binets were not out in the forsaken regions of the world for the usual constellation of reasons, for the glory of God and Samaritanism, or as some mode of escape or adventure or self-trial. They were not ultimately sentimental people, being rarely ruled by their hearts, even as they were genuinely loving and caring to their charges. They were two people who over the years had honed themselves into ideal instruments of mercy, and like any such instruments the greatest sin was to be only half used.

"I see there are some moon cakes to be had," her father said brightly, breaking the mood. They each got a quarter-cake, Sylvie eating hers in a single mouthful as the others slowly nibbled. Both her parents offered theirs to her but she refused, despite how its greasy sweetness made her insides leap. She was not some needy child. Li, the young Latin and math teacher, nudged her with his elbow and silently offered his to her but she refused him as well. A month ago she would not have taken it for the reason that others might sense how infatuated she was with him. But now she did not care anymore what the others might see. For she was infatuated, and had been practically from the moment he arrived. He had a lovely English accent and when he asked her during their private Latin lesson to translate a passage from the *Gallic Wars*, he would address her as *Miss Binet*, like some proper suitor in a novel. He was not much taller than she and although several years removed from university he could easily be mistaken for a high schooler, with his lithe, smooth-skinned build. He had the habit of adjusting his round silver-framed spectacles with both hands, delicately propping them higher on his unusually prominent nose. He pomaded his thick, coal-black hair with an English ointment that smelled of sweetened almonds, like marzipan. One day back in the late summer she had seen him shirtless when he helped her father bear large buckets of well water for the children's baths, the wiry bands of his arms and shoulders and neck tensing with the effort. He had noticed her watching and waved to her and she had felt something drop from the top of her chest to the bottom. Now beneath the table he opened her hand and tucked the small wedge of cake into her palm but she could only feel the brief graze of his fingers on her knuckles and while they resumed talking she gently pressed the cake into a damp, doughy mass, focusing now on his gift to her and her chance to eat it. Only after the conversation turned again to how best to engage the Japanese and Chinese authorities was she excused from the table, and she walked across the frozen ground of the courtyard to the room she shared with her parents. In the unheated room she let her fingers curl open, uncupping the tiny lode of heat. She ate slowly this time, simply letting her mouth dissolve the cake rather than chewing or swallowing, running the tip of her tongue on the creases of her palm to get every last tinge of the lard.

The sweetness warmed her, despite the frigidity of the room. She unbuttoned her coat, unwound her scarf. In fact she felt overheated of late, when her parents and the others seemed to have developed a waxen rime from the unceasing bitter temperatures. Even Benjamin Li could seem to stiffen in his movements. Her changing body had

become a perfectly efficient generator, somehow able to turn any meager morsel into a sustained heat. In the absence of fuel it ran anyway,
heedless of her spells of dizziness and great thirst and a waving ache
in her joints, in her bones. Worst of all was the abraded sensation, the
feeling as if her insides were in perpetual friction, flaring and rebelling
against her body. Every night now in her cot, on her side of the folding
painted screen her parents had borrowed from the Lums for some
privacy in their shared room, she'd cast aside the many layers of rough
woolen blankets and pull up her nightgown to her throat and let the
piercing air check her until every ember seemed finally to succumb and
she was as ashen as the moonlight painted her. She shivered terribly in
her nakedness and gripped the side bars of the cot until her hands grew
numb, and one morning her mother told her while brushing her hair
that one's body was never wrong and though she'd said it before, just
as cryptically, Sylvie finally understood what she meant. For hadn't she
let go, too, stunning herself to another state of waking with her frozen
hands? As with everything else, she learned this, too, from her parents.
For as long as her memory served she'd listened to them making
love (their living quarters were necessarily humble and cramped wherever they went) and she'd peered through her arms at their caresses
and then her mother's willowy body shifting above her father, tapping
out even before it happened the rhythmic tick of the bed frame and
the beautiful breathing by which she would slumber.

Out in the courtyard she saw that Benjamin Li had stepped out
to smoke. She waved to him through the window but the brightness
of the sun in the clear skies must have obscured her and he didn't
notice her. She was glad that he didn't; now she could watch him freely.
He pulled a cigarette from his etched silver case and lightly tapped it
three times, as he always did. None of the other adults smoked and he
was somewhat bashful about it and always went outside even though
no one would have objected, especially in this weather. He didn't seem

aware that he smoked with a rakish stance, his coat collar raised, shielding the match flame from the wind with his hands and narrowing his eyes as he inhaled. When they first started their Latin lessons when he arrived in the summer, he often blew rings for her, though the other day she had suddenly felt it was too childish and didn't reach out and poke through them, instead letting them dissipate on their own. He'd seemed almost hurt, if only for a moment. His Chinese name was Ping-Wo but everyone called him Benjamin, the name he'd chosen for himself while studying in England, after Disraeli. Sylvie only recently began calling him by his given name, asking him a question with the address during one of their lessons. He'd paused before answering but said nothing and resumed without mention or pause the next times she said his name.

She knew it was because he was afraid she might tell her parents what had happened one evening two weeks ago, when he returned from a dinner in Changchung. Of course she would never speak a word of it, for it would ruin everything, even if what had occurred was not his doing but hers and hers alone. No one would believe that, she knew. She didn't wish the cloud of her telling to loom above him and yet she did nothing to make it dissipate, preferring to act as if nothing real had happened except in the darkened theater of her thoughts. The light there was hushed and orangine and within it she'd been waiting in her cot for the sound of the horse, and when she heard the slow chocking of hooves against the frozen ground she put on her coat over her nightgown and told her parents, who were reading, that she was going to use the outhouse. Instead she ran to the stables that once housed five horses but now held only one, which the Lums used for transportation and sometimes to plow the garden or hitch the wagon to for hauling firewood or coal.

When she got there he was unbuckling the saddle and even through the heavy screen of the worked horse's scent she could smell the smoky whiskey on his breath. He drank sometimes with Tom Harris but he looked different now in the lamplight, his face and neck flushed and his eyes searching and distant as he patted the black mane of the animal. He startled at her presence but before he could speak she rushed up and embraced him, reaching with both arms inside his unbuttoned topcoat. He didn't move, but didn't push her away, either; and when her hands slipped down below the line of his belt and onto his flanks he didn't protest, his body tensing under her hands. She craned her face to try to meet his but he wouldn't look at her and kept his eyes shut, and not knowing what else to do she gripped more tightly at his thighs, at his backside; she felt like an obtuse child trying to figure a puzzle or lock, fraught with a dizzying conflation of ignorance and desire and self-rage. But suddenly he pressed her close with an almost frightening force and beneath his gabardine trousers something rose up against her hip and seemingly without volition her hand met it, instantly understanding the necessary meter that became its own reason and only ceased with his momentary, almost pained, shuddering. All the while she was peppering his neck with kisses but he turned her away without even looking at her and struggled off, muttering only *Good night.* Afterward he had avoided her for several days, even canceling two lessons, but then when they resumed the tutorials it was as if nothing had happened and he was exactly himself again, friendly and bright.

Benjamin finished his cigarette and went back inside. She was resolved that later on, perhaps even tonight, she would go to him in his quarters and once again press herself against him. That it might bring him some misery as well as pleasure only girded her, made her feel more mature and confident. She was sure that inside she was much older than her years and that Benjamin Li was in fact younger than his, for despite his intelligence and learning he was evidently inexperienced as far as women were concerned (once Sylvie asked him if he had had a girlfriend at university and he blurted out to her, before he could think twice, that he'd *never* had one). The moment in the stable would be their secret and she was certain that whatever he eventually wished to do to her she would comply, and wholly.

Her other self-promise was that she would not depart with the Harrises if her parents stayed behind. She could not allow such a thing to happen. She would simply refuse, as adamantly as her parents would refuse to leave a mission before they believed their work was done. (She was mostly sure it was not about leaving Mr. Li, even if the prospect of never seeing him again made her nauseous with grief.) She was old enough that she understood now how best to confront her parents. She would reveal how like them she truly was. The three of them had lived through dangerous circumstances before, and if none had yet been during an actual war, then it seemed ever more vital that they not be separated now, with its specter so near. Without her presence they'd press on despite any dangers, willfully ignore their own safety to do their work. In Sierra Leone, when she was nine, they had left her at a mission of French nuns to trek with food and medicine to a settlement caught in the middle of a tribal war. Four native men accompanied them. They planned to be away for a week but had been gone almost two when the nuns started praying hourly for their return. Then there were rumors of a massacre in the very hills where they had gone. Sylvie herself was certain that they were dead. When they did finally arrive in the middle of the night it was with only two of the men; the others had been killed protecting them, her parents and the others barely able to escape. Her mother and father woke her with their tearful embraces and had her sleep between them that night, but in the morning she could see in their eyes that although devastated they were as resolved as ever, if not more so, and she knew that they would do the same again one day, risk leaving her an orphan if it meant saving a score of the ever-inexhaustible number.

If she thought about it, hadn't they been preparing her for such a day for as long as she could remember? Hers was an education that was perhaps not intentional but certainly thorough. They had traveled all over the world and rarely ever visited a cultural site like a museum or palace or castle but instead went to hospitals and soup kitchens, to shelters and cemeteries, to every notable memorial or monument to the wronged and righteous dead. Early in her memories they often visited churches and cathedrals, but those visits became more and more infrequent as their humanitarian work increased. Just before coming to China they had been in Italy, and even there, with chapels around every corner, they didn't bother, except of course for the one they'd planned the journey around, a church that was not a church at all. Though they led prayers and carried the Bible and still believed in God (she thought), they seemed to have lost all zeal for proselytizing, and her father had even begun asking the missionaries to identify him and her mother to the locals not as a minister and his wife but as teachers from the Red Cross, to which they'd officially signed on that summer while in transit through Europe. Just as Reverend Lum did, the missionaries would naturally ask why and the Binets would simply say they wished "to work unimpeded," and though puzzled, and even insulted, the missionaries would never refuse two such experienced hands.

Her mother told her that sometimes the local people would not accept the full help they needed if they thought something was expected of them in return, especially if it went against their traditional beliefs. "No one should have to make a choice," she said. This was of course good and right. They were always good and right. But was their steady distancing from the Church a sign that they'd found the final circle of their life's passion, one that seemed to be steadily shrinking as it grew in intensity, with room enough only for two? She'd thought as she grew older that they would begin to include her in their work and all its attendant joys and dangers. Her mother had been talking to her more and more about living in Seattle, and Sylvie had begun picturing the cozy, pretty house they might live in overlooking the lake, but then her mother kept talking about Aunt Lizzie and how excited she would be to see Sylvie again, and she realized that her parents were firming the ground for a different scenario altogether, one they had planned for all along.

But in Italy that had seemed far in the future, when she'd go to college back in the States. For now they were inseparable. They'd made a trip to a town in Lombardy called Solferino, whose blood-soaked ground had compelled the bloom of the Red Cross. They had planned to join in the celebration of the seventy-fifth anniversary of the infamous battle that had taken place there, a pilgrimage her parents had been talking of for years.

It began as a mostly dull and enervating journey for Sylvie and her parents both: the incessant heat and airlessness of the third-class train cars rolling slowly eastward along the Côte d'Azur after the draining ferry crossing from North Africa to Spain, all of them suffering stomach distress and motion sickness, and when they trekked across the northern lowlands of Italy, the biting gnats and flies. To save the little money they had (money was a worldly curse), they did not break up the trip by disembarking in Nice or Milan to restore themselves in a decent hotel, but rather used the occasional two-hour waits between trains to find a rooming house near the station that would allow them to bathe for a few francs or lire, and for her father to shave. They were gypsies of mercy, her mother would remind her, and didn't require a proper bed.

So they slept on the trains, eating butter sandwiches bought from hawkers (her mother would toss the slick cured ham from the *panini* to the crows, for the Binets were the rare vegetarians, whenever they could help it), reading the Red Cross founder's account of the battle and aftermath to each other aloud, to remind them of their purpose. They still packed a Bible among their things but read it less and less, returning instead to their Marx and Zola and old pamphlets of Debs, for already by then they had become missionaries of action, a Socialist streak rising in them, which would ultimately draw them to northern China. When they finally reached Mantova her father hired a car to drive them up to Solferino, but it broke down climbing the hill to the village and they had to go the rest of way on foot in the already burning late-morning sun, her father and the driver each carrying two pieces of luggage, her mother's skirt as soiled as a charwoman's as she lost her footing on the dirt road, though of course it did not concern her. For they were here, very close now; they were on the last part of the march.

The church was built on a ridge that rose up in the heart of the village. From the *albergo* they could easily see it standing majestically up at the end of a rising allée of young cypress trees. They checked into their room and to Sylvie's surprise her father announced that instead of seeing it right away they should close the curtains and lie down for a few hours, that they were here now and should rest and rejuvenate. Of course they all knew that they had missed the commemoration ceremony by a day, having been delayed at length, first in Paris and then at the French-Italian border.

But it was a most welcome sleep, even in the lumpy, malodorous bed, which after the hard, cracked-leather seats of the trains seemed to Sylvie a lair of pure goose down. When her parents woke her five hours later it seemed as if she had slumbered for a week, and could have slumbered on for another. But their hunger overwhelmed them. The innkeeper's wife kindly fixed them an early supper of fried zucchini flowers and a pasta, its creamy egg sauce with peas so rich and satisfying they ate even all the bits of salty pancetta, which none of them mentioned. Afterward the innkeeper opened the one-room "museum of battle" across the road for them, which was mostly just a packed storeroom. It was full of bayonets and muskets and cannonballs and ornate, brightly colored uniforms with tufted headgear and avian epaulets pinned up on the walls, some of them rent and torn and blotted black with dried blood. There were a dozen framed maps and the innkeeper offered them a lengthy disquisition (translated, as he went, by her father) on the various arrays of the Austrian and French forces, a timeline of the early skirmishes and major advances, and the location of the most brutal battles, many of which were fought on and around this very foothill. There were so many dead that they were piled up in carts and buried wherever they could be buried, singly and in groups and in mass numbers. After the fighting, many more died of their wounds and were buried in the same fashion, residents of all the neighboring towns laboring to inter them as quickly as they could to ward off disease. It took weeks. The stench was historic. The rats grew to the size of small dogs. By the end, every able-bodied man and woman and strong-enough child had become, of necessity, a gravedigger. Years later, when the church was erected, the bones from the known mass graves were exhumed and cleaned and arrayed inside, transforming it into a sacred reliquary of the dead.

The innkeeper finally led them up the hill to the church. It was nearly six o'clock but still very hot, and although the incline was not exceedingly steep, to Sylvie it seemed a hike up a great mountain. She was lethargic with her fully laden belly, and the radiant heat of the pebbled ground and the battle museum room had sickened her, its smell of iron and moldering linen clinging to her like an iniquitous dust, this promise of doom. Halfway up she felt her mouth water terribly and she vomited at the side of the wide path. Though her mother said they should go back to the *albergo*, Sylvie told her that they could keep going up. She did not wish to disappoint them. At the top they stood before the church doors, the façade lighted golden by the low sun, its lines plain and almost severe, before stepping inside. The shift from brightness to shade momentarily veiled their vision. Like any church it was hushed and still, but here all breath seemed to pause. And then their sight returned and her mother loudly gasped, gripping her husband's arm. The innkeeper stood apart from them, saying not a word. Sylvie didn't understand. She looked up at the white marble altar and plain wooden cross and recognized them to be like any other, but the unusual, lovely filigree of the walls of the chancel drew her forward. And then she heard them, as if she were on the stage peering out at the audience of a macabre opera house, the coally voids of countless eyes speaking to her all at once.

Look at us, they said to her, in a single voice. We were never divine.

SYLVIE FELT THE PANE of the window buzz; it was the rumble of vehicles approaching the front gate. There was a horn blast and then another and when she looked outside she saw her father and Reverend Lum coming out from the dining room, walking across the court-yard as they buttoned up their overcoats. Tom Harris and Mr. Li followed them. The wives peered out from the dining room window, and her mother, on seeing Sylvie across the courtyard in their quarters, motioned for her to stay inside. Sylvie couldn't see what they could see, as the sleeping quarters were on the same side as the main gate, and when the men disappeared from her view she couldn't help but step outside herself.

There were two vehicles idling on the other side of the wrought-iron gate, a beat-up black sedan and a covered truck. Reverend Lum was talking to the driver of the sedan, a young soldier in uniform who kept trying to present some papers to him through the bars. Reverend Lum spoke Japanese, and though she couldn't understand what they were saying it was clear enough that Lum was being stubborn, and even high-handed, shoving the papers back whenever the soldier tried to push them through to him. The soldier was very young and despite his heavy clothing he looked as though he could slip between the black iron bars. It was surprising that he wasn't getting angry or irritated, which was perhaps an indication of his youth, or else he was cowed because Lum had unbuttoned his coat to show his minister's garb—a modest number of the Japanese were devout Christians. The soldier soon gave up and went back inside the car with the papers. The car jostled slightly but nothing could be seen as their view through the windshield was obscured by the sun's reflection. For a moment it even seemed they might back up and drive away. But then an officer emerged from the back of the car with the papers rolled up in his hand, and he gestured with them for Reverend Lum to approach the gate. Sylvie's father and Harris and Mr. Li stepped forward with him.

By this time her mother was beside her but she was no longer tugging at Sylvie to go back inside. The officer was certainly young as well but had the drawn, placid expression of a seasoned soldier. Sylvie recognized him as one of the officers who had come the week before to question the men. The officer ungloved his hand and offered it to Reverend Lum, who refused him. The officer half-chuckled and threw his arms wide, as if to ask what else he could do, and Lum finally relented, slowly extending his hand through the bars. When they shook, the officer leaned in close against the gate and whispered something to Lum, and Sylvie was confused when the reverend began to dip down on one knee opposite the officer, her mother now desperately trying to pull her away. It sounded as if Lum were humming, huffing now in singsong, and when her father and the others rushed forward to him as he was pinned against the bars he cried out in Mandarin, *Oh, please stop!*

The sound was as clean and fine-grained as a calligraphy brush being snapped in two. Lum collapsed and fell back on the frozen ground, shouting and moaning horribly as he cradled his wrist. The officer had forced it back against the iron bar until it broke. While her father and Li tried to calm him, Tom Harris began shouting at the Japanese officer about the treatment of noncombatants, how he would report this incident to the U.S. consulate, but the officer stood impassively through the epithets, staring at him as blankly as if he were deaf. He then motioned to the gate lock and, when Harris refused, unholstered his pistol in a smooth, swift movement and leveled it at his head. Sylvie's father cried, "That's enough!" and rose and quickly unlocked the gate. From the back of the truck four rifle-bearing soldiers jumped out and walked through with the Japanese officer into the mission's courtyard. The vehicles rolled slowly in behind them, the hard strum of the engines reverberating loudly in the small courtyard. Li and Harris had helped Reverend Lum to his feet and Betty Harris met them and they brought him back inside the dining room. Sylvie was hustled in by her mother right after them, Li and Harris immediately heading back outside.

Mrs. Lum was shrieking while Betty Harris attended to her husband, who sat jittering in a chair, his arm lying dead still on the table as if it were independent of the rest of him. It was a terrible ordeal simply to remove his overcoat, and at several points Lum fainted from the pain. Betty Harris tried to bind his wrist while he was out but he roused and screamed and involuntarily swung at her with his good hand. The wrist of the other hand was broken back and played freely with a gruesome range. When he finally looked at it he gagged and then vomited onto the floor. All the while Betty Harris was crying and Sylvie's mother was teary as well as she tried to calm Mrs. Lum. But Sylvie herself was quiet. She could not quite speak or move. She had seen much suffering in her parents' travels, but it was suffering caused by deprivation, hungry and sick children or adults hobbled and disfigured by chronic or untreated disease. Once, in Port Loko District, in Sierra Leone, they had come across the hacked body of a homicide victim (murdered, her parents were later told, by a neighboring tribe), and it was the first time she had witnessed intentional cruelty and violence, but never directed against someone in the position of her parents, and all she could do was stand stiffly by the window, unconsciously gripping her own wrist so tightly that later, before sleep, there was still a rawness ringing her skin.

Her gaze was now drawn outside by raised voices in the courtyard. The three men were talking to the Japanese officer, their puffs of breath quickly dissipating in the cold air. They were speaking English to the officer, her father insisting that he reconsider. The officer looked as if he understood, but he turned away and her father reached out to him and a soldier stepped between them and shoved him back with the side of his rifle. Her father stumbled, but Li caught and steadied him before he fell. Tom Harris was yelling again, but the officer ignored him completely and shouted orders to the rest of the soldiers, perhaps two dozen of them in all. They began unloading their gear, hopping out of the large truck and passing down rucksacks and crates.

When they came back inside the dining room, the men helped hold down Reverend Lum so that Betty Harris could finally wrap his wrist. She had run to get her nurse's kit and had just drawn from an ampoule of morphine and stuck the needle in his forearm, but he was still in terrible agony and thrashing in distress. Luckily the fracture had not broken through the skin or ruptured a vein, and she was able to bind it tightly for now, though she said they would have to get him to a hospital with an experienced orthopedic surgeon and should leave right away. There was a hospital in Mukden, but he would likely have to travel all the way to Peking for proper treatment. Sylvie's father's eyes narrowed and he told them what they already suspected: The Japanese soldiers would be occupying the mission.

"For how long?" Mrs. Lum cried.

"I don't know," he answered.

"This is where we've always lived! We have nowhere else to go! We can't just go someplace else like all of you."

"I'm sorry, but he wouldn't say."

"What are they here for?" Sylvie's mother asked him.

"He refused to say that, too. But I think it must be about those incidents." There had been a rash of resistance activity since Christmas, a couple of bombings of Japanese ammunition and fuel depots, and then an assassination of an officer in Changchung.

"We have to get Reverend Lum to the hospital," Betty reminded everyone. "There's risk of a blot clot, or even limb loss. We should be leaving right now."

"We can't go anywhere," her husband said angrily. "We've all been ordered to remain. We're prisoners here."

"But why?" Mrs. Lum cried. "We're only missionaries. My husband needs a doctor!"

"I'll try to speak again to the commanding officer," Sylvie's father said to her, clasping Mrs. Lum's hands. "I promise you we'll get him to a hospital somehow. But for now we have to remove our personal things from our quarters. We must do this right now. I suggest we go to it immediately and then meet back in here. We should be warm enough for the time being, if we stay together and get the stove going."

The adults hurriedly bundled themselves in their coats and rushed out to gather their things. Sylvie's mother forbade her to leave the dining room, so she remained alone with Reverend Lum. They had placed chairs in a line so he could lie down and rest. Sylvie sat beside him, holding his good hand to comfort him as her parents had instructed her. His hand was clammy and cold, but at least he was calm now, despite the uneven, makeshift surface of the wooden chairs. Like his wife, he was short and pudgy, and he hardly fit on the narrow width of the seat bottoms. She had to press her leg up against him so he wouldn't roll off. He was no longer in pain. His eyelids were heavy but he was looking up at her with a gratified expression, as if he were gazing into the face of his own attentive daughter. She wasn't uncomfortable touching him. The Lums had no children of their own and they were always kind to her, offering her sweets or cakes whenever they were at hand, at least before they started rationing.

"I wish you had not had to see that," he said. "You were watching, yes?"

She nodded.

"You're like your parents. Strong and stoic. But you are even more so, I think. Are you sure you're not a Chinese?"

"Maybe I am," she said, playing along.

"Truly? Come closer. Let me see your eyes."

She bent her head down toward him and he examined her as carefully and methodically as a physician might, slowly taking in her brow, her cheekbones, the shape and line of her eyes.

"Perhaps it is true. I see something now that I had not noticed before. Something about the inner part of your eyelids. They are not quite Occidental. They remind me of my niece's, in fact, the way they make you both look a little sleepy."

"My mother says that, too," Sylvie said. "That I always appear tired."

"But you're a vigilant girl," he said. "Always taking everything in. And it is good that you're not as scared as I am."

She immediately said she was scared, to try to comfort him.

"No, you're not," he said, faintly smiling, his eyes glassy from the drug. "Don't worry. I don't feel bad. I have never been much of a hero, that way. I always knew I was never going to be such a man."

"You stood up to that horrible officer."

"But see what it's gotten me. And now what it has brought on the rest of you. On the mission. Perhaps he wouldn't be forcing us out of our quarters had I simply let him in."

But they both knew it likely wouldn't have made a difference, and she didn't try to say otherwise. The Japanese were becoming more and more brutal as they drove to make permanent their grip on the region. Manchukuo, as the Japanese called it, was now a reality. There were unverified accounts from peasants who had witnessed how they treated the soldiers of the Communists and the Kuomintang and the civilian resistance, rumors of how they tortured and executed their prisoners and innocent villagers. It was all part of what Tom Harris had been warning about, the shift from the years of minor skirmishes between the Chinese factions themselves and then against the occupiers to a steady tightening of Japanese control, of their total dominion over the region and its resources.

Just then the officer who had hurt Reverend Lum pressed up and peered into the window and he instinctively turned away, inadvertently knocking his broken wrist against the seat back. He cried out sharply. The officer made no expression but gazed at Sylvie with a look of mild surprise. The young soldier who was the driver of the car trailed him, shouldering two rucksacks; his face was badly swollen and reddened from a fresh beating, one of his eyes pinched nearly shut. Still, he followed his superior with the dutiful bearing of a porter, only his fur-lined cap slightly askew, and they walked directly to the Binets' quarters, where her mother and father were trying to get their clothing and few possessions out of the room as quickly as possible. They were going in and out in turn, placing bags and loose shoes and sheets haphazardly out front, directly on the bare ground. The officer didn't wait for them to finish, simply passing them and stepping in without pause, as if he had been living there always. Her mother glared at him, but her father tugged at her and they filled their arms with as much as they could hold and headed back toward the dining room.

Reverend Lum was crying now, curling up around his injury.

"What can I do?" she said, her heart galloping, racing.

"I don't know," he said, wincing, breathing rapidly through his teeth. "Could you give me another dose? Betty left the kit. There it is."

On the dining table was the wooden box that held the ampoules and needles.

"I don't know how to do it. . . ."

"You saw Betty, didn't you?"

"Yes."

"Then you can, too."

"I'll go get Mrs. Harris!"

"All the soldiers are out there!" he gasped. "You must stay here, like your mother told you."

She filled a syringe and tried to find a place on his arm where she could jab him as Betty Harris had, swiftly and surely. But his wrist was bandaged up and when she tried to remove his coat for a second time he wheezed sharply, his body stiffening against the pull of her hands.

"I'm so sorry, but there's no place," she said, his suffering making her heart race. "I don't know where I should do it."

"Underneath," he rasped, tapping the bottom of his coat. "Do it underneath."

She had to lift up his coat and loosen his belt. He then turned with great effort, freeing his trousers. She pulled out his shirttail and firmly held his bare hip and with her eyes shut jabbed him forcefully with a staccato strike, just as Betty Harris had done, injecting him high on his soft, almost fleshless rump. A thick dark drop of blood welled up around the point and she blotted it with a patch of linen from the kit, pressing it tightly. His body had tensed with the shot but had just as quickly relented, going completely limp, and his mouth hung open slackly and for a moment she was afraid that she had killed him. She held his hand again, squeezing it to rouse him. Suddenly he exhaled with a visible shudder of his chest and his eyes went dull, and before disappearing again inside himself he whispered, "You did fine, my sweet girl, you did fine."

THE REST OF THE AFTERNOON and night passed without incident. Dawn was now breaking, and the dining room was frigidly cold, the windows opaque with a frozen haze from their breathing. They had all gathered here as Sylvie's father suggested and although the stove was kept lit most of the night (if very low, for the officer had his soldiers confiscate most of the mission's coal, leaving them with a barrel the size of a large garden pot, and they had no idea how long it would have to last them), the fire had died out and no one could bear to stir from beneath the thin blankets. There were just the eight of them now, as the Chinese helper ladies and their children had been allowed to leave at dusk, Jane Binet sending the two orphans off with them. They had spread tablecloths on the rough plank floors about the stove (the chairs became uncomfortable after a while and Tom Harris had already noted they could burn them, if it came to it) and slept in a communal half-circle, only Benjamin Li lying slightly off by himself. The soldiers were bivouacked in their former rooms and in the main classroom on the other side of the wall. For much of the night they could hear them good-naturedly arguing and laughing as they played cards, their youthful voices and the burnt-hay smell of their low-grade cigarettes almost making it seem as if the soldiers and they were snowed in together in some rustic isolated dormitory. Outside, gusts of wind were casting sprays of dirt against the window, knee-high funnels of dust skittering about the empty courtyard. Across the way, in Sylvie's family's former sleeping quarters, the officer had spent the night, his driver having hung a tarpaulin over the window to screen the light.

Reverend Lum slept resting his head in his wife's lap. Mrs. Lum was the only one who had remained sitting up, her back lodged against the inner wall, so that she could comfort her husband by stroking his fore-head, his thinning hair. She was sleeping now with her head bowed far forward. Her husband's wrist had bothered him all night—it had swelled into a purplish mass, the skin shiny from the extreme distention—and so Betty Harris gave him two separate, full doses of morphine. She was careful in the beginning because he had a weak heart, but the pain was so great that she couldn't refuse him. Yet they all knew the anesthesia was not going to last. Her kit was meant for emergencies, and she estimated that she had only enough to keep him comfortable for the night and perhaps the next morning. Sylvie's father, through Mrs. Lum, had informed the Japanese officer of this yesterday evening but he flatly refused to let anyone leave; in fact he had come to announce that he would be interviewing them again, this time the women as well, including Sylvie. Her father furiously insisted that the women be left alone, especially Sylvie, and for some reason the officer had finally assented, saying, "Okay, then," in perfectly accented American English. Francis and Tom Harris were stunned silent for a moment but then barraged him with protestations; yet he would still not explain why he was again conducting the interrogations, and in the middle of their entreaties and arguments he simply walked out.

Tom Harris restarted the coal stove and set a kettle of water on top. Next door they could hear the yawns of soldiers and the tinkle of their mess kits and soon the smells of boiling rice and cigarettes came to them. Sylvie and her mother served tea and some leftover moon cakes for breakfast but no one was much hungry and they were all getting back under their blankets, to wait for the room to warm up, when a large, stoop-shouldered soldier came into the room. He pointed to Tom Harris and barked an order; apparently he was to be the first for reinterrogation. Harris rose slowly enough as to appear defiant. After kissing his wife he left with the soldier, but as the time kept passing Betty grew anxious, sitting against the wall with her knees up to her chin. Sylvie's mother sat beside Betty and put her arm around the woman's shoulder, to offer comfort.

Sylvie kept looking at Benjamin Li. His jaw was tensing, and when she tried to smile at him he could only grin tightly back at her. He took out his cigarette case and got up to smoke in the small vestibule that led out to the courtyard. Last night Tom Harris had asked him if he thought they might try to conscript him—many Chinese men had been forcibly enlisted by the Japanese, to fight against the Communists and elements of the Kuomintang or work as labor—but he was confident his passport would shield him. They had no cause to interfere with a British subject, though he had indeed heard of instances of foreign Chinese being conscripted. The idea of his being taken away by them was as horrifying to Sylvie as what had happened to Reverend Lum, and she wanted to tell him now that if the Japanese did try to take him she would attempt anything for him, to prevent it. Of course she knew the idea was pure silliness, but he should know her sentiment at least and she was waiting for a moment in which she could go and speak to him.

As if he sensed her wish, Benjamin caught her eye and she immediately rose and stepped out into the much colder vestibule. The others, resting quietly in the dim room, hardly seemed to notice. He was already smoking and she asked him if she could have one, too. Bright rays of light shot through gaps between the door and jamb and coolly illuminated the small space.

She had not smoked before and he regarded her with his bright eyes but then took out the case. "I should make you ask your parents, but

I have a feeling they wouldn't mind." He showed her how to tap it, and when he lit it for her she tried to breathe it in as deeply as he did. She coughed terribly at first, and they both laughed. But she soon got accustomed to it, inhaling ever so gently, letting the smoke come out.

"Not bad," he said.

"I'm almost fourteen," she said. "When did you start?"

"I guess around your age."

"You see? And I bet you didn't have my life."

"No, I didn't. I grew up in one place. I didn't see what you've seen. And I certainly wasn't in a situation like this."

"But I'm not scared," she said.

"But you should be," he told her firmly. "This is a very dangerous situation. Please don't think anything else."

She nodded, feeling chastised. They smoked for a while in silence, though the more she smoked the sillier she felt, like a girl playing dress-up. She dropped her cigarette and stamped it out.

"Listen," he said kindly, his voice relaxed and low. "I wanted to tell you today, during the meal, that I've enjoyed our lessons together. You're an excellent student, so good in fact that you make me think I'm a master teacher."

"I'm excelling in mathematics, too?"

"Well," he said, chuckling, "you know what I mean. You should seriously consider studying Classics when you enter university."

"Maybe I could study in England," she said. "You could be my instructor then."

"That would be nice. But I doubt I'll be able to get back there again."

"Where will you go, I mean, after here?"

"I had hoped to settle in Shanghai, though it seems the Japanese aim to make everyone's plans moot. In any case, you'll require someone who's twice the scholar I am, for what you'll be reading."

"I don't care," she said, feeling suddenly that she was losing control, her voice rising. "I don't care about that at all."

"Well, you should. By the time you get to university you'll have equaled and likely surpassed me in your translations. I told your parents as much. They're very proud of you, you know. Not only because of the Latin."

"I'm just a burden to them."

"You shouldn't ever think that, Sylvie," he said, taking her by the shoulders. His spectacles glinted with the reflected light. "That's surely the furthest thing from the truth. If anything, one might say it's been you who's been burdened. I wonder if you ever minded being taken all over the world. Always moving around."

"Sometimes I wish we could live in one place," she said, though that wasn't quite true. She never minded their missionary existence, as it was the only life she'd ever known. But until now "one place" had not included a person like Benjamin Li. "I wish we could all stay here."

"You know that's impossible now."

"I know. I just don't want to be sent off with the Harrises."

"How I wish that were still an option. You probably should have left last week, when the Japanese first came through. I thought it then and should have told your parents. Really, all of you should have left then."

"What about you?"

"I'll be fine," he said, but then didn't offer any more of an answer. She asked him for another cigarette and he gave one to her. As she waited for him to light it she shivered and he leaned in close to her, cuffing his arm about her shoulders but very quickly letting go, like any teacher might.

"I have something for you," he said. He reached into the pocket of his parka and gave it to her. It was a small brass medal attached to a striped silk band of blue and white.

"What was this for?" Sylvie asked, rubbing its embossed face with her thumb. "Were you a soldier once?"

"Oh, no," he laughed. "It's an academic medal, from my high school days. Though it was a military academy. For some reason they gave these out—to make our accomplishments seem heroic, I guess. They gave great big medals for athletics and martial exercises, but I'm afraid this one is merely for Greek and Latin. I want you to have it."

"I shouldn't take it."

"Why not? I wanted to give you something for your Latin prowess, and this is just the thing. It would mean vastly more to me that you had it than my carrying it around. I just found it again this afternoon among my things and I realized I'd eventually just lose it. I'm hoping you'll keep it safe for me. Then someday you can give it to someone else. Would you do that?"

She nodded, feeling as though he were bestowing on her an eternal prize, and she already knew that she could never give it away. Beneath all the layers of her clothing her heart was bursting, and, unbuttoning her coat, she asked him if he would pin it on her. As the pin backing the medal was rusty, he did so with care, looping it through her sweater so as not to injure her, but just as he enclosed it she pressed his hand against her chest and momentarily held it there. He pulled away his hand. He looked slightly mortified but her expression was such that he smiled at her and then gave her a quick, deep embrace, her face buried in the rough wool of his coat. They were quiet then. They shared another cigarette. They stood close together but not touching and smoked without talking but in Sylvie's mind she was already leaning against him with her temple tucked in his neck, her arm locked in his, two people in the shadow of a long-mourned departure. Maybe they were even lovers. She was sure that if he asked her in the freezing vestibule to remove her hat and coat and sweaters and skirt and every other underlay of her clothes that she would do as instructed, with whatever his fancied flourish or speed, hew to the exact line of his wishes until she was all but bared.

The door opened and Tom Harris came in from the courtyard with an armed soldier, the chill rushing in behind them. She and Benjamin let them through and followed and when they entered the classroom Betty Harris jumped up to hug him, shouting, "Oh, Tom! Are you all right?"

"I'm fine," he said, embracing her. "I'm fine." He turned to Sylvie's father. "He wants to talk to you now, Francis."

"What does he want?" Mrs. Lum asked. "How was he able to speak to you?"

"He speaks English well," Harris answered. "He asked what I knew about those incidents, especially the killing of the officer."

"What did you tell him?" her father asked.

"What could I? I told him I knew nothing about it, that we had just arrived here at the mission then. But he didn't believe me and threatened me with this goon, but then in the middle of arguing about it he suddenly stopped the interrogation."

The soldier barked something and Francis held up his hand to indicate himself and they went across the courtyard. But he was only interrogated for about ten minutes before he returned, saying the questions were the same as Harris had been asked: When did he arrive in the area? In what capacity? With whose resources? Had he ever served in uniform? Where was he on the dates of the bombings and the night the Japanese officer was assassinated in the restaurant in Changchung?

The guard took Benjamin next. As he was being escorted away, Sylvie ran up and hugged him. She took him—and herself—by surprise, but he warmly embraced her in return and assured her that everything would be fine. He didn't seem self-conscious or concerned that the others were watching. After he left she sat beside her mother, who brushed her hair as she did every morning and night. But this morning Sylvie felt a strange electric tinge at the nape of her neck as the brush tugged at her hair, redolent and oily from having gone unwashed for a week; she sensed her mother was looking at her differently, taking another measure of the line of her features, as if she suddenly possessed someone else's eyes. Was she imagining what a young man, say, Benjamin Li, would desirously see and linger upon in her daughter? Surely it was an unseemly thought in this circumstance, and yet Sylvie closed her own eyes and nurtured the sensation as it flared down the back of her neck and spine, substituting the brush for a caressing hand, the hand for a cheek, the cheek for the most ravenous mouth, the exhilaration quelled only by the renewed murmurings of Reverend Lum, whose ruined wrist was coming fully awake; the morphine was wearing off. It was the very last dose: from now on he would be in his own body. And yet it was Mrs. Lum who was now crying, very softly and to herself, as if already feeling what her husband would soon have to endure. Sylvie's mother and Betty Harris had been consoling her but didn't try to do so now; there was nothing else to say or do. Soon enough his murmurs turned into shuddering, bellowing moans, the terrible sounds seeming to come less from his throat than from the body itself, as if immense sections of earth were shifting deep within a cave.

"What the hell is taking so long?" Harris said. He was standing at the window, staring grimly across the courtyard. It had been nearly an hour since Benjamin had gone.

"Sit tight, Tom," her father said. "He'll come back soon. And all this will be over."

"You think so? I'm beginning to wonder. What day was that officer killed? Early last week, wasn't it? Wasn't Benjamin away then, at least one night?"

"I don't think so," Francis said. "He was here. He ate supper with us as usual."

"But he was away a good part of the day, in Changchung, right? And he was away those other days last month?"

"What if he was?" Jane spoke up. "It's his business what he does."

Harris checked to see if the sentry outside was within earshot, then said in a lowered voice: "But what if his business is endangering the rest of us? Look at poor Reverend Lum over there. I think we all know Li's Communist sympathies run pretty deep. Even if he is a British citizen, I'm sure the Japanese didn't have to do too much snooping around to get wind of him."

"What did you say about him when you were questioned?" Jane asked.

"Nothing. But it would be no big news to me if he had some involvement in that business. I wouldn't blame him. Whether he's with the Communists or Kuomintang, here's a young Chinese man with patriotic feeling, and he's going to be fine with the Japanese taking over his country? I'd think he was with the resistance, wouldn't you? But I'm telling you, I won't abide the rest of us being imprisoned here because of him, whatever the reason. He can't use us as some cover or shield. I'll say that right to Benjamin, when he returns. I think all of us should."

"He's not using anyone!" Sylvie stood up and said, the force of her own voice surprising her. But it lifted her, too. She was angry and yet practically on the verge of tears. "He's just a teacher!"

Harris was about to respond but then kept quiet, clearly deciding not to bother arguing with her. He drifted back toward the window, looking out again for any signs. Her father took her by the shoulders to calm her. "It's all right, sweetheart. You should try to sleep now, okay? Get some rest."

"What's going to happen to Benjamin?"

"I don't know," he said, glancing at the Lums. The reverend was in great distress. "We'll just have to wait. Right now we have to get Reverend Lum out of here, somehow. But nothing's wrong yet, as far as Benjamin is concerned."

But as the time kept passing it grew ever clearer that something was indeed going wrong. No one was saying anything, and only Harris was watching the covered window. But there was nothing to see or hear except the winds. Soon the skies clouded over and it began to snow, the flurries flying sideways across the courtyard of the mission. The air had grown damp and heavy and crept inside the dining room, the coal stove burning just hotly enough to keep the temperature inside bearable. The only benefit was that the cold seemed to help blunt Reverend Lum's pain. Tom Harris also made him drink from the gin he always brought along with him on his travels. Lum at first choked on it, as he didn't normally drink, but in his tortured delirium and desperation to anesthetize himself he was able to sip down a good quarter of the bottle; he was curled up with it as he lay his head in his wife's lap, his breathing audible but controlled, only crying out every few minutes or so rather than constantly, which was a mercy to them all.

It was a mercy to Sylvie especially, for even with each small groan her own wrist ached in empathy. She had tried to sit with him and Mrs. Lum but he was so distressed and disassociated that he hardly appeared to recognize her. Then his cries made her picture Benjamin sitting vulnerably before the Japanese officer; what would he do to Benjamin, given the brutality he'd shown Reverend Lum, if he in fact suspected he was part of some resistance group? Despite the possibility, she was still furious at Tom Harris for ever stating it aloud, as if its very airing were somehow accelerating Benjamin toward a similar fate. She resolved that she would not divulge anything about Benjamin or anyone else, including Harris. Never betray a word. It didn't matter that she knew nothing to betray. She'd flashed with pride when her mother had challenged Harris, and like her mother and father she would display humility and strength of will and undying fidelity to a righteous cause, no matter the duress.

"People are coming out," Harris said from his position at the window. "It's a bunch of them."

"Is Benjamin with them?" Francis said.

"Yes," Harris said, his voice suddenly grim. "He's with them."

Before Sylvie could get to the window the outside door of the vestibule opened and closed and then a rush of freezing air preceded the entrance of armed men. The officer came in after them, followed by several others. They were all bundled for the weather—all but one of them, who wore almost no clothing at all. Clad only in his dull gray undershorts, he was immediately pushed down on his knees before them. It was Benjamin Li. A sharp gasp went up in the room but Sylvie had not cried out, though now it was not from self-control; she simply could not quite breathe. For a long time afterward, for the rest of her years in fact, her grasp of that day would function more as an ill fantasy than a memory, a dark figment she could screen for the purpose of self-torment, letting herself view it over and over until it became a kind of homily, a saying in pictures, until she lost herself within it completely.

His hands were tied behind his back. He seemed only half conscious, barely able to stay kneeling as she shivered with cold. He had been badly beaten, his shoulders and neck lashed with welts. Small angry pocks peppered his chest: he'd been burned with cigarettes. His face was gruesomely battered, one eye swollen completely shut. Blood had flowed and congealed in a branching stream from a gash in his head. He could not, or would not, look up. The soldiers, oddly, now leveled their weapons on the missionaries.

"This man has confessed to his own crimes," the officer said to them. His English voice was softer than his Japanese, its tone almost decorous, genteel. "Yet he refuses to speak further about his comrades."

"There's nothing he can say about us," Tom Harris told him. "We have nothing to do with what's happened. We're innocent."

"I know this," the officer said. "I am talking about his comrades in the province. He is not a British subject at all but a Kuomintang agent. Yet no matter what we do to him he won't answer. So I have brought him here."

The officer stepped toward the Lums and went down on one knee. He took Reverend Lum's broken wrist gingerly in his hand and as Mrs. Lum began to titter in fear he asked Benjamin to tell him what he wished to know. Benjamin shook his head, surprising them all that he could even hear anymore. The officer repeated himself and Benjamin once again refused. The officer then barked angrily in Japanese and through his blood-spittled mouth Benjamin gasped, "No!" and the officer stood up abruptly, still gripping the reverend's wrist.

The shriek from Lum burst like an explosion; for an instant it seemed to rend the room with its flash, and then there was nothing. Sylvie's father rushed to him after the officer got up but there was nothing to Reverend Lum; his heart had stopped. He was dead. The officer unholstered his revolver and spoke again to Benjamin, asking him to name his compatriots. He was now peering down at Mrs. Lum, who was unable to notice or care; she was wailing and clawing at her own eyes and hair and at her husband's chest, kissing the back of his lifeless hand. Harris was hollering to Benjamin that he should tell the officer what he knew, but he turned his face away.

"Speak now and I will let the rest of these people go," the officer told him. "It is my promise."

Benjamin bent his head lower, averting his good eye.

"Will you not?"

"Tell him, you fucking bastard!" Harris cried.

"Forgive me," Benjamin mumbled in Mandarin, unable to look at any of them.

The officer said, "Open your eyes. All of you," and then, without a word of warning, he shot Mrs. Lum in the head. She fell heavily over her husband's body. Part of her face was missing, the wound a mass of jammy, out-turned flesh. She stared into space as if she were about to say certain words to the rest of them: *Help me.* In the shock of the moment they were numbed pliant as the soldiers lined them up on their knees. And like others in such circumstances who are all too aware of their fate, they were remarkably docile and quiet in their array; even Harris simply clasped hands with his wife, who was breathing fitfully, her lungs stifled by fear. The Binets had Sylvie lodged tightly between them, her mother whispering to her not to look up, not to move. Sylvie could not have moved anyway. She could not have stirred herself a hair. Her father, however, was staring fiercely now at Benjamin.

"I can see all of you had fondness for this fellow, from the way you are regarding him now," the officer said to her father, noticing his attention. "He has surprised you. But I know this man. We met today, but I know him well enough. He is not so special. You should know that he would do the same to me, if I were in his place. He would do the same to any of you."

The officer stepped before her father and motioned for him to rise. "You are a Samaritan, yes? That's why you are out here in this miserable place, helping miserable people. You even bring your family! And during a period of conflict! It is admirable work, I am sure, but it has also led you to this. Now you can see this man has decided that your lives are not worth those of his coconspirators. Or the sake of his already futile cause."

While he spoke, the officer opened the cylinder of his revolver and let the bullets fall out into his hand. He slipped one back into a chamber and closed the cylinder, rotating it so that the single cartridge would be the next to fire.

"This man is very willing to die. In fact he is already dead. He has obviously chosen the same for all of you, and it is why I have not bothered to compel him further by simply beating or torturing him. I fear he will never talk. I am becoming curious, however, about something else."

It was then that he placed his revolver in her father's hand. The soldiers around them nervously rustled about and locked and bolted their rifles.

"Would you shoot him now? Would you kill him, for the deaths he has already caused?"

Francis held the gun in his palm as if it were a lump of coal. He had never handled a weapon, though the officer could not have known it. During the First World War he had been a conscientious objector, but rather than go to prison or expatriate he served as a medic. He'd been wounded several times and almost killed by a shell in the Meuse-Argonne in eastern France, in the last months of the war; it was the bloody fall campaign of General Pershing, when he lost 120,000 of his men. Francis never spoke of that time to his wife or daughter but it was why he had trouble sleeping at night, partly from dreams of the wounded he could not reach and then for the searing pains in his back, from still-embedded bits of shrapnel.

"You committed these murders," Francis said, speaking quietly but clearly. "You are determining the moral choices here. Not he."

"Moral choices!" The officer chuckled. "Well said! But to be philosophical about it, I could say this man set those choices in motion. And before him, many others. Yet now the rest of us, soldiers or missionaries or bystanders, we must endure the consequences. We must act out the remainder as best we can, according to our roles."

With his boot the officer shoved Benjamin forward onto his belly.

He then fitted the gun into her father's hand, pressing the stock to his palm, hooking his finger into the trigger. "You have a single round. If you kill him there will be no reason to hold the rest of you. Otherwise we will keep on."

Benjamin craned up his battered face and nodded weakly to Francis; he tried to say something but his words were barely audible. He kept nodding even as he lay prostrate, grinding his temple into the rough floorboards, as if he were offering sanction.

"Shoot him!" Harris said. "For goodness' sakes, Francis! He's nothing. He's less than nothing. End this now!"

And yet Francis could not quite move. He couldn't aim or even raise his arm. When he finally held out the pistol for the officer to take back from him, Jane whispered, "Oh, my love." Her eyes were shimmering. Sylvie was crying as well, suddenly remembering now what her mother always told her, that mercy was the only true deliverance. There was nothing more exaltedly human, more beautiful to behold. And a great searing rush of love seemed at once to cleave her and bind her back up, a love for her father and her mother and then, too, for Benjamin Li, despite what had happened, whom she could see only as her father just did, as the one wanting for mercy most of all. It was finished, even the officer could realize that, there was nothing else to be done but to cease the madness, to acknowledge this horrid interlude was done.

But suddenly Harris cried, "Damn it, let me!" and rushed to take the gun himself. The officer shouted and the soldier guarding Harris wheeled and bashed him in the ear with his rifle stock. Harris fell down, his eyes rolling up in his head. He lay dazed, his jaw broken, the hinge on one side seemingly loosed within his skin. Betty screamed and leaped for him toward the soldier and in pure reaction he struck her, too, in the forehead, knocking her completely unconscious. In the way she fell her skirt rode up her legs, revealing the soft jut of her backside where it met her bared thigh. The garter straps were unfastened, her rent stockings fallen down to her knees. Her plain undergarment glowed marble-white. The guard stood over her, transfixed, and was reaching down to touch her when the officer barked at him in Japanese and the guard stepped back. The officer regarded Betty Harris, measuring her exposed body with his gaze only, before cinching down her skirt to cover her. But then he looked long at Jane Binet, and to Sylvie, and before everything would end, it was then that the madness commenced once again.

EIGHT

AT THE BEGINNING OF EACH DAY, for a few hours or so, Sylvie could believe she was herself. She would arise just before Ames and fill the coffeepot with grounds and then get fresh water from the pump outside and balance it on the single-burner field stove while she set out the tin mugs on the table. Soon enough they would eat breakfast with the rest of the orphanage, but, as was their habit back home, they'd have coffee before doing anything else. Sitting in their nightclothes, the brief, wordless slip of time as they gradually came awake was as unburdened as any moments of their marriage. It was as though each understood the other was as blank of feelings or thoughts as himself, or herself, not yet angling on a purpose for the day, or on any previous emotions or feeling between them, comfortable in the simple animal appreciation of nearness, if not togetherness. It was almost as if they were back in Seattle, in their small, upright house in Laurelhurst, time graced by a merciful repose. But soon enough the spell would be broken by Ames getting up and dressing himself for the day,

the final punctuation the heavy scrape of his shoes against the floorboards as he pulled them out from beneath the bed, and Sylvie would
feel the first tiny tears under her skin, as though the flesh were being
loosed from beneath, pulled down toward a core that she knew had
no bottom.

By ten o'clock, an unmooring seemed imminent. She would be
teaching an English conversation class to the younger children, asking
questions of each one in turn: "Would you like another glass of milk?"
or "Which is your favorite kind of candy?" or "What is the date of your
birth?" And while the child gamely answered, she would be certain that
the rest of them could somehow sense the growing rime of hollowness
developing inside her, even if none showed anything but the usual
enthusiasms; the disparity only made her more self-conscious, and, just
as she thought her mother might counsel her, she regained a hold
and girded herself and matched their brightness and zeal, and this
carried her through to the midday meal, where she would make the
motions of eating. Although she had from the first day found the soups
and vegetables the aunties prepared to be flavorful and often delicious, especially considering the meager budget they had, her body
no longer craved the food. Now that she was on the high slow horse
again she consumed just enough to sustain her until the next meal,
spark enough of her blood so that she wouldn't grow dizzy or faint.
She was trying to convince herself as much as everyone else. She had
begun to feel again that she no longer had an understanding of hunger,
a bowl full of barley rice as significant to her as if it were mounded
with pebbles.

Her habit was as casual as was possible, and had been so since the
beginning. It was why she could almost believe it was not a habit, and
never would be. Like someone else who loved eating chocolate a little
too much and from time to time decided chocolate didn't exist and
never had, blotting it from her visceral memory with a thoroughness

that was itself a serial compulsion. She would go for many months—once even a year and a half, in the period following her swift marriage to Ames and their first attempts to have a child—and not feel the smallest prickle for that cool, sweet burning, that glimmering river, if anything marveling at the fullness of her distance from it, her perfect liberty. And yet what would spur a change was not some unhappy memory or incident or a physical need but rather a sudden, panicked thought that this free state could not possibly go on. In this sense her lapses were predicated upon what could only be seen as an evaporation of faith. Her thoughts would branch and multiply, and it was inevitable then that certain remembrances would take over, or maybe it would be her feelings of shame and guilt before Ames. He had little idea of the woman he had married, and treated her only with adoring, deep respect for her abilities and her mind; he had encouraged her plans to attend medical school, even after she became a mother, and they'd talked about her restarting his pediatric practice as he continued with his ministries.

He couldn't know how she had passed her adolescence after she returned from China, how in her second year of college she befriended a fellow volunteer named Jim while working at a mission soup kitchen. He was a middle-aged man, in his early forties. She had pursued him, always initiating their conversations and even asking him to get a coffee at the diner around the corner. He worked as the night watchman at a textile factory, and after her aunt went to sleep she crept out of their bungalow, holding her shoes in one hand and her purse in the other, trying not to breathe, and ran down the hill to catch the night bus that would take her toward downtown. Jim was gentle and soft-spoken and obviously bighearted, but there was something ruined about him and it was this that she always saw in his face when he opened the alley door, his expression pleased but with the shattered eyes of a man who could see perhaps only the drenching sadness in beauty. He never talked about his life or anything further removed than a few weeks in the past, and they would sit together in a tiny office, drinking the root beer he'd brought for them. Jim had a youthful face with a white scar that ran from the corner of his left eye to his ear, the top of which was gone. They talked about books and sang songs and eventually he apologized for being the worst kind of depraved, awful man who would have a schoolgirl as a drinking friend, and it was then that she would lightly kiss him, on the mouth, to quell his conscience. He kissed her back with his dry hard lips and she had to hold him tight, for otherwise he'd push away, and then they wrapped their arms around each other while lying down on the wood floor on which he had spread a thick bolt of surplus velvet curtain, worthless because of the malformed pattern of its brocade. He'd lined the walls, too, with other, mismatched, defectively manufactured curtains and bedspreads, and the effect beneath the dim electric light was of a carnival funhouse owner's idea of a bordello. But to Sylvie it was simply Jim's attempt to make her feel comfortable. He suffered from a severely bad back and the floor gave him some relief from the constant pain, but it was the sips he took from a dark brown bottle that finally seemed to transport him. His voice grew husky and the suddenly huge discs of his eyes took on the same shade of the bottle glass and he clung to her tightly, telling her again how ashamed he felt that she should be wasting time with such a sorry man. Of course he knew something had to be wrong with her, too, by virtue of her presence.

"You're not sorry at all," she told him, as always. "Please don't say that."

"Then what am I? Why do you keep coming here? You could be going out with any boy in your school."

"I'm not interested in any of them," she said, which was true. The boys were nice enough and certainly interested in her but she found them all too keen and bristling, like frantically spawning fish. But she didn't answer Jim, either, for although she would have liked to say that she was here because he was thoroughly kind (which he was, without any effort, to her and to everyone he met), it was in fact because he was also frail, if not somehow wrecked, that she was drawn to him. He was overtly slung with the weight of time, but to her he wasn't a pitiable sight, rather as if he had been stitched with one of the marred but still beautiful bolts, this forlorn cape, and could no longer take it off.

What he sipped along with his root beer was a tincture of opium, which he had been given many years earlier for dysentery while hospitalized in France at the end of the Great War. He always had some now and although she kept asking him if she could try it he refused, saying it was dangerous medicine, but one night when he left her for five minutes to make his rounds she dug in his coat pocket and took a small swallow, and then another. The thick, sweetly fragrant syrup instantly coated her entire insides, the sensation the exact opposite, it would turn out, of the precipitous detachment she would later suffer, hotly fusing her to herself in a manner that made her feel whole again, even if she were no more substantial than ether and light. Years later, married to Ames Tanner, she would seek out that feeling again, though it would come in the form of a vial and needle, procured in the service alley behind the city hospital by a person met, again, through a mission, though this one a client.

When Jim returned he could tell something was different and immediately smelled the tincture on her breath but before he could get cross she kissed him again. He balked at first but then melted into her as he had not allowed himself previously, the sudden force of his arms momentarily alarming her but then just as swiftly firing her desire to make love to him. She was not saving herself for any reason or person— for what propriety, what realm, would she be doing so?—and as such there was nothing stopping her from being with him now, in this oddly, lovingly enrobed little room. She tugged at his belt to unbuckle it but he twisted away and when she clutched at it again he held on to her hands.

"Please turn off the light," he said.

She rose and flicked it off and the room went completely black. She didn't know if it was the perfect dark or his medicine but she floated back to him on a silken wing and when they began kissing again she felt a wonderful new ache flooding her limbs, filling her torso. She slipped off her underpants. Then he was busy kissing her and caressing her hair and she found his belt again and undid his trousers. Her long skirt had ridden up and he lay atop her but there was nothing but his bare thighs against hers and she kept waiting for the pushing that didn't come. She reached down to touch him and when she found him he was hardly there, not tiny but empty, more skin than blood, and beneath it there was almost nothing there at all, just a node seamed by a hardened, smooth line of a scar in the flesh.

"I'm no good," he whispered to her in the dark. He was crying. "I've been useless since the war."

"You're not useless," she said to him. She guided his wet face to her chest, the way she'd once seen her mother do to her father as she peered at them through a hole in the rice paper screen. She guided him lower still, feeling the cooling trail of his tears on her belly, her hip, the crook of her thigh, but he stopped before he went any lower.

"It's all right," she said. "You can keep going, if you want."

"I don't know what to do."

"Yes you do. Just kiss me."

"How?"

"However you want to."

"Just kiss you?"

"Yes."

And when he did she was surprised by them both, their shared ignorance in the act an object lesson in how experience only mattered if one let it, his mapping of her with the gentlest, humblest fervor innocently building her up before smashing her in the darkness, exquisitely obliterating her again.

The pattern of the evening was reprised each time she visited him, once a week throughout that winter, Sylvie staying with him until five, when the first buses began running; she'd ride back up through the fogged-in hills to her aunt's house with her mind similarly sodden and obscured but her body still bounding and alive with his hands and his lips and then soon enough the taste of the tincture, craving it not in her own mouth but in her bones. Each time she'd take a little more, Jim warning her to be careful and that it was not meant for a healthy young woman, but she knew she wasn't a tenth as sturdy as she appeared to Jim or to her aunt or to everyone else who saw her as a beautiful, somewhat aloof, scholarly girl who had so quickly righted herself after such a lamentable family tragedy, whose good long years spanned out freely before her. But the recent past was a well-rutted road, still the only way she knew to get back and forth to the present, and as she went to her classes at the college, attended church with Aunt Lizzie, a part of her couldn't help but wish to run to Jim and the pitch-black room at the factory, drink in the potion and transmogrify, be anything but her mortal self.

It was soon after she was introduced to Ames Tanner, by a deacon of the church whose family was a longtime acquaintance of her parents, that she decided to stop seeing Jim. Ames hadn't even asked her out yet that but she knew, he would imminently and that if he was truly as he appeared, she would be with him always. She loved seeing Jim and loved his gentleness and modesty but it was really a love of cloistering and smallness and her own physical pleasure, all of which she already understood were signs of her ugly narcissism, her insoluble weakness.

Ames Tanner, by contrast, would compel her into the wider world: he was freshly ordained, and a pediatrician as well, and he had great plans for his new church, not only for its congregation but for the charitable works he would urge it to pursue in the wider community. He had the same incandescence in his eyes that her parents had, that cool flame that seemed an uncanny reincarnation of them both, and he had asked her right away, as they sat for tea and cookies in the warm basement of the church, if she would come to his congregation and recount her parents' dedication to improving the circumstances of the poor and powerless. Like everyone else, he knew generally what had happened to them, but he was one of the few who didn't shy away from mentioning them.

So it was with foreknowledge that it would be the last time that she went to Jim. But once there, she couldn't bear to say anything; he had brought her a bouquet of dried flowers that night, in addition to the root beer and of course the half-pint bottle, its glass the color of dark caramels. He'd tacked different fabrics on the walls. For the first time in many weeks she declined to take her sips (he'd had to buy extra bottles from his friend at the hospital), and as he slowly twisted the cap back on, his expression was that of a prisoner being led down into an isolation hole, regarding her as the man might check the sky. She thanked him for the flowers and hugged and kissed him and he hugged her back stiffly.

"Should I turn off the light?" she asked him.

"Okay."

But in the customary dark she had some trouble finding him. "Over here," he said, from the far corner. When they touched it was a minor collision, the crown of her head against his chin. He was sitting up rather than lying on the curtain he had spread out, and before she could apologize he took her shoulders and pinned her hard enough that she could feel the points of her shoulder blades grating against the floor.

He took off her clothes. He wasn't kissing her this time but using his hands, searching her out as if he had only a few scant moments to get to know her and pinching her nape, her nipples, rooting his thumbnail into her belly button until she thought it might have begun to bleed. And yet she willed herself not to tense under his hands; she laid herself open. She wanted to show him that it was all fine, that it was all welcome, that no matter what his compulsion or need she would try to take pleasure now, genuinely and not in spite, for she knew he could only feel any sexual pleasure through her. It was a surprise, then, when he tugged down his trousers and got between her legs, began driving into her, though there was nothing but a rubbing and the spurs of his own narrow hips knocking into her own; he kept on and she urged him, gripping his buttocks to pull him to the right rhythm, and when he matched it with his own fingers in her mouth and in her rear, simultaneously reaching as if he were going to clasp her in the middle, she lost herself as she never had before.

She waited to leave until he thought she was asleep and had gone on his rounds. It was cowardly of her, but he hadn't said a word to her after their lovemaking and she thought it would be a mercy for them both if she simply disappeared. But it was still an hour before the buses began running, and she walked all the way home in the steady, chilly March rain, wholly accepting the misery of being soaked to her bones. It took her an hour to climb the long road up the hill. The next two days she was fever-racked and shaky, her aunt feeding her soda crackers and beef tea in bed, wondering aloud how her skirt and sweater could have gotten so wet, then telling her in the next breath that Ames Tanner had dropped by while she was asleep, leaving a note card that he'd inscribed in the cleanest, upright hand: "Will you give me the honor of learning more about your experiences? I am eager for your wisdom! Faithfully yours, A.T."

Ames took her to lunch the following week, and to the movie

theater and dinner the week after, not making any small talk but rather asking about her family's travels in Africa and China, about the conditions they encountered and how her parents set up the ministries and schooling at each of the missions, about the other kinds of projects they instituted, in mercantilism and agriculture and disease control. He wanted to know how they had gone about learning the local languages, or if it was difficult to work with other missionaries, particularly the Catholic ones. He didn't ask about the circumstances of her parents' deaths, nor in fact speak of them as if they were even gone. She was glad to talk about them this way, for he made her feel as if they were not just alive but still out in the world somewhere, still setting up missions, still aiding and organizing and teaching, and she found herself recounting their activities of those last years in more detail than she had offered anyone else, including her aunt. He'd have her celebrate them, shout their praises if she would, make them gleam again by their brightest light.

He did ask, however, as he drove her back to her aunt's house in his Packard sedan (his family was wealthy, being prominent in the timber business), whether she'd had serious boyfriends in her life, or any present suitors, and she immediately said no, though flashing on Jim. Ames nodded, still quite serious but obviously pleased. She hadn't volunteered again at that particular soup kitchen, but she couldn't help but think about Jim sitting in the dim factory office, the various curtains still tacked on the walls, nursing his bottle of the tincture. At certain moments late at night she craved the taste of it terribly, and longed for him as well, and she found she could master both impulses by kneading herself raw with the back of her thumb until the sensation was only, solely, painful; she would make her body quell its own urges with an even sharper reality. For she knew she must not hide out any longer. She must climb out from every cave of her making. Ames's presence in her life and his interest in her parents was in fact a blessing; he would bring her forth, even if her memories of those last hours might be fully rekindled.

And soon enough, one evening, the past engulfed her all at once. She was preparing for just her fifth dinner out with Ames when she cut herself shaving, the blood running freely from her calf. She was in the tub and instead of stepping out and blotting the wound with a tissue she propped her foot against the tiled wall and let it bleed, accelerating the flow with another quick gash, letting the blood stream past her knee to her thigh, the streaked pale limb fallen asleep and coldly tingling but still existing outside her sensation. It looked as if a wave of blood had washed over her leg but it was merely a surface current, and she was never in the remotest danger; the sight froze her, however, and although she heard the doorbell (her aunt was out of town) she didn't stir, seeing only the bodies of Reverend Lum and his wife lying uncovered in the courtyard of the mission, a splotch of dark red that had spread over Mrs. Lum's face the lone mark on the ground, light snow descending upon them. It was odd, for it was never an image of her parents, but rather of the Lums, which would always spark her mind.

She could hear Ames shouting up at the opened window of the bathroom, and when she didn't answer right away he shouted again. He called her name and when she weakly responded with his he must have heard something wrong in her voice, for he pushed through the unlocked front door and bounded up the narrow stairs of the modest row house. He anxiously called and banged on the bathroom door, and when she didn't answer he came right in, his eyes instantly drawn wide in horror at the dyed hue of the water, the smears of blood on the tiles, on the rim of the tub; her leg had slipped down below the surface. He instinctively grabbed her wrists and pulled them out of the water, but when he saw they were untouched he shook them in panic and cried: "Where is it? What have you done to yourself?"

She was listless from the still-hot water and feeling she could open her throat and disappear within it when Ames reached in and lifted her out in one swift movement. She glanced toward her feet and he quickly found the two tiny slits above her heel; he dressed them with bandages from the medicine cabinet. She was dripping and now cold, but when he knelt and covered her with a towel she bared herself and blotted his drenched suit jacket and trousers. He tried averting his eyes and kept asking what was wrong, but she felt him aroused underneath and hardly knowing what she was doing undid his belt and put him in her mouth. He said no but his face was bound up and he shuddered. In just a few minutes he was ready again and they lay down right there and it was then that blood came from her once more, the ruined towel beneath them like a shock of color in new snow.

The next day Ames proposed to her, something that he was planning anyway but which was certainly accelerated by what occurred, as well as by their assumption that she might be pregnant, which she was. They were married within the month. Yet she didn't stay pregnant, nor could she remain so the next time, or the next. It was not his problem; she would become pregnant at least five times that they knew of, her body simply unable to nurture to term. The last time would be several years before they went to Korea, a three-month-old fetus with nothing obviously wrong with him, a devastating fact, though ultimately not as disturbing to him as was Sylvie's demeanor afterward. She wasn't inconsolable as she was the other times, even as those pregnancies were much shorter-lived, lasting barely a month, or two. This time after recovering from the extraction of the lifeless child Sylvie had simply showered and dressed and with hardly any despondency folded her hospital gown and placed it on the bed and silently waited for the nurse to come with the chair to wheel her out of the hospital. At their small home in Laurelhurst she left the nursery they had set up intact, which heartened Ames for a while, until he realized that she was slowly removing items from it, a book or picture, a stuffed toy or rattle, one piece at a time, until eventually the room was bare, save for the furniture and the crib. He blamed her, blamed her for the dire force her frailty and sexual abandon could have on him, and he more than she grew to be haunted by the idea that they had tainted themselves with the debased, confused desire of that first coupling. Out of anger or spite or desperation he began asking her about what had finally happened to her parents in Manchuria, as if he were sure that it was where the source of all her troubles might be found.

She refused to answer him. But was he right? Were they so easily derived? She didn't think so, and yet who could dismiss the insistent push of those memories?

For it was too easy to recall how she and her parents had watched through the classroom window as the soldiers dragged the Lums' bodies outside, her parents not shielding her from the sight. They were still in shock from the easy brutality of their deaths, Sylvie's father perhaps most of all. After the Lums were left there, he had sat back down on the blanket with his head in his hands, her mother hotly whispering something to him in the roughhewn Provençal dialect they used when they wished to obscure their talk.

Sylvie could have gleaned the gist of their conversation if she had concentrated, as she had countless others over the years; she had never let on that she could understand them at all, not intending at first to deceive but rather, like any child, simply fascinated by the sound of her parents' unrestrained engagements, whether it was joking or arguing or lovemaking. But Sylvie wasn't listening now, or even trying to listen; she could not look away from the Lums. Her eyes were alive and working but as might a bright screen playing in a suddenly emptied theater. She had fled to somewhere inside herself, and was still running, and yet the horrid sight was strange in that they didn't appear so terribly perturbed, in and of themselves, the Lums lying there almost peacefully in the gathering snowfall, the reverend's hand accidentally come to drape upon his wife's forehead, as though he were checking her temperature.

Her mother gasped, "You knew about him, Francis? My God!" with a fury Sylvie had never heard from her before. But they were done talking and her father stood up and took Sylvie in his arms and embraced her so tightly and suddenly that all the air in her chest was squeezed out, her vision near blurring. He smelled sharp with soured, dried sweat but she breathed him in as deeply as she could, burying her face in his thick brown hair. He was not a large man and she was nearly as tall as he but she felt like a little girl again in his grasp and without knowing it was coming she found herself breaking down all at once, sobbing and pressing her mouth against the smooth, curved bone behind his ear. She wasn't afraid for her own life so much as stricken by the fear that she might not see one or both of them ever again. Her mother caressed her back. It was only the three of them in the classroom now. The officer and soldiers had taken away Benjamin Li, to interrogate him one last time. The Harrises, too, had been removed, forced back to consciousness with smelling salts and half-carried to their quarters in the corner of the compound, a sentry posted in front of their door. Through all their travels they were a constant trio, Sylvie schooled by them or by someone else (like Benjamin Li), the three of them slumbering together and eating together and often enough bathing together because of the usually meager supply of hot water—she would always picture their nakedness much more easily than her own— but now it seemed that they could never be close enough, that if it were possible she'd slip inside one of them and fill herself with their tears and their blood and become an indistinguishable plenitude.

And despite everything that had transpired, did she continue to wish the same in regard to Benjamin Li? Was it still possible that all of them could get past this wretched day? Her parents, she could see, might not have any feeling left for him, but they had shown him a lasting grace and Sylvie would lead them back to accepting him and convince them to plead for his life. For her father had been ever so right: Benjamin was not the cause of the situation; he had intended no one harm; he was nearly as much a victim of the cruelty as the Lums, perhaps equally so for the mountain of guilt he would forever have to shoulder. He was a gentle and lovely man and a dedicated teacher, and that he was a stalwart freedom fighter who could refuse under such horrid duress to divulge his secrets only painted him more valorously in her mind. He was indeed a person of principle and it was why he would never take advantage of her desires, why he'd given his school medal to her instead and exhorted her only nobly, why she must wait patiently, until she knew herself to be less blatant and childish, before she could ever hope to attain a lasting, worthy love.

"Your mother and I need to talk to you now, sweetie," her father said to her, cupping her cheek. "We may not have much time, so please just listen."

"Why? What's going to happen? We're going to stay together, aren't we?"

"We will try our best," her father said, trying to smile at her now. "We'll stay together as long as possible. To the last minute. But you must promise us that if you can get away safely, you'll go. Whether it's with us or with the Harrises or by yourself. You must not hesitate. You must not think twice. You cannot be concerned with anyone else. Including us."

"What are you talking about?" she cried righteously, her face hot with a flush of angry fear. "How can you expect that of me, when all you've taught me was to put first the welfare of others? How could I possibly leave?"

"But you must, if you have the chance. Please. Your mother and I would never forgive ourselves . . ."

Sylvie shook her head, pushing away from him. "I'm sorry, Father, but after all the dangerous times over the years, you can't ask this of me now. You just can't! It's too late."

"It's not too late," her mother broke in, with her full-throated voice. She squeezed Sylvie's hands with a fierce grip. "You're going to get out of this, with or without us. Do you hear me, darling?"

She nodded. Her mother was twice as steadfast as she could ever hope to be and a certain gaze from her was enough to both diminish and exalt, often simultaneously. Her father might be the beacon, the light conveying them forth, but even now, amid even this, her mother was the great clarifier, the person who could always make her know her exact place, who could always show her what she must do, and for this reason hers was the picture Sylvie would behold brightest in her mind, this serene and beautiful figure, alabaster for flesh, marble-dust for blood.

"Say you do."

"I do."

"Say it again."

"I hear you, I do!" she said miserably, new tears wetting her cheeks.

"Here, we're going to give you these things," her mother said. "Just to hold for now." She took off her husband's wedding band and put it on Sylvie's finger, where it hung loose. She removed her own and fit it on top, the second ring a good, tight fit.

"We love you more than anything," her mother murmured, kissing her brow, her cheeks, her messy nose and eyes.

"I know," Sylvie answered, if not quite believing it was true. They loved her, yes, but the whole world was woeful, all the places they had been were so bereft, that no one could blame them for having to care for it equally or perhaps even more than for their own child. She should be more wise and serious and realize again the necessary scale of their devotions. How capacious their hearts truly needed to be. For only such would lead them now as it had before, as long as they were steadfast, the force of benevolence lighting the way. And wasn't there some hope? The Harrises were injured, yes, but had walked away mostly under their own power; she and her parents were untouched; and while Benjamin was in grave danger, he must finally see now that there was no other way, he had witnessed the vile consequences and would relent, tell the officer whatever he wished to know.

The sudden report of footfalls made her mother grip Sylvie's side with an urgent, pincering force. "Careful now," she whispered in her ear. "Stay quiet."

Before Sylvie could answer the officer entered. Three soldiers followed, pushing in Benjamin Li before them. He was still shackled. As far as she could tell he hadn't been harmed further, and was even cleaned up, his swollen face swabbed clear of dried blood. She tried to catch his eye but he kept his head bowed, as though he were still deeply ashamed.

"It's all right, Benjamin," she cried out, not able to help herself, "we'll be fine now!"

At that moment the officer's lightless eyes met hers.

"Still this man refuses to answer my questions," the officer said in the plainest, uninflected voice. "So it has led us to this."

He spoke a few words gruffly in Japanese and there was an odd pause and then without warning one of the soldiers grabbed her mother by the hair, wrenching her up on her feet. A low, feral sound came from her father and he hurled himself at the soldier's face with both hands. Her mother screamed, "Francis!" but it was too late; another soldier lunged at him from behind with his rifle, a dull glint of metal flashing in the lamplight. Her father groaned and fell. Sylvie scrambled to him, not sure where he was injured; then she felt a warmth emanating from his side. Her hand came away damp; he'd been stabbed just below the ribs. In the lamplight the blood stained her fingers dark, almost black. He was grimacing terribly, unable to speak, and he pulled her down to him. His face frightened her and she resisted but then she realized what he was doing, what he desperately did not want her to see.

The two soldiers were pushing her mother about, pulling off and tearing at her clothes as though they were flaying her, piece by piece, and Sylvie could hear her mother gasping, the rents of the fabric, the taunts of the soldiers.

The officer had forced up Benjamin Li's bowed head by the chin, to make him watch.

"Don't!" Benjamin said, his eyes closed. "Don't do this."

"Speak!" the officer cursed at him. "Speak now!"

But Benjamin shook his head, hoarsely crying out as though it were his own mother or sister before him. By now they had stripped Jane Binet naked. The officer repeated his demand but Benjamin wouldn't comply, tightly shutting his eyes. He was shuddering and weeping. He had crumpled to his knees, scraping his face against the rough, splintered boards of the floor. On the officer's command one of the soldiers dragged Benjamin to Jane as she was held down by the others and shoved him on her, making him kiss her on the mouth and the neck and the belly and down below. Then they forced them to copulate. They kicked him when he balked, but when that did no good they began kicking her instead, until he finally assented. His grunts were low and fitful; there were no longer any sounds from her. The soldiers were deriding him and laughing and when he couldn't seem to finish the large soldier with the thick neck hurled Benjamin aside and threw himself on top of her. Benjamin ended up a few feet away, suffering a few more kicks in the groin and chest before lying in a curled heap, weakly coughing up blood. When the big soldier was done the other two began bickering for their turn but the officer silenced them with a sharp order.

It was only at that point that Sylvie was able to glance up. She herself was breathless, shaking, her own throat as if throttled by a pair of invisible hands. Her mother gathered her ruined clothes and began dressing. She did so without looking at anyone. She simply threaded her arm through the torn sleeve of her blouse and then crawled back over to Sylvie and Francis, immediately checking her husband for his wounds. He tried to embrace her but he had no strength.

She rolled her coat and gently laid it beneath his head.

"I'm so sorry, darling," her father said, hardly audible for how weak he was. Tears were streaming down his face. The color seemed drained from his cheeks, his lips. "Will you forgive me? Please?"

"Stay quiet now," she said, wiping his eyes. "Don't try to move. You're bleeding too much."

"I don't care," he said. "I only care about you and Sylvie."

"We know that," she said. "Just stay still."

"I love you so much, Jane," he said.

"We love you."

"Please say you do," he said. "Please."

"I love you."

He was going to answer but his breathing suddenly became labored, his torso heaving hard upward, once, twice, and then down. Her mother was crying. Sylvie kissed his temple and there was warmth. He was still alive. She kissed him again and it was the same. It was over now. She felt a hand on her neck, slightly rough, as if her mother had instantly, terribly aged, and for an instant she leaned her cheek into it before she horridly realized it was the hand of the young officer, his short, narrow fingers chapped and scarred.

"Get up," he said to her.

But it was Jane Binet who rose instead, her expression strangely icy and dispassionate, only her hands leaping out in fury at his holstered revolver. For a moment she had it in her grasp before he wrested it from her, striking her in the ear with its grip. But she did not pause and came at him and he shot her twice in the chest. After she fell to the floor he shot her again. The officer pulled Sylvie from her father's side and dragged her toward Benjamin Li. She was too frightened to resist, or even move; her mind was bounding but in place, disconnected from her limbs. Everything came to her through the small end of a spyglass. When he shoved up her skirt she heard her own meager voice, blunted as if through a cold horn, calling out for her mother, for her father, even as she knew neither would answer.

The officer was now shouting, though not at her; he had Benjamin by the throat. He was shouting thunderously at him, lividly, if almost wearily, as if he himself were finally sick of the torment.

"You are a worthless human being! Do you hear me? Less than that! Not even a rat! A piece of dung! You are nothing! You will make no difference! You will not be remembered!"

He thrust him toward Sylvie, making him eye her nakedness. "You wish to see what will happen to her now? You wish to, yes? Is that it?"

Benjamin was shaking his head, crying something over and over to himself, his eyes now tightly shut.

"Tell me who they are!"

Benjamin curled up in a ball, as though he were trying to make himself disappear.

"Ahhh!" the officer cried. He kicked him in frustration. Then he gave an order to the soldiers and two of them held Benjamin down so that he couldn't move. The officer kneeled over him and took a straight razor from his back pocket. He unsheathed it and worked quickly. Benjamin was groaning, guffawing; then he began to scream. When the officer stepped back Benjamin's eyes were bloodied; they looked as if they had been gouged out. But the officer roughly wiped them with his sleeve and it was clear what he had done: he had cut away only the eyelids. The eyes themselves were intact, the orbs monstrous, for being so exposed. His was a fleshy skull. They retied his hands so that they were secured behind his back.

"Watch now, you son of a bitch."

The officer sharply gave an order and one of the soldiers stood over Sylvie and began unbuckling his belt.

It was then that Benjamin began screaming again. He was screaming bloody murder, all the names of his compatriots, screaming them in a litany, most loudly his own.

NINE

AT THE END OF HER WRITTEN STATEMENT to the local constabulary relating her dealings with Nicholas, the antiquities dealer in London added a coda to her testimony: *"Mr. De Nicole, or whoever he may turn out to be, was by every measure a charming, delightfully assured, extremely knowledgeable young man. Aside from the value of the stolen pieces, his departure will certainly prove a considerable loss to our firm."*

So, June thought, someone else was missing him, too.

That the sentiment was barely a month old was a cause for special heartache, and as June peered out the window glass from the back of the sedan Clines had rented for them, she realized that what she was feeling, despite the circumstance, was a deep flush of motherly pride.

Delightfully assured.

The clean type of those words was a sudden salve to her flesh, for otherwise she could hardly keep from crying out from the frightfully sharp pains in her joints and limbs. For the moment they seemed to be far-off alarums, urgent enough and real, though happening to some other unfortunate, dying woman. This dying woman, on the other hand, this one wearing a woolen skullcap and a green silk shawl wrapped snugly about her shoulders on a warm autumn evening, was in fact enjoying the first good day of the end of her life, and not even the jarring, potholed drive up the West Side Highway could call her back to her miserable bones. For she could believe that Nicholas was basically all right; that there was nothing fundamentally wrong with him; that no matter what crimes he'd committed he was essentially a promising, capable young man; that he needed, ironically, only to come back in from the world in order to thrive.

This was the mad logic of her illness, of course, and even as she understood it to be so, she took the same comfort and refuge in her thoughts of Nicholas as with the palliatives from her doctor, these new warm blankets of her life. Something had begun to happen to her body in the last weeks, and she recalled now what her doctor had warned of a month ago when she told him she was not going to see him any-more, that she was going away. Dr. Koenig said the pain would change and evolve, grow worse, much worse, and that eventually it would overwhelm her. She liked his frankness, even before she'd quit as his patient. When Dr. Koenig first informed her of the diagnosis of the stomach tumor she'd felt that horrid bleat arise in her throat, for she could tell by the grip of his unwavering stare that there was little hope for her. He wouldn't say that, of course, Dr. Koenig being famous for his aggressive, innovative techniques, but also for his utter refusal to relent, no matter the circumstance.

June's case was compelling, she was told by a resident, because the tumor in her stomach had insinuated itself in a manner rarely seen. She asked how and the young doctor told her, with unintended poetry, *Like fingers in a jar.* Eventually the cancer would spread to the other organs, but during the initial examination Dr. Koenig told her they would succeed, that they would first excise certain sections and then use other experimental regimens, some brand-new, and despite what she'd first seen in his eyes she very quickly came to believe him.

"You will realize I'm very greedy about life," he said to her, in his stripped, weary baritone. "It's life or nothing."

For a time June was a model patient, and though not trying to be she became perhaps his "favorite," a special case even among his special cases, a status she sensed whenever she had to stay a few days in the hospital, by how frequently his residents dropped in on her and wished to hear of her condition and even any complaints, none of which she ever expressed. She placed herself at his disposal, completely, never declining or even hesitating when he would request that she undergo yet another uncomfortable or painful procedure or submit to a new battery of tests. They drew blood from her as if from a tap. Of course she was encouraged by his doggedness, his decision to operate even when others believed it was no use, his aggressive regimens of radiation and then his constant calibrations of medicines, until one day, during a weeklong hospital stay, by then every strand of her lustrous black hair gone and her bones droning with a pain that was insidiously alive and the veins in her arms as brittle and ruined as Roman aqueducts and the right half of her back angrily stippled with an outbreak of shingles, June at last said no to a minor request by a resident to have an umpteenth CAT scan, for which she would have to drink a foul, metallic-tasting shake. The resident, a very smooth-shaven and bespectacled Pakistani fellow, had not quite heard her, or else believed that he had heard her assent, and ordered the nurse to prepare the concoction, to which June again said no, this time louder, and the young doctor paused for a moment before leaving her room without another word. Soon Dr. Koenig appeared at the foot of her bed with his hands splayed out as if he were a wounded suitor. His eyebrows, bushy and graying, were wilted with strain. He seemed already to know what she was going to say. Still, he quietly asked her what was the matter. "Has something gone wrong?" June shook her head. "Are you terribly uncomfortable? Are you suffering? We can address this."

"That isn't it."

She was in fact suffering, but as yet still only in the corporeal sense. Her mind, she felt, was still sharp, and steely. It could still see each moment from every side. "Then I don't understand, June. Why must you do this? Why thwart our efforts? You must appreciate how far we've come already."

"Of course I do. You're magnificent. Everyone here has been magnificent."

"Then let's keep on!" he said. She could tell he'd registered her appreciation by his rolling over it. More than anything else, she liked Koenig for this feature of his character.

"You should have a patient who wants to be here fully. There are dozens waiting, I know."

"We'll care for them in time. We are focusing on you now. We choose our patients carefully and we give everything we have and we don't let go from day one."

"But you knew then."

"What? What did I know?" Koenig gasped, waving his hands.

"That I was already dead."

"So aren't we all!" he shouted angrily. The sudden flash of his feeling animated her and deliciously, if only momentarily, suspended the pain. "We cheat time, June, all of us, whether we're ill or not. Most of us only realize it when we're not well. But I don't believe we have a certain allotment at birth or one fixed by fate or anything else. We can extend time for anyone who wants it. And I don't want to hear about 'quality of life' or some such. *Life* is quality of life. If you can take nourishment and communicate and conceive of tomorrow, then another day is riches enough."

He spoke as he always did, with the ample authority and startling egoism of a celebrated healer, and yet through his conviction and bombast June could discern the doctor as a less than invincible figure, perhaps a boy whose mother died young, or whose sibling grew up chronically sick, someone who had witnessed a wretched dwindling and instead of abiding the measured response or swift act of mercy had become an unceasing forge of the realm.

"I won't disagree with you," she said to him. "I can't."

"Then don't give up now!"

"I'm not giving up."

"You will be if you leave. We're at a critical moment. We're on the cusp of succeeding, but it's perilous, and there's no room at all for hesitation. Even the short time we've wasted this afternoon can make a difference. I believe this. Now, I'm going to call my resident back in here and you're going to allow him to do his work. Do you agree that this should happen? I know you do. You do, yes? Today and tomorrow and the next day."

He had held her by the points of her shoulders and his gaze was not so much searching as it was rallying her. Or attempting to. But even the gentle cupping of his hands felt as if he were abrading her skin, this wildfire skittering over her back and neck, and she could barely keep from grimacing. It was not that she meant to deceive him, though she knew she would be doing so. After he had gone and before the young resident could return, she dressed herself quickly and wrote Koenig a note:

My whole life I cheated days. Please give the rest of mine to some-one else.

How she wished that she could take that note back. Somehow her condition improved dramatically after she left the hospital, her body lithe and loose and vigorous, but since the day she met Clines her condition had deteriorated. She was now more and more dependent on the painkillers Koenig had had his resident deliver to her, her mind feeling sharpest when she was counting up the pills and vials (which was a way of counting time), as well as the stack of forward-dated prescriptions he'd insisted on giving her. The last few reached well into the following year, and sometimes she shuffled through them with gratitude like they were unanticipated greeting cards, salutations from a future telling of a very different longevity.

As the car crossed the bridge to New Jersey, the southerly view of the evening lights of the metropolis glinted beckoningly, showing a path to the harbor and then the open sea. She was always somewhat fearful of the water, having never learned how to swim, yet now she imagined pulling herself through the black river, her limbs motoring in purposeful rhythm, every muscle singing with heat, her body once again bristling. She saw a young Nicholas swimming beside her, instinctively trusting her to lead them and staying close, keeping up when she pushed the pace, then tucking himself against her belly to rest. She placed her hand on her stomach now and it was as if she felt him there instead of the huge dense egg of the tumor that had taken her over and had spread itself in every part. When she was pregnant with him she was terribly sick, not just in the first weeks or in the morning but constantly and nearly right up to the birthing, a welling, tormenting nausea that reached high in her throat and kept her from eating much and nurtured the horrid idea that if she were to fall so ill as to have to terminate, then let it be. When the nurse placed him on her chest after she awoke from the emergency Caesarean (he wouldn't come out, his head too large) she'd actually gagged through her tears of wonderment—she only found out later that sickness often came after anesthesia—and the first words she said to him were, *I'm sorry.*

She was sorry, was she not?

They sometimes took the ride over like this to Palisades Park when he was in elementary school; they lived in Morningside Heights then and it was easier to cross the bridge than go downtown to Thirty-second Street for an early-Sunday dinner at a Korean restaurant. They would take a taxi because she never learned how to drive, and on the rides home with a small bag of groceries between them Nicholas would fall asleep while half-holding his nose because of the sewer-smelling radish *kimchee* and dried cuttlefish beside him. They had gone only because he kept asking about where she was from and what other Korean people were like and she figured the ready setting of an eatery would do the trick. But once there her own spirit would gradually dampen and sour and Nicholas would hardly say anything and would pick at his quarter-eaten bowl of *bibim bap*. She'd harangue him to finish and maybe snap at a waitress and then they'd buy some foodstuffs she'd mostly let rot before getting around to preparing. Still, they went a half-dozen times, and then no more, June herself accepting that whatever nostalgia she was hoping to conjure for him had long been obliterated and that there was nothing she wished to latch on to. Nicholas didn't complain, but on their last time going over he asked if he could stay in the taxi while she shopped and even ate. She told him of course he couldn't and asked him why he would want to do such a thing and he replied, *Because you get so angry when we're there*. As the taxi approached the restaurant where they usually ate, June instructed the driver to take them back to Morningside Heights. At home she made them peanut butter sandwiches and after they ate he went to his room to read, as if nothing at all had happened. He was a sensitive boy but every once in a while he could exercise a remarkable composure: that perfect distance he could keep, an exquisite self-balance and suspension.

Was the letter from the antiquities dealer in London evidence that during his years away he had moderated the extremes of his person? Or was it proof of a more frightening mastery? That he had decided to work in the antiques business, of all things, made her think she hadn't damaged him. He certainly enjoyed the shop. After school

Nicholas would contentedly spend the hours until dinner polishing up the inventory with an oiled rag, or else fix things, like replacing the drawer slides of a desk. He was naturally handy without really trying, merely needing to inspect the mechanism quickly to understand what was missing, or see how an operation was going wrong. Besides furniture he could also fix mantel clocks and music boxes and really anything that wasn't too far gone or required a special tool or parts. He possessed a certain empathy for machines that in a different circumstance could have found him engineering bridges or as some gifted mechanic; but she never encouraged him and sometimes even playfully taunted him for his old jeweler's posture as he crouched beneath the spotlight of a work lamp, saying a boy should take in the fresh air (even of New York City) and run and leap and stomp on things, live with his feet and legs more than his head and hands. That she could ever utter such a thing seemed monstrous to her now, but back then it was just the two of them in the world and her focus on him alternated between being unrelentingly sharp and then dialed so wide that the boy was but a ripple in the broad field of her vision, a mark of pale, this faint smudge of her blood.

He kept mostly to the back of the shop, and whenever a customer entered he would say hello with warmth but then discreetly vanish to the tiny back workroom or the basement. The customers would invariably comment on what an attractive, well-mannered boy he was, and June could then engage in a conversation about children or parenting that would elide nicely into a talk of objects for the home. She was not a natural saleswoman or a person given to charming others, but she could sense an opening instantly and couldn't help but lodge herself in any breach. She was dogged and opportunistic, and commerce was mere play compared to what she could resolve herself to do. Perhaps it was pure coincidence that the shop did well on the days Nicholas chose to hang out, but she knew for certain that his presence helped her, that it was a necessary preface to a story she could never begin telling on her own, and for this reason she was always slightly cruel and tried to compel him to be elsewhere, not wanting to feel guilty about using him to good advantage, which she often did.

But Nicholas had not appeared to mind—he certainly never said so—though June now thought that through those early years of her shop on Lexington he must have learned something about the unhappy patterns a son and mother could fall into. When the last customer had departed and she shut off the lights of the display window, Nicholas would emerge from wherever he was working and she would say, "The mole-boy appears," sweetly enough but with an edge more aptly directed at a peer or friend than a reticent boy of nine. He would answer her with his eyes closed and a wide, exaggerated smile, freeze in his position as if stricken with palsy, and then fitfully hop away. They played at it together, but it was a strained comedy. Back at the apartment he would do his homework or make drawings while she fixed dinner (always something simple, something basic enough that it was hardly real cooking, like rice and steamed fish, or elbow macaroni with jarred sauce) and nothing would be off, but sometimes in the middle of the night she awoke to the sounds of gasping coming from his room; the first time she nearly tripped while getting up too fast, afraid that he was choking, but it turned out, then and other times, that he was crying in his sleep. He wasn't deeply distressed—it was the softest crying, self-muffled, if that was possible—and although it would have been the simplest thing to wake and comfort him, she inexplicably stood over him in the dark, staring at his racked mouth and the tight, quivering shrug of his shoulders, and it took everything in her to renounce the thought that here was a boy she would have to carry about forever.

How very different things had come to be.

"I must advise you again, Mrs. Singer," Clines said to her now, not looking at her in the mirror. He had put on glasses for driving. "You should not be bothering anymore with this man Brennan."

"Yes."

"We should be in Rome by now, looking for your son instead."

"We will fly out tomorrow night. There won't be any more changes."

"I'm sorry to be so frank, Mrs. Singer, but you're in no condition to delay."

"Then you can always drive a little faster, Mr. Clines."

She could see his lips tightening in the rearview mirror. He didn't want to drive back over to New Jersey, saying it was a waste of time, but in fact she could see it was because he was also fearful of Hector. But he did as she acidly suggested, accelerating slightly for a stretch before eventually easing back to his unusually slow driving style; he was indeed an older man than he wished to let on, and she could see him straining in the twilight to see the road. He had asked that she sit in the back because of a chest cold that he said he didn't want to transmit to her. But this was primarily an excuse. Clines, she had come to see, was a terribly formal sort; he was someone who liked the comfort of having a designated station for himself, a place. This was fine by her, for she knew exactly where she stood with him without much discussion. Discussion for her had become a hardship. She had a purpose and Clines was aiding her and there was little else to talk about.

Nicholas, of course, had always been especially subject to her commands; even as a teen he couldn't help but follow her wishes without argument. At some point she would find herself being particularly unreasonable, sometimes squarely merciless, hoping he would argue or talk back sharply to her, but he never did, merely assenting or else drifting off to another room of the apartment. Was it his character to be so compliant, or had she also formed him with those trenchant comments at the shop? Like any mother she sometimes found herself furious with him, for nothing other than his being a child. Later on the reasons would be different. In any case, she couldn't help herself and probably Nicholas couldn't either and after he left home and had been gone for months and neither written nor telephoned she wondered whether an objective observer would determine that on balance she had been the most damaging presence in his life.

That he had gone on so readily to a career of larceny seemed confirmation enough of the notion. Clines reminded her several times that these were still alleged crimes, but she knew the truth had already been long determined. For Nicholas had a history of stealing. It was not a problem before, though in truth only because he was never caught. From the time he was seven he filched candies and gum from the news shop and playing cards and felt markers from Woolworth's, and later on, when he was in middle school, he stole record albums and books from the public libraries, expensive clothes from department stores. She periodically discovered a cache tucked deep in his closet or between the mattress and box spring of his bed, once finding three brand-new pairs of designer blue jeans, another time two ski parkas, none in his size. She supposed he sold them, or gave them away to his friends. It didn't surprise her that he was never caught: he was a smart, charming, gentle-faced boy who walked easefully into rooms and could still look you in the eye and say hello while fitted with whatever goods he'd tucked beneath his shirt.

What was remarkable was that June never confronted him. Not a reprimand, not even an innocent question or comment about the loot. She would put the stuff back in its place, as if she'd found a pornographic magazine. But why? It wasn't as if stealing were a typical boyhood stage to be outgrown. She could have spanked him the very first time, on finding a dozen packs of various gums stuffed into a sock, harshly punished or scared him into never doing such a thing again. But it seemed that each time she found a new stash she'd somehow discount the previous instances, see them as isolated, even accidental, cases in which Nicholas simply forgot to pay; she'd done that herself a couple of times, once resulting in an embarrassing frisking at a store entrance by the security guard. Nicholas was naturally preoccupied, yes, that was a problem, but the truth of the matter was that June began to look almost expectantly to the stealing. She would go into his room whenever he wasn't there, half-hoping to find something. Of course whenever she did she felt frustration and bewilderment, but then a kind of dreadful curiosity about the moment itself took hold of her such that the larger, more disturbing picture dissipated and she focused too discreetly on the act; she would wonder about the particular circumstances of its moment, the part of the store he was in, if he had been nearly caught and his heart had raced terribly, and then what he was thinking, or not thinking, the faces of his compulsion.

Once she had followed him, seeing him by chance walking by on the other side of the avenue from her shop. He was thirteen at the time. She quickly closed the shop and trailed him until he went into a record store. She peered in at him from the sidewalk, making sure he couldn't see her by standing at the edge of the large display window. She was terribly anxious; she couldn't see how he could possibly take anything: as it was a warm summer day, he was wearing the lightest clothing, just a polo shirt and gym shorts. He browsed albums, lingered at a bin of tapes, a poster rack, and then, as if idly picking a leaf from a shrub while strolling by, he took an album and walked toward the entrance, which was right in front of the cashier. He was almost outside when the man stopped him and pointed to the album in his hands. Nicholas seemed to wake from a trance—and not in the least like he was pretending—and after apologies and a shared laugh, he paid for the record and left. By chance he departed in the opposite direction from her and when she caught sight of him again around the corner he was discarding the new album, paper sack and all, into a steel mesh trash can. Then he reached behind himself, lifting his shirt, and from the band of his shorts pulled out an orange-colored eight-track tape. He seemed genuinely pleased, letting the light play off the clear plastic wrapping like it was a prismatic mirror, regarding the lettering closely front and back, but then with a chilling casualness he dropped it into the trash as well.

Afterward Nicholas headed south on Third Avenue, his hands calm and empty. Was he on to a usual string of unsuspecting shops? His skinny form bobbed and then finally disappeared on the crowded lunchtime sidewalk. She tried following him but lost his trail. But she had to halt, too, because she was caught squarely by the feeling of her chest tightening around the ingot of a sudden pleasing fascination; for it was the picture of his surface equanimity, his self-mastery, that she was so gratified to see, to watch him exert himself upon the world, when the rest of the time he seemed too willingly subject to its turns. He was more like herself than she had guessed; for even though she held no illusions of being an admirable person, she had always been capable of making her way, no matter what.

"Do you have any children, Mr. Clines? Excuse me, I don't even know if you have a wife."

"My wife died many years ago."

"I'm sorry."

"I have a daughter," Clines said. They were stopped at a long traffic light. "She lives in Philadelphia."

"What does she do?"

"She and her husband are both clerks in a grocery store."

"Do they have children?"

"No."

He was clearly hesitant to continue, but for some reason June felt like querying him.

"You must see her fairly often, being nearby."

"Only sometimes."

"On holidays?"

"No, not on holidays," he said, clearing his throat. The light changed and they proceeded for a few blocks in quiet. He was driving quite stiffly, with both hands firmly on the steering wheel, his head locked straight ahead. She was ready to drop the subject but then he said, "We haven't spoken in some time."

"May I ask why?"

"I don't know why, Mrs. Singer. Nothing bad ever happened between us. There's no animosity. In fact, I would like to leave her with a decent amount of money, whenever I go. If I didn't have her, I'd probably have retired already. But she would never know that. I would have to say we didn't talk too much. Even when she was young."

"Do you think you should have?"

"I doubt it would have made a difference. Neither of us is very talkative. But I truly don't know," he said, with a sudden heaviness that revealed his full age. "Do you think you should have done something differently?"

"With Nicholas? No. I don't think so."

Clines didn't say anything else, and although she knew she was likely sounding defensive or callous she let him drive on without explaining herself further. For she had indeed offered Nicholas everything she had been capable of giving, and more, even as she knew by the time he was three that it might somehow never be enough. Perhaps no matter what you did you could never love someone out of his nature, love someone out of his fate. Love, she had come to believe, had no such power.

Was his nature hers? In the antiques business she had tried to be honest whenever possible, though with old furniture and objets d'art it was difficult to follow completely ethical practices. It was a structurally unreliable enterprise, if not, at times, downright chicane. For one could never really be sure of the provenance of a piece, no matter what anyone told you, whether well intentioned or not. She herself, especially in the beginning, had often paid more than she should have, from dealers and "original owners" alike. Certainly there were markers that you could look to on a piece of furniture—say, details of the drawer construction, the quality of the leg fluting—but ultimately those things could be contrived. Fakes abounded in every era, most of them poorly done, but there were always a few masterfully executed works. Of course, for the vast majority of non-auction-house items there was only the experienced eye and what one could say about them without simply lying or even sounding like a prevaricator. Authenticity ultimately lay in the story you could tell, a tale most effective when it was at once fanciful and mundane. You had to offer differing scales, unlikely modulations, though all based upon the firmest-seeming foundation. It turned out she was quite good at this, her upright bearing and careful, precise way of speaking enjoining her clients to trust both her and their own taste implicitly, and if over the years there were a few instances of suspicion or unhappiness, she never had any problems with the final disposition concerning anything she had sold.

Of course when she was young June had stolen things outright, too, but it had been a matter of survival, plain and simple, as with the old farmer's blanket, and dozens of other items and foodstuffs during the war and its aftermath. And yet, even after she was settled in the orphanage, where there was plenty of food, where there was shelter and safety, there were instances when she would steal things from the other children that could hardly benefit her, and only gave them great unhappiness. Certain sentimental objects drew her eye: a boy's prized marbles. A girl's silver bracelet, which had once been her mother's. A particularly egregious theft had been of a flimsy, creased photograph of a family, which she'd lifted from the back pocket of a sleeping boy. She had nothing against the boy, in fact he was sometimes friendly to her, while most of the others avoided her. Yet she waited three full days before giving it back. She watched him search frantically through his few things, comb the play yard and classrooms on his hands and knees, then could hear him crying one afternoon in the boys' quarters, blubbering to his dead parents, asking their forgiveness for losing his only image of them. She felt immense in her cruelty, but she told herself, too, that he ought to accept that they were forever gone, that he was actually cursed by having the picture, that he merely weakened himself by examining it all the time and depending on it as though it were his sole source of strength and faith.

No one found out she had taken the photograph, nor about any of the things she'd stolen from the other children. She was suspected, naturally, but nothing was ever proven. The only time she was discovered was when she returned something she openly admitted to taking. It was a book of Sylvie Tanner's, one that she always kept on the stool that served as a nightstand beside her bed. June had asked her if she could be their helper, and perhaps because of her reputation as a problem child Sylvie had agreed, assigning June the task of sweeping and dusting their cottage as part of her orphanage chores. There were always other books in the stack, books borrowed for Sylvie every other week by Hector Brennan from the Eighth Army base in Seoul, but those would change and rotate, while the slim volume would remain, the only book, besides the Bible and a hymnal, they had brought with them from the States.

June asked her to read it aloud to her but Sylvie said it was not like poetry, or a children's story, something to be enjoyed; it was an account of war, and she said that June didn't need to read about it. But June persisted, if only because she saw how Sylvie handled the book, with indeed a kind of enjoyment, a certain somber savoring. June would peer inside the bedroom when she was supposed to be dusting, or creep behind to the plot in back, and there would be Sylvie with the faded-blue cloth-covered book in her clutch, often not even reading it, more keeping it close, her form characteristically folded up in a chair with it tucked against her chest, or propped beneath her chin. Whenever June was in the house alone she would steal into the room and try to read a page. It was difficult for her—she was otherwise reading mostly English primers then, though easily—and she realized it would take her hours simply to get past the preface and initial pages of historical background.

So she took it, reading it in her spare late-afternoon hours in the cover of a natural bunker amid the hillside brush and weeds. When the account of the battle began the writing became clearer to her, the words sharpening and crystallizing and soon enough disappearing, the reading coming to her as easily as if she were viewing a picture show in a theater. What the author saw of the battle was horrifying, the grinding carnage of the cavalry charges, of the artillery rounds and chain-gun shot, the piles of sundered, crushed bodies and scattered human remains, the veritable rivers of blood, but it was in fact the days following that haunted him most. It was the unspeakable fate of the wounded that haunted him, their privation and "perfect torture" because of the grave lack of food and water and medical supplies, most of the caretakers being laypersons like himself or the local townsfolk, all willing to aid the survivors but frightfully incapable of doing so. All the churches in the area surrounding the town called Solferino were filled with miserable soldiers, the air of their sanctuaries fouled with the stench of the dead and dying.

After a few days Sylvie Tanner asked her if she'd seen the book. June shook her head, wondering aloud if Hector had taken it back by accident with some other books to the base library. It was an uncharacteristically poor lie from her, as if she intended to make obvious her guilt, but it worked, in that Sylvie told her that if they could somehow get it back from the base, she might be willing to read and discuss it with her. The next day June slipped off to the half-buried rifle-shell canister where she'd hidden it, brushed the dirt from its cover, and took it back to the cottage. Reverend Tanner recognized the book in her hands and asked what she was doing with it but Sylvie came in then from the small rear plot and exclaimed, "Oh, you sweet dear, you got it back for me!"

Yet she still refused to read the book with June, who then begged her if they might read others together regularly, after her chores. Sylvie hesitated, surely worried about showing even more favor to her, but eventually agreed when confronted with what June could contrive of her face, when she required, blunting its hardened aspects to the rounded eyes and tender cheeks of any other girl her age, back to the waif she should have been. After June quickly completed the cleaning they'd sit up in her bed and read aloud to each other until it was time to join everyone else in preparing the tables for supper. June found that her usually constant feeling of hunger would magically subside— after the war and for the rest of her life it would never quite disappear (she was like a stray cat that way, always willing to eat, no matter the state of her belly, of course except now)—and she would have stayed with Mrs. Tanner all night if she let her, losing herself in the warm tuck of her side.

Still, June kept reading the book to herself whenever she had a free moment; she couldn't help but imagine that it was Sylvie Tanner who was the witness and author of the book, as if she had seen with her own eyes the fierce fighting and wretched wounded in the churches, had toiled to alleviate the suffering without the aid of medicines or clean bandages or food. There was an inscription on the book's title page, written in a handsome, flowing, old-fashioned hand, *To our steadfast daughter. May you be an angel of mercy,* and it was Nicholas who once asked June, when he was seven or eight, what a "steadfast" person was, holding the very book in his hands. The blue cloth cover had been long burned away and the binding was crackly and exposed, though the inner pages were intact. Because of its fragile condition she kept it in a large jewelry box on her bureau.

She heard herself tell him what Sylvie had said to her, almost to the word: "Someone who is firm in his person and beliefs, who brings to the world a constant heart."

"Are you an angel of mercy?"

"I would like to be one," she told him, realizing that of course he assumed the inscription was meant for her. "We should all try to be."

He nodded, then gingerly placed the book back in the jewelry box. Sometimes she could tell that he had come in and inspected the book, tiny bits of charred paper left on the bureau top, and though she would have preferred his not handling it, and then taking such an interest in its harrowing, difficult content, she grew to see the activity as a strange kind of intimacy between them, a way to let him peek into her life and past without her having to tell him a thing. Then one day, when he was older, in sixth grade, he came into the kitchen with the book and asked whose it really was—he'd realized the illogic of the English inscription, when her parents had been Korean—and she told him it was a gift from a friend. A woman who had helped her when she was a girl but who died after the war.

"What was her name?"

She told him and though it could mean nothing to him the name seemed to spark his imagination as might a character in a story. "What happened to her?"

"There was an accident."

"What kind of accident?"

"A fire."

He didn't say anything to this. Nicholas, always very mindful of her emotions, did not push her on it. They sat in silence for a moment, and then he said, "Is that where you met my father?"

"Where?"

"Solferino."

She shook her head. "I've not been there."

"Do you know what's there now?"

"I imagine there's a small town. I know there's a church."

"I bet it's a special one," Nicholas said. "You think it's like in the book we have on the Vatican? Full of fancy stuff, like gold statues and paintings?"

"You mean great treasure and riches? Maybe so."

"We should go someday," he said excitedly. "Don't you think?"

"Yes, we should," she answered, even if she had always imagined visiting the place by herself.

"Could this be mine?" he asked her hopefully, holding the book.

"I don't know if I can give it up just yet," she replied. "Even to you." But the expression on his face dampened and she quickly offered: "But how about I write something to you in it. How's that?"

"Okay."

He quickly ran and retrieved a pen for her and opened the book to the page with the inscription. She was composing her thoughts on what to write when the phone rang; on the other end was a wholesale dealer whose call she had been awaiting. Nicholas waited patiently but when she hung up she had to leave right away to get downtown, to inspect an estate lot and make a compelling bid before any others got there. Nicholas stayed home. When she returned a few hours later (having purchased most all of the estate) he had fallen asleep in front of the television, a half-eaten salami sandwich he had fixed for himself on his lap, and she gently roused and walked him to his bed.

Only many years later, after putting him in a taxi to the airport for his big trip, did she suddenly remember that she had completely forgotten to inscribe the book for him that day. She may not have even looked at it since then. When she got back to the apartment, she went directly to her bedroom and saw that the book was gone from the jewelry box. She searched beneath the bed, in her closet, on the living room shelves, and then in Nicholas's room, still full of his things, poring through piles of his sketchbooks and records and posters (sure signs, she thought later, that he had planned to come back), but after going through everything and the rest of the apartment she was certain that he had taken it with him.

How could he? At first she was shot through by pangs of confusion, then hurt, wounded as she was by his meager regard for her feelings, by his callous act of taking perhaps the one physical object in her life that had value. Her fury the next day reached a pitch so sharp that she pictured an accident in whatever city he was in, his bus rolling over, his hostel on fire, such that he would desperately try to phone her. But just as quickly a terrible guilt overcame her and she convinced herself that it was his own sentimentality, mixed up with his particular kind of secrecy and larcenous need, that had compelled him, and she came to see it instead as a kind of loving act, as though he'd stolen in and snipped a lock of her hair while she slept. Could it be that this was where her son had gone to hide? Her heart raced with the possibility. Her mind was beginning to fail along with her body, but she couldn't believe she hadn't thought of it before. They surely must go to Solferino, too. She imagined Nicholas sitting at an outdoor café, waiting for her. Clines wouldn't like it, but she would explain to him on the plane that they could only stay briefly in Rome, long enough to rest a few hours before renting a car and driving north.

A car horn wailed behind them, the driver leaning on it an extra few beats in a show of contempt for Clines's slow driving; he'd been honked at several times already on the trip over from Manhattan. The car behind them came alongside and the driver gave Clines the finger and then cut aggressively in front of him, just grazing their bumper.

Clines swerved, losing control for an instant, the steering wheel playing jerkily as the car fishtailed wildly. June was sure they were going to crash. Somehow he steadied it but now he was driving even slower than before and when another car started honking he left the roadway at the next exit, even though it wasn't theirs. He drove for a few blocks before stopping, saying he needed to check his map, though it was clear he was shaken, his temple damp with perspiration.

June held the side of her head and face; she'd been knocked lightly against the side window of the sedan but in her condition it was as if she'd been struck with a rod, her cheek feeling like a cracked glass. And suddenly a nausea was welling up from her belly, rising and pushing against her lungs, up into her throat.

"Unlock the doors," she said weakly.

"It's okay, Mrs. Singer. We'll be moving on now."

"Please do it!"

The power locks jumped and she practically leaped out of the car, stumbling a few feet away from the door and falling on one knee in a weedy patch of the shoulder. She vomited very little, just the small mug of roasted barley tea she'd made herself before Clines picked her up, her spit tasting metallic and bilious; she was glad it was dark enough that she couldn't make out the blood in the grass. She'd begun flushing the toilet at her shop with her eyes closed after she got sick in it, simply to avoid that wash of bright, wild color.

"You're not well enough for this, Mrs. Singer," Clines said, helping her to her feet. "Let me take you back to your shop now."

"No," she said firmly, but then had to lean into him to steady herself. His clothes smelled strongly of mildew and breath mints and she couldn't help but gag and heave again, though there was nothing left in her to come out. She wiped the spittle from the corners of her mouth.

"We're not going back yet, do you hear me?"

He nodded and helped her back into the car. He still seemed un-settled from the near accident and perhaps from her vehemence, too, and when they passed a diner she told him to turn around and he didn't even ask why. Once he parked she asked him to leave her in the car for a while and go inside and have a coffee, and when he said he was fine she was sharp-voiced again and he sullenly trooped inside and sat on a stool at the counter.

She waited for him to order from the waitress before taking out a small black kit from her purse. Inside were the syringes and cotton balls and vials of alcohol and morphine that she'd received from Koenig's resident. The needle was short and tiny, as fine as a filament, the kind diabetics and addicts used, but it was important, the resident said, to insert and pull it straight out, to avoid bruising or causing herself more pain than necessary. But now, on her own, in this condi-tion, her hands shook with the screeching pains in her lower back and belly and she could hardly unscrew the bottle of disinfectant, and then jabbed her finger trying to push the point through the rubber cap of the morphine vial. She gave up, simply chewing two more bitter pills instead; she gagged on them but forced herself to keep them down. She tossed the needle into the kit; its dwarf scale somehow scared her. She was afraid that if she kept trying, one of her visions would appear along with it, that child in a perfectly sized doctor's white coat whose mouth was too gaping and wide for his shrunken old-young face. Was it Nicholas? Was it her brother, Ji-Young? Koenig had warned her that she might experience hallucinations, and this one and others were accruing to her of late, apparitions that said little or nothing and seemed only to be awaiting her. She found herself speaking half-sentences to them, faint mutterings, beseeching them in a kindly, al-most sycophantic tone she had never used for anyone, hoping that they might not wrench her away.

Please let me find him first, is what she said now, her head drifting down as she lay across the backseat. They were still heeding her and she believed that if she could endure their massing they might somehow forget about her, or else count her a kindred specter, let her soon join their number lingering in the ashen underworld gloom.

TEN

DORA, HE THOUGHT, was more than all right. It wasn't yet evening and Hector had just showered and was shaving and she was in his kitchen fixing them a dinner of pan-fried blade steaks and roast potatoes, singing an old tune his mother used to croon in her throaty, impure voice but that Dora intoned like a just-born nightingale:

> From this happy day,
> No . . . more . . . blue . . . songs . . .

Her voice was fizzy and girlish and despite the patent optimism of lyrics that would have ordinarily made him instantly contract into a leaden die he was instead humming along with her in a dusky key. His sound wasn't half bad. When was the last time he had let his voice be an instrument? He was raised in a family that valued singing, and he had performed, briefly, in the church choir, being one of its youngest boys. He showed enough talent to feature in a few solos and liked music well enough but in fact he was drawn just as much by the bodily practice of it, the used-up sensation he would get in his throat and chest after the hours of rehearsal, that blood-warmed exhaustion; but he had to quit it after the priest one day asked him to sing privately in the vestry, the florid-cheeked old man kneeling before him and tightly embracing his legs and whispering into his chest that he was a right gift from God. *You're magnificence, dear boy*, the padre said, with tears in his eyes. *You're a thing eternal.* The choir leader opened the vestry door at that moment and at the next rehearsal she made him promise not to return. After that he only went to mass with his mother, and it was the last of his singing, formal and not, this nearly fifty years past.

He wiped his face of remaining streaks of lather and dabbed on some aftershave he'd just bought himself, and combed his close-cropped hair. Dora had cut it before his shower and it seemed darker and thicker than he remembered it and with the music of her woman's voice and the smell of real cooking it seemed he was now in a wholly different life. There were already noticeable changes in his apartment. She was good about not leaving anything obvious of hers behind, such as jewelry or clothing, after he'd made it known that he preferred her not to. And yet there were clearly indications that he was no longer living by himself; the bed was made differently in the morning, with tighter corners than he ever bothered to make; his toothbrush and toothpaste were put away inside the medicine chest; his three pairs of shoes lined up neatly beside the door; and with each night she spent, another diaphanous layer of her presence seemed to settle upon him and everything else, this fine dust of her that he could almost taste on a spoon, on the rim of a glass.

For nearly two weeks now Dora had been consorting with him and they had already gone past the point in time he would have normally nudged her on her way. She was joyful and effortlessly kind to him and like a revelation these simple facts made him joyful, too, or something close to it, and he thought he should do whatever it took to preserve the feeling. He had come to appreciate her surprisingly optimistic spirit—who at Smitty's ever spoke of life actual years hence, about such a thing as traveling, or taking a college class at night? Even if her cheerfulness were more a late-rigged buttress than any natural, inner girding, the product of one of the self-help books she always carried in her handbag, he certainly didn't think less of her for it. So what if she believed that advice from a book could work. So what if she held herself to a standard far beyond any possibility of attainment. Isn't that what every normal, decent person did? Maybe she drank too much, like the rest of them, but she was dogged in pursuing her interests, this better idea of herself, paddling furiously even if she wasn't yet getting too far.

As a girl she was accidentally shot by her stepfather during a duck hunt—he was a drinker, too, a small-town Ohio banker with a temper as unknowable as heat lightning who sometimes made visitations to Dora or her sister late at night—and she told Hector that from time to time she was sure she could still feel the pellets the surgeon had to leave undisturbed in her neck and back for fear of paralyzing her; like an echo the pain was both angular and diffuse, and she suffered it all her life, though these days she said it arrived with certain kinds of weather, with the tides and the moon, with her female cycle, which had just gone intermittent.

She had been fine since spending time with him but just last night she was whimpering in her sleep and Hector could not wake her and in a ghoulish state with her eyes open wide but unseeing she'd crawled on top of him and moved her hips until he felt her wetness painting him. He already loved the ready pliancy of her flesh, the faintly damp hand of her skin, the confected, buttery odor of her scalp and hair, all these combining in an insuperable womanly embrace, which was to him a true summons to rest. To sleep. With her racked expression he wasn't sure if he ought to comply but after he did she slept the rare and peerless slumber of the gratified dead.

But he had not slept as deeply. Since hearing of June he was being hounded again by an old nightmare, the iron obstinacy of it like a railway spike fixed through his gut. The nightmare was not about June. Instead, still reigning in his thoughts was the sentinel of Sylvie Tanner, looming naked before him, perfectly alive and beautiful, her skin aglow with a pure unrivaled shimmer.

I'm too warm, she would say, and his heart would begin to skip out of time.

Please don't, he begged her.

Don't worry, she'd answer. *It's okay*. She would then scratch lightly at her shoulder, like she had an itch. But instead of simply scratching she would tuck her fingers beneath her fine skin and then, with no effort at all, no pain, peel it off as if it were a full-length glove. She'd do the same with the other arm, and then start in with her torso, pull it down with a terrible measure, down over her breasts, her belly, slowly skinning herself and revealing to him not blood and tissue but the charred ruins of her insides, all blackness and collapse.

He had awoken hugging Dora's legs, smothering his own face in her belly, as if to throttle himself in penance. She took his powerful grip for ardor and whispered that she ought to wash down there quickly but he only buried himself deeper and she let him, soon enough pulling and pushing him by his hair. He was more than glad; he wanted to be aligned with her good rhythms, to be her sightless, obliging implement. But could he devote himself to Dora, ongoing? Be good to her and adore her beyond his squalid little universe? He was almost certain he wanted to, and yet his fear of leaving her somehow in shambles ruled him, too, causing him to clam up in moments when he should have been sweetly generous, making him delay before meeting up with her, all of which, of course, only served to make her more unsure of herself than she was and seek his attentions all the more. Although she tried to hide her feelings he could see the welling anxiousness in her eyes, a grime of remorse freshly layering his heart whenever she peeped "It's fine!" when he showed up thirty minutes late at Smitty's, or said he had to get to work when he really didn't. It wasn't fine, not even close, it was rotten and cowardly and weak, and if such notions of his conduct hadn't bothered him in years, they were bothering him now.

Yesterday he had tried to take a first small step toward being a respectable mate. Dora had been worrying about his fight with Tick, not mentioning it directly but sighing and saying again how it scared her when he got into fights, that she never wanted to see him hurt. He didn't want to be hurt, either, not anymore, but it was giving-hurt that disturbed him most. Since the tussle with Tick he'd been thinking how pathetic it was for a fifty-five-year-old man to be so keen to mix it up, how sorry and shaming a picture, and then doubly so from the idea that Dora might have seen him that night standing over poor Tick, pummeling him monstrously and without pause. So at work he had roused Jung from his early-midday nap and told him they were going to drive to Teaneck, where Old Rudy lived. Jung naturally didn't want to go, saying he had just over half the money together, and that in fact he was going to go there himself next week after he gathered the rest he owed. Hector knew that "gathering" meant "betting," which would only end in more trouble, and like any comrade might he hoisted up the drowsy man by the collar and counseled him that partial payments were always accepted.

Jung cried out, "What, GI, you work for that old fuck now?"

"I'm working for you, friend."

"Fuck that, I don't want to go."

"We're going."

"Don't betray me, Rambo!"

"We're going now."

Jung saw that Hector was serious and relented, if unhappily, grabbing a fresh fifth of Chivas for the road. He cracked the seal and took
deep slugs from it while Hector drove his fancy Lincoln coupe, heading
them west on Route 4. Hector knew where the house was because he
had been there once or twice, years back, to see Old Rudy's daughter,
and only child, Winnie.

Winnie was just twenty-six at the time, a statuesque, buxom woman
with huge brown eyes and a sandbox of a voice and who was much
like her father in the seismic potential of her temper. She was volatile
and sexy and could be downright dangerous if she felt threatened or
wronged, a notorious instance of her local legend being that she'd
nearly gelded a two-timing boyfriend with a steak knife in a restaurant
bathroom. Hector was forty then, as primed and handsome as a fellow
ever was, fit for eternal bronze, and in a period of his life when he was
bedding women with an almost pathological zeal. For a long time after
leaving Korea he had isolated himself, existing, ironically, like some
toiling monk, erasing himself and all his memories of the orphanage and June and Sylvie Tanner with unceasing hard labors, and, of
course, drink. But eventually an oceanic surge of loneliness and desire
roiled him and once he let himself go it was as if he were diving through
endless, dense schools of women. He never meant to cause unhappiness or heartbreak but he couldn't bear anything but serial connections,
and with each union's demise it was their angry tears and shouts that
would echo in his head, causing him to move on only quicker.

In Winnie, Hector encountered someone as restive and inconstant
and craving as he; she had a reputation for wildness and a stout ap-
petite for sex, a nature that would have made Old Rudy proud if she
were his son but instead drove him mad. For a whole week of nights
she and Hector twisted furiously about each other in the sheets and it
might have been more had she not driven on this very road, swervy
and narrow, in a driving rain to pick him up at a job site out in Wayne.

She never showed up. He didn't much mind, figuring he'd see her the next night. He hitched a ride home with a coworker and the next morning he read about the accident in the newspaper, how a pickup truck skidded and flipped and somehow jumped the dividing median, landing squarely on an oncoming car. There was a photograph of the two vehicles with the article, the picture showing the entire front half of Winnie's white Camaro crumpled all the way back to the trunk. Hector saw it and threw up in his cereal. When he showed up at the closed-casket wake Old Rudy asked him if he was the man she was driving to meet. When he nodded somberly, Old Rudy grabbed him by the throat with both hands and held on a few scant moments short of snuffing him, which at that point Hector, despising himself all over again, hadn't minded, and hardly resisted, but a mourner who was an off-duty cop broke Old Rudy's grip and shoved Hector out the funeral home door.

He hadn't seen the man since the wake, and as Hector parked in front of the large whitewashed Tudor, he wondered if Old Rudy would even recognize him now, as sick as he purportedly was.

"This is your last chance to be my friend," Jung said, taking a last drink. "Let's go back and Sang-Mee will serve us food. I pay."

"Just give me the money now."

Jung took out a wad of bills from the inner pocket of his jacket and Hector immediately plucked it from his hand. While Hector counted it, Jung cried, "If I had that, I could make what I owe real quick! Easy winners coming up. How I'm going to make the other half now?"

"You'll figure it out."

"I'm gonna take it out of your pay."

"What, you're going to lay six dollars on the Mets? Let's go. And leave the bottle."

"I gotta stay here, GI. I hate seeing my money in somebody else's hand."

"Suit yourself," Hector told him, suddenly thinking that Jung should stay behind, being that there was a slight chance Old Rudy had somebody—or two—like Tick with him. "Maybe you should keep it running."

Jung's face flashed with alarm, and as Hector walked up the slate path he heard behind him the muted thump of the car's power locks. At the front door he rang the bell and a uniformed home nurse answered. Hector said his name, adding that he wasn't expected, and when the nurse appeared again she opened the door and led him upstairs. The house was dim and chilly, the narrow Tudor windows dingy with water stains, the air musty with old carpeting and the lingering gas of reheated food. The bedroom door was wide open and even from the hall Hector could smell the antiseptic sickroom smell, then beneath it the old-flesh smell, the piss-and-half-wiped-shit-and-fungal smell of someone spoiling from within, and he almost turned around then to leave when a raspy, cold-blooded voice weakly called out: "What are you waiting for?"

Hector stepped in the doorway. Old Rudy was sitting up in bed, dressed in a gray hospital gown, a tube for oxygen strapped about his face. Beside the bed stood an air tank in its caddy and a rolling cart topped full of medications. A plastic bag of urine lay on the floor, a line from it snaking up underneath the sheets. His bony shoulders showed through the wide neck of the gown and his once-sturdy flesh had receded, his skin stretched back onto his frame like an artificial hide. He was a menacing physical specimen, this jagged piece of Irish-German rock, and had only been known as Old Rudy because of his prematurely gray hair. But now almost all the hair was gone, leaving just the fins of his temples, the shiny, translucent skin showing through. For a moment Hector wondered what his father, Jackie, would have looked like had he lived to old age. Would his wide, ruddy cheeks have shrunken like this? Would his hand have withered even more?

Would he still insist that Hector stay at his side always, to be his best buttress and squire, to sing to in his larking, fanciful tenor?

"I figured you'd come around," Old Rudy said, having to take a rushed extra half-breath after every fourth or fifth word. "You should make your move, before I croak."

"I'm not here to hurt you."

"Oh yeah? What did you come for, then, to pay your respects? To wish me well?"

Hector showed him the thin brick of bills, saying it was from Jung and that the rest of it was coming but would be a little while. He placed the money on the rolling cart. Old Rudy didn't look at it, or seem at all to care, breathing out with some effort through his mouth like Hector had already begun pressing a board against his chest. Old Rudy groaned, "You think I'm worried about a few thousand bucks?"

"Seems like two weeks ago you were."

"Two weeks ago I was feeling like I wasn't going to die right away. Now even when the piss flows out of me I'm sucking wind."

"What's the matter with you?"

"Everything," he said, but before he could elaborate he was besieged by a long fit of nasty coughing. When he finally settled down, his eyes were bloodshot and glassy, and he gestured to a large lidded styrofoam cup on the cart. Hector gave it to him and Old Rudy took some sips through the straw, the drink the same color as the liquid in his catheter bag. He said wearily to Hector, "You don't look much different than you did."

"You're not seeing my insides."

"Fair enough," he said, handing back the cup to Hector. His voice was hollowed out from the coughing, and his body seemed emptied, too, husklike, its weight hardly pushing back into the pillows. "How long has it been?"

"Maybe fifteen years."

"You've been cleaning buildings since?"

"Other things, too. But pretty much."

"That's my doing, I guess."

"I could have moved on, if I wanted construction work."

"But you didn't."

"No," Hector said.

"How come?"

"I guess cleaning suits me, after all."

"Do you remember what she looked like?" He meant Winnie, of course, and Hector began to realize that the old man had simply wanted to talk about her, and had thus reached out to him in the only way he knew how.

"I do."

"You're the last person who spent any real time with her," Old Rudy said. "She and I just argued constantly. I stopped seeing her like everybody else did. Like you probably did."

"She was very beautiful."

"Was she? You're lucky. The last time I saw her, I had to see her in the morgue. There wasn't much left of her, above the chest. Really no face at all. You know how I identified her? She wore a ring of her mother's, a sapphire with diamonds around. When I think of her now I just try to see her hand. It was colorless and pale but it was perfect. Maybe they washed her, but there wasn't even any blood on it. You think they did that? You think they washed her?"

"I don't know," Hector answered, recalling that it was he who most often washed the corpses in the Graves Unit, as it never much bothered him, initially with a hose and then, if necessary, with a bucket and rag. In fact it had heartened him to see them come clean, even as brutally ruined as they were, to leave them again, at least in one small way, pristine. Maybe that was mercy enough.

The home nurse came in to take Old Rudy's vitals, before giving him a shot. Hector made to leave but Old Rudy waved at him to hold on. The nurse turned him over and swabbed a spot on his sunken rump and stuck him with a needle. He didn't flinch. She checked his air and refilled his drink cup and changed out his bag and told him it was time to rest.

"Rest for *what*?" he said.

"For whatever you want, honey," she answered, and then she left.

Old Rudy was fading fast and turned his head to Hector. "Tell your friend Jung not to bother with the rest. It doesn't matter anymore. I won't be around anyway."

"Okay," Hector said. "What about me?"

"What about you?"

"I want to be left alone," Hector said, realizing that for the first time in years he was meaning *we*, as in he and Dora. Which was why he would have never asked before. "That's all."

"What, you think that's up to me?"

"Isn't it?"

"You're crazy," Old Rudy said, almost smirking at him now. "Who the hell gets left alone?"

In the car, Jung had been ecstatic with what Old Rudy let pass, but then berated Hector for not trying to claw back the money they'd brought after the dying man fell asleep.

If anyone could glide through the flak, slip past all disturbances, it was the estimable Jung, but Hector had to wonder if he and Dora could ever do the same. Some did get left alone, didn't they? It seemed he and Dora had just broken into the clear. They were no more or less special than anyone else (well, maybe a little less), and maybe all it would take was for them to stay here inside Hector's little rooms, one-to-one, hidden from further view.

Dora called out that the steaks would be ready soon and Hector strode to the bedroom holding only a hand towel to cover himself. She wolf-whistled after him. He almost blushed, unaccustomed to being naked before her in the light. In the bedroom, courtesy of Dora, were freshly folded clothes on top of the rickety thrift-store bureau, his usual T-shirts, but he decided to look for something better in the closet, which she'd also organized, hanging up even his dungarees and his several shirts. He would put on a proper one for her, and maybe for himself, too. It wasn't half bad, to button oneself up in something clean and creased that didn't smell of the unreachable corners of a bar and his own sloughed skin. Of course he normally laundered his own clothes, but he never paid attention to which mini-box of soap he'd get from the dispenser, and he noticed that Dora slipped a small white sheet into the dryer of their commingled things and now he smelled of lilacs, or what he thought were lilacs, the same waft as from the narrow side yard of his family's house in Ilion, where his mother tended her flowering vines that exploded each spring in densely petaled ropes of white.

The smell of the steak and onions made his mouth water, and though Dora wouldn't have minded his sitting down to the meal in his undershirt and shorts he decided to put on clothes he hadn't worn in years. Maybe he would even take her out this Friday, somewhere other than Smitty's; there was a new place on Lemoine where younger people drank colorful cocktails at the polished metallic bar, and though he'd normally steer miles clear of such a place he thought Dora might get a kick out it, and maybe he would as well. Visit the yuppie zoo. When it came to drinking, the day of the week never mattered before but now it seemed wrong somehow to do the same things over and over again, Dora herself suddenly complaining anew about the lack of a women's room at Smitty's, where she'd otherwise peed happily.

In the closet he found a secondhand suit given to him some years ago when he did some custodial work at a thrift store, still in its black plastic coverall. He held the suit jacket to his nose and didn't like what he smelled but the trousers weren't as funky. He couldn't find a neck-tie or a decent belt but he had black shoes and when Hector stepped out into the kitchen Dora nearly dropped the spatula, as surprised as if he were a stranger come in from the street.

"My goodness, Hector," she said, catching her breath. "How you clean up!"

"You don't like?"

"Gosh, no, I like, I do. Come here." She touched his shirt collar and ran her hand down the pressed crease of the sleeve. "You could be a businessman, just home from the office."

"Yeah, but there's no money in these pockets."

"Let me see."

Dora put the spatula on the table and stepped around him and slipped her hands into his trouser pockets. Her fingertips raked gently at his thighs and then with one hand she massaged him in the soft parts but just when he was coming alive the smoke alarm went off in the short hallway to the bathroom. The steak in the pan. He was surprised there even was an alarm, and while he went to take out the battery, Dora hustled over and took the pan off the heat.

"Oh, now look!" She was wincing and getting a little panicked, frantically scraping up the onions that had stuck to the pan. "This al-ways happens in the end. Whatever I do. I ruin it."

"No you haven't."

"I have! Look at the meat. It's charcoal."

"Just one side. Anyhow, it can be good well-done."

"You're just saying that."

"Not so."

"You are."

"Okay, maybe I usually like it rare."

"Oh damn!" She nudged him in the chest and he pulled her to

him and they kissed long enough that their dinner was in danger of going cold.

She told him to sit while she made up their plates. She had roasted some potatoes and he was glad to see that the oven worked. She served steamed sliced carrots and peas, a bowl of which was set beside a stack of dinner rolls. The table itself looked remarkably nice; she had conscripted a white bedsheet as a tablecloth, folding it in half to cover the gouged and scratched wood veneer top. He couldn't remember, but like everything else in his apartment he'd either bought it at a charity shop or found it on the sidewalk, and he would still pick things off the street if he thought he needed them, for the sake of cost, of course, but really more because he'd long attuned himself to the aesthetic of the broken-down, the used-up, the worn.

But now he wished the table legs weren't so deeply scratched, that the chairs were less wobbly, that he had thought to paint the walls just once at least, rather than simply having moved in and squatted, all to match if only by half the simple, clean decency that was abounding with her presence: along with the food she'd picked a small bunch of wildflowers from the vacant lot down the street and had placed these in a glass. Paper napkins were folded in half and topped with silverware he didn't recognize as his own, for she'd buffed out the water spots. His plates were a puke-colored earthenware but Dora now dressed these up, too, by arranging the potatoes and onions in the tuck of the steak, which she'd sliced thinly on an angle and then fanned in a semicircle. She made a quick pan gravy with butter and flour (did he really have flour in the cupboard?) and a little splash of the red wine he had picked up just for her, and as she spooned the rich dark sauce on the meat his mouth watered intensely enough that his tongue ached. He waited for her to sit and poured her a full glass of wine, and then he ate ravenously and unself-consciously, like an adolescent might, mash-

ing the potatoes with his fork and slathering it on the meat and swirling it all in the sauce before wolfing it down.

"Is everything okay? How are the onions?"

"The onions are sweet," he said.

"They look burnt to me," Dora said. "How do you like the steak?
Do you want more?"

"Yes, thanks."

Dora sliced him some more, and she ate, too, but not half as exu-
berantly as Hector. She was enjoying the wine he'd bought her, which
came in a regular-sized bottle, with a real cork; he could have spent
less and gotten her four times as much of the jug wine she favored but
the label was illustrated with a pen drawing of a duck nestled among
reeds and it had reminded him of Dora, or at least the way she always
seemed snugly reposed, even when perched on a barstool at Smitty's.
She nipped at the wine to start, as it wasn't juice-sweet like her brand,
but she was quaffing it now in deep, regular pulls, saying it was lively
and tart on her tongue.

In deference to the meal, Hector was drinking beer instead of whiskey, and he was taking it with some gusto but with a different rhythm
than the usual flooding pace he'd get into with Connelly and Big Jacks
at the bar when it was a warm evening like tonight; no, he was drinking instead for the good crisp sensation in his throat, for the feeling of
being cleaned out and restored, he was drinking for the reason that to
sit down to a home-cooked meal with a kind and reasonable woman
and not want to sprint away out of fear of disappointing her or trash-
ing her already fragile life was a thoroughly bracing kind of pleasure.
Before, when he didn't normally remain in one place for more than six
months, it didn't matter, but once he saw he would be staying around
in Fort Lee he had not allowed himself to slip into the saddle of anything resembling a domestic calm.

But now here he was, focused on finishing off the steak and gathering the peas and carrots in a pile on his fork like a man come rightly home. Was he finally getting old? His body was as ever mysteriously impervious, but his mind was, like anybody else's, encumbered with time's accruals, and if over the years he'd disappeared on more than a few women at this very point, excusing himself from a table at a restaurant or from a bench in the park in the middle of a conversation and never returning, never calling again, never offering a single indication that he was even still alive, he was feeling none of that weakness now. He cleaned his plate, and while Dora got him another can of beer he topped her glass with the last of the bottle, of which he was glad he'd bought two.

"Leave room for dessert," she said. "I have a cherry pie."

"You made it?"

"Oh, goodness, no. Who do you think I am, Julia Child?"

"You're not doing too bad from where I'm sitting."

Dora didn't answer but was clearly pleased with how things were turning out. This morning when they awoke she had dressed quickly and muttered she'd see him "around" but Hector sensed she was lingering and uncharacteristically replied that they ought to have a real meal together and that's when she offered to make them dinner. Again she was slightly testy and defensive when she appeared later with grocery bags in hand and before he could stop himself he'd kissed her for the dignity on her face and right after she put away the perishables they made love, with Dora turning her back to him while holding the creaky rusted handle of the old refrigerator, the door opening and closing a couple of times before she called out his name and he hers and they swooned to the floor. Afterward she was always sweet-mouthed and proper, and he would never have imagined how uninhibited she could be, with her language and her body and her outright aggression, her pinching and scratching at his thighs, his buttocks, even his privates. It was clearly unconscious on her part, but she was thorough, each time raising small welts and marks all over him, today just as the other days, the hot water of the shower mapping a dozen good stings.

"Would you like coffee?" she asked him.

"Sure," he said. "I'll make us a pot. I can do that."

"I prefer tea," she said. "Coffee makes my heart race."

"I can make tea, then."

"You sure?"

"Yeah."

But he couldn't make tea, for he had none, and he'd run out of coffee as well. The cupboard was barren, save for a few sugar packets and take-out cups of jelly, a rusty tin of oatmeal. The oatmeal was the only thing he ever made for himself these days, and a sorry sight, but only because he wanted now to do something for her. Perhaps he'd not been exactly selfish all these years, but when was the last time he'd gone out of his well-rutted way for the sake of another? Hector knocked on the door of his neighbor, who was as unsociable as he, but the crabby fellow actually answered, and, though suspicious, eventually gave him two bags of Lipton, not waiting for Hector's thank-you to slam shut his door. Hector put the water on and while it boiled he brought their chairs outside to the cracked patio, as the small apartment had become quite warmed from the cooking. It was balmy outside but still cooler than the kitchen, and he set a folding TV table between them and brought out their plates and tea. He opened the second bottle of wine for Dora and another beer for himself and they ate their slices of pie while watching some children playing hide-and-seek in the weedy courtyard of the complex.

A girl of five or six ran over and crouched behind the low brick wall that marked the border of the patio, theatrically shushing them with a finger to her lips. The seeker ran over to them immediately and found her out and the little girl must have believed herself betrayed because she made a sour face to Hector. He made one back, but with silliness, his eyes crossed, his front teeth bared. The two girls ran off, giggling.

"We're like an old married couple," Dora said, careful to mock the idea in case he took it wrongly. Hector didn't reply but in fact he had thought it, too, recalling how his folks in their best times would enjoy sitting together on the porch of their house, wryly and good-naturedly commenting on the children's games and pouring gin-spiked lemonade for each other into tall glasses of chipped ice. Among the children there was a competition to get a sip from Jackie's glass, which he'd offer to the winner of whatever game they were playing, every now and then letting one of them down the rest of it, which inevitably turned into a competition unto itself. It was an age of such things, when they were all together during the war, his father 4-F, and at least in the private realm of the house at ease in his skin as he never was at the factory or in the pubs. His mother was in her prime beauty then, as lovely as any woman in town, but too young and naïve to know its measure, and she wore her splendor like an ill-fitting crown, half-embarrassed by the effect she'd have on perfect strangers on the street or at the green market.

"Dinner was real good," he said to Dora.

"You're being charitable. My mother certainly wouldn't have thought it up to snuff. I bet you have women cooking for you all the time."

"Yeah? How many have you seen hanging around here?"

"Well, you've just asked them to be scarce, I'm sure. At least for these couple weeks, right?"

"I suppose," Hector said, going along with her. "And maybe next week, too." And while this clearly pleased her plenty he also immediately wished to take the utterance back. He'd promised himself not to speak with her of anything outside a day in the future, even as he caught himself thinking more and more of times ahead, picturing some nice places they could escape to, some rustic fantasy, how they might drive in her car to a cold clear lake in the woods and hole up in a cabin like a pair of fugitives, eating whatever they could catch, drinking from a stream, feathering their bed with garlands of young ferns.

She clinked her wineglass to his beer and for a while they drank without talking as evening began to descend. It was an almost gracious feeling, as if they were taking the air in a park, as if he were a decent man and she a more than decent woman and the next day was a prospect they neither feared nor dreaded nor were already trying to forget. Perhaps they were even drinking for the sheer pleasure of it, for the easy communion and ritual, though they had little prior experience and were likely confusing the good feeling with the gentle weather and peachy light that was a world distant from the sorry pit that was Smitty's.

In fact, Hector was thinking how they might not go back there for a while; they'd already skipped a couple of nights in the last week, which was noted by the fellows with mentions of how they'd gone AWOL, and also a few unmistakably pitying looks, and it had struck him on entering that being with Dora had reanimated his sense of shame. He could see the old picture of himself at his spot at the bar, vainly stuck in the hard amber of his gruffness, his solitude, his strangely sound physical being, these integuments only momentarily breached whenever he was called out to fight (or, more rarely, fuck). Conversely, it was no surprise that he was feeling a little vulnerable again, as though there were a rent in his chain-mail vest, a newly opened seam along the underbelly that neatly paired with a very real scar of Dora's, a shiny inset line where she'd torn herself in youth, slipping through a deer fence. Whenever he brushed or touched her there she flinched and somehow he'd feel a nervy tickle of phantom pain and be renewed in his resolve that he would try his best not to bring her any heartache.

"I was thinking again about that woman," she said, peering down into the wine in her glass. "You know, the one who sent that man to talk to you at Smitty's?" She pretended to search her mind for the name. "Was it June? Yes, that's right, isn't it? June Singer. What was it that she wanted?"

He had already had to fib the day after the man first appeared and tell Dora that June was just someone he'd met in the war and later worked for, doing odd jobs and chores, which is what she had asked him to do again.

"She won't come around," he told her now. "I said I wasn't interested."

"Seems like she could get anybody to do odd jobs. Why should she ask you?"

"I don't know," he said, which he didn't, though it was only because he had refused to let any part of his mind alight on her. There were entire worlds of reasons for her to have sought him out, the most immense of which was what finally happened at the orphanage, and with Sylvie Tanner. But there was nothing but blackness to go over again. Of course he had been with June even afterward, a very brief and strange period that led to his bringing her over, as his legal bride, though once landed they had just as quickly separated, neither in the least inclined during the past twenty-six years to do anything but wholly forget the other existed.

"You must have been important to her somehow," Dora said. "A woman wouldn't send somebody otherwise. She would have found somebody else. But if you don't want to talk about it, I understand."

"There's nothing to talk about."

She finished what was left in her wineglass and then filled it up again. "It doesn't matter to me. You don't have to say any more. I don't care how many women you've had in your life. Past or present."

"*Present?*"

"I'm just telling you I don't care at all."

275

"I don't believe that."

"Well, I'm just telling you. You're not the only one with options, you know. I work with lots of people at the furniture store. Most of them are men."

"I'm sure they are."

"The manager even asked me out the other day, right out of the blue. I've worked with him for years. He said I was looking 'vivacious' these days. He's okay, I guess, but to be polite I said I had to think about it. What do you think about that?"

"I guess you ought to do what you want."

"That's the question for us, isn't it?"

When he didn't say anything Dora got up and asked him if he would like another slice of pie.

"Sure," he said. "But I'll go get it."

"I'm going inside anyway, for my shawl. It's suddenly getting cooler. Like a storm is coming."

"I'll move everything back inside."

"No, I like the air. Let's stay out here as long as we can. Okay?"

"Okay."

As she passed him he hooked her thigh with his hand and drew her close, a brackish-sweet air from their earlier exertions filtering through the thin muslin fabric of her skirt. The scent of them was heavy and he breathed it in deep, to let it etherize him, though it worked the opposite effect. He cupped her broad bottom and she responded by pressing his face into her belly, pinching the roots of his dark thick hair between her fingers.

"I want to stay here with you," he said. "Nothing else."

"You don't have to say that. I'm a big girl."

"I'm not saying anything I don't want to."

She leaned down and pecked him lightly and he kissed her back with a force and fullness that seemed to draw off all her blood and then fill her up again, her cheeks and neck flushed, dewy. His mouth peppered the patches of color on her pale skin, taking in her ear and then her throat, gliding down to the soft flesh above her breastbone and resting there while he guided her leg until she sat straddling him in the rickety chair, which creaked loudly and sharply.

"We're going to break it," Dora said, backing off slightly.

"You can fall on me."

"Aren't those children still around?"

"They all went inside," he said, but only because there were no more reports of their play. She didn't look around, either. Her long skirt tented their legs and while kissing him she reached beneath and unbuttoned his trousers and raised herself just enough to shift them down. Her own underclothing was in the way and he tugged at it and she simply pulled it to the side, clearing a way, recalling to him again what he liked best about her, her plain good sense and lack of put-on shame and fundamental ease with her body.

"Can I tell you something?" she said.

"Uh-oh."

"I don't have to. I can shut up."

"Go ahead."

"Did you know you are a very good-looking man? It's hard to see it because you don't wear it easily. But, honestly, you're the most handsome man I've ever seen, much less known. Only the funny-looking ones have ever gone for me. I guess poor Sloan was the last example. And there you were, every night at Smitty's, with no one to appreciate you. You don't know any of this, do you?"

He didn't answer, because it was always easier not to say that he did know it, and had known so all his life, how he was sorry for the specific misery his appearance had brought him and others, and for what? For the great sum of nothing.

"Now I've killed the mood."

"No, you haven't," he said, pulling her closer.

"You like it out in the open air, don't you, mister?" she whispered, hovering above the now high-angling press of him.

"Must be your fault."

"Mm-hmm," she said, teasing him, slowly spanning him, like a blind, knowing snail.

"You're ready yourself," he said.

"I was going in for more pie."

"You can go."

"I will."

But she didn't, nor did Hector stir a hair, both of them content to linger in the half-light. They could not know that their pose from any distance appeared to be as chastely still as sculpture. Desire in Middle Life. And it was in this marble calm that Dora took on a sudden shine, her skin and hair lustrously abloom with the wondrous feed of stopped time, her heart as well as her mind momentarily unburdened of their accreted regrets, self-lashings, those long-ingrained gravities, so that it seemed to Hector that she was thusly gliding above him at a tiny but still measurable remove, which was in fact a blessing; he could handle her quite near, though much closer and he might panic, maybe cut and run. And he didn't wish anymore to do that.

Afterward, while Dora slept in the bedroom, he found himself cleaning up the apartment. They had started early and it wasn't even dark yet, just past eight o'clock. She always dozed a little after sex. Plus, she'd had a whole bottle of wine, and the better half of a second. He'd drunk plenty himself but as usual he remained more lucid than he preferred to be, the beer more like coffee to his system, arresting nothing useful (like memory), and blotting only his already paltry need for sleep.

He quietly washed the soiled dishes and pots they'd left in their haste to get to the bed, then swept the floors and polished the counters and the stovetop. From his job he had all the supplies one might need, but since living here he had never once bothered to clean the place thoroughly. Once or twice a month he'd make a cursory pass with a sponge and broom. No one had ever visited before, and he wouldn't have cared anyway, but mostly the apartment was messy because he no longer registered the layers of grime and dust. For if you suspected you were immortal, if you were afraid you might never be extinguished, the evidence of which had accrued enough over the years to convince him to almost believe its truth—the way his wounds, even the seemingly grave ones he'd suffered during the war, healed with a magical swiftness; that he had aged in a way that appeared to the eye as if there were no other time except this one, no prior or future state—the concern for something like cleanliness, strangely enough, receded.

But Dora, thank goodness, was solely of this world, and for her sake he moved on to the living area, mopping the coffee table with a rag and knocking the seat cushions of dust outside on the patio. In the bathroom he wiped the sink basin and mirror and brushed out the toilet and then vigorously scrubbed the tub twice of its scum, the second time with a fresh rag, for she'd surely enjoy a bath in the morning. He could at least be an attendant, make things serviceable and pleasant for her, if not grand. He did such work at the mall, but there was a satisfaction in doing the same for Dora that made him think his own best usefulness was in these small, unheroic tasks, that his destiny in this realm was to take the form of the most minor of tools, a not solely metaphorical stain scrubber, or hammer, or rag. That contrary to what his father had always fantasized for him in his too proud and envious way, the ideal scale of his labors would be thusly unreported and fleeting, spot-small.

And the realization left Hector awash in the feeling that he was finally doing something right, something decent, and he quietly donned the clean T-shirt and trousers from on top of the bureau, careful not to disturb Dora from her downy wine-imbued slumber. Let her abide. He now had a good mission; headed for the bodega off Broad, he would buy some things for her, purchase not his usual canned spaghetti and pork and beans and box of saltines but what he thought Dora might fancy when she awoke, some fresh eggs and bacon and Portuguese sweet rolls and tea. He'd buy some jam as well, maybe a couple of flavors, even three. And on the way back he'd stop, too, at the liquor store for a bottle of wine for her and a six-pack of beer for himself, in case another thirst caught them in the middle of the night, or after breakfast. He checked the meager cash in his other trousers (he didn't own a wallet) and went hunting for bills and coins strewn loosely about the apartment—nearly twenty-two dollars in sum—and went out into the Fort Lee night, his pockets bulging with the scrounged change.

The skies were clouded over and where the streetlights had burned out it was pitch-dark. In the small brick row houses the older folks were turning in for the evening, their upstairs rooms lamped with bed-table lights or the colder flicker of television, the cast beams striping the tiny front yards and walks as if they were a miniature tabletop landscape, all of them stitched together by the line of mature if stunted trees growing in the median and the parked cars fitting exactly on the block in a serendipitously bespoke measure. It was mostly serene save for the droning air-conditioning units and the hidden cadres of urban locusts, whose competing songs on certain unbearable nights felt more like waves of heat than sound. On the main avenue there was disco music and thumping jungle-like music and the reports of traffic and people calling out of cars toward the grimy storefronts, where neigh-borhood youth accosted in fair share one another and the indifferent beat cops and the young immigrant couples in love, the bums rooting in the wire trash barrels for the dregs of beers and take-out food, all of them content in the now fast-cooling air. And had they carefully regarded the broad-shouldered man in the white T-shirt and dungarees stepping into the overbright bodega, his scarred, battered hands selecting from the shelves the fruits of this most modest human errand (the kind he'd avoided for decades), they might still have agreed that he was indeed cut from an antiquated cloth, this long-lost bolt of hero blue.

But of course he wasn't.

After he paid for the jams and some fresh hot fried bread he went to the liquor store across the street and spent what was left, and when he stepped outside again, laden with her morning repast, the briefest light rain drifted down. Then it was gone. The warmed, dampened sidewalks reminded him of certain sweet hours of childhood—well before he was much of a man, well before anyone (the neighborhood girls, the married women, the barmen) had found him out—when the summer torrents would interrupt the furious play of the street and they'd have to wait beneath the sagging porches for its sheets to roll past before they skipped back out, the smell of the damp concrete enveloping them in an odor earthen and stony but still creaturely, alive; he would have the sensation that he was on the broad back of an immense being, as unregistered as any sated flea, and he felt the same way now, virtually bodiless, happily ignored, free to go his unsung way.

ELEVEN

A TAP ON THE CAR WINDOW roused June; it was the drawn, dour face of Clines, come back out from the diner. She found herself braced against the throbs sharply echoing through her. The pills were not working. Or maybe she had spit them up; there was a shiny patch on the vinyl upholstery of the door panel. She felt as if someone were walking through the house of her body with a crate of porcelain vases and systematically entering each room and rearing back and smashing them against the walls. Clines got into the driver's seat and asked what they should do, and through gritted teeth she answered that they would keep going, taking two more pills in the hope that they would give her some relief.

But before they had any effect Clines informed her that they had turned onto the street where Hector Brennan lived. Twilight had just passed into evening but she could still make out the character of the neighborhood, the rows of squat one-story houses with properties separated by chain-link fencing and narrow driveways. The houses were in generally poor condition and Hector's apartment complex was even worse, decrepit and badly in need of painting, its front yard peppered with household junk and broken toys. The trees were gnarly and unkempt. A trio of unattended dogs ran about on the sidewalk, garrulously barking at one another. So this was where he lived. She thought of all the elapsed years and the other grubby details that Clines had found out about him and she wondered if this was a life that had befallen him or whether he had sentenced himself to it, as people sometimes do, in punishment right or not.

Clines parked and came around to help her out of the car. She was about to tell him not to bother in case Hector might see her needing assistance (she wanted no pity) but was instantly glad when Clines took hold of her shoulder and arm, as she might not have been able to lift herself from the deep, soft-cushioned seat.

"Which apartment is it?"

"Number sixteen, I think just there on the right. Will you be all right, Mrs. Singer?"

"Yes. I'll be fine."

But she didn't feel fine, for if stable and straight to the outward eye she was as good as gone; Clines somehow saw this and caught her arm when she lost her balance and nearly toppled. Despite an appreciative tingle in her chest she tried to shrug him off. Clines was insistent and walked with her, gripping her tightly enough that she could believe she was tugging him along. Some large tree branches were strewn about the scraggly, patchy lawn and she saw herself as the dead limb of a tree, at once ponderous and fragile, barely appended over the hard, unyielding ground. With the next good gust. Just before they reached the entryway she pushed away from Clines and bent over and gagged, nothing coming out of her except for a curdled slick of bitter, chalky spittle. The pills. It was as though her body were refusing amelioration, steadfastly denying her any comfort in order to make her cease, but rather than give in, June scolded herself and stood up straight, ignoring the shocks firing up and down her spine. She was still a relatively young woman, and if she had to die she was going to die on her feet, in beat of her own march.

Clines grasped her arm and she pulled it away.

"I'm fine."

"We can't do this, Mrs. Singer. I thought it when we first met but I'm absolutely sure of it now. There's no point. This man Brennan isn't the issue anymore. It's you. You're not capable of doing this. How much more obvious does it need to be? If you insist on flying out with me I may have to quit."

"Then quit," she said sternly, wiping her mouth. She tried to swallow the awful taste on her tongue. "Give me the files you have, and the plane tickets, and I'll pay you for what you've done so far."

"You'll accomplish nothing over there," he said. "You'll waste precious time. You won't be able to find your son quickly enough, if at all."

"I'll find him with or without you. I know that. You know how much I'm proposing to pay you, so you should decide right now whether it's worth your trouble. Or your daughter's, for that matter. Now, what are you going to do?"

Clines looked down stiffly, his eyes narrowed with a palpable anger. But he spoke to her calmly. "Okay, Mrs. Singer. We'll follow your wishes. I won't bring this up again."

"Good. Thank you."

"But please know this. While I will do everything that I can to do the job, it will be you who directs me. I will make recommendations, but it's your responsibility now. You'll determine our success."

She nodded. He asked if he should wait in the car and she told him that was fine. But as he turned she felt unsteady again and then completely parched and she asked him if he had any water in the car.

"No, but I can go and get some. There was a gas station on the main road."

"Okay. Go get it and then come back and then wait for me," she told him. "I'll see if he's here now."

Even though it was only one step up, she had to pause to catch her breath on the exposed landing for the apartments (they were set off in pairs), the thirty or so yards they had traversed feeling like three hundred. The landing itself was littered with cigarette butts and crushed beer cans and reeked sharply of cat spray. Gnats ticked nervously about the weak entryway bulb. Behind her, out in the street, Clines drove off, and for a second she wondered if he would in fact return. Perhaps he would decide to abandon her here. The metal door of number 16 was scarred and dented and there was nothing at all to indicate that anyone lived on the other side, or ever ventured out. She looked for a buzzer but there was none, nor a push-bell or clapper on the door. She tried to knock, but as with the rest of her joints, her knuckles and fingers felt like spun glass and so she rapped softly with the flat of her hand. There was no answer or any sound from inside and she tapped again.

The door opened and there before June was a woman loosely draped in a bedsheet. She looked like a life-drawing model, earthy, shapely, her full breasts pushing out against the thin fabric.

"Did you forget the key . . . ?" the woman said, trailing off on sighting her. She was sleepy-eyed. "Oh, excuse me. Can I help you?"

The woman wasn't so much beautiful as she was beautifully present, animate, with her tousled reddish-brown hair, her décolletage speckled with ruddiness, the smooth globes of her shoulders shining and delicate. She was perhaps the same age or even slightly older than June but June suddenly felt like a dried, buckling veneer in the face of the woman's lushness, this outer layer that you could chip away without effort.

"I'm sorry to disturb you. My name is June Singer. I'm looking for Hector Brennan."

"Oh." The woman held the sheet tightly around herself with one arm, the other crossed in front of her, her hand gripping the knob. Her expression had instantly hardened. "He doesn't want to work for you again."

"Again?"

"He doesn't want to see you. He made that clear already. So I think you should get on now."

"Please," June said, suddenly feeling like she ought to brace herself. "Please. It's too much to explain, and I want to speak to him now."

"I can listen. Explain to me."

"How can it matter to you?" June cried sharply, both of them surprised by her harshness. The woman instinctively stepped back but June leaned in before she could shut the door.

"I'm very sorry," June said wearily. She felt as though she were slipping inside herself, her outside stiff but her soft tissue melting away within. Her condition had now become apparent to the woman, whose eyes flashed on the realization that this insistent, brittle person standing before her was in fact very ill.

"I'm very sorry," June said. "May I ask your name?"

"It's Dora."

"Please excuse me, Dora. I'm sorry. I very much wish to speak to him. That's all."

"He's not here," Dora told her. She examined June closely. "He was just here a little while ago. I don't know where he went."

"Do you know when he'll be back?"

"I'm sure soon," Dora said, partly opening the door now. "But I don't know. Listen, are you okay?"

June faltered at that moment, perhaps more intentionally than she consciously knew or would admit, but with enough sudden gravity that Dora had to step quickly forward to grab hold of her arm; she would have fallen hard otherwise, or even let herself fall.

"I'm all right," June said, "but thank you."

"No, you're not. You're not well, are you?"

June answered by letting Dora fully hold her up; her embrace was strong but still gentle, careful.

"How did you get here?"

June said she was driven, but then she felt her legs give way again, forcing Dora to hold on to her even more tightly.

"You better come inside," Dora said, guiding her into the apartment. "Hector will be back soon enough, I'm sure."

"Thank you. You're very kind."

Dora helped her into an old armchair and excused herself, saying she was going to the bedroom to put on clothes. When she returned, she was holding a glass of ice water.

"Here," Dora said. "It'll make you feel better."

"Thank you." June took a drink and the water helped to steady her. She watched as Dora poured herself the remains of a bottle of red wine, coaxing the very last drops to fall. She had put on a nice-looking if slightly too colorful striped summer dress. Clothed, Dora appeared more ordinary-looking to her now, a middle-aged woman who had thickened around the middle, around the neck, in the upper arms, though certainly not in an unpleasing way. Life, gathering. The apartment was small but tidy and there were the remnants of what looked like a nice dinner on the table, an almost whole fruit pie. A twinge of jealousy unwound in June's gut, which was ridiculous, as she could expect nothing from either of them, but the sight of their shared domesticity made her feel that much more alone and desiccated.

"Have you been together for a while?"

"Me and Hector?" Dora said, sitting across from her with her already empty glass in her hands. "Not really. I mean, no, not long at all.

I don't know what we're doing yet, exactly. But it's good. I guess you've known Hector a long time."

"Yes," June said. "A long time."

"And you want his help again?"

"Well, yes. Did he say if he would?"

"He has a job he likes. Or at least that he doesn't mind. I don't know that he'd switch jobs."

June didn't quite understand and let Dora talk further and she soon realized that Dora was under the impression that he'd been some kind of handyman for her, and without any hesitation June found herself telling her that Hector had worked for her at the antiques shop, delivering furniture to customers. She didn't care that Dora might find out the truth later; it was now or never, for tomorrow they would have to leave if they had any hope of finding Nicholas. But all she made up about Hector seemed within possibility, given what Clines had found out about him, and Dora didn't question anything she said; in fact the more June began to tell of how reliable he had been, how careful he was at transporting and handling the pieces, how well liked he'd been by the customers, the more this widened view of him seemed to relax and please Dora, to ratify what she was clearly thinking and hoping about him. It was manipulative and cruel on June's part, yet here was Dora beginning to smile a little, warming to her, and because she felt her own strength waning June couldn't help but keep elaborating, saying how he'd been a skilled handyman (which he had been, at the orphanage), a tireless worker. It was only when she closed her shop did he move on, and she was lucky to have found him again, after all these years.

"You respect him, don't you?" Dora said. "You consider him a good man."

"Yes. I do."

Dora lowered her eyes, peering down into her glass. "Were you lovers, once?"

"No," June said firmly, deciding she wasn't lying to her at all on this; there had been the single instance, yes, but it was another for whom she and Hector had been yearning. "Not that."

"You're not very convincing."

June couldn't help but smile, but she didn't say any more about it. She said instead: "You love him."

Dora sighed. "He's not too selfish, like a lot of men I've known. He's certainly not mean, even if he rarely shies from a fight. He can be surprisingly funny. And very generous, even though he can't have much more than a few hundred dollars to his name. I suppose all that's good enough for me."

"Yes. You could do much worse."

"I have, plenty of times."

"I doubt it."

"You're nice to say that. So will you tell me now what you want from him?" Dora asked her, staring straight into June's eyes. "Please don't lie. And I'm sorry but you're sick, anyone can see that. You obviously don't really need him for your business. So how do you want him to help you?"

June paused to take a sip of water.

"I want him to come on a trip."

"A trip? What kind of trip?"

"It wouldn't be for too long, a week, or maybe two, at most." She added, if more to remind herself: "It can't be longer than that."

"But for what reason?"

"I'm looking for my son."

"Your son?" Dora said, with alarm. "What does Hector have to do with him?"

June tried to calculate whether it would be advantageous to tell her. But she was tired and muddled and she said, "Nothing. Nothing."

"Then why do you need him to go with you?"

"I just do."

"I don't think that's a very good reason."

"Maybe it's not," June said, her weariness now spilling over into irritation, anger. The little shatters of pain were expanding, the small world of her was fracturing, and she wished she had shot herself with the kit in the car, the arms of her thoughts now stretching there, desperate for the clear vials. But then she realized—or was it fantasy?—that she had a vial of morphine and a syringe in her handbag.

"Well, I don't believe you!" Dora gasped. "I don't believe you at all. There's something else. Isn't there?"

"I don't know what you mean."

"You must have something on him. He must owe you. Otherwise I can't see why he would ever agree. Not the man I know."

"Maybe you don't know anything about him," June said harshly, hearing herself utter it as would the woman she once was, who could easily wield a cold, sharp steel. "Not one true thing."

"I want you to leave now," Dora said, rising. "Right now. I mean it."

But June replied, "I'll wait here."

"No, you won't!"

"I will."

Dora took her by the arm and though she didn't grab her very roughly June gasped with the pain, this hot charge clawing and scrabbling beneath her skin, her flesh. She tried to resist, but her strength was a mere child's to this woman's and it seemed that if Dora wanted to she could crush her bones with a hard squeeze of her hand. Instead Dora tugged and June pitched forward onto the floor. Dora shouted at her to get up but June could not rise. She was kneeling, and although the floor was carpeted, her kneecaps felt like cracked glass, strums of icy pain conducting instantly up her legs, through her spine, fanning out to every last cell of her, whether good or renegade. Dora was still pulling on her and her arm felt as if it would come off easily, like a leg twisted from a roast chicken, and she cried out so loudly that Dora released her, the woman actually stepping back and covering her mouth. June was groaning, and coughing, and now retching again, spitting up the water she'd just drunk, her tears marking the worn-flat pile of the carpet, wetting her hands, her only thought being that she had better get up on her feet, that if she stayed down she might remain down forever.

"Please help me," she whispered.

"Oh, God," Dora said, mortified. "I'm so sorry. I didn't mean to hurt you."

"I'll go. Just help me, please. I'll go. My car should be back by now."

Dora first tried to lift her from beneath her arms but it hurt too much and she had to crouch and kneel herself in front of June and hoist her almost onto her back to get her up on her feet. June grabbed her handbag. They trudged this way for a few feet, until June got her legs working again, and then Dora tucked her shoulder beneath hers and it was all June could do to keep up as they walked out of the apartment. It had rained, the air moist and heavy. Dora kept asking where her car was but June couldn't answer. She was the simplest creature now, a beast trotting dumbly forth. Paradoxically, it was the pain that was now holding her up, this most rigid of infrastructures, as if she only existed through its searing lines. But she wanted to recline, if just for a moment, to feel the cool damp grass of the apartment lawn that now wove through her sandaled feet. Or was that elsewhere? Was it the pain, secretly, that she lingered upon?

So let me lie down.

Have the briefest rest.

Here . . .

Dora barely caught her, struggling to keep her upright. June was on her knees, being held up by the woman's warm, soft arms. She had to lie down. "My bag," she murmured to Dora. "I need my bag."

Dora took it quickly and splayed it out for her and June found the vial and little syringe. Her hands suddenly grew calm. She plucked off the protective cover and drew some liquid from the vial. It was too dark to try to read the lines.

"Should you do this right here?" Dora asked, standing what seemed many miles above her. "Should I help you?"

June didn't answer. She was on her side in the weedy grass, trying to open the alcohol pad. She fumbled it and Dora retrieved it for her but June couldn't wait and hitched up her skirt and blindly stuck herself, the tiny bee sting blooming into a wide, clean coolness that reached all the way up to her throat, her mouth, a temperature that she could almost taste.

And then washing back down over her was the flooding warmth, this lush, weightless blanket.

The world shifted, clicked back. Dora asked her if she wanted to get up and she said yes and without any pain—or perhaps there was pain, if unrequited—she was able to stand up. There was no sign of Clines or their car but June didn't mind, for at the moment she had misplaced her purpose for being here. All she knew was that this woman holding her was Dora, and that Dora was goodly, was basically kind, and that she would very much like to remain in her arms. The streetlamp above them went on and June had to cover her suddenly sensitive eyes from its bright, tinny light by tucking her face in Dora's neck and hair as the two of them trudged past the sidewalk and stepped off the curb into the street. The three dogs from earlier were scampering about them now, sniffing and baying playfully at their heels, each vying for their attention. Dora shooed them away. Several blocks down the wide, two-way street, headlights appeared in the distance. "Maybe it's yours," Dora said, and waved at it, and the car replied with a flash of its lights. It sped up.

"I don't want to go yet," June said, but the sounds she made surprised her, by how weak and deformed they were. She was near mute. She felt herself slipping from Dora's hold and so Dora leaned them up against the trunk of a parked sedan. Dora was turned to the approaching car, so she could not see what June saw, that behind them and across the street, beyond the cast of the streetlamp, a man with two white plastic shopping bags in his hands was strolling in his own penumbra, contented in his posture and step, maybe once and for all. Was it he? June murmured, "Hector," and Dora simply answered that she would have to leave now. The car was fast approaching and this was the end. She could see the driver behind the wheel, glasses on. But the dogs, like June, had noticed the man, too, perhaps picking up the good scent in his bags, and the three bolted across the road, directly in front of the car. The car swerved and just missed the trailing dog, but then lost control and shot wildly forward on the slick pavement, striking Dora where she stood at the back of the parked car.

Had there even been a sound? A crashing of metal? To June a new opacity reigned, as if she, or else the world, had been dipped once in candle wax. The layer was fast hardening. The car had careened diagonally across the street and bounded straight into a telephone pole. The corner of the parked sedan, just where she and Dora had been standing, was pushed in, smashed. June herself was untouched. But Dora was lying still on the pavement. The man knelt beside her, his back to June, his white bags discarded in the middle of the street. One of Dora's legs was all bloody, a mangle of flesh, though June couldn't exactly tell. Dora was crying, very softly. Then she stopped crying and was quiet and then cried a little again and then she no longer made any sounds at all. He tried to resuscitate her. After a moment the man kissed her, on the forehead, and then let go of her hand. The dogs had come back around and were rooting in the bags. The man rose and without acknowledging June's presence went past the dogs to the ticking car, where it was hitched up onto the curb. She walked into the street. Clines had slumped sideways into the door, the windshield in front of him cracked. His face was bloodied. His hand jittered up by his throat and he was lamely pulling at his own collar, as though he couldn't quite breathe, and when the man got to him it was with the feral hunch of menace. He was going to clench Clines's neck and snuff him. But before he could touch him, Clines bucked once on his own and lay back, still. The man stepped away then and faced June, and it was at last in the pale lamplight that she could be sure it was he.

TWELVE

FIVE LONG DAYS IN THIS COUNTRY, and Hector could not say if she would last another week. They were on their way to Siena. Of course anyone could see June might be terminally ill but to look at her now, riding beside him in the car, her eyes steady and sparkling with the grassy light reflected off the Maremman hills, her skin warmed by the heat of the roadway, one could believe she was safe for another month, perhaps even a season, that she could last as long as she herself willed it, that she was still in control.

She certainly had been in control back in Rome, despite being utterly exhausted after the long flight from JFK, moving them through immigration and the terminal as if she were his guardian and he were the infirm one; at one point she may have literally led him by the hand. They arrived in the early morning and her plan, as she'd explained to him on the plane, was to rent a car and drive north immediately, but he was in no mood to do so, dazed and sullen as he was, completely silent, drinking nonstop on the flight, and she'd had the taxi driver take them to a nearby airport hotel so they could gather themselves before moving on.

They were forced to share a room because a laid-over Japanese tour group had overrun the small hotel, but he was sure she had somehow arranged it that way, so she could keep him close. She would not quite fall asleep even though she had medicated herself. He was with her out of necessity and desperation after what happened in Fort Lee and she was clearly afraid that he would soon abandon her, though where he could go or what he could possibly do was not obvious to him. She kept the passports in her handbag, then transferred them to the room safe, even though he had in fact used Clines's passport to enter the country. She and Clines had planned for Hector to apply for his own, but because of events and June's hurry to leave they had taken a chance at immigration: she'd folded five one-hundred-dollar bills into her own passport, saying to the officer that he'd get another five at customs if he allowed the man behind her entry. After they collected her single bag from the carousel (he had no luggage) the officer appeared and hooked June by the arm and walked them straight through to the receiving lobby, where she paid him the rest.

In the hotel room he had continued drinking, sitting on the floor in the corner with two bottles of cheap brandy bought from the tiny shop downstairs, while she lay on her side on the twin bed with her dark eyes open wide but not quite focused, fluttering shut every once in a while, the steady traffic from the street and the harsh noise of jet engines blaring loudly enough that there was little reason to talk. She was not hungry and neither was he. He didn't want to look at her and tried to seal himself instead in the hermetic chamber of the liquor, which put him, as usual, in a state not of inebriation but of severance, though this time her presence was a steady encroachment and he ended up swigging from the bottle with an arm draping his face.

Once night fell, however, the streets grew quiet and the planes were approaching and landing on a different vector and it was then that she began to speak to him, in a voice that he suddenly remembered for its effortless, humming resonance, which was remarkable even back then because everything else about her was so abrasive and flinty. She could have been a singer, at least in another life.

"I'm sorry about your friend," she said, still on her side, her knees drawn up to her chest beneath the thin covers. She periodically shivered. She had been chilled on the plane as well, asking for extra blankets, her body as drawn as when he'd first met her on the road more than thirty years before. "She was a good person, wasn't she?"

When he didn't answer, June said, "I know she would not have been out in the street but for me. As I tried to tell you on the plane, she was helping me to the car. I'm very sorry for what happened. But I think you should know she was helping me. She was being very kind."

He ignored her but her expression didn't change and he could see that she was relieved he wasn't blaming her, at least not enough to make him reconsider his presence. He wanted to blame her; she had indeed shifted the course of events, and now Dora was gone. But he was lying to himself, for he knew that what had happened was the result of the more significant alteration of himself, having merged his grimy existence with the decent one she made pains to keep up, with her always pressed, dry-cleaned dresses and prettily manicured fingers and how neatly she was keeping his apartment. It may have appeared hers was prevailing, and yet from a wider viewpoint it was easy to see that his was the overriding condition; he was the cause, and the symptom, and the disease; he was the dooming factor for everyone but himself.

June said, "There was nothing you could do for her."

He couldn't answer, the unintended truth of the notion cutting inside his chest as if he'd swallowed the broken top of a bottle. Dora was lying there broken and unwhole in the street soaked with her blood, so frightened and confused right up to the last moments that he found himself shaking with horror and rage. Then in an instant she was gone. He tried to breathe life into her, tasting even the wine from her mouth. But she was turning cold, her face already honed into the marble-smooth mask. She had bled out. The swiftness of this final cruelty had driven him to want to hold Clines's throat until his eyes shimmered and a racked sigh arose from his lips, but the man had expired on his own. Sirens had already gone up in the distance, and it was only because Dora was so instantly, irretrievably gone that he had approached the figure standing beside the parked car, this woman who was calling him by name. He recognized her immediately and instinctively wanted to run the other way but some people had come out from the apartments pointing at him and the sirens were wailing and she told him in a sure and measured voice that she would tell the police what had happened, that Clines was already dead, which is exactly what she did while the ambulances took away the bodies.

"Why don't you rest now," she said, gesturing to the twin bed that was pushed right up against hers due to the almost ridiculous narrowness of the hotel room. The plaster walls were bare and there was a single, small window set too high and if he didn't know better he might have thought they were in a shared prison cell.

"Have you slept at all since we left New York?"

He shook his head.

"You should, because you'll have to drive tomorrow, first thing. You know, you don't look so good."

"I'm okay."

"I don't think you are," she told him. "Please, don't drink any more. Come and lie down. I won't bother you. I won't talk."

But she did keep talking, urging him to rest, and she held her hands out to him like some angel of mercy, though one who was strangely frail and wrecked, and as much as she appeared a wraith of sorry bones, her rich, plangent voice began to wash over him, envelop him as though it were the revival of Dora's living, lush body. His eyes were burning. He was not weary so much as stripped of hope and volition, but the moment he lay on the mattress the previous thirty hours suddenly accrued on the crown of his head where his consciousness prevailed and compressed him to a near-perfect erasure; oddly, all he remembered dreaming was that only his feet remained of him, and when he awoke in the middle of the night his work shoes had been removed, his rank gray socks slung over the towel bar in the bathroom, air-drying after having been hand-washed.

June was deep in sleep, her kit opened, the miniature syringe carelessly dropped on the bed beside her. When he checked her neck for a pulse—her skin was blue-tinged and quite cool to the touch—she didn't stir and he had to press hard to find it. He lay back down in the bed and tried to go back to sleep but he couldn't and so had wandered the streets of the cruddy airport town, looking for another drink. It was a hard-surfaced, unadorned settlement of low-slung concrete slab buildings, the ground floors of shuttered storefronts topped by shuttered residences above. Nothing was open, not even the gas stations, and then nothing seemed alive besides, no lights or voices or sounds of any insects or birds. It was a gritty, modern place with electrical wires sprouting everywhere from the ugly, featureless façades and the sickliest trees he'd ever seen, and with its air laced with the stink of jet fuel he felt he was in a fitting place, the kind of forlorn hole where someone like him might choose to crawl in and cover himself with dirt.

Was this Nicholas like him? Was he truly nearby? June had shown him an old school picture on the plane, and though he merely glanced at it (he had folded himself against the window seat in the most miserable mourning, walling himself off with a dozen little liquor bottles), the momentary flash of the creased photograph was enough to convince him of his paternity: the boy featured the same squared line of jaw, the prominent, gently angled brow, even the mouth, which was not quite Hector's but rather his father's, those full, ever-risible lips of Jackie Brennan. He suddenly realized how obtuse he'd been, plain dumb to the fact that June wasn't solely asking for his help but aiming to bring the two of them together before she was gone. Was it a final, sentimental gesture? The wish of a dying mother, of not leaving her son completely alone in the world? She was losing her grip for sure but even she couldn't possibly believe that connecting them now would be beneficial to Nicholas in any way. With Hector she was just saddling the young man with an unnecessary drag on his psyche. Slowing him down.

If he had any fatherly instinct at all it was that he ought to warn the boy of his presence, scare him off for good as if he were some stray dog you couldn't afford to feed. Of course he had never come close to wanting children of his own and had no feelings either way for Nicholas; but a curiosity was steadily gaining on him, too, even as he was trying to dispel it, a wonder about this elusive, apparently criminal person whose bloodlines were drawn from a most unfortunate pairing. Was he as diamond hard as June? Was he a misfit like Hector, some self-incarcerating soul? Or was he, like anybody else, desperately yearning to be discovered again, by any good stranger or beloved? It might be as simple as that. But of course a flat-out fear, too, was afflicting Hector as he turned down the dusty, unfamiliar side streets, the thought of actually facing Nicholas raising alarms in his heart, not simply for the awkward talk they would have to suffer through but the specter of something infinitely more disturbing: the prospect of his failing yet another person, even in the smallest way, someone else he should honor or protect or love better than he ever could.

Back at the hotel he had found June vomiting onto the floor between the twin beds, which they'd pushed apart as far as the room allowed, barely a foot. It was just watery mucus and he cleaned it up.

When he wiped her mouth with a hand towel she batted at him from her medicated half-sleep and Hector had to calm her, though simply folding her arms seemed to cause her pain. Her feet were terribly swollen, distended into hideous, red-purplish bags. The flight had finally caught up with her. Yet despite her condition he kept seeing her differently, as the lean, angular child he once knew, the unflaggingly angry, aggressive, icily silent girl who wouldn't let anyone touch her or get too close. Everybody at the orphanage was wary of her and kept their distance, even the toughest boys, not wanting to risk a hard shove or even a kick in the groin. One day she'd taken on two of the bigger boys at once, breaking the middle finger of one and nearly scratching out the eyes of the other; the memory of it was clear enough that Hector unconsciously reclined gingerly on his bed, so as not to make the springs creak and disturb her. And though he could have easily taken all her identifying papers and the large sum of money she'd given him and let her die there anonymously and be done with it he was amazed by her ceaseless, spearing will to persist, a life force that her physical distress was somehow sharpening rather than blunting. He was awed by the way she could push herself, ignore her obvious wretchedness, and apply herself like a tool.

The next morning she was miraculously improved, her cheeks no longer the light slate color, her movements as she quickly repacked her bag steady and efficient, like any woman leaving on a business trip. They had a breakfast of tea and stale rolls (June took only the tea) and flagged a taxi to the rental-car office and soon enough they were on the road, headed north, June reading the map for them. Hector was driving and they made it to Livorno by noon, but it proved to be a worthless trip. Directing them was a dossier of documents from Clines's contact in Rome, but they were following a trail that seemed to Hector a pathetic, frayed yarn.

It turned out they'd gone to Livorno because someone with a name similar to one of Nicholas's aliases had been was arraigned there recently on check-kiting charges, but when they got there nobody at the courthouse knew anything or could even find a file on the man. The court officer who was contracted to deal with them was on vacation. June put it down to the confusion of the aliases and the language difficulty, but Hector was not convinced; Clines's contact in Rome, a talkative fish-mouthed fellow with an Australian accent to his English, struck him instantly as a crook and a liar, the sort who maybe specialized in swindling old people and women, and after June paid what he said he'd been promised, he offered up the name of a court officer in Livorno, assuring that a sizable bribe to him would erase the indictment.

There was little point in going back to Rome, for the contact there was probably gone, too. After staying a night in Livorno they went to the medieval town of Massa Marittima, a place where her son had briefly worked in a fancy antiques shop after leaving London. They found the shop, but it was no longer an antiques store; it had changed hands recently and was in the midst of being renovated as a tourist shop, and the Czech construction workers could tell her nothing. But they got lucky: it was only because June had suddenly craved something sweet, a gelato—the one thing she felt like eating anymore—that they stopped at the stand on the other side of the tiny cobbled street and struck up a conversation with the English-speaking counter girl. June asked if a young man had worked there and the girl said that an Asian-British man named Nicky Crump had indeed worked in the shop.

June gasped that this was sure proof; Crump Antiques had been the name of her shop early on, after the original owner, before she changed it to just Fine Antiques, Nicholas himself scraping off the old name and painting the new one on the glass panel of the door in matte gold and black lettering. When June showed her the old school picture the girl had at first hesitated, scrunching her nose, but when June pressed her she agreed that it was he. Apparently Nicky Crump had told her when he learned the shop was closed that he was heading to Siena, as there were a good number of antiques shops there. The girl was gentle and bookish and not unattractive and seemed to want to say something else, maybe that she had liked him, but before she could June had whisked them away, saying they should move on, move on.

Now, heading to Siena, they seemed to be lost again, stuck on a rutted two-lane road outside yet another unsigned town. The *autostrada* had been full of tourist traffic and delivery trucks and marred by construction sites and after inching along for several half-hour stretches June decided they ought to take the smaller roads that ran alongside the main highway. But then there were countless unmapped roundabouts and side-jogs and because it was hazy they couldn't read the sun for direction. They'd doubled back several times already, even ending up twice at the same roundabout, as they were now, and June suddenly cried, "This can't be where we are!" ripping the page from the map book and crumpling it with rage.

Hector kept quiet, but while he drove them he began to wonder about the reality of this all, how Clines's contact had been able to get any of this information. He thought maybe Clines had been playing her, or been duped himself. Or perhaps he had been simply pulled along, just as Hector was being drawn along now, pulled forth in the wake of June's intensity, her inhuman stamina. And yet the questions about her son kept accruing, if more to him than to her. She seemed to ignore the fact, documented in Clines's folder, that the name of the person she'd wired money to in the last weeks—a Paul Ferro—was very different from the names Nicholas had used in the past, or that the sums requested had dramatically increased. She was simply aiming herself toward him as he kept moving and it didn't matter that hers was a likely folly of a journey and destined to end in nothing at all.

But soon they found the right road, and she retrieved the balled-up paper from the car floor, wincing as she reached for it, and then opened the map book and carefully smoothed the page out to go back in its spot. Her mood would swing erratically like this, depending on the changing matrix of the pain, the drugs in her system, or the periodic attacks of vertigo that seemed to be gaining in strength and frequency, and with it would ebb her energy and ability to reason. In the space of thirty minutes she might change their routing, or break down, or even lash out at him for driving too slowly. Every so often June tapped him to pull over at the next shoulder so she could shut her eyes for a minute and regain her equilibrium, or else so she could retch, yet time after time she'd emerge from the restroom and don her sunglasses and walk quickly back to the car like she was ready for another hundred kilometers and open the spiral map book to the connecting page.

They had traveled up well past the foothills now and the road narrowed and began to curl severely about the hillsides. The roadway lacked guardrails and the exposed slopes fell away so steeply that June was shutting her eyes as Hector marked the hairpin loops. A local bus had closed in behind them and was riding their bumper; he was driving with her in mind and didn't speed up, but soon enough June signaled him to stop. The road was too curvy and it was only after a few more switchbacks that he could turn off onto a gravel drive, pulling in a bit too fast. The driveway was even steeper than the road and the car bottomed out on the spine of the rutted path and he had to gun the throttle to get it moving. They slid perilously for a few feet, the front wheel stopping on the edge of the knee-deep rainwater ditch that was cut alongside. June promptly opened the door and leaned over and gagged, dry-heaving; the color in her face was wrong, perfectly metallic and dulled, and he simultaneously noticed through the trees the faded terra-cotta tiles of a roof and followed the road downward.

"What are you doing?" June said, wiping her mouth. "I just need a moment. Then we can move on."

"We're stopping for a while."

"I'm okay. Turn around now. Hector . . ."

He didn't reply, and for the first time in the few days they'd been together she didn't overrule him. She had already closed her eyes, holding on to the door handle as they bumped fitfully down the hill, kicking up a trail of dust. The driveway suddenly ran out around the next turn, stopping mid-hill, two large boulders marking its end; the house sat another twenty or so meters farther down, at the end of a footpath.

He helped June out of the car. She had trouble with the loose footing and he steadied her as they descended. When they reached the steeper footpath she lost her balance but he caught her before she fell, lifting her in his arms. She held on to him tightly, her hands slung around his neck. It stunned him, how she was hardly there; she was as light as a box kite. He felt uneasy, touching her. While they were briefly married he never touched her, except that final night before their agreed-upon separation, when she had plied him with more liquor after he'd come home from a night's drinking and then later startled him from his dead man's sleep, straddling him as he spasmed awake. She left their flat right then, leaving him with the feeling that he'd been not so much used as robbed.

Now he carried her to the house, where she asked to be let down, but she didn't make a move to stand and he realized she wished to recline. There was an old wooden bench tipped over in the high grass near the house and he righted it with his foot and laid her down. She was suffering, her knees tucked up into her chest. Her sandals had come off and her feet looked blanched and skeletal. The haze had dissipated and the late afternoon sunlight was still brilliant, if not hot, and Hector decided to check the house to see if she could rest where it was less bright.

The cottage was perhaps a hundred years old, made of varied stones reset and remortared over the years, with a single square, shuttered-up window in the north wall speckled with dormant moss. The place was likely a hunter's retreat, for there were ropes left hanging from a large tree nearby, for stringing up game. The short, scarred door was padlocked but the screws played in the rotted wood of the jamb and with a few hard shakes he was able to free the rusted iron and push the door in. A faint smell of ash rose up from the darkness; someone had been there in the last few days. He opened the shutters of the windows and could now see the entirety of the space, a room roughly three meters by four meters: there was a hearth on the short wall and a rough-hewn table in the center with two stools, and a canvas cot topped with a sleeping bag. The plastered walls were hung with ancient threadbare tapestries that appeared they might crumble on touch. He unzipped the sleeping bag and it smelled of a person but not strongly and he went out and got June. He laid her down. She asked for her kit and he hiked back up to the car to retrieve it. But when he returned she was already asleep, her face pinched with hurt, mumbling like she was explaining something detailed and complicated and maybe unpleasant. Did she say the name Sylvie? He thought about giving her a shot anyway, to relieve her of course, but also in the hope of quieting her, so she wouldn't make any such mention again, but he started a fire instead in the hearth, as the cottage was cool from being shuttered up.

Soon enough, however, she was awake. "Where's the car?"

He nodded up the hill.

"What are you doing?"

"Making some food."

He was filling a cast-iron pot with some ingredients he'd found. In a cabinet there was a stock of home-canned goods, jars of white beans and tomatoes and pickled meat and anchovies. There was also olive oil and bread crisps and several bottles of what looked like homemade wine, along with a canister of coarse salt.

"I don't want to eat."

"Well, I do." He was hungry, not having had a real meal in days. He'd almost forgotten to eat, being with her.

"We need to go," she said, trying to sit up. "It's probably only an hour to Siena. You can eat when we get there."

"You ought to rest."

"I've rested enough."

"You should rest more."

"Please don't tell me what to do."

"Whatever you want. But I think you should stop for a while. Otherwise you'll die. You'll die before finding him."

His words gave her pause, and then she lay back down and watched him. While she was sleeping he had also found a small terrace garden carved out of the hillside a few steps below the cottage. It was overgrown and mostly gone to seed but there were some onions and carrots and an immense zucchini, and he'd cut these up with a knife he'd also found in the cabinet. The pot had a swivel handle, which he affixed to the hook above the fire. In it he fried the vegetables and then added the jarred beans and tomatoes and a little water. There was no plumbing in the cottage or well that he could find outside, and so he used the bottled water they were carrying in the car.

Finally she said, "What are you making?"

"I guess a stew. Does the smell bother you?"

"It's okay. Is it like what you used to make?"

He didn't know what she meant, but then the sight of her face staring at him suddenly jogged his memory.

"Not really."

When he was in the army he did a stint at the base mess before his general soldiering, and at the orphanage he would make dinner for the children whenever he was able to get foodstuffs from the PX, this once every couple of weeks. The aunties usually prepared rice and a soup made from wild greens and potatoes and whatever meat they could manage, sometimes dumplings filled with bean threads and chives, but after a particularly successful trading session with the PX sergeant he'd make a "camper's stew" of everything he hauled back—canned corn, green beans, Campbell's tomato soup, frozen beef patties or hot dogs or Spam, egg noodles, and Tabasco; the kids went crazy for it, they'd yell *Campus-too!* not knowing what they were saying, and crowd too closely around the stockpots on the blazing outdoor cooker.

The stew was much heavier and richer than what they were accustomed to and a handful of the kids would eat too much too quickly and vomit, but then come back for another bowl anyway. June would stay on the periphery and wait until the clamor died down, and he remembered now how she'd insist he fill her bowl to its brim, keep pushing her hands up to him and say in her disarmingly good English, *I am very hungry today. I want more.* She was the best English-speaker among the kids, but employed it sparingly, and for her own ends, rarely willing to be a translator or advocate for anyone else. Unlike most of the other children, she was short-tempered and difficult and in certain lights insufferable but you never knew what horrors any of them had survived or witnessed or had to commit, and there was no use in judging. He'd comply and give her what she wanted, and she'd go off on her own and despite what she'd said eat her food with cold method, careful spoon by spoon, as though she were counting them for the next time.

"Maybe I'll try some," she said. "It almost smells good. To me. You know what I mean."

"It'll be ready soon."

"May I have some of that water?"

There were no cups in the cottage, so he just gave her the glass bottle, but it was a full liter and a half and a bit too heavy for her and he had to help hold it up; she had some trouble drinking straight from the bottle and some went down her airway and she had a brief coughing fit before she could lie back down. When he was finished cooking he asked if she still wanted some and she nodded. He bore the hot pot over and placed it on a stool between them, pulling up the other for himself. There were no plates or bowls and only the one wooden spoon, and he offered it to her.

"You eat," she said. She was sitting up now, her narrow shoulders pinched forward, making her seem slighter still, folded in, like she was an image in the crease of a book. "I just want a taste anyway."

"You ought to go first, then."

He handed her a scant spoonful of it, its consistency more like a soup than a stew. She took it, chewing tentatively, and then had another, two large full spoons. She rapped the spoon on the edge of the pot and offered it to him.

"You keep going," he said.

"We can share."

"You better eat while you want to," he said. Then he added, "While you can."

She nodded, and had two more spoonfuls, though the final one seemed to stick in her throat. He had opened a bottle of the homemade wine, leaving the equivalent of fifty dollars in lire for it and the rest of the things he had opened, from the money she had had him change in Livorno. In fact she'd given him her bankroll to hold, twelve thousand dollars or so in traveler's checks and cash, vastly more money than he'd ever seen at once. But he'd never cared about money and he would have likely traded a good deal of it for a corkscrew, if the cottage hadn't had one. (Though he'd smashed open the tops of bottles before.) He found one, though, and his hands were calmed by the familiar heft of the bottle, and in one smooth continuous action he pulled the cork and brought it to his lips. The wine wasn't wine at all but a very strong, clear brandy, harsh and chemical, like dry-cleaning fluid might taste, but it was right enough; he drank nearly a third of it in one slug. He sensed her watching him with hooded eyes, undoubtedly wondering whether he was that much better off than she.

"You didn't drink so much back then," she said.

"You wouldn't have seen me."

"I did," she said. "I sometimes followed you. You didn't know, but I spied on you."

He took another long slug and tried not to think of what she might have witnessed, though not because it wouldn't have been right for a young girl; he was simply shielding himself, for as much as the memory of Sylvie Tanner charged hotly through him, the picture of her milk-hued throat only made him more wary, and then thirstier. He hadn't drunk in more than a day, and if anything the craving in his body was the opposite of June's: he wasn't moving quite fast enough, he couldn't feel any of that phantom speed, the easy gearing that the drink let him slip into, allowing him to gain a merciful distance from himself, which was the pathetic excuse of a creature he had come to be: loser-for-eternity, world-class self-pitier, tireless batterer of men and embodied doom of women, this now wholly bereft last man standing.

June said, "I remember, just before the end, when Reverend Tanner was letting her have it. Telling her what a disgrace she had become."

"Where was I?"

"You were gone for the day," she said. "Maybe you had gone to the base, for supplies. It was morning and she was sitting in the patch of grass behind their cottage. She had missed breakfast again, and I had come to sweep and clean. Her eyes were bloodshot and her hair was messy and he was standing over her, so tall and high. He didn't shout. But for some reason I was sure he was going to strike her. I had his glass paperweight in my hand and I was ready to hit him, if I had to. Of course he didn't."

"He wasn't like that," Hector said.

"No, he wasn't," June answered. "But he kept telling her how ashamed he was. How she was an embarrassment to herself, and to him. She just sat there, taking it. I was so angry."

How easily Hector could see June, more than thirty years removed, wielding some sharp crystal. And then Sylvie, in a cloak of miserable penitence that she was all too ready to don. Tanner had returned from another overnight trip to nothing different except that she was obviously sluggish, exhausted, moving about as if she were the one who had been on the road for a week. She was sleeping late some days, something that she would never have done before. Tanner had asked Hector twice if anything odd had happened, whether she had seemed ill, but he simply shook his head, not wishing to have to lie outright. After that first week of their arrival, the man had been nothing but fair to him. He wouldn't apologize, but he didn't need to have Tanner know, either, that she had spent the previous four nights in Hector's bed, neither of them sleeping at all, he drinking and she drugging herself in alternation with their lovemaking, which for Hector was a revelation, this woman whose sexual hunger was both a plea and a hazard, like someone floundering in waves far from shore.

"When you were spying on us. Were you in the storeroom?"

"Yes."

His room was on the end of a long, low wood-framed building that was roofed with sheets of corrugated tin. It was a room much like this one, though half its size, with a single cot and a rusted metal shelf for his things but no window onto the dirt courtyard. It was never meant for habitation. Next to it was a general storeroom for the orphanage—study books and pencils, some canned foodstuffs, tools and rakes, Bibles, donated blankets and children's clothes and shoes, square cans of kerosene. June described how she had crouched low against the shared wall, a wall that he himself had erected with materials on hand, salvaged studs and panels of pegboard that he covered with canvas. "There was a gap in the fabric on your side, down near the floor, and if I pressed my eye up I could see through the holes."

"We never knew."

"I was careful to be quiet."

"How many times were you there?"

"I don't know."

He took a long drink, and then another. "Why are you telling me this?"

"I don't know, exactly," she said. But her eyes were enlivened, gleaming brightly against her sallow face, the last pools in a forsaken plain. "After she told me I couldn't work in the house anymore, I wanted to hate her. But then she started seeing you and I could see a way, again."

"A way to what?"

"To being with her always. Isn't that what you wanted, too?"

He didn't answer, because of course it was true. Yet at the time he didn't quite know it—he was too brutal and stupid, just a rig of flesh that selfishly craved and rebelled. He didn't understand then how deeply he needed her, that he loved not just her sharp wants and carnality but how tightly bound up those were with her decency and beauty and goodness; she was exalted and flawed, someone who required as much grace and succor as she herself readily offered, someone both he and June desperately needed, a mother and a lover and a kind of child, too. That first time they made love, when she opened the back door of the cottage for him, she had fallen upon him as if she'd thrown herself from a parapet, with the grave force of both will and surrender. She kissed him, bit him, wanted his fingers inside every part of her. She was more than thirty years gone now, though it could be a mere day, and he felt his heart suddenly unstitch, the wire twine instantly rusting, falling away, to reveal again the cold box, the great dark underworld of his guilt.

"I'm so tired," June said. She had a hand on her belly, not quite holding it, the way a pregnant woman might unconsciously take her own measure. She lay back down and slowly closed her eyes. With a long swig Hector finished the first bottle, its liquor still burning his throat. He had just opened the other bottle when she said, "I'll sleep a little now."

"Okay."

"Aren't you going to eat?"

"No," he said. He was already drinking deeply again, a broad, dry delta. "Maybe later."

"Will you stay here with me?"

"Where else would I go?"

"Just stay."

He nodded to her and waited until her breathing grew steady and more audible. He had become her sitter now. Like a child, she was acting as if his remaining within the scope of her reach and sight would somehow diminish his power or will to leave. And yet now her insistence seemed strangely valid, for he thought he needed to step outside the cottage to determine what he would do. In fact, in Livorno he had, at least temporarily, deserted her; for two hours he sat in the main station, waiting for the next train to Rome, until he finally returned to their room at the hotel and found her unable to get out of the tub. She'd been showering and had reached up to adjust the sprayer and lost her balance, slipping and falling hard on her side and back. Though she was in pain, nothing, miraculously, was broken—a folded towel on the tub edge had softened the impact—and the distress of the situation allowed them to avoid the question of where he had been. Her nakedness was unsettling, but only to Hector; she didn't try at all to cover herself, either immediately or after he lifted her up, merely sitting on the bidet in a miserable daze. Her breasts were shrunken and lined and her scarred belly was partly distended to a shine, and the patch of hair between her legs, a thick, dark broom, was the sole indication that she was not even fifty years old. He had offered her the towel but she only held it in her hands, weakly wringing it, dabbing it against her face as if it were a precious furl of cloth.

The sun was now low in the sky but still bright and he shut the door of the cottage behind him to keep the light from disturbing her. He was sitting on the creaky bench and drinking from the second bottle, feeling the day's heat radiating from the stone walls behind him. This bottle seemed even stronger than the first, and he was reminded of how Dora began her evenings by downing three small glasses of her own brand in quick succession, as if to prime her needy motor before the drinking proper. So he took three swift shots in somber deference to her, and then three more, not caring that it was harsh on the tongue and throat and smelling of petrol; but the rite fell short, for he conjured up not Dora's thirst sated, that first sip's glee, nor the soft grainy apple-flesh of her bottom, nor the furious grip she'd exert on him during their passions, grappling his shoulders, pulling his hair, but rather the horrid bed of the blood-glazed street, and her pretty leg all in a mess, and her eyes beseeching him, not to save her so much as to explain the backward mercy of the world, why it was taking her just at the moment she had finally stopped wanting it to.

Had the eyes of the Chinese boy soldier made the same petition? And the others he had witnessed die during the war? Why was he to be the angel of ironical death? It was those last few seconds that were most horrifying for Hector; at least the mien of the long-dead he had collected doing graves registration was generally one of distinct un-concern, or perhaps the mildest bemusement, if they had faces left at all. He could take their expressions blackened with rot or dried blood or else blown away, cheekless or jawless or lacking a brow, all countless mutilations, the frightful carnage, but watching a living face fade and pale was to him the most grotesque of turns, the one thing he could no longer bear. The promise of being with June at her end made him want to crawl away, to run, and he knew he would indeed have to leave her, that it was inevitable, that he must desert her before the final hour.

He wandered down the steep, arid hillside with the bottle in his hand, drinking it down as he went. The homemade liquor was coursing through him more hotly than usual, almost painfully; he could feel it drawing out into his extremities, these lines of ants on the march. He was going to drink some more, maybe drink the rest. If it was poison, let it be. He found a deer path through the scraggly brush but instead of stepping mindfully he let the pitch take him and he dropped himself headlong in its leafy track, pumping his legs in a velocity of desperate escape; to view him from above was to see, paradoxically, a man running as fast as he could in order to keep from falling.

But even Hector could not sustain the necessary speed, create enough balancing momentum, and he flew down the hill, tumbling head over knee so violently that it appeared he was there to thrash clear the greenery, the rocks, the dusty earth itself. He came to rest in a dark glade of cork trees, their sinuous trunks stripped of bark to the height of eight feet. They were old trees but now naked and smooth, and he felt as exposed as they. He was cut and bruised about the face and knuckles; he was crying, but not from any physical distress. The bottle, emptied, was still in his hand. He'd just missed an exposed sharp spine of rock and he cursed his luck and smashed the bottle against it. He was going to fight himself, pugilist as onanist, because there was nobody else to fight, nobody left to take on. Here he is, your undying low-life champion. With the jagged neck of the bottle he slashed across each wrist and also his neck, and jabbed at his side and thighs. Then he got on his feet and bull-rushed the largest tree. He rammed it with his chest, and then his shoulder, and as he grew weary he pushed against it with his now bloody carmine hands, his carmine-stained forehead, grunting and pumping his legs as if he were a football lineman toiling against a practice sled.

After a stretch of time long enough to be embarrassing, even to a man alone, he relented, his punctures already congealed and crusting over in the unnatural manner they always did. This was the only pain he actually felt, which actually registered, the sear of the too-swift healing. His exhaustion was fed less by exertion than frustration, the closed loop of his thwarted rage, and he fell against the roots and lay staring up at the stilled canopy, the sky dimming to indigo behind the web of gnarled black limbs. The sight was vaguely Eastern in aspect, like a beautiful silk-screened panel, but then lovely for nothing, and he thought that this was the diseased tableau of his life: forever there to witness splendor, while death coolly drifted upon everything else. Up the hill only the chimney of the cottage loomed. If she cried out, if she called for him, would he stay silent? And if she didn't see the morning, would he simply leave her in the bed for the huntsman to find, or else bury her, as he had buried so many others, dig the necessary hole, his best dark talent among all his dark talents?

THIRTEEN

JUNE SLEPT MOST OF THE NIGHT and on waking realized that Hector was gone from the cottage. She panicked and stumbled onto the floor and nearly hurt herself, but when she stepped outside she spotted him up the hillside from the hunter's cottage, sitting in the driver's seat of the car. She practically ran up the rutted drive and would have leaped for the bumper had he accelerated but as she drew near she saw that he was asleep.

It was the first time she had seen him so, since they'd flown from the States, and she could study him for a moment. His seat was slightly reclined and his face was turned toward the window, his reddish-brown locks untouched by a single strand of gray. His complexion was a wonder to look at, even after all these years and despite his roughness and obvious disinterest in caring for himself. He glowed like a saint in some Renaissance painting but the rendering here was of a man clearly fallen, marked by the most subtle of colorations, an incipient, brooding shade. He was a shockingly beautiful man. She had always thought him so, from the moment they crossed paths that first day on the refugee road, even if his radiance had meant nothing to her. And yet there was something definitely restorative in simply regarding him now, a momentary suspension of the sentence on her body, her demise. She had always considered beauty more perilous than useful, and yet, when it persevered, it became its own element and property, indivisible, original. Something to have faith in. She should have left him undisturbed for a little longer but she was made irrationally anxious by the fact that he was literally in the driver's seat and could easily motor away, and when she roused him with a tap on the glass he shivered ever so slightly, as might a child, the sight of which only honed her guilt.

She asked him to put the cabin back in order as best he could, and she added money to what he had left on the table for the owner, writing *Mi dispiace* across the top banknote with a grease pencil she'd found in a drawer, the sentiment of regret seeming more fitting than one of thanks. If anything, she was grateful to Hector for having made her stop and rest; she was definitely stronger today, or at least after waking him she was, the ground not shifting or rolling beneath her feet as it had been most of the last two days, her eyes able to look at an object without fixing on it so forcefully that everything else whirled about its axis in a furious, breakneck orbit. Among the many dozen complications and eventualities that Dr. Koenig had listed in his imperious fount-of-the-Maker tone was vertigo, a case of which she'd suffered once long before the cancer and was likely now not a simple disturbance of the inner ear but a sign that there might be tumors in her brain.

Of course she knew that the longer she survived, the more any extension would mean something like this, that the cancer would duly migrate and settle and prosper, and if during the past rounds of treatment she had yielded completely she would certainly give herself over now for as long as possible, endure the role of host to the last. In her painfully sentimental dreams of late, like the one she had had last night, the tumors were wards of her nursery and she was naming them as she would children, these eager clumps in her bones, in her lymph nodes, speckles on her liver and lungs, all racing to see which of them would bring her its final gift: *You're darlings*, she said to them, in a warm, matronly voice. She was dressed in white burial garments, just as her great-grandmother had been enrobed as she lay on her funeral bier. She pressed her hands against the length of herself, her still-sturdy body.

Ah, thank you, thank you.

Thank you, Mrs. Singer!

After closing up the hunter's cottage they went back up to the car. She lost her footing on a stone while walking up the steep driveway and Hector offered to carry her up and although it wasn't really necessary she let him. He lifted her easily, his arms girding her fragile spine, her fragile knees, and as her hand curled around his taut neck she drew herself close. She let her cheek lean on his shoulder and neck. He smelled grassy and sharp and there was a denser scent rising from under his shirt, like of a worked horse, and she wondered how long it had been since she'd been this close to a man. It had been David, of course, but he was admittedly overattentive to his hygiene and regularly used her body lotions and powders, and as he was remarkably smooth of skin and hairless (especially for a Jew, as he pointed out to her more than once) she would sometimes imagine when embracing him that it was a woman in her bed. Before David it was Nicholas, during his adolescence, when the air of his small bedroom was fetid and gymlike with soiled socks and clothes, and she'd briefly hold her breath on entering, and sometimes even when Nicholas hugged her. She didn't feel guilty at the time—what guilt had she felt at all, in those days?—but the regret was now keen and though it would have been fitting for Hector to repel her it was nothing like punishment at all, quite the opposite rather, and now a welling arose low enough in her belly that she could almost believe it was not a pang of the illness.

"I'm sorry you had to sleep in the car," she said to him. He was driving them slowly about the switchbacks of the wooded hillsides, braking and accelerating gently enough to minimize the tug of the turns. "When I woke up I realized there was no place for you to sleep."

"I was only in the car for an hour or two."

"You were awake the whole night? What were you doing?"

"Nothing."

"You weren't drinking more?"

"I'm always doing that."

"You weren't thinking about driving off?"

He didn't answer her.

She said, "You must be tired, anyway. I shouldn't have woken you."

"I'm okay," he said.

And to look at him was to see that he was okay, at least on the surface, the only difference this morning being that he hadn't shaved. Besides the drinking, it seemed to be his only habitual practice. He had shaved every morning they had been together (at least when they were housed in regular lodgings), which struck her as odd for a man who otherwise appeared willfully ensconced in a life so down in the mouth. But strangely enough the shadow of a day's growth on his face made him seem only more respectable, not less, for in the new, still-creased denim shirt he'd changed into (one of a half-dozen she'd bought him on landing at the airport), he could easily be one of David's square-jawed colleagues at a country home on the weekend, driving to the hardware store for a pet project in the yard.

"It must have been cold last night."

"A little."

"Tonight you'll have a decent room."

He nodded.

"I decided something, while you were cleaning up."

"Okay."

"After we find Nicholas, I want to go directly on to Solferino. For all we know he could be there right now. But wherever he is, I want to go there quickly. Even if it's late in the day."

"It could take five or six hours from Siena, judging from the map."

"I don't care. I feel stronger now, but you're right." She took a breath. "I'm going to die soon."

"I said you'd die if you didn't rest."

"I know what you said. I know what you were thinking, too. So this is my wish. When he's with us we'll start right away. We can't lose any time. I know you have doubts about finding him. I can see it in your face. But I know we will find him, and once we do he'll come with us."

"And if he doesn't want to?"

"He can't say no to me. Not the way I am. If he tries, I want you to persuade him."

"Me?"

"He won't say no to you."

"He won't give a damn about me."

"I don't mean that way."

"What? What do you want me to do?"

"I want you to make sure he comes with us. Will you do that for me, Hector?"

"You want me to threaten him? Handle him?"

"I want him to be with me. If I had to, and could grab him and hold on to him myself, I would. But I don't have any strength left. I have money but I can no longer exert myself. I have no strength at all. You're my body now. You'll be my limbs. It's best for both of us if you just do what I want. As I told you, my attorney in New York will expect to hear from you after all this. After I'm gone. Or wherever you are, you can call him and he'll wire what I've set aside for you. Then you'll be able to do what you really wish."

"And what's that?"

"You really want to know what I think?"

"Sure."

"To go bury yourself for good."

Hector drove on in silence. She didn't care that he was cross at her. He was not here for the money, or for her, maybe not even for himself, if "for himself" meant the usual reasons a person did anything: some principle, or necessity, or pleasure, or the avoidance of displeasure, pain. June had not thought it as a girl, for back then she was even more fixed in her purpose than she was now—to survive, always survive—but she had come to see over the last several days that he was a being who completely lacked desire. Clearly he had had deep feeling for Dora, but she was gone and now it seemed he had fallen back into an existence most familiar to him, which he wore like a grotty old cap. He wanted nothing. He yearned for nothing. Even his drinking was just marking the time, a busyness of the hands, the mouth. He hardly seemed to care whether he was living or dead. At moments this infuriated her, given how she herself was gripping the edge of the precipice; it made her want to push him out of the car and take the wheel. If anything, she thought, he was here to wallow in the memory of Sylvie Tanner, to punish himself over her, which she knew would also be her tightest lashing, her darkest charm, and keep him longer at her side.

She had plenty to punish herself with, too, but she was focused on Nicholas. She was becoming afraid that he might resist seeing her. Even refuse. It was perhaps mad, but she pictured how if Hector had to corral him, forcibly hold the boy down, she might decide to stick him with her syringe, in order to calm him down. Certainly Nicholas would have to accept them as the best option: either she and Hector would arrest him or the authorities would. And while they journeyed to Solferino together in the back of the car, she would tell him the things she had been meaning to tell him, since the day he left for Europe: that she was sorry for her selfishness during his childhood, her focus too narrow to include even him; that she thought him vastly talented; that his sensitivity was not, as she might have led him to believe, a weakness, but could be turned into strength, of which his stubborn distance from her was a sure sign; that she forgave him for taking her book on Solferino and that he should forgive her, if he could, if not now, then someday. Lastly, she would tell him that she had always loved him, despite her meager capacity to show it, that if she could will herself eternal life it would be wholly spent at his side.

All this was true, all this was true.

And yet Sylvie Tanner, too, was ruling the weather of her mind, like an incipient mass of stormy air; she felt disturbances and shifts, the invisible whorls of a presence, even the taste of her own tongue different in her mouth. She had to close her eyes now, as it seemed Hector was speeding up. She had long thought her love for the woman was dissipated, and had been for years, hardly a memory arising. But it was messy; love was the question that had confounded her most in life. With "loved ones"—with a mother and father, sisters and a brother, with a son—one always began with love and proceeded from there, and through time and happenstance saw it broadened, or shored up, or else steadily assailed, wrecked, and torn down.

But for June it had not been exactly so; her secret feeling was that the opposite was true. Even before they had all perished, or vanished, she had had a heart that craved more readily than it accepted, she could look upon the face of a beloved with no ill reason or malice and in an instant cleave herself from the bond. It was an effortlessly monstrous ability, as if she could simply pluck from her heel a spur called love, her own cool blood the quickest antidote.

And yet with certain unknown others, she had given herself over too deeply, perhaps a half-dozen times, with both men and women. This in the years between Nicholas's leaving and before meeting David, when her solitude was almost too perfect and she craved to be touched. It was never more than the act, though there would always be some prelude. It was this way with a woman named Stephanie, whom she knew for the length of a weekend antiques conference and would never see again. She had had no intent to meet anyone, but at a booth she met this beautiful, striking woman of Spanish descent with pale skin and a full, swollen-looking mouth, and somehow the reedy timbre of the woman's voice and her lithe, narrow-shouldered physique rendered June blind with purpose.

For two days she went about seducing the woman not with her body or character or any of the usual wiles but a furious and open desire. She kept touching her arm, brushing against her when they sat together, telling her how lovely she was, applying a constant, pressuring want that had the effect of cutting off all other avenues, all other possibilities; she would force her to relent. In the end, as if by her design, the poor riled woman finally led them from the exhibition hall past fire doors into the back concrete stairwell of the hotel, where they roughly kissed and groped each other before going up to the hotel room, their grunts echoing downward and upward in the dimly lighted well as though they were toiling in a catacomb.

IT HAD BEEN LIKE THAT at the orphanage. After the Tanners first arrived, June had actually suffered what seemed a weeklong walking illness, hunched over like one of the older aunties, swallowing back a sour burning in her throat. She might not eat much for a day, or two, then would gorge herself until she could hardly breathe, her stomach feeling like it would burst. Of course once Sylvie and June got to know each other and June started cleaning the cottage for her it eventually went away, but for a while a certain effect lingered, a mild nausea just before she knew she would be with her, the same before any imminent parting: she'd feel she was going to retch, her mouth filling with spit as she ran off. Then, one day, she caught a glimpse of Sylvie changing out of some soiled blue jeans into a skirt before dinner, her long flanks chapped pink from the rough fabric, the smooth knobs of her knees almost showing through her diaphanous skin, and June, her chest burning, finally understood her discomfort might be the expression of a desire.

She sometimes wondered, naturally enough, if Sylvie could ever have a similar feeling for her. It was pure innocence, of course; she could never link her emotions with the depraved carnality she'd witnessed during the war, for she was a child again in the woman's presence, and she gave herself over to whatever Sylvie asked of her, even when she said that they should not spend so much time together, for the sake of the other children. June didn't care a whit for the others but had agreed without hesitation or question. Still, she couldn't help constantly testing the woman:

"Would you have played with me when you were a girl?"

"Of course! We always do things together, don't we?"

"But would you have liked me, if you were just one of us?"

"Don't be silly."

"But would you?"

"Yes."

"Say it again."

"Yes! Yes!"

June never fully believed her, though it hardly mattered. That she and Sylvie were together each day, that she could work in their house from after studies until bedtime, that she could always be within arm's reach, this was the world for her, her only extravagance and riches. And it was reciprocated; even in the face of Reverend Tanner, who showed a growing antipathy to her presence, sometimes hardly even greeting her, Sylvie never minded her staying an extra hour, or two.

And although it was true that Sylvie was no longer mentioning adopting her and taking her to America, June was sure that it was Sylvie's way of respectfully allowing her husband to sit with the prospect, that he needed more time with the idea of having a child who wasn't his own. She knew about their fertility troubles, if only from having stolen peeks at Sylvie's leather-bound diaries, a collection of which she kept in a trunk beneath her bed. They were dated from the early 1930s and came all the way up to their arrival here, recounting her travels with her missionary parents and her adolescent and university days in Seattle and then her marriage to Ames Tanner. Sylvie had become pregnant a number of times but they had given up trying some years ago and June could begin to understand what they were doing in Korea, certain there must be reasons besides goodness and charity for them to have come to a place as awful as this. They could not possibly be there only to give of themselves. They were hoping for something, too, and in the tireless device of her mind she was figuring how she could give them what they wished. It was finally within her power. For the best thing about the orphanage for June was not ultimately its offer of food or shelter or schooling but that it was a world unto itself, though in a manageable scale, a world she could now exert herself upon, remake as she required.

So she resolved herself to be disciplined and not bring up anymore the question of her adoption. She would patiently wait. Her bond with Sylvie was not just of a mother and daughter but that of comrades who by the curse of war had been sentenced to be alone.

The one omission in the diaries, she noticed, was any mention of Sylvie's parents' deaths. Sylvie had already told her they had died in Manchuria, where they were missionaries in a place much like New Hope, and June imagined Sylvie to have been orphaned like herself, cast out on a solitary road, compelled to make her way back to life by the force of her own tireless will. There were many years separating them, of course, this again would be a question of waiting out time, and she saw herself in their resumed lives as Sylvie's secretary and housekeeper, her girl-in-waiting, her handmaiden, someone she could use and count on at any moment of the day or night. She would be indispensable to her, and in return Sylvie would envelop her with her passion and grace, guide her through her education to her own womanhood, when June would not marry unless she had Sylvie's blessing, indeed perhaps never abide anyone else as closely, as purely.

June knew the depth of her own feelings, for it didn't please her at all to see how deadened the Tanners' marriage had become. She could hardly bear Sylvie's unhappiness. No one else could know, as she did, how they were so wanly self-encapsulated, how they rarely touched each other anymore, not even a hand on the arm, the briefest embrace. They spoke to each other warmly enough while out on the orphanage grounds but in the house they seemed caught in their own cold amber, June stripping their separate beds once weekly, the sheets redolent of nothing but sleep. Yet she couldn't help but feel sorry for Reverend Tanner as well. Late one afternoon, while he was writing letters at his desk and she was in the back room making up his wife's bed—Sylvie was helping Hector with the last of the digging for the new sewer—Tanner called her name. She assumed she'd misheard him but he called again.

"June, would you come here, please?"

She came out holding a dusting rag lightly dampened with lamp oil and began wiping the top of the rolltop desk.

"That's all right, June," he said, motioning for her to stop. "I didn't mean that. Please sit down."

He'd never offered her such a courtesy before, and she was hesitant to take it.

"You don't have to sit," he said, taking off his bifocals. The sleeves of his white shirt were crisply ironed, the fabric against the mottled skin of his wrists as papery as the stiff white linen garments the dead were clothed in.

"How old are you, June?"

"Fourteen."

"You've been here since the end of the war, haven't you?"

"Yes."

"It's fine here, but it's not a home, is it?"

She didn't answer.

"I wonder: Do you know what you'd like to be when you're an adult? Would you like to have your own family?"

She nodded, not because she definitely wanted one or had even considered it, but because she was sure that was what he wanted to hear.

"Mrs. Tanner and I would have enjoyed our own family, too. We weren't graced in that way. But we have all of you now, and we're very pleased. I value being here, among all of you."

"Yes."

"Mrs. Tanner thinks a great deal of you. You know this, obviously. She admires your intelligence and spirit. Your resolve. Do you understand what that is?"

"She says I don't like to give up."

"That's right. You may be surprised to hear this, but I admire that about you as well."

June said thank you, not knowing how else to reply. She was uneasy in his presence always, but now only more so, given how directly he was speaking to her. With his graying cowlick loosened and flopped down over his brow, his long, narrow face seemed softer, younger. His eyes were very blue up close, the color of the fancier marbles her younger brother used to play with.

"When I'm away on my trips to the other orphanages, I'm sure you spend more time with Mrs. Tanner. You don't have to deny it. It's all right. This last time I was away, I was worried about her. She hasn't been herself of late, as you know."

"She is tired often," June said, recounting herself how many times in the last weeks Sylvie had asked her to leave so she could rest.

"Yes," Tanner said ruefully. "But one of the things that gave me comfort was that she had you to keep her company. I see the benefit of this now."

"I try to help her with many things."

"Yes, yes. Please keep doing so, especially when I'm away. She gives herself so completely to the demands of the orphanage, and by the end of the day she has nothing left. I think she has begun to suffer for it."

June nodded. Indeed she was suffering, which the aunties saw as physical illness brought on by exhaustion, the untreated water, the strange food, by having to wake each morning to a sad, destroyed land. This often happened to foreign aid workers, they said. At some point they just broke down. But June knew Sylvie's trouble had less to do with the conditions than with something else, that she had fallen into what she referred to in her diaries as "the ash pit," a hole that seemed to drain all her energy and will. It seemed to June the condition would come and go mysteriously. At first when Sylvie didn't appear at the morning meal, Reverend Tanner would announce that she had taken ill and was resting, but as the frequency had increased in the past weeks he did not say anything, and someone like young Reverend Kim would suddenly appear to teach her class for the day, and sometimes the next. And when this was the case, June would know she could simply let herself inside the cottage in the afternoon and do her chores, though not to knock on the bedroom door if it was shut. Sometimes she wasn't

329

napping but sitting as still as a stone on the wooden step out back, and when she'd see June she'd smile and beckon to her, let her sit beside her and embrace her with her long, slack arms. They wouldn't talk or even move, the woman's breathing faint and shallow. If Reverend Tanner showed up they would separate and sit up and she would notice how Sylvie would instantly brighten for him but then practically collapse the moment after he left. One day it was raining and she found Sylvie outside again on the step but this time she was sitting with her head on her knees, her wool sweater and housedress soaked through, her hair a matted, tangled mess, the shivers visibly running through her body but going completely unregistered in her face, a lifeless mirror of the chalky, overcast sky.

"It's why I ask you, June," Tanner went on, "that you let me know if she's been particularly unwell. She tries to hide her distress from me and for the most part I feel I'm in the dark. I have more traveling ahead of me and I wish you could be my eyes and ears. Even after hours, if you wish."

"At night?"

"Whenever you believe she needs you. Or seems lonely. I'm afraid she's lonely too often." His gaze wandered, like he'd lost himself for an instant. But then he said: "It's for her sake, her well-being, you understand that, yes?"

"Yes."

"Good," he said, patting her arm. "Thank you." He opened his fountain pen to resume his letter writing, pausing for her to leave.

"Do you still want a family of your own?" June asked. "Or will you stay here forever?"

"Forever sounds like a very long time," he said. "But you never know."

"What about your own family?"

"We're still thinking about that."

"There are many children here," she said, desperate to sound generous. "You must meet so many children on your visits."

"Yes, I do. So many. All worthy and good. Really every last one of you."

When he uttered those words she took his implication whole; she went back to her chores with the conviction that Reverend Tanner had made a bargain with her, that all she need do was to remain his wife's closest helper, her devotee, her constant friend, and then, if she must, let him know what trouble might lie ahead. She knew he meant Hector, there could be no one else, it was only he who was spending more time with her since she had grown infirm.

She kept vigilant of their movements whenever Reverend Tanner spent a night away, but it wasn't only for him. One night she tried to watch them but they extinguished the oil lamps and the only thing she could do was listen. There was hardly any sound to start, not even any shifting or creaking from his cot, just the barest rustle of clothing, the press of lips, the scantest murmurs, and then, finally, the breathing. His breaths came first, very low, and then hers as if it were difficult, as though a patch of thick gauze were covering her mouth. Their rhythm ticked loose and various until suddenly it unjumbled, clicked in. All the while June, tightly crouched in the peerless dark between the wall and a kerosene barrel, was suppressing her own breath, her lungs aching for release, the gleaming painting of their lovemaking begun to screen in her mind. Strangely only her belly felt alive, this yawning breaking emptiness that pushed low and hot while the rest of her went heavy, dead, and it was only when they were finally done and surely fallen asleep that she dared move, her hands and feet tingling and shaking enough that she had to crawl on her elbows from the storeroom.

The following day, having returned to the orphanage, Reverend Tanner sat down next to her during the evening meal. June sat alone now, having agreed not to monopolize Sylvie's company. She had completely forgotten about her conversation with Tanner on awaking that morning, her throat parched, her head fogged and aching, as if, like Hector, she had been drinking all night.

"How goes it, June? Is everything fine?" he asked. Sylvie was at a far table eating with the younger children. Hector was not present, being likely out in the field.

She could merely nod, not yet ready for his questioning.

"You don't seem terribly certain," he said, though almost jocularly, as though he didn't in fact wish to hear anything else.

Her memory of the previous night was a stilled curtain but its music now rose up in her chest and brought the skin of her neck to life, her cheeks feeling as though they were suddenly flushed. She thought Tanner would take her aside for an interrogation but all he did was brood a moment with a half-expectant, half-wary gaze and say brightly, "Well, I must be going. Good day, June."

For days afterward she tried to determine what to do. All her considerations foretold only trouble if they should continue, and yet she found herself hoping for Reverend Tanner to spend an evening away again. It was like the hunger she didn't suffer anymore, this grave sensation so resident that it took on its own life, its own existence, was the body within her body that now drew all her energies. At fourteen her figure was at last changing, after being stunted during the war; since living at the orphanage she'd put on more than eight kilos, mostly on her thighs and hips and on her chest, which the older boys glanced at, but warily, fearing she might catch them and take it as a provocation to fight. She noticed this and sometimes she'd sit back wherever she was and make a show of closing her eyes, let them look at her for as long as they wanted. She might even press her shoulders back, to accentuate the new fullness. Her doing so wasn't in vanity or pride, or from the slightest interest in any of them; it was pure experimentation, a trial to determine how it felt to be an object of desire, and she found that the more she felt their stares the more her own desire fired, trebled, eventually took on its own reason.

So she stayed silent when in the ensuing weeks Tanner departed on his various trips, and waited for Sylvie to emerge from her cottage in the middle of the night. Whenever she and Hector let the oil lamp burn, June could see them glide over each other with a patience and tenderness that was the opposite of the jerky, horrid couplings she'd had to witness during the war. And though she was startled by the broad, taut ropes of his body, her eye kept resting upon Sylvie's calf, her knee, the way her belly would grow shallow under his kisses and dip far enough below the spur of her hip that she appeared starved herself. She had the loveliest glow, the light seemed to stream from her eyes, from her half-opened mouth; nor did the illumination dissipate until well after they were done, when June saw her open a small black kit and remove a needle from its velvet-lined well. Hector did not take it himself but he helped her, binding her calf with the rubber cord and tapping her heel and then shooting her with the medicine that made her shiver and then go slack, turn a ghostly bone-blue.

When Reverend Tanner was present June would sometimes stay late with Sylvie in the back room. He allowed it enough times that after a while her presence after the generator went out became almost customary. They would all be reading, Sylvie and June in the narrow bed, Tanner in his own out in the front sitting room. He always retired earlier than they, and they took turns whisper-reading aloud by the oil lamp books from the army base library, children's books but also others that Sylvie had chosen for her, *Little Women* and *Great Expectations* and *The Good Earth*. Sometimes June would ask Sylvie to read *A Memory of Solferino* to her and she'd refuse at first but always eventually yield, the passages entering them, June thought, with both pain and bliss like the medicine in the kit, and making them cling more tightly to each other.

One night June fell asleep there, and when morning came she awoke to find herself wearing one of Sylvie's nightgowns and tucked in the spoon of her slumbering body. She carefully turned into her and took in the warm, round scent of her hair, the sour-sweeter one of her neck, and masked her eyes in the scant damp of her nightgown; then on succeeding nights she would pretend to fall asleep and then watch Sylvie slip outside to the chair in back with her kit, feel her when she returned, her weight seeming to have doubled as she fell against June's chest. It was then that June waited, sometimes hours, for the measure between Sylvie's breaths to lengthen, for her to descend further into deepest sleep. This happened almost nightly: she would turn, lie on her back. Her lips would soften and ease. If there was starlight or moonlight her face and long throat gleamed with its luminance, this woman an ashen statue, only half alive. Here was the only beauty in the world. And then one night June could not help herself; she pulled back the blanket as if it were the frail leaf of an antique book. Her hands crept to Sylvie's throat, where her nightgown opened, and undid the mother-of-pearl buttons that ran down to the hem; she took them one by one, the near half of the nightgown falling away, exposing the whole length of Sylvie now to the cold night air. June touched the belly, grazed the lowest rib, the small, flattish breast no fuller than one of her own. The nipple pushed up between her fingers, as dense as clay, and without knowing what she was doing she put her mouth over it, closing her eyes. She couldn't breathe again, her heart as if collapsed in her chest, this tiny leaden node, poised for Sylvie to protest, to stir. But she did not. Nor did she when June's hand slid down and nestled in the burning cup of her long legs, not moving, nor stirring, neither wanting the other to wake.

FOURTEEN

IN SIENA THEY HAD to share quarters again, as there were only six guest rooms in the *residenza*, a converted townhouse looking out over a tiny cobble stone piazza. Like everything else Hector had seen in this country it was old, beautiful, more than slightly decrepit, its façade saturated in the exact color (at least in his memory) of his mother's light-brown eyes, this burnished, timeless wood. But the constant, nearly inescapable sighting of exquisite landscapes and antique architecture was wearing on him. Maybe he was imprinted too deeply by modest Ilion, or war-ravaged Seoul, or forgettable, low-slung towns like Tacoma and Fort Lee and then the many other crumbling, forlorn places he'd drifted through in between, and after these few days he felt that he was being overwhelmed, that his eyes hurt. The feeling that he should be comforted and uplifted by the beauty only made him feel more misplaced than ever, misguided, lost in a museum of someone else's life.

Their room was very large, a half-floor suite with high coffered ceilings and marble-tile floors and rich draperies and decorated with old

rugs and paintings. The furniture, June had commented, was top quality. Hector had never seen such a place, much less stayed in one. The
bath had a tub carved from a single block of marble and the fixtures
were burnished brass and the bath and bed linens had been freshly
starched and ironed, the crisp hand of their fabric pressed to a high
sheen. Vases of sunflowers were set on either side of the single king-
sized bed (he would sleep on the red velvet sofa), its baronial walnut
headboard carved with a scene from the Palio di Siena, the famous horse
race held in the main plaza, a tight phalanx of charging horses and rid-
ers thundering to the finish, the town's huge clock tower serving as the
background. The Palio was held in July and August, but in some years
(like this one) there was also a special race in September; this was to be
run tomorrow. He had parked their car in a lot on the northern end of
the old city walls and taken a taxi toward the center. The only reason
they were able to get a room at all was an unexpected departure due to
illness by a Swiss couple at one of the most expensive lodgings in town,
which the driver knew of because he'd driven the couple less than an
hour earlier out to their parked car. The cabdriver, named Bruno, was
a brightly garrulous young man who spoke a distinctive English and
told them all about the "garish" and "anomalous" Palio tomorrow, about
the history of the race and the *contrade*, groups from different wards
of the city, each of which backed a horse. After he delivered them to
the hotel and spoke to the owner (they would pay only twice the printed
rate, normally tripled because of the race), Hector gave him fifty dollars
and explained he was looking for someone and asked him to come back
in an hour, to be their translator and guide.

June had planned to accompany them after a quick bath. But when
she was done she called weakly for him and he had to help her once again
from the tub, this time blotting her wet skin and hair with the towel.
She wavered there before him like a terribly sick child, barely able to
stand upright. She was partly revived by the warm water but perhaps

altered, too, and she spoke with a breathy delirium about how deeply grateful she was to him, saying again that her lawyer would ensure he was well compensated. She wrapped her arms around his neck and fell into him in her full nakedness and murmured that he could do whatever he wished to her, kissing his ear, his neck. He could feel the cling of her damp legs about his thigh and although he could not in a lifetime accede to so wrong an invitation, the barest instinctual shiver crept up from his groin to his chest, momentarily rousing him before a flood of shame clogged his throat. She collapsed into him and he wrapped her in a robe and helped her to the bed. She said she would just rest for a moment, but after lying down she asked him for a shot of morphine. He opened her kit and prepared the shot, unable to quell the thought of doing the same for Sylvie Tanner, to numb and pleasure, too.

"Where are we, now?"

"In Siena."

"Oh yes, yes. Will you go find Nicholas?"

"I'll try."

"Bring him back here soon," she said, a waxy veneer dulling her eyes. "Very soon."

He rolled her onto her side and injected her in her rump and she drifted off to sleep. It was easier for him to do it for her, of course, rather than watch her struggle with the vial and syringe, to twist and try to find a good spot. When he did it her breathing would quicken and she might even reach out and hold tightly to his shirt and then softly exhale with a certain ripe agony when he finally injected her. In her overly grateful euphoria she once said she loved him. He didn't know how to answer.

Sometimes he may have jabbed harder than necessary, or in a spot that wasn't fleshy enough, and she'd cry out sharply, gritting her teeth. He did so because a part of him was afraid of her, because he wanted to get away from her but couldn't force himself to do so. But in guilty compensation he now gave her more of the drug, drawing down a few more lines on the syringe. She was no longer insisting she needed to keep her mind clear. What was left of her body was in charge of her and as such she somehow seemed a bit stronger, fuller, her cheeks not so drawn and wan; she was suddenly eating more, having a butter cookie along with the gelato she had him buy her every other hour or so, which was the only regular thing she consumed, save water; maybe it was all the sugar that was plumping her up, propping her. Earlier they had stopped at the big highway cafeteria and she'd had an anise cookie and lemonade, and she surprised him by rising from her chair like any healthy, sprightly woman and walking out to the car for the Italian phrasebook in order to ask the girl at the register what the best route would be to Lombardy, after leaving Siena. But her exertions had now left her like this, and when it was clear she would sleep for a while he drew closed the heavy draperies, the place as shrouded and hushed as a mausoleum.

He bathed and shaved and put on the last of the shirts she'd bought him, which was still in its clear plastic package. Everything else of his stunk. They had been traveling without a thought of doing wash and so he gathered their dirty clothes up into a canvas drawstring sack he found in the closet, rooting through her luggage and pulling out what was unfolded or dirty. Her things smelled only marginally better than his, the odor more of dampness and spoilage than body smells. Someone could easily argue that all of him had spoiled, even as his physique remained remarkably sound, that a special scan of his abstract being would show an unsettling result, revealing a soul neither bountiful nor spare but used up, right down to nothing. Of course Dora would not have said so about him, but he couldn't help wondering during the long, silent hours in the car whether he had been fooling her and himself, whether she would have eventually seen him for what he was, agreed with June that he was a man who wanted to hide himself away forever. He wasn't useless (as a gravedigger, a janitor, a driver, a nurse, now a laundry maid), but by any weighing of the present evidence—what one might have banked via family or friendship or love or self-purpose, not even counting the mistakes or transgressions or outright crimes—he was not a worthy man. It was as plain as his thirst. His heart felt smashed every time he pictured Dora, but if he was honest it soon revived with what he had to believe was a rush of liberty, if liberty degraded, this feeling that he was released once again from the onus of having to hope or dream.

And yet here he was, dressing for an errand that he could hardly pretend had not partly become his own. He was increasingly curious about Nicholas, too, wondering about the bloodlines that he and June had given him; about its expression in his physical appearance, and then in his undeniably slippery character; what his voice sounded like; and then simply wanting to lay eyes on the young man, take in the shape of him astride the world. He wished he could bump into him and know him and trail him unannounced, peer at him as he sat at a café or on a bus. Maybe this was what comprised fatherhood, at least for somebody like him: a sorry kind of surveillance. He knew he was a thousand light-years from being a respectable adult, his only contact that was even remotely paternal being his sometime counsel at Smitty's of the slumming suburban kids, muttering they ought to switch to beer before they drove back home on the Palisades Parkway. He certainly couldn't bear any connection now, any relationship, the prospect of learning too much about Nicholas only trumped by the frightening idea that he'd have to explain himself, too, go over his background and his history and his bond to June, which would, if Nicholas pushed it, open up every other damn thing. But as he shuffled quietly across the expansive space of the suite to leave, he stopped by the bedroom and the sight of her stilled body, looking desiccated and abandoned in the gauzy raft of the canopied bed, made him think he couldn't deny her this one last thing, however it might disturb him.

At the *residenza* office on the ground floor he held up the bag of their dirty clothes and tried to communicate to the woman at the desk that he wanted to wash them someplace. She kept talking and motioning and then began pulling the bag away from him and it was only when Bruno appeared that it was sorted out; it had been so long since Hector had stayed in anything but a fleabag hotel that he'd forgotten that such a thing as laundry service was possible. He gave over the bag and had Bruno make sure she knew to leave it outside their door, as the *signora* was sleeping. Outside they made their plan. Hector had briefly mentioned to Bruno earlier that they were looking for someone and now he showed him the old school photograph and said he was likely working in an antiques shop.

"There are many numerous establishments of antiquities here in Siena, *signore*," he replied. "But I have cognizance of the very best ones, and we shall be advised to start at these."

He explained that it would be better to go by foot today. They were heading to Il Campo, the large main square, where the most prominent shops were, several of them in the piazza itself and on the street immediately ringing it. This was where they would run the horse race tomorrow.

"Excuse me if this is offensive to you, but may I inquire who is this fellow you are looking for?"

"He's her son."

"I see," he said, openly searching Hector's face. "This is dolorous. Is the situation due to an estrangement?"

"I suppose so."

"You are a good friend, then," Bruno said.

"No, not a good friend."

Bruno nodded curiously. He had a funny way of speaking and was forthright, but he still had a sense of when to keep quiet. He was just about the age Nicholas was now, and Hector decided he was lucky to have him along, so he could get at least some practice dealing with a younger fellow. All along he had assumed that June would be the one dealing with Nicholas, and that if he did anything at all, he'd do as she had asked him, perhaps physically compel him in some way. But now he wasn't sure what he'd do, and he was glad for Bruno's presence, to run interference, maybe even to talk for him if necessary.

On the way to the main square they passed smaller squares and side streets completely taken over by the *contrade*. It was as if circus gangs and their families had overrun the town. They were making preparations for tomorrow's race, making banners and decorating large chariots for the prerace procession. The banners, patterned with medieval-looking crests and designs, festooned the doorways, the motifs rhymed in the smocks and costumes of the mostly young people milling around the long tables on which older women were setting out bread baskets and plates of salami and pitchers of water and wine. Small dogs and children, also dressed in *contrada* colors, scampered after one another across the cobblestones. Tourists stood to the side, pointing and taking pictures. Some assemblages spontaneously broke into song, rehearsing traditional anthems that sounded like stadium chants crossed with folk ballads, the reports of which would prompt a competing chorus across the way, drawing out yet another chorus, echoes of the bellowed music rounding through the stone-walled city.

Hector thought back to certain summer days in Ilion, though those would too often end not in shared song but shouts and strife: a scene of mostly company families picnicking at the river park, the men playing baseball with a keg of beer stationed by first base, the mothers cheering hotly between gulps of their shandies and lemonades, all of it peppy and happily competitive until some red-faced lout (sometimes

Jackie Brennan) would shriek about a rough slide or inside pitch; there'd
be taunts and shoves, and unsettled scores would rear up and ignite a
scuffle or two, until at some point everybody quit going altogether,
staying at home and drinking on their own porches and giving familial
grief to one another. If he had grown up here instead of in Ilion, would
he look forward to sitting cheek by jowl each year with his lifelong
neighbors? Would he be drinking in celebration, crooning with them
until his chest ached? Serve as an estimable brother, or husband? Maybe
even a father? Or would he be just as unsociable as now, maybe more
so with the standing expectation that he join in? Surely there were mal-
contents and miscreants here like anywhere else, and yet to look upon
the gatherings he could believe what Bruno was telling him, that near
every last able-bodied person took part, at least marginally, that a "communal tide," as the young man put it, swept up all, even the flotsam
like Hector, who would never hold high any colors.

"How long will you be visiting?" Bruno asked.

"Just today."

"You will not witness the race?"

"No."

"The Palio is a spectacle, something not to be missed. This time it
is a special one, as I indicated, a commemoration of the Comune.
But I understand. The lady you are traveling with, she is not in good
health."

"That's right."

"My family is close-acquainted to the best general physician of our
city. He practiced in Milano."

"Don't sweat it."

"It is no issue. I will telephone him, whenever she needs."

"She doesn't need anything," Hector said. "Not anymore. That's
it, okay?"

Bruno nodded. They had reached the large main square, which

suddenly opened up from the shadowed narrow street in a brilliant wash of light. Roving hawkers peddled guidebooks and souvenirs, drinks and snacks. The antiques shops in the square that Bruno suggested were open and crowded with customers, but the proprietors, both of whom seemed to know Bruno, or at least recognized him as a local, had no reaction to the photograph he showed them. As they departed the second shop the owner eyed Hector at length, with a kind of pitying disdain, as if he were some sad sack of a parent futilely searching for someone who was no doubt wayward from very early on.

Next they went to a shop just outside Il Campo, on the way toward the *duomo* on the Via di Città; here the proprietor told Bruno that a young foreigner had recently inquired about working there. But hers was a smaller shop than those in the main square and she only needed help on Saturdays, and the young man, whom she remembered as confident and vaguely Oriental-looking, had asked her if there was another antiques dealer who could use an English-speaking helper. She had pointed him to a specialty dealer on the western end of town, a new high-end gallery that catered to wealthy tourists and whose owner was not a Sienese, and thus perhaps in need of a manager. It was near another famous church of the city, the Basilica di San Domenico, and though Bruno didn't know of it he decided they should go there; if it was unfruitful they could easily loop up and stop back at the *residenza*, to check on the lady, before trying the last few neighborhoods on the eastern side of town. Barring all that, tonight they could visit the nightclubs and coffeehouses that were popular with students and younger people; if Nicholas were indeed in Siena he would likely be out on the eve of the race.

The shop was a new glass-façade gallery across the street from the small plaza in front of the basilica. Three large oil paintings hung in the front display, tame, Impressionist-style landscapes of the Tuscan countryside. They had to push a buzzer to be admitted, and after a moment Bruno pressed again and a pretty, bespectacled young woman dressed in a tailored gray suit and white blouse appeared at the desk and let them in. The gallery was large and double-winged, as it took up the ground-floor retail space on either side, the central room a sculpture and jewelry gallery, with the wings devoted to modern and antique furniture on one side and paintings on the other. The young woman immediately took Hector for a tourist (his new shirt and trousers, no doubt) and introduced herself in perfect English as Laura, and Bruno briefly explained (also in English) why they were there. They showed her the old middle-school photograph. She examined the picture, the scantest ripple crossing her face, and when Bruno asked her again if she knew such a person she said that there was a young Englishman who was recently hired.

"You mean here?"

"Yes."

"What is his name?" Bruno asked.

"What do you want with him?" she said, her voice suddenly less friendly. "Has he done something wrong?"

"This man is aiding a lady who seeks him. She is his mother."

"I see," she said, this time inspecting Hector carefully. "His name is Nick Crump."

They both looked at Hector and he acknowledged he was the one. But he was unsettled by how quickly they located him: it was as though Nicholas were hoping to be found, making no effort to obscure his trail. At the other shops Hector thought he was prepared to come upon him, but now his natural impulse was to turn and head for the street, to get out of there before any serious complications set in, everything having revved up too rapidly to full, messy speed. Bruno asked if he was working today and Laura said he was out delivering a purchase to a hotel. He would be back soon enough. They each looked after the gallery four days a week, overlapping one day; "Nick" had apparently taken the semester off from graduate study in art history in Bologna. Somewhat coolly she asked Hector how he knew his mother, and if he lived in London as well. He didn't know how he should answer, as she clearly had a more intimate interest than just that of a fellow employee. He could only manage to say he was a family friend. But he muttered it lamely and she wasn't impressed.

She then stated: "It's terrible, isn't it, how she and her attorneys are trying to disinherit him? After his father dies, and still she can be so horrible to him. Is this why she is seeking him? Is she regretful now?"

"No," Hector said, again for lack of anything better, impressed by the passion Nick's apparent storytelling had inspired in this intelligent, attractive woman.

"Then what is it? Do you have a message for him? Something final?"

Hector's non-reply frustrated her, only stoking her indignation, and after an uncomfortable silence in the gallery, Laura walked to the door in her clicking high heels and held it open.

"I am sorry, but I feel I must ask you to leave now. If you tell me which hotel you are staying at, I will let him know and perhaps he will contact you. But that is up to him. I don't feel, however, that you should stay any longer, as you are not here as a customer of the gallery. Please respect this and understand."

Bruno began rattling away at her in a sharp Italian, but of course Hector did understand, and motioned, him to cease. All he had hoped to do was to locate Nicholas, to let him know his mother wished to speak to him and wait to see if he would agree; if he didn't, there was really nothing Hector or anyone else could do, no matter what June wanted. Yet what exactly was Hector wanting? Certainly not this. Not this at all. The prospect of having to talk to Nicholas face-to-face at any moment was making him feel as though his insides were being carved out like a gourd, which was the reciprocal sensation of wanting to fill the hollowness with a week's worth of booze, to raise a small cask of some local liquor to his mouth, to make a river of his throat.

He motioned Bruno to the door and had already turned when a tall, slim young man on a pale-green-and-white motor scooter rolled up and parked in front of the plate glass. He wore dark aviator sunglasses, dark slacks, a blue-and-white-striped dress shirt. Sleek, polished loafers. He pushed the scooter up onto its kickstand and approached Laura, who was still standing in the open doorway. He looked inside, in the direction of Hector and Bruno, but could see nothing for the reflection in the glass, and as he entered, Laura met him, and he touched her hand, only briefly, smoothly unclasping it when he saw there were customers present. Otherwise he surely would have kissed her. Laura glanced back at them and muttered a few words in his ear, but his expression didn't change; if anything, his jaw seemed to ease, and he took off his sunglasses and approached them directly.

"Good afternoon, sir," he said to Hector, extending his hand, his accent tinged British, or maybe vaguely Continental. Hector shook his cool, bony hand. Nick leaned forward and said, quite softly, "Could we chat elsewhere? All right? There's a café around the corner."

He kissed Laura lightly on the cheek and they whispered a few words in Italian. He led them down the street to the corner café. Bruno had a coffee at the bar while Hector and Nick took a table inside. Nick immediately lit a cigarette; he was a distinctive-looking person, his cheekbones jutting out quite sharply, his nose narrow and delicate. He had wide, large brown eyes and wavy dark hair that he wore in a long, loose style, the ends tucked back behind his ears. He could certainly be Eurasian, in Hector's opinion, though he didn't much look like his old photograph. Hector couldn't see much of himself there, or June either, but then what did he really know? The only varieties he was expert in were the various clans of his family's tiny Irish-blooded universe, and then maybe the demi-human strains that flourished in the dank, lightless ecology of Smitty's, identifiable by the bulbous, angry nose, the mustardy pallor, the sorry teeth and hair. Nick was very handsome, but in a perfectly original way. At the orphanage there had been a number of mixed-blood kids, a natural consequence of the war. They were sometimes teased or shunned by the others, but to Hector they looked like no one in creation with their wide, petaling eyes and buttery, earthen coloring. Yet despite their beauty and hybrid vigor he couldn't help but see them as being somehow vulnerable, too, doomed to their singularity, their species of one, which mirrored, strangely, how he had always felt inside. They could also appear so different from moment to moment, shape-shift when not even meaning to, as Nick was now, the mixing inside him veiling and unveiling this feature and that, depending on the angle, or the light. But one could make the argument: Nick was just about his height, if not build; and he thought he could see something of June's mouth in the set of his, that certain crimp in her lip, that utter resolve.

The waiter brought their order, a coffee for Nick, nothing for Hector. But Nick didn't drink his, just smoked and rolled his knuckles on the table. He wasn't looking at Hector, either, but rather glancing over at Bruno, who was standing at the bar, then to the door in the back, as if calculating what it would take to get away.

"Well, are we going to do this?" he finally said. "I'm not going to say anything more until I have a lawyer."

"I'm not a cop. I know about the stealing, but that's not why I'm here."

"You can cut the bullshit."

Hector didn't reply, just looking at him.

"So who the hell are you?"

Hector only told him what he'd said to Bruno, to Laura—that he was his mother's helper.

"Well, Jesus Christ!" Nicholas said. He nodded toward Bruno, who was watching the soccer match on the television behind the bar. "What about him?"

"He's a taxi driver."

Nicholas shook his head. He chuckled at himself and drank his espresso. Then he rose to leave. Hector got up and gripped his shoulder, firmly pressing him back down. Nicholas's eyes flashed in anger and his neck tensed but he instantly mastered himself, Hector almost feeling through his fingers how the young man geared himself back.

"So what does she want?" Nick said, lighting another cigarette. "And why did she send you? This is all very *bizarre*," he added, intoning the word like a Frenchman. Every other word of his sounded as though he had grown up in a different place. Then he said, with an attitude of propriety, "We're getting along just fine writing letters. If this is about the money she's sent, I'm sorry, but it's all spent. I'm quite broke, in fact."

"She wants to see you. That's all. She's here in town."

"Now?" He said it as a boy would say it, more non-wishing than disbelieving. "Where is she?"

Hector told him the name of the hotel.

At this, Nicholas just smoked for a few moments, then put the cigarette out.

"I can't see her," he said. "I've been away from her for this long, and it's better to stay away. Tell her I'll keep writing her, though."

"You think she'll keep sending you money?" Hector said.

"Is that some kind of threat?"

"No," he said. "Just telling how it is. She's sick. She's dying."

"You're just saying that. She never wrote of anything like that."

"It's true," Hector said.

Nicholas asked what was wrong with her, and Hector described what he knew of her condition, suddenly hearing himself as if he were indeed

some lame, defeated dad come calling on a prodigal son, finally armed
with the saddest ultimatum. He was better suited to defending himself,
or at exacting revenge, than to this soft task of convincing. Nicholas
listened in silence, his tongue slowly working inside his mouth. He
stared morosely into his empty coffee cup. Hector said they should go
now. But then he answered, "No. I can't see her. I really can't. I'm sorry
she's so sick, but I can't."

The sentiment was disturbing, but perhaps equally disturbing to
Hector was that he was beginning to feel Nick was offending him (this
when he believed he could never be offended), offending him to the
core with his callousness of course but also because of the fact of their
shared blood. It was a terrible new feeling. He wanted to grab him by
the throat, shake him silly, maybe even punch him. Their first contact,
and this is how he'd play the father: to rough up his own.

Hector said: "I won't tell her what you said. It doesn't matter to me
what you do. You can write her all you want. But you should know,
we'll only be here today. Tomorrow we're moving on. Then you'll probably never see her again."

He got up and at the bar he paid for the drinks from the rolled wad
of cash he was carrying, while Bruno told Nicholas on which piazza
the *residenza* was located. He didn't appear to be listening. They were
heading back for the hotel when Nicholas caught up with them a few
blocks later on his scooter.

"Listen," he said. "What's your name. Hector?" His tone was now
less mellifluously worldly, settling into something squarely lower-brow,
as if he now better understood the person he was appealing to. "Listen,
Hector. I'm sorry about what I said. I can see you think a lot of my
mother and I appreciate that. I was freaked out that you found me. I
wasn't thinking straight. Now I'm wondering about the other people
who might be looking for me. I know I'm going to have to leave soon.
But listen. I'll come and see her. I want to. I'm busy at the shop now

with a few more deliveries and don't have any time tonight. But I'll come tomorrow, tomorrow morning, before the races. You know about the races, yes? Okay? But can you do me a favor? I told you I'm broke, and I'm not going to lie. I'm in some trouble here. I owe money from the race last month. I wrote to her last week to wire fifteen hundred dollars but obviously you were on the way here. She's never not sent money when I've asked. I'm sure you know this. Do you think she would give me some now, if she were here? Do you think so?"

"I don't know," Hector said.

"Come on, I think you do. She'd give me what I need. We both know she would. So would you be a good fellow and front me some? I see you have a lot of cash. I'm sure she'll cover whatever you can give me."

"It's all hers, anyway."

"Well, then. I had asked for fifteen hundred. You may not have that much, but if you can give me a thousand for now, I'd be grateful."

"Here," Hector said, peeling off some bills. He didn't want to deal anymore with this, with him. Nicholas quickly counted it: the equivalent of four hundred dollars.

"Can you spare another two or three? I'll come tomorrow, I will. I want to see her. I have to. It's the right thing to do."

Although he had enough, Hector didn't give him any more money, telling him he should ask for it himself. His expression must have hardened, for without further plea or argument Nick nodded, even extending his hand to Hector before peeling away in a puff of blue scooter smoke. Hector had taken it, but grudgingly, the truth already clear to him as he walked back to the hotel with Bruno: he would never have any feeling for the kid. No feeling at all. Hector thanked Bruno for his help, paying him for his time, and asked for his telephone number in case he needed him again. Bruno gave it to him but said he was rarely at home, promising to come by the hotel several times before the next day was up. He had not said a word while they were walking, but when he got behind the wheel of his taxi he stated plainly, "Forgive me, *signore*. But I must say this to you. That is a fright of a man. I would stay far away from him."

Hector lightly rapped the top of the taxi and sent him off. Nick was not just a liar and a cheat, a world-class shit; he was a warning embodied, this alarm-in-the-flesh, a herald of no good that made even Hector's own worn-down heart gallop and shudder. He should tell June he hadn't found him, that there was no sign or further clue, and just take her straightaway to Solferino, where she could wait out her fast-dwindling time in peace. The boy would only bring her unhappiness. What struck him was how Nick didn't in the least try to hide the fact from him, as if he believed that they were somehow allied in regard to his mother, that Hector, too, was angling for something. Had Nicholas picked up on their connection, some whiff of their relation? Or was it something equally evident in Hector, his tumbled, blunted self, ludicrously wrapped in a brand-new creased shirt and cuffed trousers, this fellow masquerading as someone who could help fulfill a dying woman's hopes?

He passed the *residenza* office and the woman inside called after him as he ascended the stairs; she spoke only Italian and he assumed she was telling him about the laundry, for she gestured upstairs and then down. He thanked her and she kept talking as he went up. But when he reached the second-floor landing he realized that the laundry couldn't possibly have been both washed and dried already, for he'd been gone just over an hour. And then he saw what she must have been talking about: the heavy door of their room was ajar. He could see light from inside casting a weak beam on the carpeting of the darkened corridor. He pushed inside.

The draperies of one of the tall, grand windows directly opposite the door had been drawn back a few inches. Their mostly emptied bags

were as he'd left them in the sitting area, set between the sofa and
armchair, but he noticed her purse was not on the coffee table where
he had last seen it. He was holding most of the cash, but she had all
the traveler's checks. Across the lengthy space of the suite he could
dimly make her out on the bed, lying on her side with her back to him.
When he approached her he saw the purse on the night table. It was
open, and though her wallet was still there, the envelope containing
the traveler's checks was gone.

"Are you back already?" she murmured, turning to him, her eyes
heavy with sleep and with the drug. Her words were blunted and slurred,
running together. "Did you get one for yourself, too?"

"Get what?" Hector said.

"Oh," she said, staring at him as if she had forgotten his name, even
his face.

"It's Hector," he said.

"Oh, yes," she said, though she still didn't seem to register him.
"Where is he?"

"Who?"

"Nicholas. He said you sent him right over. He's gone to get me a
treat. It seemed like a dream but I'm sure it was real. Do you think it
was a dream?"

"No," he said, his anger at himself burning inside his chest. Nicholas must have ridden right over on the scooter while he and Bruno had
walked back.

"He didn't have any money for the gelato," she said. "I gave him a
traveler's check. I signed it for him."

"More than one?"

"Yes, I guess so. I don't know. Do you think they'll let him use
them?"

"They might."

"I hope so. God, I'm so tired," she groaned. "I want to wait for him but I have to sleep. I'd love some gelato. Will you make sure to let him back in? Please wake me up when he comes. Will you? I'm so hungry."

"Okay."

She closed her eyes. She shivered a little, and so he folded the quilted bedspread from one side of the bed over her. Then he closed the draperies and sat near her in the dark for a long while, thinking about what he would do. He'd search out the nightclubs, as Bruno suggested. He would find him, and not to retrieve any money. Let him have the money. It was by all rights his, anyway. There was no lesson to be offered; Nicholas was certainly beyond any instruction, or shaming. Still, when it came time, he wondered whether he would lose control and try to beat some decency into him. He'd never raised his fists for something as righteous as that. And he kept hearing again his father's high, rye-soaked voice chirping into his ear while he shouldered him home. *You think you're going to get away with it, boy? You think it doesn't apply to you?* Hector had never bothered asking what exactly his father meant by *it*, but now, seeing June's utter frailness, the sad, blunted topography of her beneath the bedspread, her desperate need to believe, he thought he understood at last what his old man had been talking about: *life.*

Life, still undefeated. Not just for June but for him, too. He had never gotten away with anything, could point to most every instance in his days as evidence of such. His odd father had madly suspected he was some kind of immortal, if a lowly one, but maybe his peers (in the army, at Smitty's) had like notions after certain miraculous escapes, the almost instantly healing wounds; maybe some unlucky women had caught an aura gracing him, this gleam of persistence. But any persistence, he knew, wasn't his own doing. He'd never asked for such endurance. All concerned would have been better off had he perished during the war, or in the orphanage fire, or under the bumper of Clines's car, instead of innocent Dora. And so now, at this sojourn's end, eyeing June's

demise, he was ready to cast off whatever mantle had been mysteriously bestowed on him. He would disappear along with her. To hide
wouldn't be enough. Another good person would happen across his
dooming path, start the cycle again. While driving them here he had
circled around the way it would happen, but now he was settling on
the idea. His was juvenile imagining but he knew it would have to be
catastrophic: accelerate before a tight hill turn and burst through the
railing. Wind heavy chains around his ankles to bury himself at sea.
Drape his head over the steel train track and listen for the clang. He
had tried in earnest, in fact, soon after Sylvie died, looping a rope over
a tree limb far away from the orphanage (so no kids would have to see
him), cinching the noose, but when he kicked away the stool he'd
brought with him the cords of his neck sprang up in protest and jack-
eted his windpipe and after a while he had to cut himself down, his
skin abraded in a mocking necklace of futility, his heart sodden with
the full deadweight of defeat. For what was worse than dying, if not
being able to die?

But there would be no more enduring for him now.

June stirred, moaning terribly. He could already tell the kind of cry;
the morphine was wearing off.

"Nicholas?" she gasped. "Are you here?"

He froze, not wanting to tell her otherwise. She drifted off again.
He quickly went downstairs and across the piazza, to where there was
a gelateria. He brought her back a double cone of *limone*, the refreshing
scent of which was somehow enough to rouse her from her sleep. She
sat up all by herself and took it from him without hesitating, licking it
with the eagerness and focus of a child. Her world was becoming quite
small, centering on the simplest things. A sweet, tart flavor. A salve of
cold in her parched throat. Sometimes there was nothing better than
to offer a little succor. While she ate the gelato he prepared her a heavy
dose and when she was finished she surprised him by hugging him as

tightly as she was able before lying down again. She even turned herself over when she saw him holding the syringe.

"Is Nicholas here?" she said afterward, gazing up past him, searching, her pupils huge, dark.

"Not yet," he answered.

"He'll come back. I know it."

"Yes," he told her, now looking her straight in her eyes. "He will."

FIFTEEN

THEY WERE TRAVELING at what seemed to June a great, soaring speed. Really a wonderful speed. It was Sunday morning and the *auto-strada* was still mostly empty. The sky was shimmering, an electrified vault of blue. They were flying north. She was not up front with Hector anymore but reclined in the back of the sedan, propped up on one side with the pillows he'd bought from the innkeeper of the *residenza* back in Siena. It was too uncomfortable for her to sit upright or lie flat, and with her knees lifted up toward her chest she could clasp her hands around the backs of her thighs and steady herself with the pressure the way one might tightly press on a bad cut or wound. Of course, she was the wound, but he was being good to her with the needle and although the pain was constant it was routine weather and what she mostly felt in her belly and limbs and in her groin and neck was that certain cling-ing weight, an ineluctable density that while phantom took its form in a woman's voice: *I'm here, I'm here, I'm here.*

She took it as Sylvie's voice, then the cancer's, and then, finally, a version of her own. It was melodious enough and yet at the same time washed of human feeling, its notes echoing coldly through her bones. But she could endure it. She could endure most anything now. Even if she could hardly walk more than ten paces at a time, her will was un-diminished and perhaps even strengthening; she was convinced that if she could remain at attention and make her thoughts hew to the neces-sities of each moment, string herself from one to the next, the focus of her mind would not allow her flesh to cede. One need not surrender. It wasn't always the case. She wasn't crazy. Although she could hardly distinguish anymore between waking and sleep, each state having bled over into the other enough that she could close her eyes and still see, she felt sure she was right about this. She was almost certain that she could hold on for a long time, maybe indefinitely, croon along with the voice ringing in her head and thus stay hinged to the present. Never let herself go.

That they would be in Solferino later today was a blessing, for she could rest after they arrived and still have some good light to see the church. Or they could take their time, maybe even leave it until the next day, or the next, and the thought occurred to her that instead of an inn or hotel they might stay in an efficiency or even an apartment or villa—they had enough money—where Hector could cook again if he wanted to, make that camper's stew she loved back then and loved now for its sweet, tomatoey smell, the way it had made her mouth water and ache in the hunter's cottage like she was truly about to eat again.

In fact Hector was being quite kind to her, maybe even gallant, exiting at rest stops before she had to ask and helping her in and out of the low-slung seat of the car. He'd even grabbed a surly cashier who made a remark when she fumbled and dropped her change, holding his collar over the counter and telling him in English to be polite, which by his expression the fellow seemed instantly to understand. Maybe a villa would be better, for they could sit together in its garden and finally talk about all that had happened between them. They would have plenty of room, too, in case Nicholas changed his mind and decided to train up and join them in Solferino.

Nicholas said he wanted to come, to visit the place with her, but he decided that staying behind in Siena, so he could keep working at the fancy art gallery and make a way for himself, would be best for him at the moment. Eventually, it was understood, he would return to New York. She wished now that she had not sold her business, but of course he could start his own. He *should* start his own, sell only the highest-quality pieces, unlike her. He had promised to keep out of trouble, to write regularly as he had been doing, and in kind, she said, she (or her attorney) would wire whatever money he needed. Maybe Nicholas had been a bit selfish and greedy and his requests somewhat inappropriate but in the end everything would be his anyway, so there was no real obstacle for him as long as he could right himself. She was certain he could master his impulses.

Hector had brought him up to the hotel room practically in the middle of the night and squired him over to her bed with a hand on his shoulder and although she was but a sliver of her normal self it gave her a great joyous boost to see him again, her legs feeling as though they could sprint up a stair, to look upon his still boyish, handsome face (beneath some bad bruising, he told her, from a recent motor scooter fall) and hold his hand and listen to his stories of traveling through Great Britain and Europe. How worthwhile, to have been so persistent with her letters to him! She was glad not to hear any more details of the riding accident, and to see that his leg seemed healed. In fact he showed no limp at all when Hector ushered him away, though perhaps he was making a special effort to mask it for her sake.

She was as certain as ever now that the nightmare of his death and that one middle-of-the-night phone call had been the resulting figments of the almost lethal dosages of the cancer drugs that Dr. Koenig had convinced her to take at the time. But now she saw that the whole horrible nightmare had been a purposeful self-alarm, a stern warning from her unconscious mind that she make amends before it was too late.

The one unsettling element was his amazing equanimity to her present condition. It had stunned her, at first. Although she kept telling him she was going to be all right and that he ought not to worry, it was disappointing that he didn't ask even once how she was feeling or what her prognosis was, that although he was gentle-faced and soft-spoken as he stood above her in the dimness of the canopied hotel bed, his hand on hers was sweaty and almost twitchy, as if he wanted to shrink from her. And yet she could empathize, honestly and deeply, how scared he must have been to see her like this, to have to know in his heart that there was nothing to be done. He could hardly meet her eyes. But when she told him that he ought to let her rest and should go, he kissed her, leaned down and quickly pressed his lips on her forehead and bravely did not gasp or cry out, did not pause or even linger, and thus offered, ironically, the best proof that he was indeed her son.

Perhaps there would be a future, too. Hector, she noticed, had even given him some money before he left, for which she had to remember to thank him (which in her state was like trying to remember the scene inside every picture in a random pile of photographs after having glanced through them once), to thank him for showing decency in a circumstance that would be unsettling for any man but that he was never cut out for. She kept telling herself not to pressure him to keep up with Nicholas. They were loners both, they certainly didn't need each other yet, and there was nothing to be gained by compelling any bond. If anything, she imagined that it would be Hector who would someday look again for Nicholas, wish as she did to make a final connection with his son, if for no other reason than not to die alone. She had been wrong to believe she could have ever preferred a solitary end, for the prospect now terrified her, made her think it would be the last true horror. But nothing like that would happen now.

"You haven't told me what you thought of him," she said. "It must have been strange for you."

"I guess it was," Hector answered, one hand propped on the steering wheel. The other was cradling a bottle of beer. That he was drinking while driving didn't concern her in the least. He was calm. He wasn't sullen or angry, and for the first time she thought he looked almost contented, if a little tired, as though the long night into day he'd spent dealing with Nicholas had in fact been a worthwhile effort for him. Perhaps something he would be glad for always.

"I'm so happy he was healthy," she said. "His leg seemed completely healed."

"Uh-huh."

"You don't sound so sure."

"Don't listen to me," he said. "Nick's going to be fine."

"I'm sure you told me already but I forget. Did you talk a lot with him?"

"Not so much."

"He must have asked many questions. Especially about you."

"A few."

"I assume you didn't tell him you were his father?"

"No, I didn't."

"I think he suspected something, anyway."

"How's that?" Hector said, taking a long sip from the bottle.

"When Nicholas finally came back, when you brought him to me again very early this morning, I asked him the same thing. I asked him what he thought of you. And do you know what he said?"

Hector shook his head.

"He said, 'You have a decent man there, Mother. He'll look after you. I think you should keep him around.'"

"Nick is some kind of boy."

"You keep calling him Nick. I like the sound of that. It's nice to hear."

"Sure," he muttered, though suddenly sounding to her as though he wanted to change the subject. But she wasn't yet ready to let it go. At the moment there was hardly any discomfort in her body, even the expansion joints of the road giving her none of the usual painful tremors as they sped over them. And her mind suddenly felt right again, or at least geared in, her thoughts interlocking, turning forward, exerting some force.

"Maybe you'll check in on him sometimes."

"I doubt it."

"But why? You don't ever have to tell him anything. You could just be his friend. Someone he could contact, if necessary. He obviously respects you."

"It won't happen."

"Why not? Because you don't want the responsibility? There wouldn't be any. He'll have enough money. You wouldn't have to do anything. What I'm thinking is that you'll just be someplace he could find you. If he wanted to talk to you. That you'll tell him, or at least my attorney, where you might be."

Hector suddenly braked, slowing down enough that she had to hold out her arm and brace herself against the headrest of the front passenger's seat to prevent going face-first into it. They were on the shoulder of the roadway but it was very narrow, as they had been crossing a long bridge. They were stopped midway across the two-lane span, the valley and planted fields receding majestically below them. He shut off the engine and got out and opened the rear door. A truck thundered by at full speed, blaring its air horn and only missing him, it seemed, by inches. Yet he didn't flinch or even seem to notice, his glare trained only on her as he bent down to speak.

"You have to stop talking about him and me," he said sharply. "Or this can't work. I found him for you but that's all I'm going to do."

"Don't you have any feeling for him? Any feeling at all?"

"I don't want to see him, okay?" he shouted, with as much vehemence as he'd displayed since being with her. "I don't want to think about him anymore. He's gone his way and we've gone ours."

"We could go back for him."

"Is that what you really want?" he cried. "I'll turn us around and take you. I'll do it right now. Well?"

She couldn't say anything and she thought he was going to slam the car door and walk off forever but instead he crouched on his haunches in the opened doorway, his head cast down with the kind of exhaustion that she had always counted on engendering for her own benefit. But she didn't want to see it now. A car shot past, again too closely.

"Please don't stay out there!" she pleaded. Two more cars careened by, in either direction, each honking at him in ire for impeding the road. "Please, Hector! I don't know what I'd do if you got hurt. I couldn't even drive you to a hospital. Please!"

Finally he got back behind the wheel. He drove them to the other end of the bridge and pulled off onto the grassy shoulder. He cut the engine and got out of the car, wandering off into the woods. She was going to tell him how sorry she was for upsetting him, that she was deeply grateful for his efforts, that he had been quite wonderful to her when all she was offering him was this toilsome, perhaps disturbing errand, but her body was once again rudely alive, shuddering with pain, and before she could summon any words he was gone.

When he hadn't returned after fifteen minutes she wedged her swollen feet into her flats and lifted herself out of the car. She followed his direction, finding a deer path that snaked through the high weeds and into the woods. The undergrowth was brambly and dense at first and she didn't think she could make it through, but then the brush gave way to firs, the higher canopy looming dark and cool above the open forest floor. The ground was covered with soft needles, and as it sloped steeply toward the valley floor she had to step sideways so as not to slide down or fall. Her legs were quivering and the pains from her belly and up her back and neck jolted her with each measured step, but she clenched her teeth and told herself as she had throughout her life whenever she needed to persevere that it was wartime again, those days between what happened to her siblings on the train and when she met Hector on the road, when every last cell of her was besieged by hunger and fear but was utterly resolved not to flag, and never did.

Yet a terrible feeling about Hector was overwhelming her and she quickened her pace and stumbled over a tree root in the path. She fell on her hands. An ugly, sharp squeal flew up from her throat. Her left wrist felt shattered. She tried to squeeze away the pain. On looking up she thought she could see something through the silvery green of the trees and she got up again, ignoring the pain—or, better, forcing herself to meet it differently, as if it were the embodiment of her own harsher self, the one that had mostly ruled her life, this cold, cruel woman she had relied on and befriended and to whom she would now lash herself in punishment.

The stand of firs thinned and the slope bottomed out to more level, open, arid ground and she found herself pushing through some large wild rosemary bushes to see an exposed ledge of rock. To the right of her was visible the long bridge they'd just crossed, at the same level as she, but before her was just air, in the distance a lovely expanse of dry rolling hills and verdant farmland and terra-cotta-roofed houses, the vista like any of the third-rate landscape paintings she'd periodically sold in her shop, except that this one was dotted by a single brush of dark, reddish hair in the foreground, the crown of a man's head floating somehow out beyond the ledge. What was he doing? Suddenly a panic speared her chest and she called out his name, but he didn't answer. She stepped gingerly to the platform of the rock, but once there she had to drop to her knees for the sudden attack of vertigo, the high clouds in the sky twisting about her. She had to crawl to the edge. Below her on a short spit of outcropping Hector sat with his legs hanging over the steep hillside that fell away below him. He took a last slug from the bottle of beer he'd taken with him, then tossed it into the chasm. It made no sound that she could hear.

"Please, Hector," she said, fearfully gripping at the weather-worn face of the granite. Though it was only slightly canted she was certain she was about to slide off. Her mind was racing, desperate not to focus on the horizon. "Please climb back up. We still have many miles to go to Solferino. I won't talk about you and Nicholas anymore. I'll shut up, I swear. Let's go now, all right? Please, Hector? I don't like it up here. . . ."

She started to cry, the sudden flood of which took her by surprise, for there was no calculation or aim behind it, no stratagem, just the involuntary release of someone who was genuinely spent. Her cheek lay against the warmed rock, this giant headstone. A marker for them both. She was going to witness him disappear, fall away from existence. But then he stood up and without the least regard for his precipitous position or the poor footing he simply turned and hauled himself up onto the ledge.

"Okay, now," he said, his hand heavy on her back, "take it easy."

"I'm so sorry for what I've done."

"You've done nothing to me."

"I have!"

"I'll handle it."

"It's not about Nicholas!" she gasped. She was going to say more, to tell him everything, but she was coughing hard, just as she had begun to over the past few days, the one store of energy left to her, hacking violently enough that some blood was starting to come up, and he gathered her in his arms and held her up so she wouldn't buck herself against the rock.

"What is it, then?" he murmured, his eyes wide but lit inside by a flicker of dread. "Is it about her?"

But she could not talk, could hardly breathe, and he kept patting her gently on the back, caressing her, and it was in this instant that she decided not to speak another word, retracting herself into the ever-slackening coil of her body. This pile of frayed rope. She shut her eyes, trying to fill her lungs, fill them again. He hoisted her up and she could feel the strength of him as he piggybacked her up through the trees. She would not open her eyes, fearing she might be sick. He lowered her into the pillow-strewn backseat of the car. He started the motor and rolled onto the road, heading again in the same direction.

The ride was smooth, which calmed her. He said he could stop at the next town and look for a doctor but she shook her head. There was no more time to pause. She could recall very little of the past thirty-six hours, could not even remember if she had said farewell to Nicholas. But she knew this: she was being borne on this swift raft, the taste of blood like that of an old coin on her tongue. Would she be allowed to cross over? Would her family be awaiting her? The Tanners? Her parents had not practiced any faith, nor had she, but it seemed reasonable that there should be simple questions now about all that one did in one's life, and whether those commissions were on balance decent, humane. Whether she would do them again, or else they were regrettable enough to disavow, to try once more to forget.

HECTOR GLANCED in the rearview mirror every twenty or so kilometers to see if June was awake, but all he saw was her mouth hung open or shut depending on the depth of her slumber, her head lolling back to one side or the other. He was skeptical of her regret for whatever she had "done" to him, figuring she was characteristically angling to get her way, contriving to move him forward, yet her outburst had seemed as genuine as her physical misery, which he knew from both wartime and peacetime (if the hours at Smitty's could ever count as the latter) was as good a truth serum as anything else. Had she told Dora something hurtful about him? Taunted her with the fact of their brief union, and the existence of Nicholas? She was definitely capable of that. He wanted to be angry with her and a flush of heat rose up in his neck but it wouldn't build to rage, or anything else. What was there, really, to be concerned about now? It was just the two of them from here on in, a pair of souls in a barrel floating down the last stretch of the river, twirling in one of the quieter eddies before being drawn into the chute toward the falls.

In truth, he ought to be asking for June's pardon, for that final night. His selfishness and need for Sylvie's love had caused him to neglect his nightly duty of checking the stoves in the orphanage, and one of them had erupted into flames. His lame mode of apology to June was their sorry marriage and even sorrier tryst, which he should have known then would only lead to further difficulties. It was easy for him to imagine how she would have had an entirely different existence, had he simply stayed clear: a chance at a full and relatively benign adolescence; a decent family and husband; and then an enduring bond with Sylvie herself, who would be nearly seventy years old by now, certainly a doting grandmother, or great-aunt, to June's children, who, in that reality, would never have dreamed of running away. But in the present reality, in this dwindling timeline, June had ended (by her choice or not?) back with him, pitiably dependent on a person who in the span of a single breath could decide to step away from the perch he'd sought in pure desperation just moments before.

So he felt at least right, if not righteous, for bringing Nick again to her for a final time. Back in Siena, he had met up with Bruno in the piazza. He told him how after talking to him in the café Nick had doubled back to the hotel to get there before him and had June sign over the traveler's checks. Bruno nodded, not even asking what Hector wanted to do, and said he had an idea where they might find him: there were some clubs that were popular hangouts for students and younger revelers. In the hotel, June had risen and slept and risen again, Hector getting her another gelato before putting her down for the rest of the night with another heavy dose. He had begun drinking in the room, a four-pack of beer to fill his empty belly, but he wasn't yet sated in the way he needed, which was the feeling of being completely sodden, like some corpse long suspended in the water. He was drinking because he wanted to be sure that he wouldn't hesitate when he saw the young man again, so that he wouldn't decide to let him go without leaning on him, maybe like any disappointed father; he wanted to eye the boy once more, too, offer a last word, but here his impulse was not to reform but rather to be the bearer of ill tidings, a malediction from the world.

The first club they tried was mostly empty and quiet, as it was still early, only eleven p.m. By midnight Bruno said they ought to try the other club, which was nearby. When they got there it was more crowded and smokier than the last, the dance floor spilling over with people, which kept him and Bruno from moving too far inside. They stood in one of the vaulted nooks near the entrance of the underground club. They got drinks and stood where those entering had to pass by to get to the bar. But after another hour Bruno shouted over the music that they should try another place and Hector agreed. He was finishing the last of his drink when Bruno tapped him.

It was Nicholas, striding in with Laura, the young woman from the gallery. Bruno stepped forward but Hector cuffed him and had them stand back in the shadows. Something made him want to observe the boy for just a few beats longer. Was there a certain smug gleam in his face? A wholly remorseless light? The couple looked contented, even happy, as though they had no great worries; or at least Nicholas did. He seemed taller, more upright than earlier, as if he were rigged inside with new girding—the prop of fresh funds. Hector could tell that Laura didn't know a thing about it from the way she brightened when he kissed her, perhaps more deeply than he would have on another night, and as Nicholas ordered drinks for them and made a toast, Hector could figure this was the eclipse of her as far as Nicholas was concerned. He would be leaving her, along with everyone else.

At the side of the short bar a scuffle suddenly flared up, two men in brightly colored shirts pushing and taunting each other; they were from different *contrade*, by their shirts. The men tipsily grappled with each other, not punching or kicking, as if there was an acknowledged code of battle, rather clasping each other in a palsied, theatrical manner, like in a silent film. But they rolled back hard into Laura and made her spill her entire drink onto Nicholas; a large splotch bloomed darkly on his light-blue shirt and white linen pants. The *contrada* man was very short and built thickly and he held up his hands in clear apology, but Nicholas kept shouting at him, tugging to show him his soaked shirt, and the scene would have been over quickly enough had Nicholas not become instantly, unreasonably, furious; he even brusquely dismissed Laura's attempt to blot his shirt as he accosted the man. Standing much taller, Nicholas hotly scolded him as he would a child, and in a lull in the music Hector could hear that he was doing so in English, though this time with a much sharper British accent, and though Hector didn't know enough of the world to place it or give it a name he would have said it was a workingman's tongue, what you'd hear dockside or in an alleyway bar.

This confused Hector; maybe Nicholas was an accomplished and elusive thief (this gleaned from the papers in Clines's folder) but this openly volatile temper didn't quite jibe, not to mention how sensitive and quiet and artistic June always said he was. He wasn't someone who would strike a match in a place he shouldn't. To his momentary credit he was impressively aggressive, enough that both *contrada* men and their respective mates were initially silent, slightly amazed that this lone foreigner would address them so; but then, soon enough, as Nicholas persisted, they pushed in around him with anger in their faces. This was a locals' club, after all, and as locals' clubs went, Hector could see from how the bartender and bouncers now stepped back without pause that this was a serious one, intramurally run, a place where a certain kind of visitor could get himself in trouble.

Laura evidently knew this and had stepped forward to get between him and the local men, pleading with all for calm, but from behind her Nicholas got right up in the faces of them, and they right at him, the shouting escalating into finger-pointing, nudging, hands raised and ready. Hector instinctively approached now, Bruno close by. Someone behind the *contrada* men shoved forward, jamming one of them hard against Laura and Nicholas, and it was then it began, perhaps because Nicholas saw Hector, while Bruno tugged Laura away as the first punches were thrown.

Hector approached to help, given that he was here to retrieve him, but in the mess of the moment, in the mayhem of fists and grunts and flying sweat and spit, a region in which most decent folk perceived only senseless blurs and flashes but was pacific and deep-etched for Hector, a life-sized diorama he could move about in at his own pace and pleasure, he decided that the extent of his help would come in the form of not allowing Nicholas to be maimed or blinded. He had no issue with the *contrada* boys, doing the same as they plenty of times at Smitty's, and he only had to pull off one of them from doing uncalled-for damage, the others allowing him (this gentleman-appearing tourist) to move in and cover the offender from more kicks and blows. When they stopped, he hustled Nicholas out to the street. Bruno and Laura quickly trailed them. Nicholas, who was propped over his shoulder, tried to break from him and run but caught his foot on a raised cobblestone and fell. He rose to get away but suddenly a very different impulse compelled Hector to trip him, sending him hard to the ground. He lay there prostrate, and instead of helping him up Hector pressed his knee on the back of his neck.

"What are you doing to him?" Laura shouted. "Why are you doing this? Get off of him!"

Hector didn't answer her, but Nicholas did, surprising them all by telling her to go away. His face was swollen, his lip puffed and cut. His entire head of hair was sopping with sweat and he was breathing heavily. Laura was still yelling at Hector and not listening but Nicholas now screamed at her, cursing her, so cruelly and profanely dismissing her that one could believe he could have slit her throat in a slightly different moment. She stepped back, horrified, incredulous, perhaps waiting for him to explain himself or try to amend his words, and Bruno took it upon himself to take her by the arm and accompany her home. But she wouldn't let him touch her and she began cursing Nicholas in Italian, stomping on his legs, trying to kick Nicholas in the groin, spitting at him, Hector collaterally receiving a part of her fury, which was no doubt trebled by what she had likely suspected of Nicholas from the beginning but had not heeded and was now wretchedly taking the full measure of. Finally Bruno was able to corral her and lead her away, though she kept her eye on him as they went, as if she were still unsure of what had occurred, wondering if Nicholas might still call for her, say everything was a mistake, that nothing was what it seemed.

"Get the hell off me," Nicholas cried, getting up after they had gone. "Get off me!"

Hector did, pushing him forward with a firm hold on his shoulder.

"Where are we going?"

"To the hotel."

"The traveler's checks are already gone. I sold them, to pay my debts. I've got a couple of hundred from the cash you gave me, that's all."

"Give it over."

"Those checks were mine, you know, she said they were mine."

Hector punched him hard in the kidney, Nicholas buckling as if he'd been shot.

"What the fuck?" he groaned, down on one knee. "What the fuck is wrong with you? Here, here, just fucking well take it!" He threw Hector his wallet. "Now leave me alone."

"You're coming with me," Hector said, lifting him up by the shirt collar.

"I'm not who you think I am," he cried, struggling to keep up as they walked. "I'm not him. I'm not her son."

"I know."

"You want to know my name?"

"Isn't it Paul?"

"That one's fake. It's Nick."

"Nick?"

"That's right. Isn't that a laugh?"

"Yeah. Let's go."

"But what for? She must know I'm not him."

"You'll tell her where Nicholas is."

"She knows where he is! He's dead. He's been fucking dead since last year. We were decent enough mates, I suppose. He was a pretty good player, really. Maybe a little soft, a little too nice where our marks were concerned, but I was getting him into shape. We were getting to be a fantastic duo, really. We were up at some *nouveau* lord's hall in Sussex. Full of primo stuff. But Nicholas fucking fell off a horse and broke his leg and in the hospital a clot got up into his lung and killed him."

"But you've been writing to her as him."

"Just once. But she kept on, like he was alive. Didn't she know? So I wrote back, and was flooded with letters from her, saying this and that. How sorry she was for treating him like dirt all his life. Well, boo hoo. I wrote that it was okay. I wrote that I forgave her. I forgave her for him, and that's all it took. And when I answered that I had her book, she sent a lot of money. Lucky for me. I had kept it only because Nicholas always had it with him."

"What book?"

"Some stupid book about an old battle up north, in Lombardy. I stopped there, actually, when I first got to Italy. Nicholas said it was a special place. But it was nothing much, in my view. I half hoped there was something to be got there."

"You still have it?"

"The book? What if I do? What's it worth to you?"

"You'll see."

"Why have a go at me? I only gave her what she wanted. What the fuck do I care, if she wants to pretend? She was still pretending when I saw her this afternoon."

Hector pictured her there, this ripple in the bed, talking to the blur holding her hand, the blur riding her conscience and memory.

"How about giving me back my wallet, then, huh? If she doesn't care, why should you?"

But Hector thought he did care, and in a way that surprised him, and with a sudden, furious grip on the back of Nick's neck he made him march, march to wherever his apartment was, and then march to the hotel.

"What do you want? What else is there? For God's sake, I've told you all there is!"

Hector didn't answer, for there was nothing more he needed to know. Nothing more June needed to know. And yet he felt it would be best if her son Nicholas made a final visit with her. Brought a lemon ice for her parched throat. Returned her book. Sat with her for as long as she could manage, him telling her all she wanted to hear.

SIXTEEN

IN THE DAYS AFTER SHE SLEPT tucked beside Sylvie, June crept about quietly as she dusted in the cottage, departing without saying a word. Sylvie was distant and distracted, staying and reading in the bedroom while June did her chores in the front, and then whenever she was outside it seemed she would allow herself to be surrounded by other children, who instantly formed about her like a buzzing hedge. June was afraid that she had somehow defiled their bond, had imperiled everything she had been planning. She didn't dare ask if she could stay overnight again, not wanting to remind Sylvie in the least of what might have happened.

For what had happened? She wasn't sure herself, save for the imprint of Sylvie's body on her hands, the arid, smooth skin that had been almost burning to the touch, if perfectly stilled, solid, this live ingot. It was only at night, in the girls' dorm room, well after the lights were extinguished and the other girls finally fell asleep after their incessant chattering, when she was on the threshold of slumber herself, that a seam of pressure pushed up through the trunk of her body, this ache coursing through her arm and to her hand, and which made her reach again for Sylvie, though there was only herself. Throughout the bunks there was stillness, but in her own cot there would be movement, shifting, the tiniest travel in the cot's metal feet, and in the morning she'd awake enervated and bewildered and loathing herself yet again for pushing away the only person she loved. Her desire, she could see, was only ruining her chances for the future. She must only be a good daughter. She knew the grip of her thoughts had better be as steely as ever, as though she were alone again on the road, when her body was wild with hunger, every last cell of her about to burst in all directions with its emptiness but her mind furiously gripping at the rails. She had to be the implacable train. The unswerving force. She must do whatever she had to, to keep moving ahead.

One night, when June thought Tanner was still away, she'd awoken by habit in the early hours and peered outside to check for any lamplight from the cottage and on seeing a faint glow stole to the back to see if Hector was there. She crept beneath the window along the wall and listened for any sounds. The night air was frigid but she held herself tightly so as not to shake. But it was Reverend Tanner's voice—he must have returned very late, contrary to plan, perhaps even to check on her—and to June's surprise he was speaking without a stitch of suspicion or anger, in fact quite tenderly, his voice a high, soft reed.

"You're only thirty-four, dear. Other women we know have had children as late as that. My mother gave birth to my brother at thirty-six."

"Dorothy had six of you, before him."

"She lost several, too, you know."

"She didn't lose five," Sylvie said miserably. "Not every one."

Tanner was momentarily silent. But then he said: "We can't think about that anymore. Being around all these children has heartened me—but, I see now, in an astonishing way. Their spirit and ceaseless energy have brought me renewal. I feel very strong inside. And I was thinking as I drove back tonight how lucky we've been to have this time here. What a rare chance this is, to be amid so much possibility! So many hopeful beginnings! And here you haven't been well and my frequent trips to Seoul and to the other orphanages have only made things worse for you."

"It's not your fault. It's not at all."

"It *is* my fault. Perhaps I'm not the cause, but I've exacerbated the situation, and I'm as culpable in the end as if I were. I've been negligent. I've been a poor husband, by every measure. Not only these past months in Korea but for years now. It's why I returned instead of staying over in town, to tell you how sorry I am, for the way I've willfully disdained your unhappiness, when I should have redoubled my efforts to help you. To be with you. I've been selfish, and terribly self-righteous, too. I'm asking if you'll forgive me, Sylvie. If you'll try to forgive who I've been and let me come back to you."

"Forgive *you?*" she cried. She was trying to say something now, but she was gasping from low in her chest, shuddering, and June was sure that she was going to confess to him, admit what he may have already known, but he was shushing her, telling her that there was nothing she needed to say. June slowly stood up to peer over the sill and through the gauzy curtain and saw him embracing her in the lamplight as she sat up in her bed. He stroked her mussed-up hair.

"Let's start again, darling. I've come to have a renewed belief in our chances. I want to try for us again. We can still take children home with us, but I want you to believe that we can have our own. Can you do that for me? Will you?"

"Yes," she said, wiping her eyes, her nose. "I will, for you. But I think it's too late, Ames."

"It doesn't have to be."

"But it is," she said hopelessly. "It's too late."

"It's not!" he said, his voice loud enough to buzz the window glass. He paused, then spoke gently again: "It's only too late if you believe it so. We have no chance otherwise. None at all. We must want the same thing, which hasn't been the case for a long time. It's not mysterious to me anymore."

He bent down and kissed her on the forehead, and the cheek, and then on the mouth. She didn't turn away. Perhaps she was not wholly with him but she wasn't fleeing, or flinching, and when he pulled on the sides of her nightgown she simply raised her arms so he could lift it from her body. Her ribs showed starkly. He clasped her there and pressed his face into her breast and as they lay down on the bed he put out the oil lamp, sending the room into perfect black. June ducked, afraid her silhouette might be visible. For another half-hour she remained crouched in the near-frosty night air, listening for the scuttle of lovemaking as she did in the storeroom next to Hector's quarter but hearing in the end only Tanner's low, sharp breaths, half pained.

The next day was bright and glorious, the hillsides awash in a gaudy autumnal display. The shimmering glow was bounding inside of June, too, despite the terrible headache and congested chest that she'd awoken with after finally going back to the dormitory, her hands and feet and face numb with the freezing air. And she was finally realizing now how she ought for the moment to desist, pull back, force herself to recede from Sylvie, and from Tanner, too. She saw how amazingly shortsighted she had been, what a stupid, silly child, ridiculous in her neediness, mistaking her unwavering insistence on wedging herself into their lives for a strength, a necessity, when it was in fact only helping to dismantle everything she wanted. It didn't matter if they would still have their own baby or not, or if they adopted another child or children along with her; all that mattered from this point on was that the Tanners remain as is, that they work together, as before, that they be at least accepting of their union, even if they were no longer deeply in love.

She had enough love for Sylvie, she was certain, to sustain them both forever.

As for Reverend Tanner, June had already begun to practice her new way: in English class and Bible study she spoke up regularly, clearly surprising him with a new enthusiasm and the demeanor of a girl who was respectful and demure; he even took her aside afterward and asked if she was all right, as she'd steadily coughed throughout the class.

"I am fine," she said, trying to smile for him, even as her temples pounded.

"Perhaps you ought to rest for the day. You don't sound yourself." He patted her shoulder. "You can see if Mrs. Tanner is inside, if you like."

"I don't want to disturb her," she said, and instead headed for the dormitory, imagining with near certainty that he was nodding approvingly behind her. She would show him her restraint. Show him that despite all the fights and other troubles she had caused she was a worthy girl at core, exactly the kind of hard soul he must be here to save. She was not being so crafty or calculating, as she was exercising a differing form of the same capacity for self-discipline and self-direction she'd always possessed and counted on, but now applying it to self-reform. Was true maturity to be found in this measure of control? If so, it was a jubilant feeling. Yet as she lay down in her cot in the empty dormitory, the first rush of a fever welling in the back of her neck, in her joints, the thought occurred that it was in fact Hector Brennan who must be changed. Or even, somehow, removed from the scene; she was already painting him dark with pitch. Blacking him out. It was ironic because if there was anyone in the orphanage besides Sylvie who seemed to understand her or accept her it was Hector; he never judged her or acted as if she ought to behave differently, even when she was raging and belligerent. There was nothing conditional about his regard. He seemed amused by her, if anything, and unlike everyone else (including Sylvie) he was impressed by her regular fisticuffs with the boys, once even demonstrating from across the play yard how she ought to rotate her fist when she threw a punch, drive all the way through.

She did not spend any extra hours with Sylvie; there would be ample time in the future. Rather, she was vigilant of Hector and his movements, noting when he was at work outside on the grounds, or at the sewer ditch, or else left the orphanage at night for the red-light section of the city, which he was frequenting again. Maybe Sylvie had broken it off with him. Certainly the Tanners seemed closer than before, often sitting together at meals among the children. June was practically joyous on seeing Hector return early one morning with his fatigue jacket ripped at the shoulder, his lip bruised, not because he was injured but because he was going into town and drinking and fighting again, which in her ever-grinding calculus was a sure sign that he had relinquished any hope of a civilized future with Sylvie. Whenever Hector did emerge from his room he was always in his soiled work clothes and boots, heading for the ditch digging, which he had almost finished. He'd been working continuously and even set up an oil lamp and dug for a few hours at night before driving late into Seoul.

June openly followed him one morning. He paid no attention to her. He went straight past the Tanners' cottage on the pathway down the hill to the end of the dig, a mere ten meters to go to the as yet empty pit, setting to work immediately, pickaxing as if he were attempting to injure the ground or himself. But neither seemed to give, the soil at that spot so rocky and compacted that the ax would viciously rebound every so often and almost strike him in the face. Eventually he prevailed. He didn't seem to tire, only the force of his blows slightly diminishing, his rhythm staying true until he was finished and simply stopped, his chest bellowing deeply in and out.

She approached him and told him that she would fetch him some water if he liked. He didn't look up or reply, just shoveled the loosened earth and rock. She stood there for a moment and then ran back to where the kitchen aunties worked and made sure to catch the eye of Reverend Tanner, who followed her with his gaze as he conducted Bible study for the younger children beneath the pavilion. When she got back to Hector she offered him the tin bowl of water. Hector paused from his shoveling and quickly drank it all.

"Thanks," he said, again gripping his shovel.

"Do you want more?"

"No."

"I can bring you some food."

He shook his head and turned to resume working.

She said, "Could I help you?"

"No."

"I'm strong. Let me try," she said. It was then that Reverend Tanner and the group of younger children approached the edge of the low hillside. Hector's back was turned to them. Seeing her chance, June reached around him for the pickax.

"Leave that alone," he said. "It's too heavy. Just go, okay?"

But June was already removing her light wool sweater, rolling it up over her head. Her blouse was untucked from the band of her long skirt and as it was pulled by the sweater she let it ride up, over her bare chest, taking her time to unfurl the sweater from her head before the fabric naturally fell and draped down again. From his downcast eyes she knew her breasts were clearly showing through the thin white shirting. She let her sweater fall to the ground and when he didn't move she stepped quickly to him, as if he'd pulled her in an embrace. He tried to push her away but she clung tighter to him the more he squirmed and she was exhilarated by how tenacious she could be, how resilient, though a reciprocal, near-hungering ache uncoiled in her gut from the hard pads of his hands. Finally she pushed away from him, letting herself fall to the ground.

"What the hell is wrong with you?" Hector shouted.

She expected to hear Tanner's voice but when she looked up she glimpsed only his dark minister's jacket and the tops of the children's heads bobbing away as they hiked back toward the compound.

"Don't you ever do that again," Hector growled. "Don't you ever touch me like that."

"I won't!" she said defiantly.

She put on her sweater and ran off. In the central yard it was nearly lunchtime, the younger children playing tag while the aunties set up tables outside, as it was a warm fall day. Sylvie and several older girls were bringing out utensils and cups and she joined them. Reverend Tanner was already sitting at one of the tables, watching their play with an opened Bible before him. June was ready to tell him a broader story of what Hector had done, or tried to do, but Tanner said nothing to her. He only glanced at the freshly soiled patches on her skirt, on her sleeves, and although this surprised her she realized that he couldn't talk about such things in front of his wife and other girls. In fact he didn't need to talk about them at all, for she had done the necessary work, and as she began setting down chopsticks and spoons she felt that she was a wellspring and that Hector was a leaf just fallen on the surface, soon to be tided inexorably away.

YET HECTOR DIDN'T GO AWAY. It seemed impossible to her, but Reverend Tanner made nothing of witnessing her and Hector down in the ditch. He didn't seem to care. A whole week went by, and at the end of it the reverend even talked animatedly with Hector about the sections of concrete piping just delivered by truck. Tanner even decided to help Hector with the job of joining the sections, suspending his schedule for two days while young Reverend Kim from Seoul came down to help Sylvie with his teaching and liturgical duties. June and some other children watched them from a perch above the gently sloping hillside. Each thick-walled concrete section was a half-meter round and as long as a man and it took them past dusk of the first day to lug all the sections of pipe down the run of the ditch. It was simple work and they didn't have to say much of anything to each other and labored in a steady rhythm, lifting a section from the pile beside the main outhouse and walking it down sideways or with one of them backpedaling. As night fell one might have thought the two men were interring corpses in a strange, threading line of a mass grave. The next day it rained lightly and they shifted the sections, using shovels for leverage in order to connect them, and by the end when they shook hands ever so briefly they were covered brown-gray from head to toe in mud and joining mortar.

Sylvie was again not well. Maybe it was the pressure of her husband's new wish for a child, or her own guilt about Hector, or else that she was craving him even as she knew she should not have him, but June could see the parched quality of her skin, the streaks of red at her elbows where she constantly scratched at herself showing through her blouse sleeve. She needed medicine for her kit.

June kept telling herself that she could be the remedy. She told herself to keep disciplined, to stay the course she had laid out, to remake herself along the lines of an entirely different girl: someone who was not an orphan at all, had not lost anyone in her life, much less witnessed any horrors or degradation. She was a normal child who would soon have a normal life. And it was shortly borne out: after the morning prayer Reverend Tanner announced that at the end of October young Reverend Kim, who substituted for him when he was away, would take over as director of the orphanage. "But what will you do?" a boy obtusely asked. "Mrs. Tanner and I must be leaving," Tanner solemnly replied. "We have to go back to America." There was a long second of silence and then all the children were crying, many outright wailing, some fallen to the ground, the rest crowding around him and Sylvie, both of whom were crying, too.

Only June did not fret, knowing that she would soon be asked to prepare for the journey. She knew from others they would fly first to Japan, then go on to either Alaska or Hawaii, before landing in San Francisco. From there they would take a shorter flight to Seattle, where the Tanners were from, a place that Sylvie had once described to her as a city shrouded in constant rain and fog, a place on earth but stuck in clouds, where one always felt the weight of dampness in one's clothes and hair and skin, which was strangely comforting, once gotten used to. Naturally some found it oppressive. But June liked the idea that the weather was a near constant, like a too-loyal friend, something to bear around and tolerate and maybe cherish, even if it would never leave you alone. And she knew that she and Sylvie would be just that for each other, and in time perhaps she could prove the same for Reverend Tanner, who would come to see her not as a bane he had yielded to but the living picture of his grace.

So she organized and reorganized her small footlocker, which every child had, discarding the pairs of socks that were past darning, resolving to wear the ugly olive-drab trousers as often as she could to preserve her two decent blouses and skirt, which she snapped in the air to rid of dust and then tightly folded. She polished her ill-fitting leather shoes, knowing that she would have to wear them on the plane. She went through her workbooks and tore out the pages marred by idle sketches or doodles and she honed her three pencils against the floorboards to sharp pinpoints. She cleaned the footlocker itself, removing the grime from the handle with a kerosene-dipped rag and sanding the rust from the rivets and steel-clad corners. Lastly she borrowed a pair of good scissors from the aunties and trimmed her own hair (which was in a rough, unkempt pageboy because she never sat long enough for them to cut it properly), smoothing out the line of the ends and pinning up one side like some of the other girls did but with the fancy, large tortoiseshell hair clasp Sylvie had given her very early on. It was in the shape of a butterfly, which she loved, but she had not used it even once out of fear of losing or breaking it. But she was wearing it constantly now, to remind herself to keep her hair and face and fingernails neat and clean, to be polite, even smiling and pretty, just as the younger girls who had been adopted before had been polite and pretty, so eager to please, but mostly because she was confident that her time here was truly ending, that her life was about to begin anew.

Thus it didn't bother her in the least that the atmosphere of the orphanage was lifeless for some days after the announcement of the Tanners' departure, the boys not even playing soccer or tag during free time. The aunties seemed less patient with the children, scolding them more hotly for not clearing the tables fast enough, or for making too much laundry. In fact it was mostly just Hector who seemed as active as ever, maybe more so, as the winter would soon be approaching and countless repairs needed to be completed before the frightful cold descended again upon the hills. As June watched him work at reframing a window—his face unshaven, his hair unruly, his eyes unwavering from the task at hand—a pang of recognition struck her low momentarily: his life was about to begin again, too. She almost felt sorry for having tried to bring him trouble. What would he do, after they were gone? It was why she could smell him from a distance, the boozy smell and the sharp body smell and the faintest ashen smell of someone's embittered heart.

It was with the news that visitors from a new adoption agency in America were coming to take photographs of the children that the compound came back to life. The aunties heated water the entire day to draw enough for bathing all forty children, separate boys' and girls' tin tubs accommodating three or four of them at a time.

June refused at first to bathe, for there was no reason for her to do so, she was already spoken for, but as one of the aunties berated her she realized she ought to take every chance to better herself, as much as stay in line. And so she got in with three much younger girls, soaping up their hair for them, reminding them to shut their eyes, even drying them off quickly in the chilly air and helping them get dressed in their best outfits. She put on her own good clothes and accompanied the younger ones out and waited in line with them for their photographs, except that the kindly-faced, plumpish older couple who arrived by taxi had no intention of taking portraits but rather wanted to meet all the children in the hope of taking home as many as they could manage. They had a camera, but only for taking snapshots of their journey. Reverend Tanner was confused, as he'd obviously received erroneous information from the church office in Seoul, but he still had everyone meet the Stolzes, who sat in chairs in the central yard and shook each child's hand. Sylvie had not yet reemerged from the cottage after the midday meal, Reverend Tanner making her excuses to the couple, telling them she had a bad cold.

Reverend Tanner introduced each child by name and age, adding some humorously flattering description or anecdote, and when June stepped up he didn't hesitate at all, saying she was self-possessed and highly independent, adding that she took and gave no quarter to the boys during games, eliciting approving nods from the Stolzes. When they asked him about her English, she answered that she spoke it well, surprising and impressing them. Mrs. Stolz, wearing a dark green dress and black shoes, asked how she had learned the language and June explained that her father had been an educated man, a teacher, and had attended a top university in Japan.

"And what about you, June? Would you like to be educated?"

"I am already. Mrs. Tanner has been teaching me."

"I can see that!" Mrs. Stolz said to her, with a spark of delight. "And do you have any brothers or sisters here?"

She didn't answer but Reverend Tanner pursed his lips and shook his head, which Mrs. Stolz immediately understood to be a topic for another time. She took June's hand and patted it tenderly, her hands thick and fleshy and warm.

"What do you think about living in America? Mr. Stolz and I live in a place called Oregon. Do you know where that is?"

She shook her head.

"It's near Seattle," Reverend Tanner said, his mention of it significant to June but not in the way he was thinking.

"You know Seattle?" Mr. Stolz asked her. "That's way too big a town for me."

"We're close enough, I suppose," Mrs. Stolz added, if perhaps somewhat confused herself. "It's a half-day's car ride."

June said, "I will go there soon."

"You seem quite certain of that."

"I am."

"Well, I guess why shouldn't you be?" Mrs. Stolz said, gently squeezing her palm. "You're a very strong girl, aren't you?"

June was about to tell her it didn't matter what she was but Reverend Tanner answered for her, pronouncing with a strange, surprising tone of pride that she was "as strong as they come," and it was then that Mr. Stolz stepped forward and aimed his tiny camera right at her and quickly clicked the shutter. He had taken pictures of only a few other children. June's instinct was to put her hand over the lens, but Reverend Tanner immediately introduced the boy behind her and Mrs. Stolz tightly pressed her hand in farewell as one of the aunties ushered June away.

By the time the Stolzes got around to meeting the last child in line June was back to the girls' bunk room, where she changed out of her good blouse and skirt. She had first gone straight to the Tanners' cottage, tapping on the front door and then going around to the back, but a new dark brown window shade had been put up, covering the glass right to either edge of the frame. There was no answer at the rear door, either. Despite her resolve not to bother her, she needed now to see Sylvie right away, not to interrogate her or make her promise anything but simply to stand before her and read her eyes, her face. Did she know what the old couple was here for? Was that why she had not come out? Was she hoping that someone like them would take her? Relieve her of this burden?

"May we come in?" a voice said. It was Mrs. Stolz, her head poking in the doorway of the bunk room. When she saw that June was dressed she entered, her husband at her side. They seemed somehow shorter and even plumper now that they were standing up: these two smiling folk dolls, their cheeks round and pink. He was dressed in a denim work shirt and rough wool trousers and scuffed-up shoes, and though they seemed to her as impossibly rich as all the other civilian Americans she had ever seen, she understood now that they were probably country people, small-town citizens like those in the village where she had grown up. But rather than feeling enmity toward them for how those villagers had treated her mother and father with suspicion and resentment and ultimately callousness and cruelty, instead a tide of longing unexpectedly washed over her, this longing for the days before her father yielded to his demons and retreated to his study, longing for her mother's proud face, longing finally for her two brothers and two sisters who could not even stand here as she was in an ugly, too-large pair of trousers, and all at once June was not mature or resolute or strong in the least but a fallen pile of child, sobbing and shaking.

"Oh my dear, oh my dear, dear," Mrs. Stolz cooed, embracing June and pressing her to her ample breast as they sat on the cot. "It'll be fine now."

"Easy there," her husband said, leaning over them as he patted June on the back. "You have a family again. We're going to take six of you. We have plane tickets for six."

"For goodness' sake, John, we haven't even asked her yet!" she said to him, shushing him. And then to June: "Would you like to come live with us, sweetheart? As my eager husband said, you'll have sisters and brothers. We'll have plenty of room and plenty to eat. We have four of our own but they're pretty much grown up. We have a big farmhouse and barns and surrounding us are all the fir trees you will ever want to see."

"Not like here."

"John, please!"

"You should know we have animals, too," he went on anyway, as though he had practiced his pitch and didn't wish to lose the chance. "Horses and milking cows and chickens, not to mention dogs and cats. Do you like animals? Do you want to have a pet?"

She didn't know whether she did want one or not, but she nodded, weakly, for it was all she could manage, the rest of her gone slack in Mrs. Stolz's arms. June had no feeling in her limbs. And if she felt no love or kinship yet, it was enough to be absorbed into this kind stranger woman's flesh, to lose herself and still be alive, to shed the tyranny of this body, always aching and yearning, always prickly and too aware. Even more than death, she was sure, she hated this enduring. This awful striving that was not truly living. But maybe it was ending now . . .

"You don't have to tell us right this minute," Mrs. Stolz said. "We'll be staying here for a couple more hours. We're going to go talk to some other children now, but we made sure to see you first."

"Nobody chose me before."

"We're all the more fortunate, then! We're lucky. There must be a reason. You have a spirit in you that is wondrous, anyone can see it, and you're going to be happy in our home."

"You'll be the oldest," her husband said. "You can help with translating, among other things. There'll be some chores, naturally, just like the jobs Reverend Tanner says all of you do around here."

"You don't have to help with *anything* you don't want to," Mrs. Stolz said, glaring at her husband. "I can't imagine what you've gone through already. What you've had to live through and see. But I can promise that you'll be safe and sound with us. You'll always have our love and support. And God's love, above all. You're going to begin a whole new joyous life."

She hugged June closer, and despite a seam of unease, June shut her eyes, bracing the woman tightly in return, while Mr. Stolz took a step back to snap another picture, this time of the two of them; but he found he had run out of film. While he turned the crank to wind in the roll, Mrs. Stolz stroked at June's temple, her hair.

"What a lovely thing," she said, touching the tortoiseshell clasp. "You know, it's the first thing I noticed when I saw you. I thought it made you look so beautiful and graceful. Just like a fluttering butterfly."

No sooner had Mrs. Stolz spoken the words than June tried to break away from her. The woman, not understanding, clutched at her again, holding on, but June warded her off with a forearm that pressed stiffly enough against her clavicle that the woman gave out a panicked cry: "Oh no, what's wrong? Please!"

Her husband took hold of June, more in confusion than anger, but she rose and stamped on his foot, causing him to drop the camera, the back panel springing open and exposing the stretched film. June heard him curse loudly as she ran away, Mrs. Stolz weeping beside him as she sat crumpled on the bunk room floor. She ran as fast as she could, up into the bare hills, climbing until she started to descend, the sun following her down in the next valley until it grew dark.

When she finally returned, just before lights-out, the Stolzes were long gone. No one knew the Stolzes had come to see her, and she had only missed dinner, which she sometimes did before, staying in with Sylvie Tanner. The ten-year-old girl in the next bunk, So-Hyun, told June that they had adopted six of the children, just as they said they would, three girls and three boys, of varying ages. They were in Seoul now, and in two days they would be leaving the country. They didn't have room for the children's footlockers and so they'd left them behind, each child taking only one sentimental object, like a doll or book or blanket; the rest of their things were distributed to the others. So-Hyun had gotten a sweater, which she showed to June, a red wool one that was of good quality but was pocked with several moth holes in the chest and back.

"Did they seem upset?"

"They were all crying," So-Hyun said, a bit glumly. She was a bit of a smart aleck, which made June admire her. "But I think it was in happiness."

"I meant the American couple," June said.

"Oh, them," So-Hyun said. "The woman was crying, too."

"In the same way?"

"I don't know."

"Tell me!"

"I guess so. Yes."

"Did Reverend and Mrs. Tanner see them off?"

So-Hyun said, "Just the reverend."

"How was he?"

"He wasn't crying," So-Hyun said, sleepy now as she lay in her bed. "He asked where you were."

"And what did you tell him?"

"What we always say. 'Who knows! Who cares!'"

The lights went out then, one of the aunties padding through the bunk room with an oil lamp to make sure everyone was in bed. When she got to June she gave her a cross look, but June didn't care. She didn't care, either, about what So-Hyun said, even if she acidly added the latter line, because of course it was only the truth. All that was important now was that the Tanners would soon depart, as the couple from Oregon had, but with her in tow. She didn't care anymore if there were others they might take along as well. Or whether Sylvie became pregnant again. In fact she herself was hoping for it now. For if they had a baby, June would cherish it as her own, give her life over to the child, if necessary, in all the ways that she had not been able to do for her siblings.

She couldn't sleep that night, overeager to bond with Sylvie again (after their weeks of observing a mutual distance), to go over the plans she surely had to make for their imminent travel and resettling in Seattle. She would explain, too, if Sylvie asked her, what had happened with the Stolzes, that despite the woman's kindness and the very fine life she described, June had realized just in time that she was not meant to go with them. She could not be a part of any other family again. In a different lifetime she would have her parents back, her older brother and sister would be healthy, the twins happy and whole; but in this one she had been paired up, she and Sylvie aligned like twins themselves, if by one of them not quite acknowledged.

Just before dawn broke she got out of bed, her mind feeling as honed and ready as a newly forged blade. Though her belly was unfilled from not having eaten supper or lunch the previous day, the emptiness felt more like purity than privation, what she imagined a pilgrim might feel at the end of an arduous journey, this state of cleanly ecstasy that suddenly became, in the last meters, both its own great fuel and flame. She dressed quickly as the others slumbered and went across the yard and knocked on the door of the Tanners' cottage. She knocked again when there was no answer. Finally the door creaked open and Reverend Tanner looked out at her in his plaid pajamas, putting on his spectacles in the blue morning light.

"What's happened? What's the matter?"

"Nothing," she said. "I want to talk with Mrs. Tanner, please."

"Mrs. Tanner is asleep," he said angrily, "and I was as well. What is wrong with you, June? You make everything so difficult!"

"I do not mean to."

"I don't believe you!" he said, barely in control of himself. He stepped outside, closing the door behind him. "Or else I must think you have a wrecking force within you. Mrs. Stolz was terribly, terribly upset. She actually feared she'd done something awful to you."

"She did nothing to me."

"Of course not! But I can't imagine what you said or did to make her think she had. If she weren't such a generous, humane woman, they would have fled. Certainly her husband wanted to leave right away. Do you realize that? Do you realize that you near ruined the other children's chances as well? Did you ever for one moment think about them?"

June was silent, though not in acquiescence. Not in remorse. Rather she had receded, deep within the whorl of her thoughts. She was simply waiting for Sylvie now to come out and embrace her just as fully and breathlessly as Mrs. Stolz had, to welcome her inside.

"You have nothing to say, do you?" Tanner said. "Nothing at all?" He glared at her as the first warm light arose, the cowbell for reveille suddenly clanging from the direction of the kitchen. She had heard it hundreds of times before but today the rounded hollowness of the sound struck her deeply, the echoes mapping her empty reaches. It would be breakfast soon but she did not wish to eat, despite what she would normally know as well as anyone alive to be the welling pangs of hunger. But it was not that now, she was certain, for instead of distress or panic she felt rather the strangest satisfaction, a peerless morning calm. She would remain right here until Sylvie came out, and she didn't move or speak, even as Reverend Tanner ascended the stoop and without turning to look back at her firmly shut the door.

SEVENTEEN

EVERYONE BELIEVED she had been suffering from the flu.

Sylvie tried to believe it herself. It was the same as the other times she cut herself off, no better or worse. In Seattle there would be a period every few seasons when she fell ill and she would have to gather herself into a normal, presentable state of sickness before Ames returned from his work at the synod offices. He was always tender to her, his renewed concern that she was innately sickly lining his forehead as he peered down at her while he took her temperature. She was volunteering then in various organizations run out of the church so it wasn't such a problem to stay home for a few days, but here she had impetuously quit her habit and disrupted everything.

She had not been able, for example, to come out and embrace and kiss the children the Stolzes adopted, and by this she felt doubly sickened. The three younger boys, Sang and Jin and Jung, were a boisterous, puckish threesome unrelated by blood but who always roved in a tight pack, playing pranks on their playmates and the girls and sometimes even the older boys, who'd chase them into the hills. Sylvie was the only one who was spared the odd frog in the shoe, a brigade of crickets under the bedcovers; once even Ames had found an oversized bird's nest constructed from twigs on his classroom chair—he was nicknamed "Big Crane" by the children because of his lankiness and skinny legs. The three girls were the Kim sisters, who along with a dozen others regularly knitted with Sylvie, and each had given Ames her unfinished project to leave with Mrs. Tanner, three pairs of woolen mittens and matching caps, graduated in size. They were small enough that she could have finished all of them in the morning and sent them with Ames on his way to Seoul to deliver them before they flew out of the country, but her hands were too twitchy and she had to poke at her palms with the knitting needles to try to quell them, as she kept dropping stitches or stretching out the knitting too much.

She had felt this before, though this time it wasn't the steady, drenching enervation that laid her low but a pointed, angry sickness, her flesh and skin feeling as though they wished to pull away from her. Finally she had to give up the knitting, her nose running and her eyes hotly welling up with a relentless, involuntary flow that kept steady even after her frustration waned. Her head was sodden, as with a bad cold, but her limbs felt alternately prickly and numb and just as after the other times when she had suddenly thrown away her kit—this time tossing it, three days ago, in the fire the aunties built to heat the children's bathwater—in a matter of a day harsh flashes of hot and cold swept through her body like vengeful weather.

She was suffering because she had to suffer, because she needed to, every pincer and tremor and hard drum of craving a deserved punishment, yes, but also a reminder that she was still vital, still alive. She had little hope that she could ever bear a child and was not certain she wanted one of her own anymore, but for her husband's sake she would endure. She could keep down only a few saltines and some sips of roasted corn tea. Ames brought these to her, insisting that she allow him to take her to the army hospital in Seoul. But she refused him, afraid the doctors would instantly recognize her ailment. *I'll be myself again in a couple of days*, she told him, though she was fearful who *myself* might be this time when the sickness finally lifted; after the previous quitting, it felt as though her soul had been worn down by half, and by now the math was surely pitched against her. She didn't believe he knew. But whether he did or not didn't matter: this was the very last time, she was done with this ugliness, and when they returned to the States she would devote herself as never before to the work of his next ministry, which had been rearranged by Ames to be not in Seattle as planned but in southeastern Washington, outside of Spokane, where both of them knew there would be nothing around them but boundless fields of alfalfa and barley.

She stayed in the cottage, seeing no one but Ames. She didn't have to ask him why June was not appearing for her chores; the other morning the sharp tone of his voice had reached into her racked sleep, June's soft, flat murmurs echoing there as well, and when she arose she could see in his face that it would only make things impossible if she brought up anything about June. He was furious with the girl. There was not even two weeks remaining in their time here were and though she felt utterly wasted, she would somehow convince Ames that they must take her. But each time she tried to talk about June when he brought her tea or mentholated compresses for her neck, an easy reason to defer presented itself—he'd earnestly ask about where she was in her monthly cycle, or he'd simply tell her, as he did this morning, that he loved her, the locks at his temples appearing grayer than ever, his cheekbones jutting and sharp from his constant traveling, and all she could do was think again of his irreproachable character, how he had never sought anything but good for her and for everyone else, that he was just as fair and constant a man as he'd been every other day of his life.

But look at you, she said to herself now, peering into a hand mirror to check the condition of her neck, which was tormenting her with its itchiness, the skin now scratched raw and almost bleeding. Look at this Sylvie Binet, with two bloodshot horrors for eyes, the fever-matted hair, the ghoulish pallor that would certainly frighten the younger children. But she wondered if she wanted to be cured. Ames once said that although an awful thing happened to her in youth she had pulled herself far past it, but in truth she wondered if she would ever possess the necessary strength. She often felt a great part of her had been fixed in time, that despite appearances she had been simply stuck in place, never quite getting anywhere. Maybe that's why the children liked her; it wasn't her bright, golden hair or even her obvious adoration of them but their instinctive sense that she was as vulnerable as they, as desperately keen for a lasting bond. That she had never quite grown up. She remembered her father telling her in Manchuria how this world was littered with those cut off in mid-bloom, all this wasted beauty and grace, and that it was their humble task to gather as many as they could and replant them. It didn't matter that they were stomped and torn. That the soil was rocky and poor. She must be the sun and rain. As long as she kept vigilant, as long as they never gave up, the blooms could thrive again.

She was sure this was true of the children. But what of a person like her? Could one ever reroot her own long-trampled self? Or would you in perpetuity need someone to pick you up at certain intervals, pluck you from the slow rot of your being? It was a good thing that people buried themselves in mostly shallow graves. If she thought about her adult life, it was an existence of constant exertion and work, but also one marked serially by the compulsion to yield. And however

miserable and dissolute she ended up, however wretched in that suspension of utter fall or erasure, there was an undeniable seam of what
must be gratitude, too, a kind of relief in finding yet another path to
giving herself over.

Hector was still angry with her. By the time Ames announced the
news of their departure last week they had already ceased their trysts—
during Ames's last absence she had not shown up at Hector's door—
and he had stopped speaking to her as well, avoiding her, steering
himself away from wherever she was and taking his steel pail full of
tools to do some job or task in another part of the compound. After
lights-out he had begun to head into Itaewon again, and if it showed
in the clouds darkly shading his brow, in his unruly, unshorn hair that
made him look even younger than he was, like a gruff teen, there was
no change in his habit of working all through the day. He was almost
out of work to do. She was not afraid that he would confront Ames,
or tell him about them. Hector was the least of talkers. The nights they
had spent together they hardly spoke, and at the end of only the second
night he had told her, unprompted, that they shouldn't have an affair.
She didn't know if that meant she shouldn't come visit again.

Yet it had been an affair to her, for it wasn't only the carnality she
craved (which was as sharpened, as ardent, as she had ever known),
but even more the easeful, inertial pull of the hours together afterward,
as if they were floating on some quiet water instead of a bed. He'd
drink his liquor and she'd bind her arm or thigh and soon they dissolved
into each other in the tight well of his cot until she felt them become
the pool itself, shedding all their mortal properties. It was a feeling akin
to when she was a child and slept between her parents in a stifling hut
in West Africa and the heat of their three bodies put her in a near-trance
of fever that let her hear their blood coursing together like a wide,
whispering river. In her dreams she became that bloody river running

out far past the land and into the sea. For what had she witnessed daily from her earliest memory of their missions but the fragility of the body, every needless face of sickness and hunger, of merciless injury and death? Even then she imagined how she could make it so that the people they lived among could change form in waking life as she did in her sleep, somehow live without this living, and it was when she helped relieve Reverend Lum of his terrible pain that she saw a first kind way.

But she was at the end of her own ruinous clemency. She had to release herself. She must cease. When Ames left on his last brief over-night she found herself again at Hector's door after midnight and saw the weak yellow lamplight through the slats and was about to push inside when she saw herself in the clutch of her kit and her hand began to shake, both in anticipation and in dread. The tremors subsided but then a hard knob rose in her chest and she could barely breathe; she had to walk back to her cottage by propping herself against the exterior walls of the dormitory, and once inside she dropped hard on her knees to the floor.

The next day after the midday meal Hector caught up with her in the kitchen and asked where she'd been and although the aunties spoke no English anyone could tell he was confused and hurt. She turned away from him and he trailed her across the yard and in an odd reaction that only drew more unwanted attention she broke and half-ran, feeling a tightness in her chest. He followed her to her cottage and without knocking stepped right inside and embraced her. His smell was gamey and sharp. She asked him please to go but he kissed her and she couldn't help but kiss him as well but the door had drifted back open to the sight of some children in the central yard, paused in their games, and she panicked and pushed up hard at him. Her hand glanced him on the cheek, but he shrank from her as if she had smashed his face.

He bolted from the cottage just as the sedan transporting Ames from his overnight drove through the gate. She couldn't tell if Ames had seen him leaving.

It was only several evenings later that Ames asked if there had been something amiss or in need of fixing in the cottage, not mentioning Hector at all, and when she told him there wasn't he nodded and didn't pursue it. Later Ames came into her bed and wanted to make love and she must have surprised him with her intensity for he was as physical with her as he had ever been, so lost in the moment that he was unaware of his hand pressing her throat, nearly to the point of her losing consciousness. Yet she had not resisted him in the slightest. He seemed to know that he could do whatever he wished to her, that she would give herself over to any extent, and in the veil of perfect darkness he was not so much a man as a fury, this starved force that sought out every peccant part of her. He fell asleep half atop her in the single bed and by morning the one side of her was numb. He dressed quickly for the day and kissed her but wouldn't meet her gaze; it was always like this after their lovemaking, from the very beginning, a pale light of shame in his eyes. Perhaps it had nothing to do with her but this time she felt the depth of all her lies. As if he sensed something awry Ames embraced her, and she held on to him. What would she be, without him? That afternoon, while he took the children on a hike, she removed her kit from its hiding place in the trunk beneath her bed and threw it in the fire, aware of the miserable hours ahead of her but knowing that they would be so for the very last time.

Ames now returned from breakfast with a bowl of beef broth for her. It was milky white, made as it was in the Korean style, shinbones completely boiled down. She didn't want it but he asked her to try some and she took a sip and then another, the soup dense and rich and salty. Her stomach felt calm and she sipped some more. But then something seized and turned and spit up in the washbasin next to her bed. Ames braced her as she gagged. She wiped her mouth, her burning eyes.

"I shouldn't go tomorrow," he said. "You're not getting better." He was scheduled to go on his final trip to visit two recently opened orphanages along the eastern coastline. It was a slow journey on the poor roads across the coastal mountain range and down along the peninsula, three full days to go out and return.

"I'll be okay."

"I don't see how," he said. "You look as if you're dying."

"I'm not dying."

He looked down at his hands. "Do you want me to go?"

"Of course not," she said. "We have so little time left. No one wants you to leave. The children as much as I."

"I can have Reverend Kim go in my place."

"Do you truly think he can? Do you think he knows yet how an orphanage ought to be run?"

Ames didn't answer. "Sometimes I wonder if he knows much besides conducting the liturgy. "

"And how to eat," she said.

"He's a champion eater, isn't he!"

They laughed easily, the first time in a long while. Ames said: "He's a good man, though. He's smart, if a bit dreamy. He'll learn."

"I hope so," she said. "But sometimes I worry. He never spends any extra time with the children. He has no natural feeling for how to be with them."

"Perhaps sending him now would do him some good. Force him to connect."

"That would be fine if we weren't leaving, and you could go visit. But this is your last chance. Why should those children have to lose the benefit of your being there? Just because I'm not feeling well? I don't want you to have to go anywhere, but should you take a chance with their welfare because you're worried about me? I'd only feel worse, knowing they would be shortchanged."

"I wish that you could come with me."

"I will if you want."

"How can you? Look at you. You have no strength. Besides, if you did come we'd be leaving Reverend Kim in charge."

"The aunties and the children can handle him."

"But of course Hector would be here."

She would have wished for Ames not to say his name. But he went on: "You know, I've been thinking it might be best if he could stay around. I mean after we've gone. I know I've told him otherwise. But now I think I was wrong. Hector still doesn't seem to know it, or perhaps he knows and doesn't care, but he's good for the children, in his own way."

She nodded but was silent.

"I was thinking that perhaps it's not so terrible, to have an adult around who's not telling them what to do all day. Who's not a preacher. I think I've been too strident about what I expect of them. Sometimes I think I'm not seeing who they are. They're children, yes. But they're not innocents, and maybe it's not the worst thing to have someone like Hector around, who is obviously not so certain of his future. Who clearly struggles. But he works as hard as anyone I've ever seen and I know the children recognize that, too, and I wonder if that's not better for them than any sermon from me."

"You've only done wonders for them. Here and at all the other orphanages. No one could say anything otherwise. They love you."

He clasped her cheek. "I have to teach now. Will you be all right?"

"I'll be fine."

"I'll bring you something again at lunch."

"Please don't," she said. "I can make myself tea. That's all I need."

"All right. Will you do something for me, dear?"

"Yes, of course."

"I was hoping that you would speak to Hector. When you're feeling better, I mean."

"What about?"

"I'd like you to ask him to remain here, after we're gone. I doubt my asking him would do any good. Don't you think it would be best if he stayed on? I don't know how I or Reverend Kim will find someone else who would know to do all the necessary things, before and after the winter comes. I think only you have any chance of convincing him."

"He won't listen to me."

"Why not? He's always thought so highly of you. Am I wrong?"

"We haven't spoken very much of late."

"I have noticed that," he said, his wire spectacles still in his hand. The late-morning sun was streaming in from the window and brightly lighted the side of his face. He looked tired himself, worn down, and then oddly childlike, his sky-blue eyes appearing immense against the tight, drawn skin of his brow.

"Did something happen?" he muttered, looking down at his spectacles. "Did he offend you in some way?"

"No."

"Then what is it?"

He waited, but she didn't answer. Finally he pulled on his eyeglasses. She was sure he was going to say something difficult now, something irreparable and lasting, but he paused in mid-breath, literally swallowing the words. He reached for her then, and she shut her eyes, a flinch tensing her neck, but all she felt was his tender stroking of her hair.

"You should rest now," he said, his own voice weary. He got up and put on his black suit jacket. "I'll be back after lunch, to look in on you."

"I'll pack for you."

"Just rest. I'll do it. This is as good a time to learn as any. Because you were sick I had to help the three boys gather their things. We ended up simply stuffing what we could in each of their satchels. Nothing stayed folded. Jung wanted to bring his collection of rocks, Jin his live beetles. It was such a mess that Mrs. Stolz had to take everything out and start again, and I must admit I felt completely useless. You've spoiled me."

"I'm the one who's spoiled," she said.

He leaned down and kissed her. "When I get back, I think we should tend to each other as much as we can. And do so right up to the time we settle down again in Spokane. Can we do that, dear? Can we promise each other?"

"Yes."

They kissed and embraced again, but before he could leave she said, "I'll talk to him, Ames. I'll try."

He nodded from the bedroom doorway. "I won't expect that you can change his mind. I won't expect anything."

She was asleep when Ames departed the next morning, the driver from the church office in Seoul picking him up before dawn. She must have woken just as the sedan headed out beneath the arched gate and down the hill; in her dreams she heard the squeals of children but it must have been the car brakes and she had quickly risen but by the time she opened the front door of the cottage there was nothing in the frigid air except the lean, sweet perfume of motor exhaust. When it dissipated she felt even colder in her nightgown, the buildings about her barely discernible in the dim, rising light. Ribbed batons of clouds underpinned the sky. They would blow away soon. Ames had told her he wouldn't rouse her and yet she still felt as if she had been abandoned. He had gone not a kilometer and she felt the loneliness already. Her body wasn't frantic anymore but now felt instead like a forlorn hive, every chamber of her desiccated and empty. As if she were made of a thousand tiny tombs. Of course it was having been left now to her own devices that was most disturbing, making her wish that it was mid-morning already, with the Reverend Kim long arrived, the children bolting about with the aunties keeping after them, the pitch and shout of the day careening them all forward. She needed time to speed up. But there was no sound or light or movement, and rather than just turn back in and shut the door, she stepped in her bare feet onto the chilly ground. The shock of it made her gasp. But her mind was finally clearing and the cold air was bracing her and she didn't want to sleep anymore despite her physical exhaustion, for she was sick of sleep, and she stepped forth in the darkness toward the dormitory, her thoughts alighting on the children.

She wiped her feet on the towels the aunties placed before each of the three inner doors in the small vestibule; the doors led to separate dorm rooms, one side for the boys and the other for the girls. The one in the middle led to the chapel Hector had built. The vestibule itself was filled with their shoes, which because they were donated were of an unusually wide variety, sneakers and sandals and dress shoes and boots. Her eyes had adjusted to the dimness, everything made stony-looking in the weak blue light. And though she wanted now to peer in on June, missing the sight of her pretty, round face, a face so much more placid than her soul, she could not bear to speak anything of the coming days. For what could she have said to the girl? How could she ever console her? With the fact that she and Ames were not going to take any children at all? That she was finally as unfit to be a mother as she had been a wife, and even a mistress? That she was a bleeding heart and a coward, a person unfit, it turned out, to be herself? Their departure was imminent and Ames had not mentioned the subject of adoption and she could not breathe a word of question. As far as she knew, the arrangements they made on arriving in Korea to adopt some to-be-determined number of children had not yet been canceled. But it was no matter; Reverend Kim had confirmed as much the other day, when he gave Ames an envelope with the tickets for the first flight to Japan. There were just two, as Ames had specified. They had always assumed that they would take four with them, or five, or ten, as many as they could. But now they would return childless, which, she could now begin to see, perhaps as Ames had already seen, was a mercy for all.

She slipped into the boys' room. She had ventured into both rooms before on certain restless nights, the sight of slumbering children a calming medicine. Here, as in the girls', they slept in rows broken in the center by a large potbellied coal stove that the children took turns feeding through the night. There was no central heating and in the heart of winter it was important to keep it hot because there was no insulation in these walls, but this time of year it didn't matter so much and the stove was now barely warm to the touch. The air was heavy and dampened with the smell of their bodies, and of sleep, and at this preadolescent stage it was much the same scent as in the girls' room and though Sylvie could see how it might be off-putting or unpleasant she didn't mind the sour fatness of the smell, in fact half-adored it, like day-old cake. She was tempted to lie down for a moment in one of the three newly empty beds. Their sleep was hard, so deep as to appear almost deathly, though one of the older ones looked as if he were being beset by awful dreams, his face pinched up like an infant's, his fists guarding his head.

"Mrs. Tanner?" said a voice behind her.

It was Min, leaned up on an elbow in his cot. Despite what had happened to his foot he had remained the target of pranks by the three boys who were adopted by the Stolzes. He was the only boy who used to come to the knitting group; he told her he wanted to make a present of scarves for whoever eventually adopted him. The boys kept teasing him and he stopped coming before he could finish, and Sylvie had had to complete the second one for him. But the teasing had still continued, particularly by the just-departed trio. Once she'd had to wash his hair, which was full of ants, as they'd dribbled some syrup in the lining of his cap. Hector made the boys help him shovel out the latrines as punishment.

"You are okay, Mrs. Tanner?"

"I'm checking the fire," she whispered. "I'm sorry to wake you. Please go back to sleep."

"I am not sleeping," he whispered back. "You are cold?"

"I'm fine." She crouched down beside him, covering her chest and knees with her arms. She realized she wasn't even wearing a robe over her thin nightgown, that her hair was an unruly, matted mess. It had been nearly a week since she had bathed. "Are you cold?"

He shook his head. She cupped his cheek but he wouldn't lie down again, his face full of concern. He said, "You are sick, still?"

"Not so much anymore. I feel better."

"I am happy," he said. "I am waiting for you yesterday."

"What for?"

He swung out his legs and quickly ducked beneath the cot and tugged out a canvas bag. From it he pulled two neatly folded scarves, both camel-colored, and handed them to her.

"For you and Reverend."

"Oh, no," she said. She tried to give them back but he immediately understood her fear of their implication and so he insisted, if somehow confusingly, "Not for me. Not Min."

There was stirring, and murmurs from some boys nearby, and Sylvie took one of his blankets from the cot and led him out of the room. It was cold in the vestibule and she wrapped him in the stiff woolen throw, then wound one of the scarves about his neck. She tried to hand him back the other but he pushed away her hands.

"You must keep it, Min. Please. They'll be wonderful presents, just as you intended." She paused, carefully measuring his eyes. "Whoever is lucky enough to become your parents will cherish them."

"No."

"Please. This scarf can't be for me."

"I am not needing them anymore," he said. "I am staying."

"For the moment, yes, but not forever. The children who just left, you'll be leaving someday just as they did."

"You and Reverend are leaving first."

"Yes."

"I know you must go."

"Yes."

"I wish they are staying," he said.

"The other children?"

He nodded.

"Even the boys who left?"

"Yes."

"Truly? They were not always the kindest. Especially to you. Things will be better now. No more surprises."

"I don't care about that," he said, with a perfect equanimity. "I wish they are not happy. I wish they are here."

She didn't know what else to say. He held out the scarf to her and she took it; she wrapped it around her neck. She bent down and hugged him and kissed him on the crown of his head and he suddenly clung to her, his bony little arms strong enough to press painfully against the back of her neck. It surprised her, how much it hurt, like something would fracture, even snap: chalk against chalk. But she didn't steel a grain of herself, or try to shed him, letting him clamp her with all his might. She lifted up but he wouldn't let go and he was hardly anything, or else everything; like every child here he was an immeasurable mass, and she cradled him for what seemed a very long time, waiting him out until he was drained of all force. His shoulders sank and then his head lolled on her, like he was suddenly asleep, like he was lifeless, or wanted to be, but when she turned to carry him back inside, gathering the end of his blanket in her free hand so they wouldn't trip, a flash of pale in the darkened vestibule caught her eye. A hand or half-hidden face. She expected the sharpest glare. But glancing at the girls' door, she saw there was nothing there, it was fully shut, and she took Min inside and settled him into his cot.

"I'll keep this for now," she whispered, tucking the blanket beneath his chin.

"Present."

"But I'm going to give it back to you."

To this he shut his eyes.

"Okay? Before we leave. Please promise me."

But the boy pinched his eyes tighter, and then slipped beneath the covers, making his wafer of a body disappear in the well of the cot.

THE REST OF THAT DAY was the coldest of the year yet. At most forty degrees Fahrenheit. Despite the open skies and the clarifying brilliance of the unimpeded sunlight it seemed only to grow colder as the hours progressed, winds from the north racing intermittently through the compound. In danger of dispersal were the fallen leaves and pine needles all the children had gathered just yesterday into several large piles that were to be collected and composted for the gardening next spring. Reverend Kim, who had arrived mid-morning and given the lunch prayer with Sylvie standing tall beside him with a new woolen scarf banding her throat, idly paged through a newspaper inside the main classroom while everyone else tried to sweep and rake them now into a central, mountainous pile. There were no classes this Saturday, with Reverend Tanner gone.

But as if the winds had some deep objection to their efforts, each time they came close to clearing the ground once again a fierce gust would shoot across and instantly erode the top third of the new pile. The winds died down and they raked quickly, but another hard gust blew through and made a sail of the thin canvas tarp with which they were trying to blanket the pile, the muslin-colored sheet kiting wildly up in the air. It ended up festooning the peak of a short, lone pine at the far edge of the field. In frustration one of the boys gave a feral, guttural shout and ran and dove headfirst into the still-huge pile. He went in practically to his calves. Hector, who had been directing the work silently and joylessly, stepped forward to pull him out, but perhaps on seeing the boy's feet waving comically, and the children cheering him on, he relented and dropped his rake and let himself fall as stiffly and heavily as a dead man, hands at his sides. The children shouted with joy. A boy followed, next two of the girls, and soon the rest of them were jumping in, paddling and writhing in the crinkly mass of leaves.

Soon even June wanted to take a turn and after waiting for the others to clear out set her feet for the run. There was no cheering as with the others. But Sylvie clapped for her and June sprinted, sliding headfirst into the dispersed pile, which at that point was barely knee-high. When she got up, the knees of her trousers were scuffed reddish from the ground. Her face was tight with a strained smile, and as the others began collecting the scattered leaves to rebuild the pile she drifted away with her arms crossed, her hands tucked tightly in her armpits. Hector tried to see if she was okay but she kept them hidden and walked off. Sylvie caught up with her as she headed toward the dormitory.

"June? Are you all right? Look at your poor trousers." There were dirt-smudged rips in the fabric and Sylvie knelt and brushed them off. "Are you hurt?"

Sylvie lifted her pant cuff but June drew her leg away, and it was then that Sylvie saw the condition of her hands. They were torn and bleeding, tiny black pebbles embedded in the fat part of one of her palms, a triangular flap of skin on the other roughly peeled back, exposing raw tissue.

"Oh goodness, June! We have to wash and bandage you."

"I am okay."

"No, you're not."

"I will take care of myself," June said, pulling back her hands. She sounded not so righteous as strangely overexcited, as though she had eaten an entire box of sweets or been given the wrong medicine. "Please, Mrs. Tanner, I do not want to bother you!"

"You're not bothering me, June. You never have."

"Please, I am fine," she said, and before Sylvie could do anything else she ran off, sprinting behind the dormitory. Sylvie followed her but by the time she rounded the far end of the building the girl had disappeared. At the head of the path that led through the thick underbrush of the foothills Sylvie stopped to listen for movement. There were no sounds except for the threshing by the breeze of the tall, dry grasses and spiky weeds. And yet she suspected that June was still there, just as earlier, when she was with Min in the dormitory vestibule.

Back in the yard, the children and Hector were beginning to regather the leaves onto the tarps so they could be dragged to the compost pile near the gardens. Sylvie felt strong enough to help them, and once she began sweeping she was glad for the exertion and the closeness to the children. Her heart suddenly heaved with the realization of the time she had wasted: four days spent inside the cottage, and now there were only ten more before they would depart. Min worked near her, gathering errant leaves with a rustic hand broom made of bound twigs. He was obviously pleased to see that she was wearing his scarf but didn't point it out or say anything. He was a mindful boy. His small stature was painfully obvious now that he stood among others his age, and when they momentarily crossed paths she couldn't help but quickly press his oversized head to her coat. A broad smile lighted his face.

Several girls then joined them and they worked together and soon the rest of them spanned the width of the makeshift field, everyone sweeping and raking in a single row, making one another brush faster, if mostly in the spirit of play.

Hector worked at the far end of the line, his back to her. If he had been in a good humor when they were all jumping in the pile he had all but shed it now. His wide shoulders pivoted powerfully as he raked, the reddish dust kicking up in low billows about him, the sound of his tines rasping loudly against the hard ground. His strong, steady rhythm was easily distinguishable from the rest. She could almost feel his scouring through her feet. He hadn't spoken a word to her yet and although she was thankful he was keeping his distance she wondered if he could sense her attention. She was trying not to look at him but the sight of even his heavily clothed form after nearly a week of not seeing him kept drawing her eye. It was not so much a desire to be with him or to touch him that made her glance but her own wonder at how willfully she had forgotten his shape, which was so unlike Ames's, and frankly her own, his body completely un-angular, blockish, as if he were made of sections of trunks cut from various-sized trees. Even his fingers about the rake handle had the property of a certain primary thickness, while all her life she felt herself as being composed of only the thinnest reaching branches, third- and fourth-order limbs.

She knew with Hector her feelings were base and wrong and in every way contemptible, but there was the truth that she desired his form, the magnificence of which he was completely unaware. She hadn't ceased to feel its density, the uniform heft of his flesh when she drew him into her and she rowed them, he the heaviest oar. She had always tried to make herself invulnerable to beauty, her parents acclaiming only the sublimity of deeds, of selfless effort. The beautiful work. The last person who had so arrested her breath was Benjamin Li, whose outward beauty had been completely unlike Hector's but had infiltrated her all the same, this beauty that was disrupted beneath the surface, veiling some errancy or even wreckage.

The leaf pile had again grown mountainous and Hector told a few older boys to grab hold of a corner of the tarp, while he took another. They pulled together but their corner didn't budge and the boys lost their footing and fell down. The children cackled wildly. When they were ready again Hector counted to three and they pulled in unison; the pile began to move, Hector gripping the forward corner of the tarp, and when it looked as though the boys would falter, some of the others, including Sylvie, took hold of the lead sides. Several children stood between her and Hector. He glanced at her bloodlessly but her gaze didn't waver and he had to look away. She could not give in to him now, let him keep shunning her, for these few days Ames was gone would be the last chance they might freely speak. She had not lied to Ames about wanting him to stay or about how much the children at the newer orphanages would benefit from his visiting, but it wouldn't be untruthful at all to say that she had hoped for this chance.

Hector counted again and all together they dragged the pile about fifty meters, to the spot near the garden where they collected the compost. Once there, Hector went around to the other side of the pile and then waded through it while pulling the tarp in his hands, crouching and using his weight for leverage to flip the huge load over onto itself; for an instant it completely covered him before he stepped out, his hair and clothes tagged with pine needles and leaves as though he were a wild creature of the woods. The children brushed him off and after a moment's hesitation he stretched out his arms and even bent down so they could reach his head, letting them pick him clean.

Since the field was cleared, and with no other work for the day, the older children organized their usual afternoon soccer match, the younger ones playing jacks with stones or running about in games of tag. Reverend Kim had not yet come out from the dining hall and would probably remain there until supper, after which he would drive back to Seoul. Hector was now gathering the various brooms and rakes, and when he knelt for a hand broom, the high raft of the tools he was balancing on his shoulder nearly toppled and Sylvie stepped forth quickly and picked it up. She neither moved nor handed it over and without speaking he walked to the garden shed where he kept the tools. He came out and went right past her and she watched him transfer a load of firewood to a wheelbarrow and push it to the main dormitory building; he was replenishing the fuel for the woodstoves in the dorm rooms and the chapel. She waited until he was inside and then made her way over. He was coming back out for more when he saw that she had an armful for him. He took it and went inside the vestibule.

"You're not going to talk to me anymore?" she said. He didn't answer and she followed him into the chapel, where he deposited the wood next to the stove in the far corner. He was responsible for preparing the stove in the chapel for services, though now because of the cold weather he was lighting and extinguishing it nightly as well. The chapel was aglow with light from the small window he'd put in the roof, the gray-painted pews, the gray-painted walls, the plain wooden cross suspended by wires attached to the backs of its arms. "Is that it, then, Hector? Is that all?"

He said to her: "You're leaving the day after Thanksgiving."

"Yes."

"Maybe you ought to go the day before."

"Why do you say that?"

"This way we'll all know the blessing we're missing when we're giving thanks."

"Please don't be cruel."

"I'm not being cruel. I'm just saying it like it is."

"You know I don't want to leave."

"I don't know that," he said, his voice rising. "How would I know that?"

"You do," she told him.

"Then you can stay."

"I want to, yes. But if I did, what would happen? Do you think anything good would come of it? Do you think we could work together like simple colleagues?"

"You mean like you are with your husband?"

"Please don't be like that. Don't act like a boy."

"Isn't that what you want?"

"Please stop."

"Isn't that why we were together? Because you wanted someone you didn't have to be righteous and responsible with, and who gave you a good screw besides?"

"Fuck you."

She turned to leave but he caught her by the wrist and pulled her in and tried to kiss her and she turned away, covering her face. He persisted and she slapped him. But he held on to her anyway, not even flinching when she raised her hand again. She tried to wrench away, but his grip on her was fierce, unbreakable, as though she were manacled to a rock wall.

"You've taken pity on all of us, haven't you?" he said, tugging her closer. "I'm talking to you now! I want you to listen to me now! Before you came this place was no better or worse than any other orphanage in this damned country. Which was just fine for the kids and the aunties, and even for me. There's enough food and a roof and no more killing, and so what else is there to want? But you're leaving, and what do we have now? You know what I found one of your girls doing after your husband announced you were leaving?"

"Just let me go—"

"It was Mee-Sun. She was at the well pump, drinking water straight from it like she was dying of thirst. I passed her twice before I noticed she wasn't stopping. She was just drinking and drinking, getting her sweater soaked, and I had to pull her off it. I thought she was going to drown herself. I asked her what the hell she was doing, and she said she felt funny inside, because you weren't going to be here anymore. For some reason she felt like she was hungry again. She said she used to do it during the war, so she wouldn't feel so empty inside."

"What would you have me do? Don't you think I want to take every one of them?"

"Then take them!" he said, grabbing her other wrist. She resisted him and he pushed her against the shed wall with enough force that for a moment she thought he might hurt her. And if he did she wouldn't care. She wouldn't fight. "Did you think you could come and go so easily? Is this what happens in that precious book of yours? I want to know. I thought it was about showing mercy to the helpless, to the innocent. But I think that book of yours is worthless. In fact, it's worse than that. It's a lie. It's changed nothing and never will. That battle he describes, when did that happen?"

"A long time ago."

"How long?"

"Almost a hundred years."

"A hundred years! How many people got slaughtered in that time? Got ground up to nothing? How many went up in smoke? I'm not even counting us leftovers. But you, you do your part, don't you? You offer us hope and goodness and love. You're indispensable. But no one can help you. Isn't that right?"

"No."

"So you have to help yourself. Finally I know why. I've figured it out. Because you know in your heart that once you've come here you can't give up anyone. Because when you do, you leave every last one of us."

He let go of her then but she held on to him, afraid all at once of his absence, of being left alone, and though she turned her face away, he pulled off her knit cap and tightly clasped her hair and kissed her roughly on the face. Then he kissed her mouth and she turned but he held himself against her and when her own mouth softened all of his fury seemed to find her, his hands running over her as if she were difficult clay and he was desperate to remake her. But there was no need. She pulled him against her on the wall and she kept her mouth on his while his hand pressed her from beneath, rocking her, anchoring her on its hard seat, and after the days of unwinding wretchedness her body came wholly awake, alive. She didn't wish it but it was true. She was cured.

EIGHTEEN

THE HUNGER. It had come for June again. Yet this time, unlike on the road, when she was marching with her mother and her siblings and with the twins and then finally alone, it was not a lurking angel of oblivion. An angel of death. None of them had succumbed to hunger itself but it had driven them to exhaustion and carelessness and ultimately to peril and she always believed it would do thusly to her. Push her to the precipice. But this time, she wasn't hiding or running from it; she was inviting it along in a kind of dance, as a partner, a companion that would mark her every move. She knew that hunger would clarify her mind, strip away all extraneous thought, and leave her with the focus of pure, unswerving will.

She was eating almost nothing. The first couple of days were difficult; she could not have a thought that didn't involve breaking off from whatever she was doing and sprinting to the kitchen where the aunties were stirring the pots and push them aside and plunge her hand into the large cast-iron vat of rice porridge as if she were a bear reaching into a beehive. Fill herself to bursting. But after the second full day the panicked tremors began to subside, and on the third and fourth diminished enough that the chasm inside her was not of any need unrequited, nor a body forlorn, but a version of herself that she did not know until now existed, this June in quiet thrall. It wasn't an emptiness at all. It was the truer sculpture of her, the more deeply worked shape, and rather than feel her strength drawn down she was girded as she went forth about the orphanage, the ground hardly apparent beneath her feet.

Yesterday one of the aunties had regarded her suspiciously and kept glancing her way after she took her bowl of rice mixed with soup. After that, June made sure to eat a couple of bites whenever the old woman was looking her way but then would quickly spoon her food into the bowl of whoever was beside her (she made sure now not to sit off by herself), some younger boy or her mouthy bunkmate So-Hyun, who made no fuss or complaints about getting an extra helping, even though there was plenty of food. Orphans never declined.

Otherwise she was still mostly avoided or ignored, which suited her. She was no longer doing chores at the Tanners' cottage—an auntie had informed her that she should not go there anymore—and as no other job was assigned to her she could simply slip off after classes and meals where attendance was noted and wander in the hills. The foliage of the bushes and young trees had mostly fallen to the ground so that she was wading through puddles of brilliant color. She would have liked to pick up the pretty little leaves or even lie down in a pile of them but the strange thing was that she had to keep moving, for when she kept still she grew dizzy, this wild ball of a storm twisting within her like a gyroscope. She gagged if she stopped for too long. So she took to running, running fast in her too-tight shoes, the raw throbs of the blisters marking the distance on the deer trails that the boys and Hector used in their forays to gather firewood. With each step the grating pains flashed up into her chest and throat but she didn't whimper or even grimace and she swallowed them as if they were sweet sustenance.

The other day, after English class, Sylvie had offered a wave and a smile and though June was desperate to rush forward and press her face into the woman's chest she knew Reverend Tanner might see them. And even if he couldn't, she would show Sylvie her resolve. So instead she just nodded and scurried away. Since rousing Reverend Tanner out of bed a week earlier she had not spoken to Sylvie at all. Not a word. She knew earlier had been wrong to be so stubborn that morning and she would do what she could to get back into his graces enough so that he'd let his wife adopt her, and if that meant denying herself and Sylvie for a brief time, then so be it. June had faith: if he loved his wife, he would yield. She had never known anything like faith before but she was quite certain she knew what it was now, at least the bodily expression of it, the privation in her belly paradoxically convincing her of her way.

And the way, she realized, included Min. She had become his friend. It hadn't been at all her intention. She was keenly aware of him, yes, she couldn't keep from thinking about him, seeing the scarf he'd given Sylvie, how she always wore it now around her neck. On one of her wanderings down near the main road of the valley she'd found the rusted, broken-off tip of a bayonet in the dirt and she couldn't help but think of him darkly, pressing the edge against her own scabbed palm to test how sharp it was, drawing fresh blood. But the other day she had gone to the dormitory to retrieve a book and while in the space of the new chapel heard some scuffling coming from the boys' side. She cracked open the door to see four boys standing about a cot in the middle of the room. Min, undersized anyway, cowered amid them, trying desperately to slump down into his cot. He looked as small as a toddler. But he was being held up on either side, while one of the boys stood in front and grabbed Min's hair with one hand and with his knuckles of the other ground down hard at his scalp. The boys sometimes did this to one another, as it could be very painful but showed no marks, and Min cried out with each slash. "You think you're clever, don't you, you little bastard?" the next boy snarled at him. His name was Byong-Ok. He was one of the bullies in the orphanage, older and already very pimply. "You think you're going to go away with the Tanners so easily? Did you think we wouldn't find out?"

"I'm not going away!" he pleaded. "I'm not going anywhere!"

"That's not what I heard Reverend Kim telling one of the aunties," Byong-Ok said. "He said you were going to get all new clothes and shoes from the church office in Seoul. And maybe some spending money, too."

"Why would I get anything, if the Tanners were adopting me?" he cried. "It doesn't make sense! The Tanners would just give me whatever I needed!"

"Shut up, you bastard," Byong-Ok said, and knuckled him viciously. Min groaned sharply. Byong-Ok said, "How would I know why? Maybe that's the way they do it. Maybe the Tanners don't have as much money as those other people who were here. All I know is you're going to give us whatever you get. All of it. You hear me?"

Min murmured something.

"What?"

"I think you will be eating . . ." Min said.

"What? What are you saying? Speak up, you little bastard."

"When you're on the streets," Min said, now quite slowly and clearly. "I think you will be eating your own shit."

Byong-Ok punched him hard in the belly. Min doubled over and fell to the floor. He spit up his lunch, a muddy puddle of barley rice and soup. The boys standing about him jumped away, laughing disgustedly. Byong-Ok then grabbed Min again by the hair and was about to push his face into the vomit when June found herself running at him. She knocked him over with her lowered shoulder. He rose, ready to fight, but he dropped his hands when he saw her. June was as tall as he, taller than his friends, and she stepped forward and pushed him, making him stumble over the corner of Min's cot. When he tried to get to his feet she pushed him down again, and then again, and finally he shouted from the floor, "Okay, stop it! Stop it!"

She let him get up and the boys trudged out. They cursed Min on the way, cursed her, too, though she could tell from the low huff of their voices that it was for the sake of their own pride so she didn't respond. Min seemed to understand this as well and he stood beside her in silence.

"Are you okay?" she asked him.

He sat on the cot, cradling his belly. "Why did you do that?" he said. "I've got nothing to give you."

"I know."

"Then what do you want?"

"You can tell Reverend Tanner. Or Mrs. Tanner."

"Tell them what?"

"You can tell them that I helped you."

A flicker of something momentarily lamped his face. "All right," he said. "But you have to protect me. You have to keep me safe from them. They hate me."

"You don't try very hard to make them like you."

"Why should I? I hate them. They're dumb as oxen. They just play marbles and soccer and eat all they can, and they don't think about anything."

"What should they think about?"

"What you and I are thinking about. What's outside of this place. What's going to happen. What we're all going to have to do. Isn't that what is going on inside your head, *noo-nah?*"

She didn't answer; she didn't like how he addressed her, much the way her younger brother might, with a lingering plaint. But of course he was right. There was no other consideration in her mind. It was becoming ever clearer to her, transparent, all the other concerns dissipating as she could feel her own flesh dissipating, cell by cell, the needless layers dropping away to leave only fresh, hard bone.

"So will you protect me?" Min said.

"I can't be with you everywhere," she said. "At night you'll be in here with them."

"I can sleep out in the chapel."

"What would that do? They'll just come for you."

"You can sleep there, too."

She shook her head. "It's cold enough in the rooms."

"I'll relight the fire for us in the stove, after Hector has come and gone. We can sleep right in front of it."

"I'm not going to sleep out there."

"You would if you were my sister."

"Yes," she said. "I would."

"Well, you're going to be my sister. I'm going to be your brother. Soon enough we will be in America together."

"How can you be so certain of that?" She found herself pinching his meager forearm. "What did Mrs. Tanner say? Is that what she said?"

"You're hurting me, June."

"What did she say!"

"She didn't say anything!" he told her, wrenching himself from her grip. "It was Reverend Tanner. He said he was going to take us with them."

"I don't believe you. You're lying, just like you were lying to Byong-Ok."

"I'm not lying to you."

"Did you get spending money like Byong-Ok said?"

Min nodded. "But it wasn't from the church office. It was from that old couple. Maybe they thought I wouldn't be as useful on their farm, with my foot. They were going to take me but decided at the very last moment on Sang-Ho instead and they must have felt guilty. It was twenty dollars. I don't know why they bothered. I wasn't going to get any of it anyway. But of course I couldn't care less now. Soon we won't have use for anything like money. We'll have everything we need."

"How do you know?"

"Talk to Reverend Tanner, when he returns. Ask him yourself."

"I will," she said, though already knowing—as Min undoubtedly surmised—that she would not talk to him, or even approach him, out of fear of further sullying her chances. She made to leave but Min hooked her arm and hugged her with every ounce of his little boy's force, his scant strength, and although she could have easily nudged him aside she let him hold on to her the way one of the twins might, his face mashed hard against her breastbone, his fists digging into the small of her back.

"Very soon," he murmured, his voice muffled in her sweater. "You'll see. We'll be living a new life."

That evening, well after lights-out, Min tapped at the door of the girls' room, just as he'd told her he would. It was freezing in the chapel but he had just relighted the fire in the stove. It was enough to blunt the chill. He had dragged the two front pews before the stove and put them together front-to-front for the planks to be wide enough to lie upon. He pointed her to the pews and she climbed over the back. He had spread a folded blanket as bedding. She asked where he was going to sleep and he scooted quickly beneath the pews onto the bare floor. It was quiet and she was vigilant for any sign of Byong-Ok and the others. But Min kept turning on the floor beneath her and groaning with the discomfort and she pushed apart the pews and scolded him for making too much noise. He said he would stop but after a few more minutes of his tossing she gave up and pushed apart the pews and he scooted up between them. She made room and spread his blankets over hers and without hesitation he tucked himself into her side as snugly as if this were a nightly ritual and almost immediately fell asleep. She bristled with annoyance, but the faint, high sound of Min's breathing made her think of her brother, and though the smell of his hair and body was not at all pleasant she instinctively wound her arm over his cheek and neck, to keep him warm.

They both awoke before reveille and June went to her cot in the girls' room, leaving Min to set the pews back in place; he didn't want to go to the boys' side until everyone else was awake and waited in the chapel until the kitchen bells rang. The rest of the day proceeded like any other with Reverend Tanner away, Reverend Kim arriving in time to give the breakfast prayer, and then he and Mrs. Tanner conducting the classes. She was clearly no longer ill: the color had returned to her face and she appeared as vigorous as ever, and in English class she led them in a few songs, the last being "Rise and Shine." There was always an unofficial competition among the children to see who could sing the chorus the loudest, and for the first time ever it was June's voice that sailed above the others, everyone (including herself) surprised by the force of her sound, its pleasing pitch and carry. Min was in the class and he stomped his good foot loudly in time to the rousing chorus. The other children and Mrs. Tanner did the same. It was strange, but June had slept very deeply, and despite only eating over the last three days what she would normally take in a single square meal, she felt as if she were the very ark they were singing about, her hold filled to capacity with the vitality and promise of the world.

After class she did not linger or even try to catch Mrs. Tanner's eye, rushing out along with everyone else to the lunchroom, where she would take her bowls of food but merely touch the spoon to her lips, leaving the food for her bunkmate So-Hyun and Min to split. She calmly watched them finish her food. Lick clean the bowls. It was not for them she felt satisfied but for herself, sure now she had mastered herself, transfigured the great foe within.

Outside, the boys were organizing the usual post-lunch soccer game. She had not played since tussling with the other girl back on that warm autumn day, but she felt a new electric strength in her legs, a need to run. When she stepped onto the field Byong-Ok held the ball underfoot, telling her to go away. She stood quietly and waited. He kicked it to start the game only when Reverend Kim and Mrs. Tanner came out to watch. Soon both of the adults joined in the play, even Reverend Kim, who rarely spent any time outside. Everyone expected him to be stiff and awkward but he moved easily with the ball, flipping it up and deftly trapping it on his thigh, then on his foot, before floating a perfect cross to Mrs. Tanner, who deflected it for a goal between the two dirt-filled petrol cans. She raised her hands and a hearty whoop went up on both sides, though perhaps it was one more of commemoration than celebration, as if everyone saw that this was one of the last times Mrs. Tanner would be here among them.

June had now joined in the game, too. She was as carefree as any of them, feeling as though she was moving to the rhythms of the play, following the track of the ball and the others, when before all she would look for was an opportunity to avenge any slight with a shove or collision, a kick in the shin. Though no one except Mrs. Tanner was intentionally passing the ball to her it regularly ricocheted her way, and instead of rearing back and booting it as hard as she could at someone or out of bounds she tapped it to her surprised teammates. Min was on her team and she tried to stay close to him whenever she could, warding off those boys with a glare. They couldn't goad her today. On one play, as she was dribbling toward the goal, one of the boys who had threatened Min tackled her hard, his foot riding into her ankle, but she popped right up from the hard ground and kept running after the ball. She felt remote and light, almost bodiless, as if she could no longer feel pleasure or pain; or else the pleasure or pain existed somehow outside of her, in some ghost of her old self. She was not the same vessel anymore. She was simply moving, playing, and she was certain that Mrs. Tanner was seeing her fully once again, appreciating her anew.

It was not even a question of Hector anymore. Since Reverend Tanner's departure he hadn't appeared in the mess hall, instead taking his meals to his room or to wherever he was working. He was at last keeping to himself. He was not outside now but from habit she kept an eye out for him. Although she knew they'd not been together for some weeks, June had still awoken late last night and crept out in the frigid dark to check for any sign of light from either the Tanners' cottage or Hector's quarters. But there was nothing but blackness and the cold, no sound but the whining gusts of the harsh wind jetting past the long dorm building, and she had quickly returned to climb next to Min in the warm box of the butted pews.

A pass was now booted down the field nearest June and Byong-Ok and they sprinted after it. He had a few steps head start but she propelled herself with all her will and she got to the ball first. He was a much more skilled player than she and should have been able to take the ball from her easily, but she thwarted him with her hip, her shoulders, leaning back into him so he couldn't reach the ball. His flagrant kicks stung her ankles and calves but she didn't give in and when she noticed Mrs. Tanner and the others running toward them, she faked a kick as she'd seen Byong-Ok do and then jabbed the ball through his legs with the back of her heel, sending it toward the approaching players. Byong-Ok, frustration twisting his face, shot after it, reaching it just as Mrs. Tanner did, both of them stretching out a foot at the very same time. But at the last moment, perhaps realizing that it was Mrs. Tanner, he slid to the side and averted the ball just as the sole of her shoe met it. Her shoe rolled over the ball, her leg extending unnaturally, and she fell in a heap. The ball came loose and Reverend Kim took control of it but he stopped when Mrs. Tanner remained on the ground. She was wincing terribly and gripping her leg at the knee. Everyone crowded around them as Reverend Kim knelt beside her but when he touched her leg to examine it she cried out, pulling away.

Hector suddenly appeared, though no one had fetched him. He pushed through the tight throng of children. Reverend Kim would not yield at first but when he saw Hector he moved aside to give him room. Hector didn't have to say a word to her, to make her yield. He didn't even look into her eyes. He simply pushed up the wide cuff of her trouser leg past her knee, taking her stark, pale limb in his rough hands. His fingers grazed the soft underside of her thigh. He handled her with great tenderness, cradling the back of her knee with one hand and clasping her calf with the other, telling her he was going to try to move it in certain directions. She nodded, to say she was ready. He slowly bent her knee, and then gently straightened it and this was fine, too, but when she turned her foot to either side she winced. "Be careful," he said.

"I'm all right. Please help me up."

"You think you can stand on it?"

"Yes."

He raised her up and braced her under the shoulder, his arm hooked around her waist. But when she put weight on the leg she instantly fell into him and in one motion he lifted her from the ground and walked toward the cottage, the whole orphanage following. Though she had been right beside them, June was now trailing everyone, her own legs suddenly gone weak, her chest clenched, her belly razored by a double saw of rage and desire. For it was at that moment, while Hector ascended the step of the cottage, Mrs. Tanner's arm slung casually about his neck, that June realized that they were lovers again.

Reverend Kim announced he would leave now and bring back a doctor from Seoul.

"I'll be fine," Sylvie told him. "I'll be fine."

"It already looks swollen. I will come back tonight after I find someone. It may be late, but I'll return."

"Please, Reverend," she said. "There's no need."

"It's not as if he's a doctor," he replied, regarding Hector coldly. Hector was silent.

Mrs. Tanner said, "You're not even supposed to return tomorrow, are you?"

"No, I have to be in Seoul for something else. But now I feel I should be here, especially since Reverend Tanner won't return until the following night. I shouldn't leave while you're in such a condition."

"Please don't bother making any trips. I'll be fine. Thank you."

"We'll see," Reverend Kim said, as Hector took her inside. A couple of the aunties had retrieved bandages and ice hastily chipped from blocks delivered in the morning. The reverend went in and observed Hector wrap her knee, the children trying to push in and watch as well until the aunties shooed them all out. Soon enough the two men emerged, Hector heading to his room, Reverend Kim collecting his briefcase and coat in the mess hall before getting into the church car. He started it and rolled out on the worn path of the drive. June ran after the car and had to rap on the trunk to get him to stop, this just beneath the orphanage gate.

"What do you think you're doing?" he said, rolling down the window. He brushed her hands from the door of the dented old sedan. He didn't know any of the children particularly well, but if there was one he knew, it was June, at least by reputation. "Now stand back."

"Will you be contacting Reverend Tanner when you get back to Seoul?"

"It's no business of yours."

"But he should know Mrs. Tanner has been injured, shouldn't he?"

Reverend Kim nodded, clearly annoyed for having to speak with her, but now giving pause. "He should be. But as with this place, there are no telephones at those orphanages. There's a popular inn at the pass near the second one. I suppose I could leave a message there. But whether he'll stop in is pure chance."

"Please leave a message, Reverend."

"Maybe I will," he said, his eyes growing curious. "But tell me, girl, why are you so concerned?"

"I care about Mrs. Tanner."

"Is that right?"

"Yes! More than anything!"

"And I take it you think it would be best if the reverend came right back?"

"Yes . . . I don't know. It just seems Mrs. Tanner shouldn't be alone."

"No," he said, somewhat thickly. "She shouldn't."

"So will you return tonight?"

"Mrs. Tanner does not wish it."

"What about tomorrow? You'll come back tomorrow?"

"She doesn't wish that, either." He put the car into gear. "Step back now."

She clung to the door, tears in her eyes. "But you must! Everything will be ruined!"

He let out a begrudging sigh of solicitude. Normally he would have rolled up the window, right there and then, but she looked particularly desperate, her round face unusually tight and drawn.

"Nothing will be ruined that won't be ruined anyway," he said. "Do you understand me?"

"Yes, Reverend," she said, "but you're wrong."

He sighed again. "Look here. I can't explain it to you now. They'll be leaving very soon. You children should make good use of your time with the Tanners."

"Not Min."

"Why, does he not care that they're leaving?"

"Of course he does. He's going with them."

Reverend Kim said gravely, "Is that so?"

"Yes. And I am, too."

Something sour flashed across his face, as if he had just smelled spoiled porridge. "You had better step back now," he said to her, nudging away her hands. He rolled up the window, and before she could do anything else he drove away, the rear bumper of the rusty sedan rattling as the car bounded down the rutted drive.

SOON THE BELLS RANG for supper. June lined up with the others. The children were orderly—they were always quietest on the line—and she took her bowls of soup and rice and sat alone at the far end of the mess hall. So-Hyun and Min ambled over just as they had the last few days, knowing she would only pick at her meal. But she didn't acknowledge them when they sat beside her, and when So-Hyun reached out to take her bowl of rice, June grabbed her wrist and held it, with increasing pressure, until the girl began to whimper.

"What's wrong with you?" So-Hyun cried, finally able to pull back her hand. She rubbed at her wrist. "Are you crazy or something?"

June made no answer. So-Hyun scooted down on the bench, continuing to complain, while Min had already picked up his bowls and left. He was no longer even in the mess hall. June thought she ought to go find him. It was then that she noticed one of the aunties leaving the mess hall with a tray of food. She caught up with the woman just as she was nearing the cottage. "Dear auntie," she said, "let me take it to Mrs. Tanner."

"What are you doing out here? If you're done with your dinner, then it's time to get ready for bed."

"I'll wait and bring the dishes back for you when she's done. That way you don't have to make another trip."

"I do have some radishes salting." The woman sighed, weary from the long day. "I should get them seasoned before I go home. Okay, then, but just bring it to her and wait outside. And don't bother her! If I hear anything different I'll strap you, you hear me?"

June agreed and took the tray. When she knocked on the door she could hear Sylvie say in Korean, *You may come in.* June let herself inside just as Hector was coming out of the back room, some balled-up bandages in his hands. He walked out without saying anything to her. In the bedroom, Sylvie was sitting up in bed in a robe, reading by the lamplight, her knee newly wrapped and propped on a pillow. She seemed startled when she saw it was June but then warmly smiled, putting down her book. "You're nice to bring me supper."

"Does your leg still hurt?" June asked.

"I'll be all right," Sylvie answered.

June nodded. "Would you like to eat now?"

Sylvie said yes and took the tray from her, setting it on her lap. She removed the newspaper covering the porcelain bowls of soup and rice and prepared vegetables. The aunties had prepared some extra dishes for her.

"My goodness," she said. "It's so much food. I'm not terribly hungry, to tell you the truth. Have you eaten, sweetie?"

June said she had.

"But I just heard the bells a few minutes ago. Did you even have a chance to finish your own meal? Why don't you share this with me? You use the spoon and I'll use the chopsticks. Sit up here with me, it'll be easier."

Sylvie shifted to make room for her, June sitting cross-legged with the tray on her lap. She didn't want to eat but Sylvie kept saying she should, patting her shoulders, and before she realized it, before she could stop herself, she had already begun, eating half the bowl of rice and all the radish *kimchee*. It was like breathing after holding one's breath for too long, the inhalations at first quick and deep but then settling right back into an automatic rhythm, her body in command, cribbing her sight with opaque blinders, the dull glow of the bowls the only halos before her. Sylvie was saying to keep on, and very quickly June finished the vegetables, the fritters, the last spoonfuls of rice, and by the end she had lifted the soup bowl to her lips and drunk it down, the hot, rich broth scalding her tongue. But when she was done she felt immediately ashamed, the barely chewed morsels lodged in her gut as if she'd swallowed fistfuls of coal. She slipped off the bed to take the tray and leave, but Sylvie grasped her arm. "You don't have to go . . ."

"Please forgive me!" June said. "I ate all your dinner! I will bring you more!"

"Oh, sweetie," Sylvie said, now trying to hug her. "I didn't need any of it. Not a bit."

"I have to go," June gasped, and then pulled herself away, just quickly enough to open the back door and retch onto the ground. It smelled almost good, simply like food, but she coughed up some more. Sylvie was now holding her shoulders as she stroked her back, the hollow feeling in June's belly strangely confirming to her that this was the state in which she felt most honed, elemental, most purely alive.

"Are you feverish?" Sylvie asked her. "Are you feeling sick, otherwise?"

"No, no," June said. "I should not eat your dinner. I am sorry."

"Please don't apologize for that," Sylvie said. "Never for that." They stepped back inside, Sylvie limping but bracing June as if she were the one who needed help walking. She pulled up a stool for herself and had June sit on the edge of the bed. She clasped June's hands. "I'm glad you came here tonight. We haven't talked very much of late, have we?"

"No."

"I've missed spending time together."

June didn't answer, for she realized she had not come here to speak but rather to hear what Sylvie would say to her, to hear her utter what she of course knew was the truth. Yet all at once June found herself beset by a great flowing rush of tears. She did not feel sad or afraid and yet here she was with her face awash, her eyes burning, its salty run trickling into her mouth.

"Please don't cry," Sylvie said, gently wiping June's face with her hands. "Please, sweetie. You're going to break my heart."

June steeled herself, rubbing her eyes. She was not going to falter. She was not going cede to childish need, to weakness. "I am sorry, Mrs. Tanner," she said, in her clearest voice. "I am fine."

Sylvie said, "Of course you are. May I tell you something? These months that Reverend Tanner and I have been here, they've been the most joyous times in my life. The reason is being with all of you children. There's nothing else that has given me more happiness, and I'm sure nothing ever will. But above all, most precious to me has been our friendship."

"What about Hector?" June said, unable to help herself.

Sylvie bowed her head. She looked at June and said, "I've done many regrettable things, here as in the rest of my life. I don't know if I'll be forgiven. Perhaps you can someday forgive me, but I will not ask you for that. I deserve nothing of the kind. I simply hope you know something about yourself. Early on, I didn't know if I was being unfair to the other children by spending more time with you. My husband certainly thought I should have gone about things differently. But you have always lifted me up. And I see now how much you've grown and changed, in such a short time. I've been watching you the last weeks. You've been so thoughtful, and kind, and wonderfully willing to help some of the younger girls, and I notice how you've now taken Min under your wing. When we were playing the game earlier today, I was so pleased that you wouldn't let Byong-Ok provoke you. You don't even seem to have your famous temper anymore! You've become the girl I always believed you were. And I know only a small bit of that is because of me. It's more because of this place, and everyone's hard work and care, but most of all, it's because of you. No matter what you do or where you go in this world, your undying spirit will see you through. You have a singular perfection, that way. Nothing will ever halt you. But you should know something else, too. You have a great and passionate heart, June, one as capacious as you are strong. Soon, I know, and forever, it'll be full of love's riches."

Sylvie reached over to the shelf that served as a night table and pulled out a book and gave it to June. "I was hoping that you might like to have this. Would you accept it from me? Would you keep it safe, after Reverend Tanner and I have gone?"

June stared at the thin volume in her hands. It was the one covered in blue cloth, the one of the long-ago battle in the long-ago war. Here was the sole possession of Mrs. Tanner's she had truly wanted, and had once stolen, and had given back. And so this is what she would have. This was her prize.

"Yes," she said, gripping it tightly. "Thank you."

She rose to leave. Sylvie hugged her and almost fiercely held on but June did not yield a hair to the embrace, a breath, even a prickle of her skin. How quickly she could check herself. She was only a child but she was a right hard stone. When Sylvie released her, June did not have to look at the woman's face to know that it looked as if it had just been struck, brutally smashed.

June left the cottage. In the twilight the children were coming out of the mess hall, chattering and running around in the last weak lamp of daylight. They streamed past her as she carried the tray of empty bowls, the book pinned under one arm, staring at her for a moment and then fluttering by like the tiny, carefree birds that nested in the bushes and small trees around the orphanage and under the eaves of the buildings. During the summer there had seemed to be scores of the mouse-brown wrens perched about, hundreds of them, but now their numbers had rapidly thinned, culled by the growing scarcity of the season. After returning the tray, June watched the other children, and she thought how their numbers were thinning, too, but rather because of their character, or young age, or plain luck, and that those who remained would be only less fortunate, and grow older, simply settle ever deeper into the fixed molds of their selves, the selves that had already been passed over.

When the bell rang once again, the children scattered and dashed about in a final frenzy before being ushered inside by the aunties. June stayed outside in the leading shadow of the darkness. She crouched on her haunches well beyond the far end of the field, right by the rickety gate, her hands and neck and face steadily stiffening in the chill. One of the aunties called out for her and waited for an answer but didn't call out again. They had become accustomed to not bothering with her. The kerosene lamps were now lighted in the dormitories, the windows aglow on both the boys' and girls' sides. In recent weeks she had indeed helped the youngest girls brush their teeth and dress for bed and had even read to them a few times, but tonight she would stay out until she couldn't bear the cold. Or maybe she would simply remain here, lie down on the hard, gravelly dirt and close her eyes and hope that this would be the night that brought forth winter in its first full, harsh form. She remembered sleeping on the train with the twins, the same icy fingers grasping at them as they had huddled tight, and how she had hoped they might get all the way to Pusan without having to march again, to eat again, without fearing any more misery and privation. It was June's decision to climb atop the overcrowded train. Since that night she had often wondered if it would have been better to wait for the next one, or to have taken their chances on foot, or else steered the twins and herself far off the main road without any provisions and simply waited for the one merciful night that would lift them away forever. The twins would not have suffered and she would not be here now. For what had surviving all the days since gotten her, save a quelled belly? She had merely prolonged the march, and now that her new hunger had an altogether different face, it was her heart that was deformed, twisting with an even homelier agony.

She was just about to lie down on her side when a kerosene lamp emerged from the main dormitory door, swinging to and fro. From the clipped gait she could tell that it was Min. She didn't move or speak, and she could see him stepping back and forth in the dark, lifting up the lamp to try to see. He headed back to the building but a wind whistled past the sign at the top of the arch and the sound made him turn around and venture out past the field. He must have seen her shape against the thin lines of the gate door, for he lowered the lamp and approached her quickly.

"What are you doing here, *noo-nah*?" he said, his shoulders hunched up tight against the cold. He was wearing a sweater over his pajamas. He turned down the wick of the lamp. "It's freezing. You should come inside."

She didn't respond. During dinner, before Min disappeared, she had resolved never to speak to him again, or maybe to do worse: she had flashed with a rage, wanting to pummel him, make him plead and cry. But the sight of him slightly limping, the kerosene lamp still too big for his hand, momentarily disarmed her.

"Please come now, *noo-nah.*"

"Just leave me alone."

"I went in the chapel and made the fire in the stove. It's been going for a half-hour already, so it's nice and warm in there."

"Go back inside, then."

"You don't look right. You're going to get sick in this cold. You could die."

"I don't care."

"I do," he said, kneeling down beside her. "And it's not because Byong-Ok might beat me. He doesn't care about me anymore. The others don't care, either. Nobody does."

"You're better off that way."

"Are you still my friend?"

June stood up and began walking away. Her feet were tingling, nearly numb, her fingers cramping, and she thought that she should go now down the dirt road and veer off on a trail deep into the woods, where no one could find her.

"Well, are you?" he asked, following her closely. "I want to know. I don't want to live here anymore if you don't even care about me."

"Why should I?" she said, turning and shoving him roughly. He fell to the ground, just barely keeping the lamp upright. She put her foot on his hand as she stood over him. "I should strangle you. Why did you lie about our being adopted? Didn't you think I'd find out?"

"I didn't know!" he cried, trying to pull his hand away. But she just stepped more heavily on him.

"You're a liar!"

"I didn't *want* to know!" he said wretchedly, trying with his free hand to push her foot away. She let him go and he curled into himself like a wounded snail, holding his hand against his chest. "Isn't it the same for you? Don't you have to make believe, too? Everybody knows I've got little chance, with my foot. Not when there are so many others with nothing wrong with them."

"There's nothing wrong with me," she said, clutching the collar of his sweater. "Not with me!"

"Nothing?" he said, and almost laughed. "You can say it ten thousand times over, but it's not going to make it true. You're the way you are. Everybody knows it. The way you'll always be. You're trouble, just like me."

She grabbed him by the throat with both hands, her fingers monstrously vitalized by the heat of his neck, his windpipe like the gently ribbed sections of a delicate reed, and had he not turned his face to the lamp, revealing the willing forfeit flooding his eyes, she might not have let go.

But she did. Min coughed horribly, shudderingly low, as if he were a dying old man, and after he regained his breath she got him up on her back and carried him to the main building. The chapel was lit by the bright honeyed light leaking out around the edges of the door of the old steel stove. Min had already moved the front pews together and close to it, as they had done the previous nights, their shared blanket was neatly laid out, his pillow set to one side to make enough room for hers, and she gently tipped him over the pew back and let him down on his side. She leaned over him, to make sure he was okay. He wasn't speaking but he was breathing shallowly and steadily, and in the odd crib of the pews his body seemed even smaller than it was, loosed of stuffing, like some worn-out, sunken doll. He was staring up at her, not with wonderment or anger or even hurt but with the plainest appeal: Stay. Please don't go. She didn't know what she wished to do but what else was there now? He was not her brother or her friend or someone to care for or love. He was all right now and she owed him nothing. And yet she let him take her hand. He gently tugged on her and she climbed over the pew back to lie beside him, and when he turned and rolled right onto her, his face pressed into her chest, his hands seeking the pits of her arms, she wanted to push him off. But there was something in his certain sorry weight that seemed to seep down into her, suffuse her, until a strange new fullness had risen up in the stripped caverns of her belly.

They fell asleep. After some time June awoke to a dying fire and climbed out of the pews to feed a small log into the stove. The fire flared quickly with new heat.

"Could I have some water, *noo-nah?*" Min said to her, peeking up over the pew back, his voice raspy.

She said all right. Outside, the sky was clear but moonless and the stars barely thwarted the darkness. But her eyes quickly adjusted and she made her way to the well. It was by the kitchen, and after she worked the hand pump five or six times the frigid water splashed out of the spout. Beneath there was a wooden ladle in a bucket, and while she filled its large cup she noticed a tiny, weak glow at the far end of the field. It was Min's kerosene lamp; they had left it by the gate. She went across the field to fetch it and was about to head back to the chapel when the low groan of a door broke the silence. June instinctively crouched down, thrusting the lamp behind her to shield its light.

A dusky figure emerged from the Tanners' cottage. It was Hector. He must have gone over while she and Min were asleep. Hector turned and held out his hands toward the pitch-black doorway and then it was Sylvie, in her light-hued robe, stepping out gingerly on the stoop. He helped her down, her one leg unsteady, and though it was obviously painful for her she appeared to want to walk by herself, if closely braced by him. But as they made their way across the yard she tucked her face deeply into his neck, not so much with ardor but rather as if she were trying to blind herself, as if she were unwilling to see.

They had not noticed her. June waited until they were long inside Hector's room before rising. The night air had grown even colder now but June did not feel its sharpness. She stood stiffly before his quarters, staring at the lamplight or stove light knifing out from a vertical gap near the bottom of the door. She had no picture in her mind of what might be going on inside, whether they were speaking or kissing or making love, but that was no matter now. She did not desire to see them or hear them as she had from the other side of the shared wall, for she did not want any image of their animate bodies, or the sounds of even chaste breathing, any signs of life.

June crept into the storeroom and took a can of kerosene. Outside she silently doused the wooden stoop, the walls, splashed the ground in front of his door. She raised high the wick of her lamp, the height-ened brightness surging through the clear glass globe to illumine the whole side of the building and the night as though she were still in search of someone, still bearing the light of everlasting devotion. She lifted the lamp and was ready to hurl it against the door when a shadow inside interrupted the slat of light at the bottom. It was a moment's pause, a mere flicker, and yet it was enough to send a shudder through her bones.

She extinguished the lamp. She picked up the square-bottomed ladle from the ground. It was night again, and she suddenly felt the full chill of being alone. Inside the chapel, Min had pushed open the pews so that he was sitting directly in front of the fire, the door of the stove opened for light; he was looking at the book Sylvie had given her, flip-ping through the pages. When he realized June had returned he quickly put it down. He said, "You were taking so long."

"You can have it," she told him. "I don't care."

"I don't want it," he replied. "I don't want anything anymore."

"I brought you water."

She gave him the ladle and he drank half of it, saving her the rest. She took a sip and offered it back and he finished what was left. Then, with a surprising indifference, he threw the ladle into the stove. It was not worth ten grains of rice, but like many things in the orphanage it was a shared object and therefore of communal value, and the ease with which he tossed it in startled her. They watched it closely. The ladle was waterlogged and at first it only hissed but soon the twining and edges began to burn, smoke starting to billow from the bamboo cup, gathering beneath the long handle, and then in a whoosh it was aflame, its light hot on their faces. Min got up and left. When he returned he was carrying two of the small footlockers. One was his, the other June's—he had stolen into the girls' side. He opened the lid of his locker and began taking out the few items it contained, inspecting them for a moment and then tossing them into the stove. She did not say anything or try to stop him. He started with his box of pencils, and then a deck of Korean playing cards, and then he put in two special pairs of dress socks that he'd received from a church group in America. Next were some letters and greeting cards from the same people. Then he drew out the fine scarf he had made; aside from his everyday clothes, it was the last thing he had. He handed it to June to put in the fire, and after he nodded to say it was all right, she balled it up and dropped it in. It burned not quickly but rather steadily and well, the fire consuming it with its own slow savor.

"You want to try?" he said. "It feels good."

June opened her footlocker. One by one she began tossing in her possessions, which were nothing at all, letting Min throw in every other, a straw doll she had never played with and old magazines and a yellow summer dress that she had worn only once and knew now she would never wear again. The fire flared with each item and they had to lean back from the blasts of heat. The last thing of June's was not in her footlocker but on the pew, beside Min, and he picked it up now, the little book. "How about this?"

She regarded it for a long moment. "Okay," she said.

"Are you sure?"

"Yes," she told him. "Put it in."

Min leaned in toward the stove, one hand shielding his face. He then flipped it into the seething vault. It lay on the coals, its cover pristine and cool blue. It appeared as though nothing would happen, that it was miraculously immune to their private inferno. And then she knew how wrong she was to give it up. She was wrong to ever let it go. There were things not bound for oblivion. But all at once the book was in flames, blazing as brightly as anything gone in so far, and without hesitation June reached deep into the stove and grabbed at the heart of the fire.

"Noo-nah!" Min gasped, trying to pull her back. "Noo-nah!"

There was pain at first, pain so sharp and great and pure that for a moment June felt that she had become the burning itself, that she was the crucible and not the iron, and as she grasped the book a lightning flashed into every last part of her. She fell back onto the floor, Min immediately snuffing her hand and the book with the blanket. He was frantic because she would not let it go, and when the flames were finally out he was crying at the sight of her hand and arm. The horrid, bubbled skin was like half-molten, bloody wax. But to June it belonged to someone else, for there was no feeling at all, the nerves seared dead up to her elbow. It was the untouched rest of her body that was shuddering, as if buffeted by the wake of all the phantom pain from her hand. Yet her mind was clear.

"Somebody must help us!" Min said, panicking. "I'll go get Mrs. Tanner!"

She told him no. He was frantic but she calmed him with an embrace. They were on their knees. She let him go and the boy sat on his haunches. She reached for the big oil lamp that she had fetched from outside. It was still quite heavy with fuel. She gave it to him and he hefted it from the bottom; he knew what she wanted him to do. He threw it into the stove, the glass globe shattering without much sound. June shut the hearth door, neither of them moving back. Min hugged her tight now. She was still holding the book, its cover charred but the inner pages still intact, and she could smell the smoke and her ruined skin as she wound her arm around his neck. She thought she heard voices outside but it was too late. She kissed him on the cheek.

"We don't need anyone," she said softly in his ear. "We're going to stay here now."

NINETEEN

SHE KEPT TALKING about *la chiesa dell'ossario*. The Chapel of Bones. She was still flush with the double dose Hector had given her, riding in the splendid chariot. The three-hour drive had taken nearly five because of jammed traffic and then getting lost several times, Hector having to pull over and check the map himself. June was no longer able to help him. There was a question as to what she could even see, her eyes opaque and darkened, the color of muddy coffee. But they were close now, ascending the road to the village on the next hill, and as if she knew they were making the last approach, she was preparing herself, reviewing. She had not been to this place before but she spoke as if she had seen it many times, as might a guide, telling him how the church was consecrated in 1870 as a reliquary of the fallen soldiers of the Battle of Solferino. It was the simplest church, nothing about it ornate, the only spark of color on the cream-and-white façade a mural of Saint Peter in a blue robe, a red shawl about his shoulders, a golden halo encircling his somber head. She said he would know it by this.

But the car had sounded funny in the last half-hour, and now something was clattering in the undercarriage, and as Hector careened ponderously on the steep curves banking up the hill, he wondered if this last effortful stretch would prove its demise. He shifted to a lower gear and lurched the rest of the way, the heaving strain of the motor shaking the tinny sedan, and when he looked in the rearview mirror he saw her slumped against the door, her face pinched up as if she were tasting something bitter. The road widened on a plateau and he stopped across from a small hotel whose patio and cocktail tables were set practically onto the pavement. He was simply going to park, to give the machine a moment's rest, when to his right he saw the church. It shined starkly in the late-afternoon light. It stood atop a brief rise of land opposite the old hotel, a wide gravel walking path lined with cypress trees leading up to its dark wooden doors. Above the doors was the figure of the saint, his colors just as June had described.

"Look," he said to her. "Up there."

But now, in the lee of the drug rush, she was too weak even to turn her head. Her color was ghastly.

"Is your back hurting again?"

"I want to lie down," she said breathily, talking through her teeth. "I want to lie down right now."

He was going to circle tightly in the wide street and let her off in front of the hotel, but when he tried the ignition it cranked and cranked, and then it simply clicked. Finally it didn't even click anymore and he told her to hold on and he walked across to the hotel and arranged for a room. When he returned she was nearly passed out and he had to catch her head as he opened the rear passenger door so that she wouldn't tumble out. He lifted her and held her as several cars and scooters passed, one of them peppering its horn at them. He bristled until he realized they were probably being taken for newlyweds. The honking startled her and she gazed at him as if waking from a long and restful sleep, craning her neck back before resting her cheek on his shoulder, happy to be once more cradled in his arms. And yet he wasn't completely sure she recognized him. The elevator was out of order and so he carried her up the four flights of stairs to a room in the tower, led by the manager of the hotel, a gaunt-faced young man in a crimson tracksuit. He let them into a large spartan room with two double beds and an armoire with one of its doors detached and leaning up against its front. There were large armchairs in the corners, placed, it seemed, more for the inhabitants' punishment than comfort. But the main feature of the room was its tall, large window, which framed perfectly the church on the hill. The manager pointed it out in Italian and broken English, obviously accustomed to hosting its visitors.

Hector laid June on the bed next to the window, but she didn't turn toward it, as if she had no desire to see the church, or had even forgotten why they had come. The young manager considered her gravely, and when Hector extended some lire for a tip he refused it, saying instead that he would fetch their bags. Hector pointed out their car, parked across the way, but couldn't explain that it had just died.

"I wish Nicholas were here," June said, after the manager had come back with their bags and then left once again. She was somewhat revived. She wanted to change her clothes, for some reason, rather than have him bear her immediately to the church on the hill. He didn't say what he was thinking, which was that she might never leave the room, or at least leave it alive. They were finally here after the fitful sojourns of recent days—and now she would devote precious minutes to this? But he didn't protest.

She said, "He would have liked this place."

"You think so?"

"He was always an artistic boy. He would have liked the landscape here. The colors and the hills, just like in the art books he used to look at. All the cypress trees."

447

Hector was surprised, wondering when she might have noticed.

"I don't much like those trees."

"No? Why not?"

"Makes me think of cemeteries."

June nodded, waiting as he unpacked her bag to look for the pieces of clothing she wanted. "Of course you're right," she said, almost able to smile.

"Are these the ones?" he asked her, holding up the things she'd asked for from her bag. An outfit constructed from a stiff, coarse white linen.

"Yes."

He placed them on her bed. June explained to him that the outfit wasn't a traditional death robe exactly, except for the fact that it was white. The mourners would wear white as well.

"I don't have any clothes like that," he said.

She laughed weakly. "You're not going to mourn me, so what does it matter?"

He didn't answer. Back in the car she had told him what to do with her after she was dead: she should be cremated and then her ashes spread about the grounds of the church, or perhaps even snuck inside, dispersed however and wherever he saw fit. She joked that he might perhaps prefer to do the job himself, though following the old manner, swathing her body in cotton dressings and then building a wooden bier on which to set her aflame.

"Do you think we should have had Nicholas come with us?" she said, now lying on her side, her head propped on two pillows.

He peered into her eyes to see what she was thinking or could possibly be hoping for now. But there was only flatness in her gaze, an unfocused stare, as though she were looking upon a shape more looming than defined. What she believed or wanted to believe, he couldn't tell anymore.

He said, "It's better that he stayed back in Siena."

"Yes. You're probably right. What would he do here? Except I was thinking just now that perhaps he might have wanted to spend more time with you."

"I doubt that."

"Why not?"

"I don't think he took to me much."

"How could you tell?"

"It wasn't hard."

"Did you take to him?"

He didn't answer, for although it was obvious how she hoped he would reply, he couldn't bring himself to say anything good about "Nicholas." In fact, this renewed mention of the fellow was making his chest pound, his fists ache. On the road he had scolded himself for not beating him to within an inch of his life. And now he wished that he could have met the other Nicholas, her true son, and his, if even for just a few minutes, not for any longing or want of a bond but simply so he could say something that wouldn't be such a burning, raging utterance. To simply greet the boy. So he pictured the old school photograph of Nicholas, the color washed out, yellowed, his long hair parted in the middle, framing an expression that was more a question than a statement, as though he were waiting for some long-hoped-for instruction.

"Maybe I could have," he said. "But it would have taken a long time."

"Doesn't everything?"

He nodded, startled by this seeming flash of lucidity. He had un-packed the rest of her clothes and put them into the armoire and begun emptying his own small satchel when he saw the book that he'd forced Nick Crump to hand over to him in Siena. He couldn't bear to handle it and had immediately thrust it beneath his clothes. But earlier, at a rest stop, while she was napping, he couldn't help himself and had peered once more into the book. It was the same, except that the cloth of its cover had been burned away, its pages made brittle by the trauma. He noticed two inscriptions on the title page. The first, to Sylvie, he recognized from all those years before; the second was in a different hand, the ink newer: *To Nicholas, my dearest wayfarer. May you find great treasure and riches.* He was confused as to how June had come to possess it, whether it had been singed in the terrible fire, and how, if so, it had ever survived. But like a promise of ill reckoning, the scent of smoke that rose up from its binding quickly quashed his questions and he had pushed it back into his bag.

Now he gave the thin volume over to her, the thing literally falling apart in his hands. When June took it he could see her fingers straining against it, as if she wanted to press it back to life. She opened the book and turned its first pages to a photograph of the author, a young-looking man with muttonchops and a gold watch chain on his suit vest. Opposite was the title page, twice inscribed, as he'd seen, and June seemed to linger on the handwriting, her expression one of confusion. Finally she caressed the page as if it were the cheek of an infant. With hardly any difficulty she stood up before the large window, her hands braced against the wide marble sill. In the framed vista the church at the top of the hill gleamed in the late-afternoon sun, the rising gravel path darkly ribbed with the long shadows of the cypress trees, and though it must have been the first time she'd seen it her eyes only narrowed coldly while taking its measure, her gaze no pilgrim's.

"I didn't mean for him to be alone in the world," she said. "Not forever, anyway. I thought it would be good for him to get away from me. Not to depend on me. But I haven't asked you. Was he still angry with me? I mean to say, did it seem to you that he had forgiven me?"

"Forgiven you for what?"

"I told you," she said, wrapping the book with her arms. She looked strong all of a sudden, her posture as straight as when she was a child, her chin forward, elevated. That orphan girl, carved from rock. For a long second, when she turned back to look at him, she appeared as if she might not be ill at all.

"Didn't I? When he was injured in England while riding. After the hospital called. I waited until I got a postcard from him. In the end it was okay but I keep asking myself why I didn't try to reach him right away. I wanted to talk to him so much. I wanted to see him. It had been many years. I could have told him I'd fly right over and be with him. But for some reason I just passed the hours. I opened the shop the next day. I went to dinner by myself. For two weeks I didn't sleep. Then his postcard came and after that the nice letters, and it seemed that he cared about me again, but I've been thinking it was only because he was angry for so long that he ended up being kind. Do you think that can happen? Do you think that's what happened to my son?"

She then stepped back from the window and sat down on the bed, her head heavy and bent, all the girding of the prior moment now fled from her body. She set the book aside on the bed beside her. He asked her if she wanted to change now into the special clothes.

"I don't know," she said.

"I can leave if you like."

"That's not it."

"You don't want to?"

"I don't know," she said, her voice suddenly sinking. "I don't know."

She began to cry, which took them both by surprise. She was weak enough that it hardly seemed to be crying at all, more as though she was having trouble breathing, her meager tears barely wetting her cheeks. But he had never seen her cry, not at the orphanage, not once since, and the sight broke open a fear in his chest: here, about to perish, was surely the strongest person he had ever known. She wiped her face roughly with her palm. "Give me another shot now, okay? I want a little more time, without it hurting so much."

"I gave you one just two hours ago."

"I'd like another."

He obliged, another heavy dose. Hector drifted into an armchair across the room, trying to avert his gaze. He could have loaded up another half-dozen syringes and instantly extinguished her but he couldn't help but think that she might somehow come back for him if he did, in a malign form, hound him for eternity for cheating her of even a few hours.

"I'm sorry, Hector. But I think now I want to rest."

"Okay. I'll leave you alone."

"But just for a little while. I don't want to fall asleep for too long. I can't let this day pass. I don't know if I'll be able to do anything tomorrow. Where will you be?"

"Downstairs, I guess."

"Would you come for me in an hour? We'll go up to the church then."

"Okay."

"Would you bring me back something?"

"What do you want?"

"Something to eat."

"You're hungry?"

"I don't know if I can really eat anything. But I want to try."

"I can bring something. What do you want?"

"It doesn't matter. I just don't want this to be the last feeling I have."

He went to close the curtains but she told him to leave them drawn open, so the room would stay awash in the light. It was good light, being reflected light, as it was now late in the day, all of it fully drenching the room, the tops of the trees and the terra-cotta roofs and stuccoed buildings illuminated by the strong, low sun, the color of their lower halves in the warm penumbra glowing in a muted scale, the white church atop the rise of land as brilliant as a lodestar. "Just an hour, Hector. Don't let me sleep any longer. You'll remember to come back up? Won't you?"

"You think I wouldn't?"

"I don't know," she said, the shot having settled deep into her now. From her loosened posture he could see that it had already met and quelled the harshest pain. She was almost herself again.

"I know you must hate me," she said. Her eyes were narrowed. "You do, don't you? You're the only person in the world who knows anything about me now, and I don't want you to hate me."

"I said in the car I didn't."

"Even after everything I told you?"

"That's right."

"I don't believe you."

"I'm not going to talk about this anymore."

"Please just say it again."

"I already did."

"Please say it, Hector, please!"

"What do you want?" he shouted. "What the fuck do you want from me?"

"I don't want this!" she shouted back, slapping at her own shriveled, wasted thighs. Her face was a cracked, broken mask. "Not this! Maybe you wouldn't care if this were happening to you! Maybe you never cared whether you lived or not. But I do!"

He was about to tell her she would rot in hell when he realized he was arguing with a woman who had in almost every way disappeared. She immediately said she was sorry, trying to follow him to the door in her feeble hobble, and she might have caught him had he not leaned forward in the last quarter of a second, half-bolting onto the landing and down the steep steps of the tower; he was a world-class sprinter, at such distances. As he rounded the corner he caught sight of her ruined silhouette, halted at the end of the landing with her hands outstretched like a flightless bird, her desperate apologies echoing down the stone well of the tower after him, and though he felt ashamed for the velocity of this easy escape he kept going, his rage making him want to punish her.

Downstairs, in the bar that doubled as the hotel lobby, he slumped at a corner table. The young manager came over and asked if he wanted something and Hector didn't answer and the manager suggested a beer. After serving him the bottle, the manager stole glances at him as he stacked cups on the coffee machine, as did an older German-speaking couple sharing a plate of cheese and salami and a carafe of white wine. The couple had been just sitting down when he carried June into the hotel, and the fleshy, ruddy-cheeked woman now regarded Hector with kindly eyes and a sympathetic purse to her mouth that made him helplessly think of Dora. He drank from his beer but after a sip he put it down, despite the fact that his insides were crying out; for once in his life he didn't want to douse the parchedness, that driest, coldest flame. He wanted his own sentence, for all his deeds and non-deeds, for every instance when he had failed. For when had he not? If he were truly eternal, as his father Jackie madly fantasized, the sum of his persistence had so far only added up to failure. Failure grand and total. Ask Dora what she thought. Ask Patricia Cahill. Ask the Chinese boy soldier if Hector had done right by him. Ask Winnie Vogler about the collateral calamity he had wrought. Ask the Reverend Ames Tanner if his end was the one he had envisioned for himself. Ask them all if Hector had been their right attendant fate.

His failing found expression now in even the small measures, too, like the fact that he couldn't quite summon the hatred even June assumed he should have for her. In the car, in her delirium, or perhaps under its cover, she told him what she had done. Yes, she had caused the fatal fire. Yet in his own way he had stoked it, too, with his rank, blinding want, and he had always believed that it should have been he who never emerged.

On that last night, Sylvie had begged him to let her be. Why had he not heeded her? Why hadn't he simply stayed in his room? Once the fire started, surely he would have rushed inside the dormitory first and gotten them all out. He'd been drinking all evening, sitting in his dim room with a bottle of harsh Japanese-brand scotch whiskey, feeding his accelerating thoughts, which alternated between wanting to flay Sylvie with harangues, with the lowliest of sentimental entreaties, with self-pitying rants and outright attacks, and trying to figure out how he might lovingly convince her to stay on. To love him back. But he was useless at romance. He had no profound or pretty words. He thought she had made up her mind on the day they had all collected leaves around the orphanage, when she had followed him into the chapel. Afterward they left the chapel and headed in different directions but she met up with him as he had asked, about one hundred meters along the most southerly trail, where there was an obscuring thicket of woods. They didn't make love but had still fallen upon each other in a primed, overdesperate state and in a matter of minutes they had clawed and tasted one another with the privation of ghouls. They had hardly undressed, and yet later, when he was bathing, he could feel the tines of her fingernails striping his back, his neck, his thighs. He'd done the same to her but with his mouth, his ravenous teeth, biting her wherever she pointed to herself, as if they were playing some curious grade school game. She had gasped with each snap, tears filling her eyes, then pointed again. It was then that Hector was sure that he had won, mishoping, misreading her erotic fervor for a deeper devotion; for he was too young and ignorant to know that she was not acting or dissembling but rather offering herself to his pure and towering want, surrendering to his great keen need, which to her was as lovely as he.

It was already midnight when he finished the bottle and went to her cottage, knowing that the next day Tanner would be back. He and Sylvie had not yet made love while her husband was presently away, his carrying her after she twisted her knee in the soccer game the first time he'd time touched her since the brief, furious moment in the woods. Simply holding her was an alert of his craving but a kind of anchoring, too, how he needed the literal burden of her to offset the hateful, numb condition of his being. His unassailable body. And as he went around to the back of the cottage he realized how vulnerable he felt whenever she was close, as though he were at last mortally subject, as prone as the next. His heart a boy's, brimful and shaking. Yet he knew, too, though he was still resisting it, that it was already finished between them, or that it had never truly begun, and it was this dire feeling that pushed him to try to be with her again. The window shade was down and when he tried the door it was locked and he rapped at it harder and harder until the sound was loud enough to rouse the children across the way. She opened the door and let him in. Her knee was still just as he had wrapped it and she limped away without even looking at him.

"Does it still hurt a lot?" he asked her, following her to the bed.

"Not anymore," she said wearily, her head bowed. He knelt before her and took her knee in one hand and her calf in the other, gently and carefully testing the joint. She winced with its play. "It'll be fine. Please go now. Please."

"I said I would come."

"I asked you not to," she said, pushing off his hands.

"So you don't want to see me anymore?"

"Maybe I'll see you tomorrow."

"He'll be back tomorrow!" Hector cried, the instant thunder in his voice surprising even him.

She was silent. "Please, Hector. You can't be here now."

"Why? Because you've changed your mind?"

"I've never changed my mind. Not about you. It was never a question of that."

"Then what was it a question of? Would you tell me? Because I'm stupid. I'm confused. Are you in love again with your husband?"

"I've always loved him," she murmured.

"You've always loved him," he scorned her. "I guess you were loving him right from the beginning. I guess you were thinking about how you loved him when you were fucking me on this bed. You've thought about him so much that every time he goes away you come around to wherever I am."

"I didn't come to you tonight," she said.

"It's because you're strong," he said. He was standing now, glowering as he angled his words sharply down at her. Had he not had a voice he might have actually struck her. "You don't pace around your room like an animal in a cage. But I'm an animal that's too awake. Before you showed up I didn't care one way or the other about anything. But now here I am, waiting to be petted and fed. Told how much I'm loved. Here," he said, holding his open palms before her. "What if I need comforting? What if I need some ministering to? What will you do for me, Mrs. Tanner?"

She didn't move. She was silently crying, the tears running down her face. Her natural paleness was warmed in the honeyed lamplight, her brow and cheeks a vital, gleaming shade, and as much as he was raging he couldn't help but see that she had never appeared as lovely to him as now. Which only made him burn. "You won't help me?" he said. "You won't come to my aid? It's okay. You do me good just like that. I've told you some of the things I've done and so you know that I'm not a good man. I'm an awful person, by any account. But looking at you makes me feel better about myself. You know why? Because you're like me. You're frail and selfish, but you're reckless, too. You're a whore for love. Hope is your drug. To me that adds up to a pretty sorry religion."

Sylvie didn't answer. But a different color had now risen in her face. She said, "My mother once told me something. I never quite understood her, but I think I do now. She said there was a surplus of benevolence in this world. Of loving mercy. Surely too much of it went begging. But it was worse, she said, when it was misspent. Because then it was no good at all."

"I don't care if it is," he said, fiercely gripping her shoulders. "Misspend it on me."

She took his hands then and had them cup her face, blot her eyes. She turned them over and kissed his palms. She kissed his fingers and his wrists. He kissed her madly in return and began pulling off her robe but she said not here and so they made their way slowly across the yard to his room, Hector bracing her. Once inside they made love. Or a kind of love. He was overwrought. It was as if the entire army of him had fallen upon her, overrunning her in waves, the breakneck charge of a thousand faceless troops. He kept waiting for her to try to slow him, or tilt against him with equal fervor, with the disquieting roughness he craved from her, but even as she mirrored him and was strong enough it was as if she drifted outside of herself and was watching them from across the room. After a short while he was done. He got up and pulled on a pair of trousers, a mountain of shame in his gut. She lay in silence on the cramped cot, her back to him. Then she rose and put on her robe. She was looking for her slippers but he told her that she had come barefoot. He asked her not to go but when she opened the door he didn't try to bar her.

Outside, the smell of kerosene oddly prevailed. But it was a car that made her halt. It was rolling up through the gate, following the path that went around the field and then led in front of the buildings. It was too late to be Reverend Kim. The glare of the headlamps swept across her like a harbor light as she stood in Hector's doorway and the car imperceptibly slowed, as if the driver momentarily had taken his foot off the gas, before resuming speed again. Sylvie stepped off the stoop and onto the ground but she didn't move. The car had turned and was tracking straight for her and for a second Hector was certain it was going to run her over. But it stopped just short of her and when the driver came out it was too dark behind the bright beams to see but of course he knew it was Tanner.

"Sylvie," Tanner said, his voice throaty, beseeching. "What is this? What's going on? There was a message you were hurt. I drove myself back all night. Why are you out here?"

Sylvie stood barefoot in her white robe directly in front of the car, the stars above them gone out for her brightness. She was clearly naked beneath. She drifted toward him, her hand outstretched, but Tanner slapped it away. When she tried to get close to him he hit her, once, quite hard, and she fell beside the wheel of the car. "What are you doing to us?" Tanner shouted down at her. "What are you doing?"

Hector made a short sprint and rammed him, knocking him to the ground. Tanner lay gasping for wind. Hector was kneeling and checking on Sylvie when a sound like a mortar round, a plosive, metallic thump, went off from the direction of the dormitory. As he craned to see what had happened a dead, sheer weight struck him, this broad, leaden plate meeting the back of his head, his shoulder blades, like the angry hand of a god. Hector crumpled from the blow, his mind momentarily emptied as he fell forward on his face. He couldn't quite move. He could see but not yet speak. The cold ground tasted almost good to him, clean and flinty, like a freshly etched stone. And he could hear Sylvie shouting at her husband, who loomed tall above them; Tanner had walloped him from behind with the heavy sedan door. Hector got up on his knees and would have been struck again but for the sudden bright dawning of firelight, sharp licks of flame spearing up around the chimney pipe on the roof above the chapel.

"My God," Sylvie said, getting to her feet. "The children!" Though faltering, she ran to the chapel. Tanner went after her. Some of the children were already fleeing the building, smoke billowing from the top of the chapel door, oozing out from under the eaves. None of them could see it yet but the flames inside were spreading quickly, flying through the parched wood of the old structure, and by the time Sylvie reached the main door others were climbing out of the windows from the dorm rooms on either side. Sylvie frantically counted the children, making sure the youngest ones were out. Tanner was asking everyone to check for his bunkmate, each calling out a name and waiting for a reply, when Sylvie said, "Where's June? Where is she?"

"She's not here!" one of the children said. "Neither is Min!"

"Where are they?"

"They were in the chapel," Byong-Ok said.

"But why?"

"They were bunking there together."

"Oh, my June!"

Sylvie was headed in but Tanner grabbed her. She fought him but he commanded her, "Stay here! Stay here with them!" Tanner took off his suit jacket and used it to cover his mouth and nose. He took a few quick breaths and then held the last and rushed inside the door. Although his skull felt smashed Hector was now on his feet, and he could see Sylvie drifting toward the door. She was calling for them to come out. She was calling their names. But before he could gather himself enough to try to dissuade her she stepped inside and disappeared.

Hector went in after her. The vestibule was choked with smoke. He bent down so he could breathe and when he pushed through to the chapel there was a blast of heat. The roof timbers were aflame.

The front pews were on fire, as were the altar table and the cross, which had fallen to the floor. The back wall of the chapel was burning, part of it fallen away or blown out where the woodstove had been, and nearby were Sylvie and Tanner, huddling over a child. A fierce draft was being drawn in from the gap in the wall, feeding the conflagration. Hector felt his own hair begin to singe, the skin on his shoulders begin to prickle and burn. The heat was turning, it was on the verge, as though a sun were just about to push into the room. And in a flash a plumed beast of flame leaped up from the flooring to enfold the couple and child, for a moment cradling them in an almost placid repose before swallowing them whole. Hector gave a bloody cry. The walls gave a shearing squeal and a terrible crack and then the chapel roof fell in. There was a great burning pile where there had been a room, the black sky exposed. He was trapped at the edge of the pile by burning beams across his legs, shattered clay roof tiles searing his arms, his chest. He was in the bonfire now. The adjoining walls of the dorms would collapse next. Yet he didn't try to move. He was more than ready to pass; maybe at last transmogrify. But a hand gripped his wrist, another lifting the beam from his back. The girl was inordinately strong. And she dragged him through the collapsed back wall and out into the cold, quenching night.

"THERE YOU ARE," June said softly when he finally returned to the room. Nearly two hours had passed. He could tell by her eyes that she had not quite expected to see him again. Somehow she had managed to move a stuffed chair to face the vista of the church on the hill, and she was sitting in it before the now opened window. Though it was nearing dusk the breeze was still quite warm, faintly fragrant with pine and earth. She repositioned herself now and sat up, as if to try to demonstrate that she still had a measure of control. But even this tiny exertion was too much for her and her head lolled over the chair back at an unnatural angle, her mouth hanging open. "Did you bring me something?"

He had: the proprietor had arranged a few cookies and bite-sized café pastries in a basket, as well as a pink plastic parfait cup with a scoop of lemon ice. Hector put the basket on her lap and she beheld it like a girl at Easter. She picked up the spoon and was about to take some ice when she paused and asked if he would like some. He shook his head. She dug out a dollop and placed it upside down on her tongue, holding the spoon there as she closed her eyes, her drawn cheeks clenching with the tartness, or the sweetness, or both. He couldn't help but watch her swallow, the mechanism ponderous, wholly voluntary now, and he imagined the melting ice finding the besiegement of her insides, how utterly thronged she was with disease, that there was nowhere to go. She didn't take another taste, just clutching the spoon at her belly as she sat for a moment with her eyes closed, as if she were counting the seconds before the first kind swells of a drug washed over her. He asked her if she wanted a shot and though her face had gone suddenly ragged and chalky she firmly said no.

"Do you remember when we first met?" she said, gazing again out the window. "On the road?"

He said he did.

"I was thinking about that day while you were gone. It was such a hot day."

"It might have been a hundred degrees."

"I was so thirsty. The days before I saw you, I was searching less for food than for water. It hadn't rained for some time. The one well I found had gone dry."

"Didn't I give you some water?"

"You did, but your canteen was almost empty," she said. "You had chewing gum. To this day, I think that was the most wonderful thing

I've ever tasted. But mostly I was dying of thirst. I was truly close to death. There was only thick, stinking mud in the paddies, and I was so thirsty that I tried it. I scooped some with my fingers and put it in my mouth. It was terrible, but it was wet. So I ate it, two full handfuls."

"You kept it down?"

"For a little while. In the middle of the night I woke up with a terrible stomachache and threw up about a dozen times, right up until morning. I thought I was going to die from that. But if I hadn't eaten it, I doubt I would have lived to see you. You would have walked past my body on the road. Perhaps that would have been better for you."

He didn't answer her, though maybe less out of decency or compassion than to shield himself, such that he wouldn't have to consider a timeline that featured him alone, in sole steer of a likely unaltered fate. Like everyone else, he was at the helm, whether he wished it or not. Very soon he would be on his own again, and he thought about what June had said earlier, that he was the only person in the world who knew anything about her, or at least anything significant, which made him realize, now quite obtusely, that in this case the opposite was true, too.

"I haven't asked you," she said to him, as if she were reading his thoughts, "what you're going to do, afterward. Where you might go."

"I don't know yet," he said. The car was broken down and he had no interest in or idea of how to be a tourist, and although she had already given him the rest of the money (enough to buy, she said, a couple around-the-world plane tickets), he had no thought of where else he might go. He had finally telephoned Smitty the other night to let him and the fellows know he was still breathing, and Smitty told him how broken up everyone was over what had happened to Dora. Scenes of the accident had been on the ten-o'clock news. They figured that's why he'd been scarce, holed up someplace with his hurt. Hector didn't bother to say where he was calling from, nor did Smitty ask.

Smitty simply said, *Well, stop in soon, we'll be here,* as though Hector were just across town, and Hector replied that at some point he would. They would go on in their inertial drag, more or less, hang around in the dimness until the time of the reckoning. Then have one last drink and shuffle into line. The question was again what he would do. Nobody in his right mind would want to be immortal, as he was in the mad dreams of his father. Still, Hector feared his own persistence. He flashed on her request of cremation and her suggestion that he do it himself; he could pull off on some rural road and find a clearing on which to build the pyre, and torch not just her body but douse the pile of brush and sticks with gasoline and, having filled his gut with fuel, climb atop the heap himself, before striking the match. He would make the hottest fire, burn up even their bones. Send them both far and nigh.

She said: "You could stay in this place for a while. You could live here for a long time with the money you have. Maybe you'd even find someone. Someone who would take care of you."

"I wouldn't want that."

"Why not? Every person needs the love of a good woman. Don't you think that's true?"

Of course he didn't dispute her. How could he? Think of a world in which we all had such succor. The problem was that succor bore the sentence of frailty, infirmity. It expired too soon. And then what were you? Lost. Bewildered. A sack of broken things. It was cruel, and he meant it to be, but he asked her, "I wonder if you would have taken care of me. If I was the one who was sick."

She looked at him unwaveringly. "I don't think so," she said. "I've never taken care of anyone."

She took another spoonful of ice, but that was all. In the warmth of the breeze, the rest quickly melted in the bowl. The clouds were

tinting amber and red with the falling light. This long day would soon
be at its end. She rested the basket on the arm of the chair and tried
to get up. He helped her to her feet. He asked if she wanted to change
now into the special clothes.

"I want to bathe first. All of a sudden I feel very cold. Would you fill
the tub for me? I tried to do it myself while you were out but it was too
hard to bend down. And the hot tap seemed stuck. Do you mind?"

"No."

"Don't be afraid to make it hot, all right?"

He drew the bath for her, as hot as he thought she could bear. As
the tub filled, he wondered if once she got in she would come out
again—alive, that is. All this ferocious will and effort and now she might
not make it up the hill. What did she think she was going to encounter?
What does the pilgrim hope for at journey's end? Her beliefs confirmed? Revelation? Or does she secretly wish that the destination never
quite materializes, that it keeps receding, ever shrouded in the distance,
all the more to feed an inextinguishable devotion.

June came into the bathroom and without shame took off her
clothes. It was as if he weren't there. She had trouble twisting her arm
out of her blouse, and so he helped her with that. Her belly was distended but it appeared full and vital compared to the rest of her, her
drawn shoulders and limbs, the blades of her hips. He turned off the
water and dipped his hand in the tub but before he could warn her
she had already put one foot in. She sharply inhaled, wincing, but she
gripped the side of the tub and eased herself down into the water. He
rose to leave but she grabbed his hand and wouldn't let go as she rested
back against the tiled wall. She wasn't going to take a last chance. Her
eyes were shut and they didn't speak for a long while and when her
hand relaxed he was afraid she was gone. But the bathwater welled
and sloshed over the edge and she was suddenly on her feet, wrapping

herself in one of the towels from the rack. The hot water had pulled up a color in her legs. Yet her expression was sallow; she was only cheekbones and eyes, as though the flesh had melted away into the bathwater, and she said, "Please, Hector. Let's be quick now."

He sat her up on the bed as he helped her with the clothes, gently manipulating her limbs as if he were dressing a life-sized doll. The outfit consisted of very loose pajama-style pants and both a blouse and a vest, all made of the same coarse white linen. The shape of the papery clothing took on a boxy, formal allure, the whiteness making her look like a strange kind of bride; showing through the diaphanous fabric were the dark nipples of her breasts, the patch of hair between her legs, these final notations that she was still a woman, still alive. She tried to knot the waist-strings of the vest herself but she kept fumbling it, so he tied it for her in a double bow. He slipped a pair of his own large socks on her feet, not bothering with shoes for how swollen they were; and then, it was obvious now, he would have to carry her anyway.

"Are you ready?" he asked her.

"Yes." When he lifted her she groaned, so he paused, but she tapped at his arm to keep them moving. "We have to go," she said, her voice barely above a whisper. "We have to go right now."

Hector carried her down the tight dark turns of the tower stairs, making sure of his footfalls on the slick, worn stone treads. He'd already half-tripped back on the threshold, just barely regaining his balance, though he'd accidentally bit his own tongue. He was stepping as lightly and carefully as he could and yet the descent for her seemed an agony, her hand gripping the hair at the back of his head, squeezing the strands between her fingers in time to each step. The bath had only sped her ruin. In his arms her body was warm and damp, but she didn't smell quite right, not off or spoiled, but rather like she'd been mostly rendered away, or diluted, like the faintest trace of blood or flesh that lingered even after he'd disinfected and scrubbed and hosed off a canvas litter during the war, somebody's clinging half-life. She was already a presence residual. When they reached the empty lobby the hotel proprietor put down the book he was reading and instinctively moved to aid them but he stopped at the end of the bar when he got a good look at her, his head solemnly dipping as they passed. Outside, they crossed the street and mounted the wide pea gravel path that led up the hill, the dark sentinels of the cypress trees marking either side.

"I can't see," she said.

He turned to walk sideways so she might have a better angle on the church but when he looked down into her eyes they were dull and black, inkier still for the soft, late daylight, her pupils straining to hold off a welling darkness that was not apparent to Hector but that was falling more swiftly than the evening.

"I can't see."

Hector quickened his pace. Her face was turning a watery shade. She felt heavier now, taking on that weight. All his life he was present at such ends and yet each time it filled him with a raw astonishment. He felt himself begin to cave with panic. And a realization: he did not want to watch her die. He did not want to have to stoke her fire. He would stoke his own but no one else's. Had he the power to save her he would do so, he would trade places with her, let her go on, if she wished, for the rest of time.

"Wait," she said. "Wait."

He stopped. He had reached the plateau of ground before the shallow steps of the entrance. One of the double doors was open. But she was not addressing him. She was craning at the sky, her eyes unfixed. She was almost gone.

She murmured: "Not yet."

"It's okay," he said, suddenly drawn forth. There was a strange gleam in the church. He took her inside. Between the entrance and the altar the space was completely open; there were no pews in this church. And somehow it was illuminated, somehow it was brighter than outside, the sunbeams stealing in through the side windows at a last, impossible angle. For the moment everything was awash in a light pewter shade, this rubbed, high-burnished grayness, a hue, he realized, long known to him. On top of the white marble altar stood an immense wooden cross, as severe and plain as the one he had once made, the vault above it rising more than twenty-five feet. How was he here again? And it was now that he recognized the patterning of the circular walls of the chancel, the odd mottle of its ornamentation. It was not fresco or fabric or artful intaglio. It was the most basic design. What Hector perhaps understood best in the end: an array of bones.

They were not entombed as he'd expected but rather on open display. Behind the altar, at a subterranean level, open to view, were built-in shelves stocked tight with the bones. They were arranged by kind—piles of femurs and tibias, nested pelvises and jaws. There were bins full of the smaller bones of the feet, of the hands, like countless pieces of chalk. Many bundles of ribs. Then, rising to the cornice of the vaulting, even stacked above it, were rows upon rows of skulls. There were hundreds of them, if not a thousand, all neatly lined up, one beside the next, like some vast, horrid hat shop. Some of the skulls had jagged holes punched out of their temples, blown out from their crowns; some were smashed through at the cheek, at the nose. Missing a brow. But he saw that most of them were touched only by time, their color bleached or tinged pink with rust or a moldering gray. He could not picture their pristine faces save by the distinctive set of their teeth, crooked and straight, protruding and curved. All the grinning, grimacing dead. Hector grimaced back, his own teeth tasting of iron and blood.

"Are we inside?" June murmured, her eyes shiny pieces of coal. "Are we here?"

He said yes.

"It must be beautiful. Is it beautiful?"

It is beautiful, he whispered, not hearing his own voice. *This is our place.*

NOT YET.

She was running for the train. The very last car. It was moving away from her, it seemed, at an insurmountable speed. Voices were calling for her to run. Run. Not to give up. She had no shoes on her feet—when had they fallen off?—and the ground beside the tracks was gravelly and sharp. Laced with burrs and prickly weeds. But she had no mind for the pain that had taken her over now. Her legs were working, straining, madly pumping beneath her like pistons, pushing her to make this brief sprint she had been running the whole of her life. She could not look back. She loved them all but she knew if she looked back she was done. She would come to a stop. And she did not want to stop, not just yet. Not now. To crave anything, alas, is to crave time. She was simply hungry for more. The wheels of the last car squealed and flashed; it was accelerating, about to pull away. In defiance she leaned forward and cried out, suspending her breath, and reached for the dark edge of the door. The world fell away. Someone had pulled her up. Borne her in. She was off her feet, alive.

THE AUTHOR GRATEFULLY acknowledges the support of several institutions during the writing of this book: the Punahou School in Honolulu; the American Academy in Rome; and the Lewis Center for the Arts at Princeton University.

Chang-rae Lee is the highly acclaimed author of the novels *Native Speaker*, *A Gesture Life* and *Aloft*, and the recipient of the Hemingway Foundation/PEN Award and a Guggenheim Fellowship. He lives in the United States, and is the director of the Creative Writing Program at Princeton University. *The Surrendered* is his fourth novel.